CLINT IE

BESTSELLING AU STICE

"MCKINZIE HAMMERS HIS ACTION AND SUSPENSE HOME LIKE A BOLT INTO A ROCK FACE."
—Perri O'Shaughnessy

POINT OF LAW

High Praise for
THE EDGE OF JUSTICE

"One of the strongest debuts of the year . . . McKinzie takes us to the mountaintop, dangles us over the precipice with good plotting and realistic characters and then slowly reels us back in with death-defying suspense. . . . Strong courtroom scenes and a breathtaking view of Wyoming."
—*Chicago Tribune*

"A fast-paced and promising debut." —*The Washington Post*

"Action-packed . . . [a] page-turner." —*USA Today*

"This book signals the start of a great new career. Clinton McKinzie delivers a story pulsing with intrigue and character that is as poetic as it is harrowing. This one's a true winner."
—Michael Connelly, *New York Times* bestselling author of *Chasing the Dime*

"A riveting and powerfully unique thriller."
—Iris Johansen, *New York Times* bestselling author of *Dead Aim*

"A tremendous debut novel, a high-octane, adrenaline-powered rise that features **a terrific new hero."**
—Phillip Margolin, *New York Times* bestselling author of *The Associate*

"Action soars in court, on the peaks. . . . Hair-raising climbing sequences . . . [Burns] is a complex character with all kinds of potential for growth and involvement in spellbinding dilemmas. One of the more fascinating aspects of *The Edge of Justice* is how McKinzie delves into the climber's mind, revealing the complex emotions fired by the addictive thrill of extreme climbing. . . . McKinzie has made **an admirable beginning to what is likely to prove to be a long and distinguished career as an author."**
—*The Denver Post*

"An **exciting** crime novel . . . adrenaline-filled story . . . **A nail-biter all the way."** —*The Toronto Sun*

"An adrenaline-pumping, heart-pounding thrill ride with a terrifying climax that left me clenching for a handhold."
—Tess Gerritsen, *New York Times* bestselling author of *The Apprentice*

"An exciting, clever, and whip-smart action thriller."
—Robert K. Tanenbaum, *New York Times* bestselling author of *Absolute Rage*

"You can almost feel the rock beneath your fingers and the air beneath your heels as you race through the pages. McKinzie brings the bizarre and exciting world of climbing addicts to life with **such skill and passion that there can be little doubt he is a novelist with a bright future."**
—Kyle Mills, *New York Times* bestselling author of *Sphere of Influence*

"Adventure fiction that lives up to all the label implies. The story moves along at a rapid, believable pace, and the characters are written with authenticity." —*The Decatur Daily*

"McKinzie packs his first novel with a wealth of rock-climbing detail while **winningly depicting the clash** between the new-century West's yeoman and yuppies."
—*Daily News* (New York)

"A superb thriller . . . Antonio Burns is a unique and likeable detective who creates adventure and suspense at every turn and crevice in the rock all the way to **an exciting mountaintop climax."** —*Mystery Lovers Bookshop News*

"A tough, taut thriller with fascinating insights into the world of extreme rock climbing." —Perri O'Shaughnessy, *New York Times* bestselling author of *Unfit to Practice*

"A heart-pounding thriller. McKinzie creates a taut read filled with psychopathic killers, monstrous cliffs, and hair-pin twists that **will leave you gasping for more."** —Lisa Gardner, *New York Times* bestselling author of *The Survivors Club*

"McKinzie has talent: a sense of character and dialogue, the imagination to construct a **unique and complex plot."**
—*Booklist*

"McKinzie knows his wild Wyoming, and also how to keep things moving briskly. . . . **A nail-biting climax** on a mountain in a storm." —*Publishers Weekly*

"Clinton McKinzie gets so much right in this novel— mood, place, character, prose—that you have to keep reminding yourself that this is his first book. . . . **He knows how to tell a story that won't let go."** —Stephen White, *New York Times* bestselling author of *Warning Signs*

"**A stunning debut by a gifted writer.** This book combines two of the most exciting things on earth—rock climbing and courtrooms—to produce a **spellbinding thriller.** Clinton McKinzie knows how to grab your attention and hold it to the very last page—and beyond."
—William Bernhardt, author of *Criminal Intent*

"An altogether smashing debut by an author who will clearly be with us for years to come. McKinzie's fast-paced tale of murder and political intrigue set against the backdrop of Wyoming rock-climbing wilderness will leave readers breathless. . . . **Don't miss it."**
—Les Standiford, author of *Bone Key*

Also by Clinton McKinzie

THE EDGE OF JUSTICE
TRIAL BY ICE AND FIRE

POINT OF LAW

Clinton McKinzie

A DELL BOOK

POINT OF LAW
A Dell Book / May 2003

Published by Bantam Dell
A Division of Random House, Inc.
New York, New York

Cover design by Yook Louie

ISBN: 0-440-24080-8

Manufactured in the United States of America
Published simultaneously in Canada

OPM 10 9 8 7 6 5 4 3 2 1

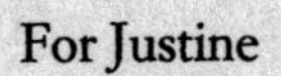
For Justine

PART ONE

Nor law, nor duty bade me fight,
Nor public men, nor cheering crowds,
A lonely impulse of delight
Drove this tumult to the clouds

—W. B. Yeats

"An Irish Airman Foresees His Death"

ONE

"WATCH ME. KEEP it tight."

My father's calm voice belies his precarious position. He clings to the vertical granite forty feet above where I sway in my harness, another one hundred and fifty feet above the canyon floor. Although my vision is slightly blurred by the waves of early-morning heat the sun is generating off the cliff's face, I can see where his right hand grips a tiny edge barely thicker than a pencil. His left hand sorts through the rack of protective gear slung around one burly shoulder. The toes of the old man's climbing slippers are splayed on nubbins of quartz that look as if they could pop off the sandstone wall at any moment. But there's no quiver in his muscles, no panic in his voice. I glance at the last piece of protection my father had clipped to the rope twenty feet beneath him and feel a familiar admiration swelling in my chest.

"You say you want slack?" I shout up, pretending to have misunderstood. My hands shuffle over the belay device—a slotted piece of cold-forged steel appropriately called an Air Traffic Controller—and take in the few inches of loose rope between us.

My father drops down a hard look before he returns to the task of finding a cam to fit in the narrow crack above his head. From that look I guess he isn't in a humorous mood. My mother had warned me about this: in recent months his tolerance for frivolity has suffered a dramatic decline. Resolving to remain silent and simply focus on my job, I study the forty feet of vertical space between us.

The rock is a combination of sandstone, gneiss, and pinkish pegmatite. Its texture is sometimes smooth and sometimes coarse under my fingertips. The entire five-hundred-foot canyon wall overhangs slightly from where it's been carved out of ancient bedrock by thousands of years of rushing water and tumbling boulders. The distance between my father and me appears almost featureless but for where a single recess mars the wall—a short and flaring horizontal fissure, the only opportunity for him to have placed some gear to protect against a fall. Above his head begins the comfort of the deep vertical crack into which he's working the spring-loaded camming device.

According to my father's tattered guidebook that describes the route, called "Big Balls and a Puckered Ass" (the route's name could just as easily describe my father), and which credits him with the route's first ascent, this second pitch is the toughest of the four rope-lengths up the cliff. I had led the easier first one hundred and fifty feet or so and had expected that this crux pitch would be mine as well. Dad hasn't been climbing much lately and the years have to be taking their toll. But the old man insisted on keeping the crux for himself, taking what is known as the "sharp end" of the rope from me rather than being safely belayed from above, where a fall could be measured in inches rather than feet or broken limbs.

Dad has something to prove today, I realize. It is the last time he'll be able to climb here at the scene of his glory days thirty years ago. And this is the hardest single pitch of the numerous routes he'd pioneered on the isolated canyon's walls, when climbs of this level were only rarely attempted and the land around the canyon and the entire Wild Fire Valley region was believed to be forever in the public trust. It must pain him to know that in just weeks this land—his land—will become private property and climbing will be forbidden.

The narrow gorge is sacred to me, too, because of a sort of mythology I'd invented about the place when I was a child. Although my brother and I had never been to the canyon, we grew up listening to stories told by our parents' friends about Dad's long-ago exploits here. For me in my childhood this was Mount Olympus, where the gods frolicked in ancient times.

For a moment I try to imagine my father in the old days, before my birth and before the war that turned him into a career soldier. I can see him laughing and joking with equally loose-jointed and tight-muscled young partners, clad in felt-soled boots while trusting their lives to primitive gear, made delirious by the heights and the virgin risks they faced. At night they camped around bonfires up in the broader valley where the canyon walls begin their deep cut through the red and gold sandstone. There they drank cheap wine from jugs and relived each day's thrills in a sort of Olympian bacchanal. They would wake in the morning, groggy and heavy-headed in the damp meadow grass, but ready to lay it all on the line once again. If the stories were true, Dad must have been a far more effusive man back then. The tales his friends told my brother and me made him sound wild-ass crazy and larger-than-life, not at all like the somber, cautious man above me now.

Refocusing on the present and the expanse of steep rock between us, I can see that there's good reason for caution. If he slips, he'll be looking at more than a forty-foot fall before the rope locked in my belay device can catch him. And that's only if the one lousy piece of protection he'd placed twenty feet beneath his heels doesn't fail. If it blows, then the rope will catch on the anchor I hang from. An eighty-foot fall for Dad. A serious whipper for any man; one that few could walk away from unscathed. I take a quick look at the boulder-strewn ground well over a hundred feet below me and reassure myself that at least he won't deck out. As long as the rope and my anchor hold, he might shatter his bones on the cliff's face but he won't hit the ground. Then I look at the three pieces of gear that compose the anchor in front of me, suspending me from the wall, and wish I'd done a better job of positioning them.

My father gingerly slots the mechanical cam in the crack over his head. A good fit. He finally calls for slack in that same terse, unconcerned voice. I give him a few feet so that he can clip the rope to the cam's nylon runner. My lungs release an unconsciously retained breath as the carabiner's gate snaps shut.

"Want to rest?" I yell up, unable to restrain myself.

He doesn't even bother to give me a look this time. My question had been meant as another joke, but as far as I can tell he never even smiles. Either he climbs or he falls—Dad never hangs on a rope. But he does spit out a brown glob of tobacco juice that I watch float down toward me then past, barely missing my arm. After a few seconds I hear its soft smack on the boulders below. Above me he resumes his deliberate crawl into the sky.

I start to shift in my harness, trying to ease where the nylon straps are cutting into my crotch. But after a quick glance at the sketchy anchor, I resolve to stop squirming and simply endure it. If the anchor fails, I will plummet, pulling Dad off with me. It isn't the danger that concerns me, as in all likelihood the cam he's just placed will hold us both on our separate ends of the rope, but the shame that will result. Above me my father continues upward with apparent ease although I know his forearms and calves must be burning, his shoulders pumped with lactic acid. *Christ. Closing in on sixty and the old man's still an animal.*

By the time he pulls over a small roof and disappears from sight, I'm beginning to wonder if I'll ever be able to have children of my own. My harness's crotch loop feels as if it's attempting to sterilize me with a cutting pressure. With great relief I hear his deep voice call out, "Off be-lay!" There are two sharp tugs on the rope.

"Nice work, Colonel," I shout up into the sky. "You've still got it!"

I feel another two tugs on the rope, signaling that he's

anchored and it's my turn to be belayed. I disassemble the anchor, wipe my sweaty hands on my shorts, dip them in the pouch of chalk that hangs just below my butt, and ease onto the hot rock.

After pulling over the short, difficult roof, I find my father comfortably belaying me from a wide ledge. He sits with his back propped by the sandstone wall and his legs spread before him. He's removed his shoes; his bare feet and ankles protrude off the edge and into space. His eyes are half-closed against the sunlight. I step to the anchor he's built out of two hexes stuffed deep in a constricting crack and clip a bight of rope to the carabiners connecting them. I shake the anchor a little and try to make another joke.

"Jesus, Dad, whatever happened to not trusting just two pieces? Remember the way you used to yell at 'Berto and me for that?"

His eyes remain half-closed but I can sense a sudden heat in them. Even his bald, sun-freckled scalp turns a little pink at the mention of my brother's name. For a moment I want to stuff a stinking climbing slipper in my mouth, thinking I've spoken the name too soon. But then I remind myself that Roberto is the reason we're here. The primary reason, anyway. This trip is supposed to be an intervention with Roberto, my drug-addicted brother, as well as a holiday in which our father can relive his glory days and say goodbye to a remote piece of Colorado that's soon slated to become a part of a massive ski resort. Roberto will arrive this afternoon or maybe the next day, and it's time for Dad and me to get some things out in the open.

So I slump down next to my father. I offer him the

bottle of warm water that I've carried dangling from my harness. He speaks first, and I suppose he's trying to head me off from the direction he must know I'm traveling.

He asks without looking at me, "So, how are you liking this cop stuff?"

His tone sounds vaguely condescending, as it does every time I see him and he asks this same question. He has to know the response this will provoke from me.

And I can't resist falling into the trap. "I'm not really a cop, Dad. I'm an agent," I explain as I always do. I try to keep the annoyance and defensiveness out of my voice. "I don't wear a uniform, I don't write speeding tickets, and I don't eat donuts. I investigate drug crimes—mostly meth—and that's it. Anyway, I like it. I run my own ops and I make my own hours."

This last part is something I add in a juvenile attempt to make my father appreciate my job. His dead-ending career is as an Air Force officer in command of an elite Special Forces unit known as the Pararescue Corps, or PJs. Being harnessed to a rigid chain of command, he never runs his own ops or makes his own hours. And he seldom takes a leave that isn't interrupted. We've had this discussion a hundred times.

With a self-deprecating smile, I add, "And I get to take vacations like this whenever I manage to get myself suspended."

That almost makes Dad chuckle. I can see the lines around his mouth deepen for just an instant. I've been suspended twice in my three years as a special narcotics agent for Wyoming's Division of Criminal Investigations, a part of the state Attorney General's Office. The first time had been the result of an officer-involved shooting.

Anytime a law enforcement officer is forced by circumstances to pull a trigger, especially if he or she manages to put a bullet in someone, there is a mandatory period of suspension during which the shooting is investigated by the office's version of Internal Affairs and ruled either justifiable or not. These bureaucratic inquiries take a long, long time. During the investigation the officer is supposed to seek counseling in order to alleviate the guilt and grief of having shot some scumbag who'd been trying to kill him. I hadn't felt the need for any counseling, but then, I didn't kill anyone. I just winged the bastard. And the only thing I felt even a little guilty about was my lousy aim and the terrific amount of climbing I'd gotten in during the prolonged period of suspension-with-pay.

My current suspension is for three months without pay. It's part of a negotiated plea agreement to avoid having criminal charges pressed against me for assaulting a fellow peace officer. The charges would have embarrassed both my office and the local sheriff's department the so-called "victim" was a member of. I've accepted three months without pay, an official reprimand, and been forced to make a half-assed apology. Kind of like with the prior suspension, the only guilt I feel is for not having hit the deputy harder.

Instead of continuing our usual subtle but tense banter in which my father will attempt to degrade my career choice and voice his preference for something more "professional," I'm surprised when he tries a new tack, mentioning Roberto for the first time himself.

"Do your bosses know about your brother, *Agent* Burns?"

"They know I've got one, but they don't know about

any of the trouble. It probably wouldn't do my career much good if they found out."

This is something my father knows about firsthand. Just a few years ago he'd been on the verge of becoming one of the youngest generals in the Air Force. Then the crimes of his eldest son had come to the attention of the military. Dad ended up being denied further advancement. You don't become a general, the ultimate leader of men, when you've sired a felon. Fortunately for me, though, the Wyoming AG's Office doesn't concern itself much with background checks on family members prior to promotion. I make a mental note to mention this additional benefit the next time we argue on the career subject, but don't want to bring it up now that we're finally talking about Roberto.

"Do you know what he's using these days?"

"Not for sure. He's banging—injecting—I know that much."

My father nods. Even in magazine photographs, the tracks of scabby pinpricks on my brother's arms are hard to miss.

"So that leads me to guess it's either crank or heroin," I say. After a moment I add quietly, "There's not much out there that's worse, Dad. At least we don't have to worry anymore about him turning to harder drugs."

My father doesn't say anything for a while. He just takes a few short pulls from my water bottle and stares up the canyon.

The ledge is narrow where I'm slumped next to him. My feet and calves dangle over more than two hundred feet of space. I lean over and look down for the large black shape of my dog. Oso lays under the shade of a green-leafed cottonwood, staring straight up at us with his red tongue parting sharp white teeth. The dog is the cause of my current suspension—the deputy I supposedly assaulted had been trying to spear him with a shovel. I wave my hand at him and see the ears twitch forward.

Taking back the water bottle from my father, I notice that one of his thick fists still holds the rope locked tight through his belay device.

"By the way, Dad, I tied in. I'm off belay."

He nods. "Waiting for you to say it, son. Belay off." Finally he releases his grip. I'm annoyed and embarrassed. I've violated one of his cardinal rules by failing to announce my status, but at least he's too preoccupied to comment further.

"Do you have a strategy for dealing with your brother when or if he shows up?" he asks.

I take a deep breath. This is something I've been thinking about for weeks, ever since my suspension and the news about the pending development of Wild Fire Valley as a part of a Forest Service land swap. I'd convinced my father to fly in from the Pentagon to meet Roberto and me for a last climb here together—and an attempt to save my brother's life. Despite a lot of mental effort, I'm still uncertain what our plan should be. A hard-core user like Roberto needs confinement and careful medication, something he's not likely to submit to voluntarily. One thing I know for sure is that my father's unconcealed animosity, born out of the impending termination of his career, won't help things. Nor will my own distaste for the hard drugs I've devoted my professional life to combating. Persuading Roberto to swerve away from the path of self-destruction he's speeding down won't be easy, and there's no place in any strategy for anger and recrimination.

Climbing has always been the Burns family's first drug of choice. *La llamada del salvaje,* as my mother describes it. The call of the wild. According to her it's a sort of genetic flaw on my father's side that has descended to Roberto and me. It's a hunger we learned to feed by getting lethal amounts of air beneath our heels. The fear you feel free-climbing, hundreds or thousands of feet off the deck, and with just a skinny rope as backup, is like an illicit substance—once ingested it makes the sweet stuff called noradrenaline just ooze out from the adrenal glands. It blows through all the panic that comes from deadly heights, replacing it with a tingly sensation. Ecstasy. Exaltation. Rapture. The negative side effect is that it's a little harder to replicate that feeling after each session. You have to push it a little further. Dad and I have learned to control our addiction—we've learned that there's pleasure in just crawling up into the heights without needing to lay it all on the line for that hormonal surge. Roberto hasn't.

He reached for something even stronger. Starting in his early twenties he turned to pharmaceuticals to pump up the volume. He began with pot, mushrooms, and acid, then moved on to methamphetamine, cocaine, and heroin. He was chasing the dragon, looking for a better and louder amp. On the frequent climbing trips we used to take together in my college days, he would sometimes offer me some. I'd never been interested. Even then, before having really seen the damage those drugs could do, I preferred a natural high, although I had occasionally smoked marijuana with him in my teenage years (something I still consider no more dangerous than beer). Roberto once told me he'd discovered that cocaine mixed with heroin—a speedball—could push him beyond climbing's natural rush. It could take him places far further than the thrill of fighting ordinary gravity.

"It's just an ice cream habit," he'd explained when I'd given him a hard time about the hard drugs. "I got it under control, bro."

Right.

But it isn't just the drugs, although they've become the center of Roberto's life. It's the way he interacts with people, the way he thinks, even the way he climbs. Roberto has become addicted to living on the very edge. If he isn't climbing, he's slamming a needle deep into a vein. If he isn't surrounded by the circle of fast-living friends who worship him as the fastest of them all, then he's brawling with anyone he perceives as having done something unjust. And if he isn't utterly free, then he's caged in a county jail somewhere. Recently there had even been a brief stint in a federal prison. Roberto has happily danced so far out on the edge and for so long that it's a miracle the void hasn't yet sucked him in.

Do I really believe we can change that? It would require almost a repolarization of my brother's soul. I know, even now, that this is simply a last hurrah before the odds catch up with him. There's no chance in hell he'll ever become an ordinary citizen, responsible with his life and his future, and constrained by the rules that civilization demands.

So I say to my father, "No strategy, Dad. Just show him that we love him, that if he keeps this up we'll be the ones who suffer."

My father shakes his head and uncharacteristically expresses some emotion in his voice while looking at the red and gold stone of the canyon's opposite wall. "Shit, Anton, it'd be hard to suffer much more. It'd be a relief if he were dead."

You'd think a son would be shocked to hear his father talk about his brother like that. But I'm not. In my darkest moments I often think the same thing. I'm tired of waiting for the telephone to ring late in the night; waiting for the quiet voice of some Colorado police officer to tell me that my brother's dead.

There isn't much more to say than that.

I close my eyes and recall a scene from this morning, just a few hours ago, when my father and I sped on the highway out of the seemingly endless suburbs of Tomichi in the predawn blackness, on our way to the valley. I'd been glancing over at my father's deeply lined face while we talked, noticing how old it looked in the glow of the dashboard's lights. His mouth opened suddenly. His eyes narrowed. I snapped my own eyes forward to the road. A big coyote was braced facing us in the middle of the lane. His eyes burned with green fire in the reflected heat of the headlights. The silver-tipped ruff of fur around his neck and shoulders was standing straight up. I swung the wheel hard to the left, onto the wrong side of the road, mashing the brake and throwing my big dog in the backseat across the truck. The coyote never even flinched.

That coyote was just like Roberto. Totally defiant in the face of law and civilization, even when it's coming at him seventy miles per hour in the form of three thousand pounds of rusty Japanese steel. Utterly audacious, reckless, and not long for this world. But beautiful all the same.

I realize that my brother's luck must soon run out, that the world won't swerve away much longer. And that Roberto's nuclear-powered élan combined with whatever sort of shit he likes to spike in his veins will vastly magnify the force of the inevitable collision. What I don't yet realize is just how many lives are about to be lost in the crash.

Opening my eyes to the blue sky, I take up the sling of gear my father has laid between us. Without a word I add the pieces from the anchor I'd pulled below and slip it clanking over my head and one shoulder. Standing, I arch my neck upward and try to plot the course that will take me another rope length into the sky. My skin touches the warm, rough rock as I slide my fingers over the lip of a small contour above my head. The familiar texture of it for the first time in my life fails to give me a small thrill. For a moment I'm caught off balance, experiencing a sense of vertigo and dread I've never experienced before. This is a mistake, I tell myself, as I will the web of well-conditioned muscles in my forearms to grip with my fingers and hold me on the ledge. Something bad is going to happen. A cold sweat seeps out of my skin. I glance at my father and see him looking back curiously. Concerned.

"Locked and loaded?" I ask, trying to reassure myself with the start of the short litany he'd drilled into Roberto and me as children. We examine the harness buckles and knots at each other's waists.

"Tight and right," Dad responds, his voice puzzled.

"On belay?"

"Belay on."

"Climbing."

TWO

IT TAKES MORE than an hour to rappel down the cliff's four pitches. Oso's yellow eyes track me all the way. But the beast doesn't come out from the shade of the cottonwoods until my feet are on the stony canyon floor. There I pop the ropes out of the ATC and yell up to my father, who's waiting on a ledge halfway down, that I'm off rappel. Oso finally lumbers to his feet, shakes some brambles from his woolly black coat, and approaches me with his head held low. His stump of a tail quivers in the air, not really swinging at all, when he bumps my hip with his broad snout. Over the rushing of the stream just a few feet away, I hear a low rumble from the dog's chest. It's his version of a purr. I rub Oso's ears while watching my father slide down the last two pitches with the controlled grace of a spider.

When Dad touches the ground, he too holds out a

hand to scratch the beast's massive head. Oso lifts his lips with a more audible growl and my father jerks back his hand.

"Damn it, dog, I'm just trying to make friends," my father growls in response.

"He'll come around," I tell him. "He's got to get to know you." Then, after a moment's thought, I add, "Actually, you may be better off trying to be someone else." I can't picture Oso warming up to my father in his current mood.

Dad makes a mirthless noise like "Uh-huh" and turns away.

I've already explained to him how it had taken a long, long time for the dog to even let me touch him. And I'd shown my father the parallel scars on one forearm from when I'd tried to take the liberty too soon. Eight weeks and eighteen stitches. It took that long to tame Oso's savage heart enough for me to stroke him.

I'd found Oso nine months before. He was chained to the back porch of a decrepit house outside Rawlins that was being used as a clandestine methamphetamine lab. The shaggy beast was supposed to scare away both cops and rival dealers. During my undercover investigation of the meth lab's operators, I'd heard one of the suspects claim to have fed the dog a missing informant. Although I doubted it was really true, he'd certainly looked the part—a hundred and fifty pounds or so of unidentifiable breeding, malnourished muscle, open sores blowing with flies, and those enormous white teeth. He had the appearance and the demeanor of a starved grizzly bear.

One hot afternoon, with the help of some deputies from the Carbon County Sheriff's Office, I took down the lab and arrested its operators. At one point in the short fight, the monster on the back porch had to be pepper-sprayed when a deputy chased a suspect out through the rear door. Oso was lucky not to have been shot right then.

Later on, after the arrests, the interviews, the paper-work, and the dismantling of the lab, I returned as the local officers managed to get him into a cage provided by the state's Wildlife Control agency. They'd wrestled him in by using wire nooses on the ends of long metal poles. One of them was jabbing at him with a sharp-bladed shovel, seeing just how crazy he could make him before they carted him away. Blood from the beast's lips and teeth ran down the cage's steel bars as he tried to crunch through to get at his captors. Something about the plight of the tormented beast made me lose it. I knocked down the deputy with the shovel—I kicked his legs out from under him and punched him in the ribs as he fell. It took the three other officers to keep me from doing worse. Like jabbing *him* with the shovel, to see how he liked it.

Despite the resulting and now-deferred charges for assault on a peace officer, I adopted the monster as my own. In some subconscious way, Oso reminded me of my brother.

After weeks of giving love and receiving only the occasional slashing wound (for which I was lucky—his jaws have the power to snap bones), I finally convinced Oso that his days of abuse were over. Now he is cautiously devoted to me, yet reluctant to accept another's touch and still, at times, even a little uncertain about mine.

Because of his size and disposition, Oso continues to be an immense pain in my ass. In addition to the eighteen stitches, he's torn apart three different rental homes when

I left him alone for too long. He got me evicted from each of them. I've learned that I need to take the beast with me pretty much wherever I go. Even when I'm working, Oso is happiest to remain hunched massively in the passenger seat of my ancient Land Cruiser, his weight causing it to tilt to one side, where he can glare out the windshield and watch for his only friend.

"Is that stinking pile of teeth and fur worth it?" Dad had asked yesterday after I'd picked him up at the Denver airport. He'd been visibly tense on the long ride down to Tomichi with the beast lurking in the backseat, just inches behind his exposed neck.

"Yeah, he is," I answered, smiling. It's a rare thing to see my father nervous.

When Oso wanders away to slurp at the river, I begin stuffing gear in the packs. My father pulls the ropes and then coils them. I notice that every few turns he stops and looks around, gazing up and down the canyon walls, probably reminiscing to himself about the summers he'd spent here three decades ago. I pull a small tube of sunscreen out my pack and hold it out to him.

"Want some? Your head's starting to look like a ripe tomato."

"That's funny, son. You'll see how funny in a few years."

"Not me, Dad. I've got Mom's hairy Latin genes."

I smear some of the lotion onto my fingertips and rub it on my face. Touching the left side of my face, I feel the unnaturally smooth strip of skin that runs from my eye almost all the way down to my upper lip. It's from where a falling flake of jagged rock the size of a dinner plate had split my face a few years earlier. I massage in the lotion with care—at one time I'd hoped to prevent the scar from baking into something permanently disfiguring. It's a habit I've clung to ever since the accident. Maybe someday the scar will disappear. Between climbing and the dog, soon I'll be nothing but scar tissue.

I take off my sunglasses and stare at my distorted reflection in the mirrored lenses. What I see isn't pleasant. I look like some sort of desperate fugitive, with my close-cropped hair and the short beard I'd allowed since my suspension began. The beard is an experiment with trying to hide at least a portion of the wound. But it just makes things worse. I quickly put the glasses back on.

Dad is again staring up the canyon to where it opens into a wide valley, and where beyond that there's a broad mountainside containing valleys, forests, and streams of its own. It is the twelve-thousand-foot mountain that's soon due to become a ski resort.

"Feel like home?" I ask my father, thinking about how he'd spent every summer of his late teens and early twenties camping on this land.

Dad shakes his head. His mouth is turned down at a tight angle. "Nope. Not anymore." When he turns back around to continue up-canyon, his shoulders, still bulging with muscle beneath his olive T-shirt, sag a little to match his frown.

I imagine this place in a few years' time: the forests bulldozed to make ski runs, the ridges lined with chairlifts, the valley sprawling down-canyon with condos, asphalt, traffic lights, restaurants, and liquor stores. Already a lodge is being built halfway up on the mountainside. I can hear the distant whir of an electric saw and the faint, erratic pulse of hammers. Olympus is dying.

Both of us are quiet as we leave the canyon and enter the broader valley. Ahead of us, directly to the north, is a small, densely wooded hillside with a red cliff in its center shaped like a heart. The cliff is only a couple hundred feet high and is composed of crumbly sandstone, unsuitable for serious climbing. At its base lies a steep field of broken boulders that had, over the centuries, spilled from the cliff's face like drops of blood. Two small figures, barely visible, are rappelling down it. I wonder why anyone would bother when there's such fantastic granite in the canyon. People do strange things, like tearing up a place like this.

To our right is the 12,500-foot massif of Wild Fire Peak. Its westward face is a complex series of low-angled glades, forests, and ravines. About halfway up is the source of the distant construction noise we hear—a crew is hard at work building what's to be the mid-mountain ski lodge. I can see a winding path of torn-out aspens and pines leading up to it.

A short way to our left is the end of the Forest Service road, the only way into this place. The road terminates in the broad meadow where we're camped. The construction trucks have torn a new series of paths through the valley that don't come together until they begin their winding climb up the mountainside.

"Stay close, Oso," I call before we come out of the screen of trees and into the valley. I don't want him to scare the other campers in the meadow. Due to his size and cut-down tail, more than one nearsighted person has mistaken him for a shambling bear. As we walk through the pines toward where I'd left my Land Cruiser, my jaw is tight with tension and my teeth feel sore.

Will Roberto be waiting for us? The question is crawling around in my mouth but I don't interrupt my father's thoughts to let it out. Like an unpleasant chore, his arrival is something I'd be happy to put off for a little while longer.

When we'd come through the meadow earlier in the morning, before the sun had risen, there were only a few other cars parked near quiet campsites. Now, at midday, there are more like thirty. And the meadow is full of activity. The articles I'd read about the coming land swap mentioned that some of the local environmental activists intended to hold a protest vigil in the valley this week. It looks like the vigil has begun.

Near the meadow's center a group of seven or eight youths are standing in a circle and kicking a small, brightly woven sack the size of a lemon back and forth with their feet. They're either college-aged or in the wandering postgraduate years. Dirty white tape clings to some of the kids' fingers, marking them as climbers. A few mountain bikes have been tossed haphazardly in the grass nearby.

Around the fringe of the meadow, where it's bordered by thick stands of spruce and aspens, are the other campsites. There's more than one rusting VW bus among the battered cars that stand in the grass near tents patched with duct tape and smoke-blackened fire rings. More young people gather around some of those, and the sweet scent of marijuana from shared joints wafts in the meadow's gentle breeze. Music plays from a boom box—Phish, I think. I see a few backpacks with chalk bags and climbing slippers clipped to gear loops with shiny carabiners. A few older women, even fewer older men, are seated in lawn chairs next to the motor homes they've somehow managed to bounce up the rough road. Through the trees comes the occasional shout of laughter from the hot springs by the creek.

The entire scene has a sad festival air. A sort of wake. Soon the entire valley will be torn down and replaced with bright condos and neat landscaping.

There's no sign of Roberto. Things won't be so peaceful when he gets here. His frenetic energy is like a tornado. It never fails to stir things up, to throw shit all over the place.

We dump our packs beside the truck. I check the locked glove box, where my badge, gun, and cell phone are stored, and find everything still there. From a cooler in back I get out a couple of jars and a loaf of bread and start smearing together peanut butter and jelly sandwiches while my dad mixes powdered Kool-Aid into two water bottles. Oso rolls in the tall grass nearby. He's grunting with pleasure and bicycling his hind legs.

I look up when I feel more than hear his deep growl vibrating over the beat of the boom box, which is now playing Blind Melon. Two women are walking toward us. One is blonde and young, college-aged, with a pretty face. I can't help but admire the expanse of smooth, pale skin that extends below her brief shorts down to her bare feet. Her hair is a rat's nest of dreadlocks and tight beaded braids. On her upper half she wears only a purple tank top that is cut to reveal a flat stomach. Braless. She has an unconscious spring in her step, as if she's delighted to be here, half-naked in the meadow.

The other woman is smaller, older, and darker but even more striking. She radiates intensity. My eyes are drawn to her despite the lush blonde's obvious appeal. She's thin, almost to the point of being gaunt, with lean muscles carving down from her shoulders to her wrists. I guess her age at middle thirties, and that's only because of her clothes, her confident manner, and unlike the other youths in the meadow, her face is unpierced. She wears a white sleeveless shirt that she's buttoned almost to her neck with old jeans and a pair of worn-out running shoes. Her face is all angles. High, sharp cheekbones, a long jaw, and a slightly oversized nose. The most striking thing about her is that despite the dark hair that spills over half her face, a black cord is visible where it stretches across an exposed part of her forehead. Beneath it there's the oblong shape of an eye patch.

"That dog's not going to bite, is it?" she asks as they approach our camp. She looks from the beast to us warily. Our appearance, mine in particular with my damaged face, probably doesn't inspire much confidence.

"Oso!" I call to him. "Cut it out. Get over here." I click my tongue against the roof of my mouth, and Oso sullenly turns, coming to sit at my side. "He's harmless, really," I say to the women.

My father chuckles from behind me, not at all persuaded. It's the first real bit of mirth I've heard from him all day.

"We saw you guys come in this morning. My name is Kim Walsh," the one-eyed woman tells us.

"I'm Sunny," the blonde girl says, smiling down at the dog and displaying perfect white teeth. The name is totally appropriate for her.

I introduce us as "Antonio and Leonard Burns,"

leaving out our respective titles of Special Agent and Colonel, then ask if they want some Kool-Aid.

Kim shakes her head but Sunny says, "Sure!" and takes my father's bottle from him.

I have a hard time taking my eyes off Kim's face. It isn't the eye patch but something else, some sort of feeling in my gut that I'm destined to know her better. That sort of feeling has happened several times before, like when I'd seen a particularly beautiful girl in class the first day of school and *knew* she'd become my girlfriend. It has always proven true. The thing that surprises me about it now is that this woman seems to be almost a decade older than me, probably a more appropriate age for my father than me. I've never felt much heat for an older woman before. Yet I suppress an urge to self-consciously run my hand over the scar on my face.

"You guys are climbers, huh?" Sunny asks.

When I nod she says, "I'm learning how to climb. A guy I met here in the valley's teaching me, but he's kind of a beginner, too. Am I going to get muscles like yours?" she asks with a laugh.

"You might," I tell her. "And scabs and scars and all that."

"God, I hope not!"

"It depends on how hard you want to climb."

Kim breaks in, "I was hoping for the chance to talk to you gentlemen about what's going to happen to this place. Have you been here before?"

I wait for my father to answer but he doesn't. So I glance at him and say, "Dad put up a bunch of the routes in the canyon, like a hundred years ago. Before anyone even knew about this place."

Kim looks past me at my father for a long time while neither speaks. Measuring him. Sunny seems on the verge of saying something to break the silence, when Kim says softly, "Then you must really love this place."

Again Dad doesn't answer. I'm used to it but still annoyed at how he can be so closed-mouthed with strangers, bordering on the impolite. I know it's probably a habit he'd picked up from years of semisecret missions and training exercises as the leader of Pararescue teams, but it doesn't seem like an effective technique to me—it just makes the strangers all the more curious. It's my father's commanding presence and impassive features alone that usually keep people from asking more.

Kim doesn't push, but doesn't look particularly intimidated either. From the steady way she watches us with her one good eye, I'm willing to bet she's as tough as he is. Speaking to us both, her voice now hard, she says, "It's about to be made private land in a crooked swap with the government. A group of us are trying to do something about it."

I nod. That was what I'd read about in a newsletter from the Access Fund, a climbing-oriented environmental protection organization. It was the reason I'd wanted to bring my father here before it was forever closed to the public. I tell her that.

"I've seen the plans," she goes on, her coffee-colored eye blazing with a zealot's gleam. "You men are climbers, right? Well, a developer named David Fast"—she spits out his name with such venom that I guess she must be taking his assault on the valley personally—"is going to make that canyon down there into a bunch of high-priced homes on the river. This meadow"—she turns and sweeps her brown arm past the Hacky Sackers and other campers—"it's going to be a goddamned golf course. And the hot spring up-creek is going to be some sort of massive concrete bathing facility." She points at Wild Fire Peak looming to the east and tells us that it will be the ski area proper once they've stripped it of its forests and built lodges all over it. "In about two weeks Fast will start the serious construction, when the Forest Service makes its approval official. He'll begin with a guarded gatehouse down the road to keep us out." She pauses to look at each of us in turn. "We need help fighting him."

I ask, "What are you going to do? From what I read, the Forest Service has already announced they're going to approve the swap. It's kind of a done deal, isn't it?"

"No, it's not," she says fiercely, her hair slinging back to fully expose the eye patch. "Not when there's fraud involved. Fast bribed some scientists and then lied to get a positive environmental assessment. We're still trying to keep the local Forest Service manager from approving the exchange. If that fails, we'll try to get an injunction in federal court. Tomorrow we've got a local TV station and one from Denver coming up here for a rally. What we need is more bodies, to show the Forest Service and the media we're serious about this."

Sunny chimes in, "And it could get nasty, with the townies—"

Kim cuts her off with a glance and then explains, "Fast has managed to convince some locals that his ski resort will be good for the town. A lot of them are investors, too. There's a rumor going around that they plan to disrupt us tomorrow."

My brother's impending arrival momentarily forgotten, I look to my father. He's methodically chewing on his sandwich, leaning against the Land Cruiser, his face as expressionless as ever. Almost imperceptibly he shakes his head at me. Turning back to Kim, I say, "I'm interested, but I don't know yet how available I'm going to be. My dad and I are waiting here for my brother, who could arrive at any time over the next couple of days."

Clearly that doesn't seem like a very good excuse to her. She gives us both a one-eyed scowl and says, "We're having a campfire meeting tonight, over there near our sites on the other side of the meadow. At least come by and listen."

Hearing nothing from my father behind me, I tell her I'll try to stop by. Kim's turning to leave when Sunny speaks up again. She's kneeling in the grass, a few feet from Oso, with one hand tentatively extended toward him. "Is it all right to pet him? God, he looks like he's thinking about taking my arm off," she says, laughing nervously. My eyes are drawn straight down her loose shirt where two perfect breasts, as pale and smooth as the rest of her, float above the purple fabric. It takes a conscious act of will to lift my gaze.

When I look up, I see that Kim is watching my face. I wonder if this is why she's brought Sunny along with her—to try to recruit us. She's the honey to attract some worker bees. If my father and I had been women, Kim probably would have brought some shirtless stud from the Hacky Sack circle. It shows she's pretty cunning for an environmental activist. I kind of admire that.

Grasping Oso's collar, I hold his head close to my hip. "Go ahead," I tell Sunny, "just be careful. He was abused." It seems like a good time to start socializing the beast.

"You poor thing!" Sunny says, touching his chest with her hand uncomfortably close to my thighs. Oso starts to lift his lips but then rolls his eyes up to meet mine with a sort of annoyed resignation. His lips droop back down as Sunny continues murmuring and stroking him. "Who would do such a thing to you, you big, beautiful creature. You're really sweet, down deep inside, aren't you?" Behind us my father makes another noise that might be a chuckle.

They walk away a few minutes later. Watching them, I focus on Kim's slender back instead of Sunny's, and I feel that strange, inevitable attraction.

"What do you think?" I ask my father.

"Not bad, but I'm still married to your mom."

"I mean about the meeting tonight. The rally tomorrow."

"Sounds like a lost cause to me." After a minute he adds, "There are two things worth fighting for, son. The things you can win and the things worth dying for." He looks around the valley for a long time before meeting my eyes. "This isn't either one."

THREE

ROBERTO DOESN'T SHOW up in the afternoon. I'm not too surprised that he's late—promptness has never been among his few virtues. And he'd been reluctant to agree to meet us in the first place.

"*Che*, what the hell do I want to see that asshole for?" he'd said to me a few weeks ago when I finally reached him through his parole officer in Durango. "Haven't seen the dude in years and I like it that way."

I did my best to explain that Dad was different now, that he'd mellowed a little since accepting the fact that a ceiling had been imposed on his career and that his days in the Air Force were numbered. The time was right for reconciliation. My words on that count weren't too persuasive—Roberto wasn't interested in apologizing for ruining Dad's career or not living the kind of straight life our father wanted him to. Finally, I got him to agree to meet us by simply begging. "C'mon, bro, do it for me. Do it for Mom. Do it for the family. What have you got to lose by climbing with us? Besides, I hear you're getting weak, that you can't climb for shit anymore."

The last part made him laugh. A few months before, I'd received a postcard from him that was forwarded from the AG's Office in Cheyenne to my current assignment in Lander. The scrawled message told me to watch a certain cable channel at a certain time. Not owning a TV, I'd tuned in to the program at a local bar and found it to be some sort of special called "Generation Why?" on a sports channel. It featured extreme athletes doing all sorts of high-risk things and discussed the psychology that made them do it. A primary segment showed my brother free-soloing the Painted Wall in the Black Canyon of the Gunnison.

I'd watched the segment with a combination of horror, envy, and awe. A camera team filmed Roberto moving easily, ropeless, up over two thousand feet of vertical rock on Colorado's biggest wall. At one point, when he was climbing inverted beneath a granite roof that jutted from the massive cliff's face with his hands and his feet stuffed deep in a crack, Roberto turned to the camera with his movie star's grin and streaming black hair, then hung from just his feet and one jammed hand to shake his other out over the void. His eyes were lit up with either rapture or methamphetamine. In another scene he was resting on a tiny ledge, slumped against the wall with his feet dangling in space much the way I'd sat the day before with my father. Only I'd been wearing an anchored rope. Realizing the camera was on him, he quickly popped up into a handstand with his fingers curled over the edge. The inside of his left arm was exposed just beyond his tangled hair, and there were tiny red scabs tracked down it. Over the pumping music I could hear the cameraman's panicked shouts for him to *cut it out.* I realized I was quietly saying under my breath exactly the same thing as the cameraman, watching my brother on late-night TV, as the rest of the bar hollered and whooped.

After Dad and I soaked in a hot spring that was crowded with naked and frolicking environmental activists (sadly, neither Kim nor Sunny was among them), we cook dinner over my blowtorch of a camp stove. The noise it makes is loud enough to preclude much conversation. And that's fine with me, as the tension between us, a tension born of Roberto's impending arrival, has been steadily increasing. Oso drools on my thigh when I crouch by the stove to fry turkey sausage and boil pasta. My father slumps nearby in a low sling-back chair, watching the night descend on the meadow. As a sort of peace offering I take a bottle of wine from one of the plastic gear crates in the back of my truck and toss it to him. He nods his thanks, then pops the cork from the bottle with his pocketknife.

We eat in silence. When the food is gone and the bottle's drained, I scrub the pans with sand in the stream where it cuts close to the meadow. Coming back into our camp, I see that Dad has built a small campfire. He's also taken out a bottle of Yukon Jack from his own gear. Across the meadow, near where the activists have parked their cars and erected their tents, is a much larger fire. In its orange glow I can see ten or fifteen people already gathered around it.

My father holds out the bottle to me, making a peace

offering of his own. My nose automatically wrinkles at the cheap whiskey smell.

"No thanks," I tell him, my stomach twisting with memories of when Roberto and I used to steal the stuff from his liquor cabinet. I'd gagged it down and thrown it back up more than a dozen times in my high school years.

"I'll be back in a little bit," I say as I tie Oso to the truck's bumper with a chopped-off piece of an old climbing rope. Dad responds with a disapproving grunt.

Everyone eyes me with suspicion when I stroll into the group. I know that my damaged, scratchily bearded face makes me appear dangerous, so I try to compensate by smiling. Judging from the way people move away from me, the result is an appearance of being both dangerous and demented. I end up standing alone, buzzing from the wine and uncomfortably scanning the dark faces, until Sunny comes out of the night and takes my hand.

"Hey, Antonio. Glad you could make it, man. Where's that sweet dog of yours?"

"Back at camp. With my dad."

Her bright teeth flash. "Leonard, your old man, he didn't seem too into things. Guy seemed a little hostile, you know?"

"He's got a lot on his mind right now."

"But I fucking love your dog. You should have brought him."

Sunny's looking up at me, staring openly. I should be flirting back. She's wearing the same high-cut khaki shorts she'd had on earlier, now with a flannel shirt that's unbuttoned halfway down her chest instead of the loose purple tank top. Cannabis Sativa is her perfume of choice. Even though she's a few years younger than me, her sexuality is so obvious and so powerful that I toy with the image of a sleeping-bag fling. But I'm still feeling the lingering effect her friend Kim had on me in the afternoon. And I'm a little wary of Sunny, because of what I suspect is her job as a recruiting tool. I don't want to be manipulated. At least not so obviously.

"C'mon," she says, tugging my hand, "there's people you should meet."

She introduces me to a few of the younger activists. Their faces are bright in the firelight. The flames glint off the studs and hoops that adorn many of their eyebrows, lips, and noses. Studded tongues click against teeth when they speak. They seem so alike, all working so hard at distinguishing themselves and yet so disappointingly similar. Because I know it will be hard to differentiate them in the daylight, I don't worry too much about trying to remember names. But one stands out—a skinny young man named Cal, who puts his arms around Sunny protectively from behind. He wears a Gore-Tex jacket that's caked with dried mud.

"Antonio Burns, huh?" he says after being introduced. "Sunny told me about meeting you this afternoon. I've heard your name, dude. Used to read about you in those climbing magazines. Your brother, too."

I smile at him to convey that I'm not a threat, that I'm not hitting on Sunny. I'm probably not convincing, though, as Sunny still has a warm grip on my hand.

"Are you the one who's teaching Sunny to climb?"

"Trying to. But I'm just a recreational climber, you know? I don't do anything serious. I'm more of a cave rat."

"Oh yeah?" I ask. "Is there a lot of that around here?" My dad had never mentioned finding any caves.

Cal shrugs, meets my eyes for a second, and then looks at the ground before meeting my eyes again. "Sure. There's caves everywhere. If you know where to look."

"Was it you guys I saw this morning, rappelling down that red cliff?"

Cal looks away quickly now—it looks almost like he's blushing but it's hard to tell in the dark. "Could have been us. I was just teaching Sunny to rappel."

I assume he's embarrassed to have been caught rappelling instead of climbing, and even more embarrassed that it was on such an ignoble bit of rock compared to the higher, more vertical, and more solid stone down-canyon. Even Sunny looks away and drops my hand as if she knows enough about climbing to be embarrassed. Cal seems eager to change the subject.

"Haven't heard much about you lately, although your brother's still pictured in the mags all the time. You get a job or something?"

"Yeah, something like that" is all I will admit. It's my turn to be evasive.

The night is loud with voices, low laughter, the crackle of the giant campfire, and beyond, the rhythmic chirping of crickets. I can't help but keep glancing around for Kim in the reflection of the flames.

She finally shows up when just about everyone else from the environmentalists' camp has already appeared. The fire is well fueled from the enormous pile of dead wood that I'd seen the activists gathering in the forest all afternoon. Kim steps close to the fire, wearing the same jeans and shoes she'd had on in the day but with a sleek-looking black fleece coat to protect her slim frame from the night's chill. She begins to speak while the rest of the activists squat on large branches they've dragged off the woodpile.

I don't think she's noticed me until she starts off by saying, "There's a new person with us tonight—his name's Antonio Burns—so I'm going to review the situation here in the valley for his benefit and for those of you that haven't been around lately."

The shifting orange light from the campfire dances over her as she explains how Wild Fire Valley is a part of the San Juan National Forest, created in 1937, and supposedly placed forever in the public's trust for the use and enjoyment of the nation's citizens. Several times over the last twenty years various developers have attempted to lease the land from the federal government in order to build a ski resort that would rival nearby mountains like Aspen, Telluride, and Purgatory. Wild Fire Peak, the broad mountain that stands above us blocking out the moon and the stars to the east, is considered to be the perfect ski mountain due to its abundant winter snowfall, moderately steep glades, and quick access to the nearby town of Tomichi. For years the Forest Service, with the strident support of environment groups, rebuffed the developers' proposals. The prospective developers grew more and more excited as profits in Telluride and Aspen skyrocketed with the influx of stockbrokers and movie stars in the 1980s.

Finally a local timber baron and developer named David Fast got the attention of the Forest Service by proposing a land swap. He had recently mortgaged himself to the hilt in order to purchase a huge private inholding to the north in the White River National Forest. That piece of land was at the top of the Forest Service's "must have" list, as it was in the very center of a proposed habitat for the reïntroduction of the Canadian lynx. But there was no way a Republican Congress, which was vociferously opposed to the reintroduction plan, would ever approve the millions of dollars it would take to buy the land for inclusion in the National Forest. Fast bought the inholding, placing his bet in a great gamble, and then offered to trade it for the entire Wild Fire Valley. The Forest Service was definitely interested, as the trade would cost them nothing and give them something they very much wanted.

Federal law requires that an environmental assessment be performed on any proposed land swap. Unfortunately, the Forest Service did not even have the available funding to undertake it. So David Fast volunteered to cover the expense himself and hire the necessary scientists and environmental engineers. According to their assessment, the Forest Service would benefit tremendously by allowing the exchange—the value of the White River land was appraised at twice that of Wild Fire Valley due to the discovery of a vast amount of coal buried beneath its rolling forests.

Public hearings were held. Various environmental organizations, including Kim's small group of locals who called themselves "the Wild Fire Tribe," decried the proposed swap. When it appeared that the Forest Service would deny the developer's plan, David Fast announced his "reluctant" intention to develop his White River land if the swap wasn't approved. He was going to strip-mine it for coal, he told a reporter, as that was the only way to recover something from his gamble and keep himself from bankruptcy. The resulting excavations would render his land and the entire White River National Forest around it forever uninhabitable for the tuft-eared cats.

"Fucking blackmail," one of the young activists next to me mutters.

The national environmental organizations were horrified—they desperately wanted to reintroduce the lynx. They had worked for years toward that goal. Their position switched overnight from condemnation to eager enthusiasm for the swap. The small and powerless Wild Fire Tribe found themselves alone in opposing the trade. With the support of the larger environmental groups, the regional manager of the Forest Service announced his intention to formally approve the exchange. This valley would then belong to David Fast.

A few weeks ago Kim's group learned from one of the engineers who performed the assessment that the whole thing was a "bunch of crap." There was no economically extractable coal to be found on Fast's White River land. The land had no significant economic value at all. It was too remote for tourist cabins. It was too wooded for ranching. Its trees were too gnarled and diseased for logging. Yet the Forest Service and the environmental groups who'd fallen for Fast's blackmail remained adamant that the swap must go forward. For the sake of the lynx.

The Tribe's allegations of fraud on the part of Fast and his hired engineers have once again put the developer's plans in jeopardy. Fearing for his project, Fast has hired a "consultant," a man named Alf Burgermeister, a.k.a. Rent-a-Riot, who is considered an expert in combating environmental groups. It's rumored that Fast may have even made him a partner. In any event, the resulting harassment has been petty for the most part. Like the Tribe's members receiving fake flyers that changed the time and place of where the Forest Service was to hold community meetings to get public feedback on the swap. Some of it had been irritating—members of the Tribe had had expired license plate permits stuck over their current ones so that the local police would frequently stop them. And some of it had been mildly frightening.

Kim talks about how at one of the Tribe's recent meetings at her house a window was shot out with a pellet gun. Tires on the numerous cars parked outside were slashed. Someone threw red paint on her front door, which she took as a threat to spill blood if necessary. Members of the Tribe received crank calls late at night. Some of them were verbally accosted by the developer's local supporters in supermarkets, restaurants, and hardware stores.

"But we won't let them scare us off," she says grimly.

A chorus of "Right on!" comes primarily from the older portion of her audience. To me, though, there seems to be a lack of defiance in the voices. A meekness. I have the impression that many of them are very close to being scared off—maybe many of them have been already.

While she talks, I sit in the damp grass near the fire. I listen and take a polite pull on a bottle of rum when it's passed to me. Like a good narcotics cop, I decline the occasional offer of a toke from a joint. Again I'm struck by the intense hatred Kim appears to bear for the developer, David Fast. Her lips are thin when she says his name and they pull away from her teeth in almost a snarl. It seems out of proportion to his simple greed and schoolboy bullying. I wouldn't want to be on her shit list.

Her damaged face taut and passionate in the firelight, Kim goes on to discuss her strategy of legal and media-inspired challenges to the land exchange. Tomorrow they'll have a rally, she explains. Two television crews, one local out of Durango and a second out of Denver, have both promised to send cameras. A rumor's been going around that the developer, his timber and ranching employees, his investors, and his friends are going to try to interrupt it, but they can't be allowed to stop the Tribe from getting their message out.

"Waste of time," a voice says dismissively when she pauses. Every head turns to where the speaker is crouched in the dark grass.

I worry for a moment that Kim will explode. But instead she says evenly, "Okay, Cal. Tell us why you think it's a waste of time."

The skinny young man, the caver who'd earlier put his arms around Sunny, stands up. " 'Cause that guy Fast is all sewn up with the politicians, the judges, everybody. His mom was a fucking *United States senator*."

"So what do you propose? That we just give up?"

"We should fight 'em dirty, the way they fight us. Burn down that fucking lodge they're building. Burn their trucks and tractors. Shit, we should burn that Fast guy's house. Screw this media crap," he says.

Kim appears unprovoked, as if she's heard all this before. She calls for a show of hands—who wants to seek a legal solution instead of responding with harassment and violence? The vast majority of the activists around the fire raise their hands. Only a few, Sunny hesitantly among them, raise their hands when Kim asks in a half-joking tone, "Who wants to burn stuff?" Some of Cal's young friends hoot and whistle with both hands in the air. As a peace officer and a man more than a little interested in Kim, I voted for her plan.

Cal is as calm as Kim had been a minute earlier. Still standing, he looks around at the activists and says, "There's another way, too. Something I can't tell you all about right now. But I'm working on it. It's something big. Fucking huge."

Kim isn't able to keep the condescension out of her voice. "Cal, I've heard you talk about this big surprise before. If it's for real, then let us know. Tell everyone about it."

The young man looks into the fire and shakes his head. "I can't. Not yet."

"Then we'll go with the vote and continue to pursue a media-based and legal means of stopping the development."

She turns back to the group and explains how the rally scheduled for the next day will work. She instructs everyone to not react to the counter-protesters no matter what they say or do. Just ignore them—that's the only effective way of dealing with them. She tells us that she asked the county sheriff in Tomichi to have a few deputies around but was rebuffed. The sheriff doubted there would be any trouble. Then Kim asks if anyone else wants to speak.

A few of the older activists stand up and detail the harassment they've received from the developer and Burgermeister, his hired gun. They complain about being jostled in Tomichi's main grocery store, about the hang-ups late at night, about paint thrown on the walls of their own houses and cars, about threats from Fast himself that a local bank where he serves as a director will not be able to refinance their loans. They want sympathy for the deprivations they've had to endure by trying to save the valley. They want their suffering documented and recognized. They want it deemed excusable if they decide to bow out of the battle because of what it has already cost them. It's clear to me that many of these people are afraid, although they still try to sound determined. And I think that Kim may have a problem keeping her Tribe together if this goes on much longer.

Kim tries to stir up their blood. She glares from face to face and says sharply, "Listen. It's not over yet. This man and his plan are *evil*. He wants to destroy *all this*. And if we don't fight David Fast, no one will. He'll tear this place apart. But if we keep our courage, we can beat him." She looks at Cal. "By using the law."

I suppress a sardonic smile. Despite being a sworn peace officer, the law is not something I have a whole lot of faith in.

FOUR

AFTER THE MEETING ends, when quiet groups of activists begin to walk or stumble away in the dark toward their camps at the meadow's fringe, I finally have a chance to speak with Kim alone. Sitting in the damp grass, I wait for their voices to fade until they're just a background for the crickets. Somehow one of the bottles of rum the younger crowd had been passing around the fire has ended up in my lap. I take a final swig and contemplate Kim's silhouette. She stands near the edge of the dying campfire's glow, looking less tough than she had when speaking, looking even a little forlorn. Maybe the softening is just a trick of the light. She doesn't smile as I walk up to her, but I am buoyed by the rum and the knowledge that she must want to talk to me, too, otherwise she would have walked off to the campsites with the others.

She starts just a little when I speak.

"Hi, Kim. I'm glad I came tonight. Thanks for inviting me."

I stand next to her and watch the popping embers. She's been studying them as if they were tea leaves that can tell the future. The only message I perceive in the coals is that this place is going to be destroyed, or maybe that we're all going to burn in hell. I wouldn't make a very optimistic fortune-teller. Especially not after a few too many pulls from a bottle of cheap rum.

"Thanks for coming." Her voice is gentle and sad, not nearly as passionate as it had been a few minutes earlier. Maybe she's getting the same message from the glowing coals. "I guess you couldn't convince your father to join us."

I shrug and repeat what I'd told Sunny, "He's got a lot on his mind right now." I don't explain further and she doesn't ask.

"Do you want any of this?" I offer her the bottle but she waves it away without taking her eyes off the fire.

"I don't drink."

We stand in silence. There's a bark of laughter from a nearby campsite. A playful cry follows it. More laughter from a few more people, then once again the crickets take over with their pulsating rhythm. The heat from the smoldering logs is hot on my face, and the rum is warm in my belly. With my eyes half-closed against the smoke, my brain lazily wonders about the future of this valley that Kim and my father love so much.

"Who's doing the legal work, moving to get the injunction and that sort of thing?" I ask, thinking I know some attorneys in Wyoming who might be able to help.

"I am."

"You're a lawyer?"

She nods, still staring into the embers. That's a strike against her. Two, actually, with the not drinking, because I'd really like to see her loosen up. But my attraction remains undiminished.

"Your group, the Wild Fire Tribe—are they the only one protesting this thing?"

"Yes. It's just us—me, a bunch of college kids, and some retirees." Her voice is tired. "Not enough people know about this place. Even fewer care or are willing to take the time to do anything. Most of the people in town believe the development will bring them money from tourism. They don't seem to understand that it will be a private, self-contained resort. It will be good for the construction business for a while. A few locals may get jobs waiting tables and cleaning bathrooms, but aside from the tax revenues, that's about it. And as for the out-of-towners who come here to camp, bike, and climb, well, they can just go somewhere else like Moab or Durango. They don't have the time or the interest to help save this place."

Despite the fact that I'd shown up at the meeting, I feel as if I'm being reproved. Maybe for not having gotten involved sooner, when I'd first heard about the proposed swap in a climbing magazine. In any event, I feel guilty. "What do you think your chances are?"

"The law will be on our side if I can convince a federal judge that there was fraud with the environmental assessment."

"You should be able to do it, right? Get that whistle-blower engineer to tell his story and subpoena the rest, make them testify under oath? Then a judge will grant a restraining order to keep the Forest Service from approving the swap?"

For the first time she looks straight at me. "You sound like you've had some legal training, too." I see her lips quiver with the start of a smile, and I can read what she's thinking but is too polite to say—*You sure as hell don't look like a lawyer, so you must have been a defendant.* I touch my scarred cheek. I wish I'd shaved and not drunk so much wine and rum.

"I've had some experience with the law," I say vaguely. I don't want to tell her I'm a cop. Not yet. People tend to get defensive when I tell them what I do. It's often better to be thought of as a criminal. I change the subject back to the valley. "Are you going to have Fast's engineers subpoenaed for your hearing?"

"I wish it were that easy. I can't even request a hearing for a TRO—that's a temporary restraining order—until the Forest Service Supervisor, who's an old friend of the Fast family by the way, has approved the exchange. And my whistle-blower's been sent to India by his company. The others are all over the country. I've tried to interview them on the phone but they very politely tell me to fuck off."

The word "fuck" sounds particularly harsh coming from her lips. She's becoming animated again, and angry. "To tell the truth, things look bad. But I couldn't tell them that," she says with a gesture toward the camps. "I'm left with very little evidence, just some hearsay really, to convince the judge to grant me an injunction and the right to continue the suit and then subpoena all the guys who did the assessment for Fast."

"You should see them in person. Appeal to them, threaten them. Now, before the hearing. From what I've seen, you can be very persuasive." I admire her fierce, pretty features in the shifting light. Her single eye is a hot orange in the reflected glow of the embers.

"If I had the money, I'd do it. But this group of mine doesn't exactly look wealthy, does it?"

No, they didn't. They looked like a combination of broke-ass college students and octogenarians eking out a retirement on their social security checks. "What about other environmental groups? Can't they help?"

She shakes her head and laughs again in that humorless way. "Most of the big ones fell for the scam, and now they're too embarrassed to admit it. And the smaller ones have their own troubles."

"I've seen bigger groups of protesters show up to complain about the paving of a trailhead parking lot." By the tightening of her mouth I can tell I've said the wrong thing. The rum has loosened my tongue and made me say something she could only take as an affront.

She doesn't respond right away. Instead she studies me in the firelight with her good eye. Her gaze is hard enough that it feels almost like one of her small hands is at my throat. "You look like a tough young man, Antonio."

I shrug, but I'm pleased at the way my name sounds coming out of her mouth. "Call me Anton. Everyone but my parents does."

That pleasure is lost when she asks, "Tell me, Anton, what the fuck do you care?"

I can only shrug again, taken aback and a little offended. "I like this place. I've heard my father talk about it since I was a kid. I don't want to see it go down without a good fight." Then my annoyance at her tone and words catches up to me. I remember my father's advice about choosing fights. "It doesn't look like it's going to be much of a fight," I comment, unable to resist the rum-fueled urge to provoke her a little further. To see what will happen.

"Screw you, kid." She turns away from the dying fire and starts to walk in the direction the others had gone.

Her words hit my ears like a slap. It chases the alcohol right out of my blood. The realization that she is walking away with the belief that I'm nothing but an obnoxious jerk is almost painful. Things aren't going at all like I'd hoped. I'm going to be left alone by a smoldering campfire, rejected by a woman who has some strange hold on me, and with nothing to look forward to but a tense confrontation with my brother and the destruction of the temple of my father's youth.

I call after her, "Kim. I'm sorry—I didn't mean it the way it sounded. I want to learn more about this. I'm on your side."

She turns quickly and walks back up to me. She stops only when her forehead is just a few inches from my chin. "I'm sick of hearing how hopeless it is. I'm sick of all my old friends telling me that. And I'm sick of guys like you, people who look and sound like they might be able to do something, chickening out. If it's not much of a fight, it's because everyone's too afraid of this guy to fight. Everyone wants to just roll over for him. Let me tell you, Anton, I'm not going to do that. And I'm not going to listen to any defeatist bullshit."

A little alcohol sneaks back into my voice as I try to

lighten her mood. "Hey, you saw my dog. We'll just turn him loose the next time Fast's around."

But it doesn't work. She snorts and starts to turn away again.

"Cal and his crowd don't seem too afraid," I say, trying a more serious tack. "What about them?"

"That's because they're too dumb to know better. David Fast and his hired pit bull eat kids like them for breakfast."

"Listen, Kim, I'm not a dumb kid and I'd like to help you." I talk quickly, hoping to keep her from walking off again. "The thing is, my brother is coming up here and he's more than a little messed up right now. My first priority has to be dealing with him. I've got to keep him and my father from killing each other." And Roberto from killing himself.

But Kim isn't paying attention to me anymore. She's facing the nearly dead fire again, listening to the smoldering logs crackle and pop. After a few seconds her rigid posture seems to slacken a little, as if the anger's draining away. I step up beside her and suppress an urge to put my hand on her shoulder. *Go away, rum.* Then she starts speaking to the embers.

"The thing that makes me sick is that Cal might be right. If this rally tomorrow doesn't work out, and if the judge won't go for an injunction, then Cal and his cigarette lighter and this 'secret' of his may be the only way to stop David Fast." She looks over at me quickly and adds, "It might be the only way to save the valley."

I wonder what's more important to her—saving the valley or ruining Fast.

After a minute I ask, "What's Cal's secret?"

"Oh, he claims to have found some important cave but he won't tell anyone where it is. He says there's an Indian ruin in it, Anasazi maybe." I recall that the Anasazi were an ancient tribe in the Four Corners region. They were famous both for the hidden cliff dwellings they inhabited and their sudden and mysterious disappearance many centuries ago. She pauses to look at me. "Do you know any cavers?"

I shake my head.

"There are a few in town I know. They're all obsessive about keeping the places they explore secret. Anyway, Cal believes he's found some undiscovered ruin full of artifacts. He says no one's found it before because it's hard to get to and because it was partially buried by an old rockfall. It's supposed to be part of an enormous cave system that is so valuable it will keep the Forest Service from approving the swap. He says it's bigger than Carlsbad or Kartchner, and valuable enough as a unique resource to throw off the land appraisals. He actually wants to call it 'Cal's Bad Caverns'—a play on words."

I nod and smile with understanding. "Is it for real?"

She shrugs. "A few days ago he showed up at the campfire looking kind of scared and sick, and all covered with red mud. He said he'd gotten lost in it. Only he won't tell anyone where it is because he's afraid the government won't let him be the one to explore it. He says they'll put a lock over the entrance and only let government geologists and archaeologists go inside. And then they'll turn it into a tourist attraction and destroy it. I think he's probably full of shit, but he's adamant that he won't tell anyone where the entrance is until the Forest

Service agrees to his terms. They're supposed to be considering it, but I wouldn't count on it."

"Why not?"

"I've talked to some people there. They don't believe him—they think he's a crank who's found some worthless little mud hole. And even if he were telling the truth about the size and importance of the cave, federal regulations wouldn't allow them to agree to his conditions anyway. The rally tomorrow and the legal challenges are still the best hope we've got."

Reading her better now, I know not to try a joke or even a comforting word. "Tell me about Fast," I ask. I recall the venom I'd heard in her voice each time she'd spoken his name.

She answers slowly, still looking into the dying fire, choosing her words carefully. "David Fast is an arrogant prick. He more or less runs this county. He thinks he can do what he wants without consequence." Then she smiles. "I think I've got him worried, though."

After another quiet minute in the darkness she glances up at me. "Stick around for the rally tomorrow, Anton. You'll see what we're up against. It's going to get ugly."

FIVE

I WAKE UP even more thickheaded than usual, groggy and dry-mouthed.

The sun is rising to the south of Wild Fire Peak, and the meadow is noisy with birds. My father is already sitting up in his bag. He's gingerly touching his sunburned scalp with his calloused fingertips. The other campers and protesters, the "Wild Fire Tribe," are still sleeping off the excesses of dope and rum that had been freely passed around the campfire. As I shed my bag, the sunlight touches my bare skin with a caress despite the cold night air that lingers in the valley. Oso rouses himself from a wool blanket by my side. He'd been curled on it in a huge, tight ball, with his nose a few inches shy of being able to bury itself in the stump of his tail.

Dad and I shake the dew off our sleeping bags, then stretch them to dry on the Land Cruiser's hood. I pull on a pair of shorts and a fleece vest. After taking care of some urgent morning business in the woods, I set up my tiny stove and spill a little gasoline on the primer. Nearby, Oso pees on the same tree where my father had just relieved himself.

"Guess he's showing me who's top dog," Dad grumbles.

"I don't think he liked being relegated to the backseat yesterday."

When I sleepily flick my lighter at the shallow pool of fuel I'd dribbled beneath the burner, flames shoot three feet in the air. I jerk backwards before my hair catches on fire. The sudden motion causes a heavy ache in my skull. The wine and the rum I'd helped myself to around the campfire last night feel as if they're sloshing like mercury in my brain. For several years now, ever since my brother began his excessive experimentation with substance abuse, I haven't been much of a drinker.

I glance at my father when I think I hear a grunt or a chuckle from behind me. He's frowning, but his blue eyes sparkle with amusement.

"I think I'll do the leading today," he says. "You're going to be useless."

"Bite me," I say under my breath.

According to my mother, the old man was a legendary drinker in the old days. It fitted with his wild-man image in the stories she told my brother and me. But these days he never drinks to the point that you could tell. The new Air Force frowns on excessive alcohol consumption. And I know that as Dad gets older he's having a harder time keeping up with the young Pararescue soldiers he commands.

We haven't even finished our oatmeal when the first car rolls into the meadow from the Forest Service road. Soon it's followed by several others. Most of them are muddy, oversized pickups with gun racks visible in the rear windows. I guess that they belong to the counter-protesters—I doubt many environmentalists would drive one these diesel-guzzling beasts. Some of the trucks are equipped with oversized tires that even at low speeds chew then spit out the meadow's grass.

The trucks park haphazardly in the clearing. Some of them appear aggressive in stopping very close to where the Tribe members are waking up and rubbing their eyes as they stare in confusion at the snarling engines. The people who get out of the trucks are, without exception, young to middle-aged men. I remember Kim's warning from the night before—that things could get ugly—and think that the fact that no women or children have been brought along is a very bad sign. The men look tough when they get out of their trucks. Physical laborers, it appears from the broad forearms and sunburnt necks. Probably construction workers promised work on the new development in the valley.

The majority of them wear what could be a uniform of jeans and work boots and baseball caps, the only concession to individualism in what tobacco or beer company logo is displayed on their T-shirts. They stare at the protesters with what looks to me like a sort of grim amusement, the way a pack of coyotes stare at a herd of sheep.

Only one of the trucks is even remotely new looking—a huge Chevy Suburban painted a glossy black beneath the thin layer of dust the Forest Service road has sprinkled on it. The license plate reads "FSTRNU," which, after a moment's thought, I decipher as "Faster than You." It must belong to David Fast, the notorious developer. *An arrogant prick,* I remember Kim saying. She also called him evil.

The driver of the black Suburban steps out. David Fast is dressed more expensively than the others, in a creased pair of khakis and a white shirt with pearl buttons. He looks around the meadow with a concerned, proprietary air. While the license plate gives credence to Kim's description of a self-satisfied jerk, his appearance isn't evil.

He's a tall man, a little heavy with too much fat and too much muscle. Like an aging football player ten years past his prime. Although he's probably Kim's age, he looks a few years older. His graying hair is buzzed short on a handsome head.

Another man looks evil, though. He climbs out of the Suburban's passenger side and slams the door shut behind him. He does it hard enough so that the echo bangs off the forested hillsides surrounding the valley. The sound reminds me of a bull elk's territorial bugle. This man has a pumpkin-sized head, no neck, and the powerful torso of a prison weight lifter. The prison part is emphasized because of the tattoos that cover his arms. Even from this distance, I recognize some of the tattoos as a mark of membership in a jailhouse white supremacist gang. And I remember how at the campfire meeting the night before, several of the activists had complained about how Fast's harassment had only become serious after he'd hired a professional enforcer named Alf Burgermeister, a.k.a. Rent-a-Riot. Someone had mentioned that

Burgermeister sells his services to antienvironmentalist causes all over the country. This guy certainly looks like someone who would be called Rent-a-Riot. His menacing appearance is accentuated by the way his head is carefully shaved but for the long, red sideburns that meet above his upper lip.

The men who look like construction workers sit on the tailgates of their trucks or stand around them in the grass, talking, laughing, and watching the Tribe members in the meadow. Burgermeister calls to them in a deep baritone—a sergeant summoning his troops. For a moment I wonder who's in charge—Fast or his enforcer. The men respond instantly, wandering over to gather around the developer's shiny truck.

"What are we going to climb today, Ant?" my father asks, ignoring the spectacle around us. "It doesn't make sense for us to wait all morning for Roberto."

"I think I'm sticking around to check this thing out. There's something nasty in the air."

"I smell it, too. That's just your brother, on his way," he says in a rare try at a joke.

It's a sign that he's feeling a bit of stress. In my grumpy mood, I find it kind of amusing. This man can jump out of planes at over sixty thousand feet, climb runout 5.12, fire just about any weapon known to man, run and swim in the worst of conditions for hours at a time, and perform every type of emergency surgery, yet he's nervous about a reunion with his eldest son. To be fair, though, he should be nervous.

I pour myself some coffee from the kettle I'd placed on the hissing stove and keep watching the meadow. I glare at a new pickup coming into the meadow when it rumbles too close to us. The lone driver, a burly young guy with his sleeves rolled to his shoulders, hesitates while looking back at me. I can almost read his thoughts as he takes in my scrappy beard, scarred face, and the climber's arms that I've folded across my chest. He slows, considering how to respond to the challenge in my eyes, and looks over to see just how far away his friends are. Then he glances at Oso, who places himself between the truck and our camp, and wisely decides to pull to another part of the meadow.

My dad touches my shoulder.

"There's nothing you can do, Antonio," he says gently. "We're in Colorado. Your badge isn't any good here."

I answer without looking at him and try to make a joke of my own. "Badges? Don't need no stinking badges."

My father clips his rock shoes and chalk bag to a small pack. He shakes his head at me before he walks into the forest and heads in the direction of the canyon. He's going bouldering, I guess. He's too cautious these days to solo on the steep canyon walls.

David Fast and his hirelings don't outnumber the Tribe's mostly youthful protesters, but they certainly outdo them in intimidation. Their physical presence is bigger. Harder. More confident. After disassembling the stove and washing the dishes in the stream, I walk among the pickup trucks and SUVs with my steaming coffee mug and observe the bumper stickers that attest to membership in antienvironmental organizations such as Wise Use and the Rocky Mountain Legal Foundation. Some are even amusing, saying things such as "Are You an Environmentalist or Do You Work for a Living?" and "The

Only Good Trees Are Stumps." My favorite reads, "Hungry and Out-of-Work? Eat an Environmentalist."

While the newly arrived men mill around, shaking hands, slapping backs, and trying to get a look at the young hippie girls writhing out of their sleeping bags and putting on their clothes, Kim directs a few of her followers in stringing some sheets between trees. Painted on the sheets are slogans like "Save Wild Fire Valley" and "Stop the Development." The banners are arranged around a prominent stump that I suppose will act as a speaker's platform.

As I amble I receive suspicious looks from both sides. None of the environmentalists seem to recognize me from the campfire meeting the night before. Without obvious tattoos and facial piercings, I probably look more like one of Fast's men, except that I wear sandals, shorts, and a purple fleece vest instead of boots, jeans, and a Jack Daniel's T-shirt.

I'm wandering near Kim, drawn to her as I had been the night before, and wondering if I should offer to help, when a large white van from a Denver television station bounces up the dirt road and into the meadow. At a gesture from Burgermeister, the construction workers eye the people inside with what can only be taken for menace. They shift themselves slightly to be in the way as much as possible. Slowly, the van works itself through the human obstacle course and stops at the small stage-area Kim is arranging. A middle-aged woman climbs out as Kim hurries forward to greet her.

"Kim!" I hear the woman say as they embrace. "So good to see you again!"

The construction workers snicker and I hear one say something about lesbians.

While glaring at the men nearby, the Denver reporter tells Kim, "They put a couple of logs across the road, trying to stop us from coming in. While we were trying to get around them, some thugs in boots and cowboy hats had a talk with the guys from the Durango station, and they turned back."

"Damn," I hear Kim say. She joins her friend in glaring at the counter-protesters. One of the men waggles his tongue at her, then toasts her with a coffee mug, to the amusement of his colleagues. Kim catches sight of me watching them and nods slightly. *See*, her look says, *I told you it was going to get ugly*. Then the two women turn, walking back toward the stage.

It's evident that Kim is too busy to talk to me, so I walk back over to the Land Cruiser and sit down in my father's soot-stained camp chair. I watch as Kim continues to organize the small rally. It doesn't appear that it's going to be much of a protest—with the road blocked down-valley, Kim is stuck with just the thirty or so protesters already in the meadow.

David Fast does a little organizing of his own. He pops open the back of his gleaming Suburban, revealing a few boxes of donuts, an ice chest, and a huge urn of coffee. His workers gather around as he jokes with them. Burgermeister stands directly beside him, as close as a bodyguard would. But he doesn't smile at the jokes. Instead he squints angrily at the environmentalists.

After a few minutes Fast takes a heavy roll of canvas from the Surburban's backseat. With Burgermeister's help, he carries it over behind Kim's makeshift stage.

There they unroll the canvas and start to string it between two trees right next to where the Tribe's banner proclaiming "Save the Valley" is hung.

Kim hurries over, probably asking him what the hell he thinks he's doing. Fast just smiles—maybe even a little apologetically—and ties one end of the banner to a tree's trunk. His enforcer pulls it tight at the other end while glaring at Kim. I suspect he says something rude, too, because Kim's back stiffens although she remains in the developer's face. The canvas reads in neatly printed letters, "Support Local Jobs! Support the San Juan Economy! Wild Fire Resort."

Kim keeps arguing with him, but Fast never loses his thin-lipped smile. After securing his end, Burgermeister comes to stand beside his boss. Then he reaches out with a thick finger and pokes Kim right in the breastbone. I start to get up. As tightly wound as Kim is, I expect trouble right there. And I'm feeling protective toward her even though she hasn't really done anything to encourage me.

Fast does something sensible—he grabs Burgermeister's arm and tries to pull him away. But Burgermeister jerks free. Before I even take a step, Kim spins away and marches back to where the television crew is still setting up. She speaks hotly to the reporter or producer who'd hugged her earlier, but her friend just shrugs and shakes her head. They hadn't seen it. Kim's face is red when she walks back to her makeshift stage.

Two people on foot come up the Forest Service road and into the meadow. Even from a distance, it's easy for me to recognize pretty Sunny and her boyfriend, Cal the Caver. The sunlight glints off Cal's pierced eyebrows and nose. Sunny's blonde dreadlocks bounce with each step. Fast sees them, too, and I watch him pause, then start to stride toward the couple with brawny Burgermeister in tow. Cal slows. He looks over a shoulder, back down the road, as if he's considering running away. But Sunny tugs his hand toward the gathering activists.

Fast intercepts them near the center of the meadow. It looks like there's a brief argument before Sunny tugs again and leads Cal past the two big men. Fast and his enforcer talk to one another while watching the young couple walk away. *What's that about?* Both Sunny and Cal glance back at the men nervously.

Then Kim's voice rings out across the meadow. "Let's get started," she says. She calls the Tribe around her makeshift stage and arranges them so that they're in view of the television crew's camera but not in its way. I stay where I am, wanting to be able to watch the activists' backs.

She steps up on the stump and begins to speak. Her voice is loud enough for me to hear across the meadow as she decries what the development will do to the valley. Almost as soon as she starts speaking, Fast, Burgermeister, and the other men move in behind the activists, encircling them. They begin chanting, "Local jobs! Local jobs!" drowning out Kim as she does her best to shout over them, her beautiful, damaged face getting redder and redder beneath her tan. A few of the activists, led by Cal, do their best to exhort the workers to shut up and listen, but it's a halfhearted shushing—they're clearly intimidated by the big, rough-looking men.

It's over even more quickly than it began. Kim simply steps down from the stump, her head low but her jaw protruding sharply. She stalks away into the forest. I see the producer of the camera crew shrug her shoulders again and they begin packing up the equipment. The activists disperse back to their scattered camps at the meadow's fringe while the construction workers slap one another's shoulders and hands. I can hear their jeers.

When the television van bumps its way out of the meadow and down toward the road, the workers cheer again. This isn't my fight—as my father advised, I'm not going to get too involved in a lost cause—but I'm angry. Fast and his hired muscle are simply bullies. Their tactics are dirty. I make myself stay in my chair and trace my hand over Oso's heavy head where he's laid it on one of my knees.

It looks like the show is over. I'm thinking about going to look for my dad down the canyon when Kim comes back out of the woods. She's moving fast, her face determined, walking straight toward where Fast is distributing beer to his victorious minions. Cal and several of the activists stand up to watch from their scattered camps around the meadow. Burgermeister stands protectively in front of his boss, his hands on his hips and a nasty smile on his face.

Kim jabs a finger into the middle of his thick chest just as I'd seen him do to her earlier. Burgermeister laughs and pushes her away by placing his hands on her breasts. As she stumbles backward, her feet tangle in the grass and she falls. A small group of the workers encircle her like a grinning pack of wolves. Others back away, Fast among them, probably realizing that this is going too far. Things begin moving very quickly.

Before I can push myself out of the chair, Cal, the

skinny firebrand, is stalking toward the group. Sunny trails behind him. Oso is at my side as I begin to run. Glancing over my shoulder, I check that the beast is still securely tied to the old truck with the long rope. "Stay!" I shout at him just as the rope snaps against his throat. I hear the truck creak behind me with the impact of his weight.

I'm still fifty feet away when Cal reaches the group. Through the bodies of the men, I can see Kim struggling to get up but the men keep pushing her over with their boots as Burgermeister leads them in pouring their beers on her. Fast looks as if he's trying to intercede on Kim's behalf. Cal leaps on somebody's back like he's mounting a wild horse. One of the man's friends peels the wiry caver off his steed.

"Hey!" I yell as loud as I can. The grinning men all turn to me, but not before one of them slugs Cal in the face and sends him reeling back into the tall grass.

"Let her go! Let her go!" I'm almost to them. Their attention diverted, Kim struggles to her feet looking like an angry cat. Her wet hair is plastered across her face, her white shirt stained yellow from the soaking, her pale yellow sports bra visible through the transparent cotton. She sputters and spits.

Burgermeister steps through the throng of men and faces me. "Who the hell are you?" he asks as I stop just a few feet from him, breathing lightly from the run across the meadow.

"A witness." I turn to Kim. "Get out of here." She looks at me with her one good eye wide in outrage. She doesn't move. Cal stands up, one hand held to his face, blood dripping between his fingers. "Get her out of here," I snap at him.

"This is none of your business, buddy. And besides, the bitch touched me first."

"You grabbed her breasts and pushed her. That's assault. Then your boys held her down. That's false imprisonment."

"Alf!" David Fast barks, stepping forward and interrupting us. "That's enough!"

For a moment I think I'm going to get out of this okay. But then Burgermeister turns to Fast with a growl. "Shut up, Dave. Let me do my job. You hired me and made me your partner, so this goddamn thing is as much mine as yours."

Fast says, "Alf," again, but this time his tone is plaintive. He's ignored.

Cal has taken one of Kim's arms and is trying to pull her away. Sunny takes the other. The construction workers move in a loose circle around where I face Burgermeister. This is what they'd wanted all morning, I realize. They'd come looking for a fight. I size up the man called Rent-a-Riot, taking in his considerable bulk. He probably weighs in at two hundred and twenty or so, forty pounds more than me. Even if I could take him, through speed and cunning and luck, his men will step in and rip me to shreds. I'm in serious trouble. A rush of fear floods through me. But for some reason the corners of my lips twist up in an expectant smile. My blood starts to tingle with a touch of my brother's madness. Far behind me I can hear Oso bellowing across the meadow. I should have let him off the leash.

Grinning back, Burgermeister says, "She pushed me

first, Scarface. Just like this." He steps forward and shoves a thick finger hard into my chest. "Now what would you do if someone did that to you?"

I knock his wrist away. Oso roars again in the distance.

"If it were a woman, I'd walk away." I have the familiar sensation of my vision somehow widening, my sense of sound and smell and taste all expanding while time seems to slow to half-speed.

"Are you saying I'm a woman?" Burgermeister demands, his voice sounding to my ears like a tape playing on low batteries. He tries to jab me again with his finger, and I step back, again knocking his wrist away. I'm aware of the hollow rustle of my own breath flowing in and out of my lungs.

The men gathered around us laugh. Cal and Sunny are half dragging Kim toward their friends at the screen of trees. Kim's good eye is locked on me, open wide now in panic rather than anger. She's talking fast to Cal but he's just shaking his head. With his free hand he still holds the blood that's leaking from his face. I can hear Oso roaring and slamming against the heavy rope that binds him to my truck.

I turn to walk away but a heavily bearded man in a Harley-Davidson T-shirt blocks my path. In his hand he holds a Heineken bottle by the neck, ready to swing. They aren't going to let me go. No way. The mob of Fast's men is totally pumped up for this. The fun they'd had with Kim on the ground at their feet, her thin shirt transparent with beer, has stirred up a violent sexual energy that I can taste in the air.

My dad's words come back to me. "There are two

things worth fighting for, son. The things you can win and the things worth dying for." I add a third: *You fight when you've got nothing to lose, just to get in as many licks as you can.* I spin back toward Burgermeister and shoot a clenched-fist jab at his face.

He has both hands raised like a boxer; he easily bats away my fist. But it was never my intention to hit him with my hand. That was another rule my dad had taught me about fighting—never hit a man in the face unless you want a broken hand. With my hands high in the air, I snap a clean front kick into his crotch. Then, as he doubles over with an explosion of exhaled air, I bring my left elbow down on the back of his head. I might as well be striking a boulder—a lightning bolt of pain shoots up my arm.

"Anton!" Kim shouts my name. The two syllables come out as crisp as hands clapping twice. A warning.

I whip my head toward the sound while dropping into a low crouch. A body is coming at me in a flying tackle. I shove into the air, coming out of the crouch like a whale breaching, and lift the incoming body high, flinging it into the air and sending it crashing into another man. Out of the corner of my eye I see another object arcing toward my skull—a green bottle clenched in someone's raw-knuckled fist. There's a flare of bright light as the bottle shatters against the side of my head.

SIX

THE PUNCHES AND kicks of seven or eight big men fall on me with an almost mechanical rhythm. It feels as if I'm being run through a threshing machine. At first their blows just cause sharp explosions of pain before a sort of numbness overwhelms my body. And the realization that once they're done beating me, there will be a lot more pain to come. Over their grunting curses and occasional barks of laughter, I can hear Oso roaring as he throws himself against the rope. I kick and punch back as best I can from where I've been pummeled onto my back in the grass. But every time I strike out with a leg or a fist, a new blow sneaks in to bang some exposed, vital part.

Over the whoops and the laughs of the men all around me, there comes an immense thundering sound, as if some gigantic tractor really is tearing its way through the meadow to finish the job of chewing me up. At first I think it's my consciousness taking flight, lifting off a runway in my brain. But when my world doesn't fade to black I realize it might be one of the trucks coming to run me over.

I picture the huge ribbed tires I'd seen churning the grass when the trucks had first pulled into the meadow. A part of me can't believe that these men would actually intend to kill me—when it began it had seemed like a little fun, a simple mauling, and a lesson not to interfere, was all they were after. I ignore the sharp blows that hammer in every time I open myself up and fight back with every savage ounce of strength I possess.

Suddenly the men are leaping off me like flies swatted away from a piece of rotting meat. A shower of torn grass and dirt pelts my skin. When I twist my head to figure out which way to roll to avoid the thick rubber treads, all I can see are two spinning tires instead of four, smaller than I expect, and the chrome and glossy black paint of a speeding motorcycle. The bike's just a few feet from my head. And then it's gone. The machine races past me, chasing the fleeing, shouting men. The bike's rider is screaming the Highland war cry Dad taught my brother and me when we were kids.

I prop myself up unsteadily onto my hands and knees. It's Roberto on the bike. His black hair streams out from behind low-slung sunglasses. He's wearing a pair of heavy brown jeans, faded to the color of buckskin, below a black T-shirt. A leather jacket is rolled on the bike behind his back, above the saddlebags. He looks like an avenging Apache ghost.

I feel a familiar thrill rush through me; it's the same exhilaration I'd felt in a dozen schoolyard fights when older boys on some new military base sought to teach the new kid a lesson. So many times my brother had magically appeared, apparently out of nowhere, rescuing me, punishing my older tormenters, and finally chasing them off as they bawled like frightened children.

With confident ease he slams the bike's rear brake while turning the handlebars, slewing the bike through the grass and turning it one hundred and eighty degrees. Even from across the meadow, I can see the wild grin I know so well on his face.

Burgermeister runs toward my brother. He moves with surprising agility for a bodybuilder. In his hand he holds a piece of metal—a tire iron or maybe a crowbar he's lifted from the back of a pickup. I shout a warning at Roberto. The motorcycle gives a throaty roar as he spins the rear wheel in the grass and heads straight toward the threat. Over the engine's noise, I can hear my brother laughing. The scene looks like something out of a medieval joust, only Rent-a-Riot is horseless. I can't help but be impressed by the big man's courage. Or stupidity. He's about to feel the full force of my brother's madness.

Fast and his remaining men gather near the safety of their parked trucks. They're staring at the action in the center of the meadow. Someone yells at Burgermeister, "Get that crazy fucker!"

Roberto weaves the bike back and forth as he gooses the throttle. I can see every sinew and muscle in his lean arms where he grips the handlebars. Burgermeister keeps running toward him, bobbing from side to side in answer to my brother's changes in course. The burly man with the linebacker's muscles dances with an odd, determined grace as he runs. His face is set in an intense scowl. It looks as if he's hoping to step aside like a matador at the last moment, hoping to have the chance to swing the piece of iron and take my brother's head off with it.

They come together just as the big man raises his weapon. Roberto gooses the throttle again and shoots forward in a sudden burst. With one hand he grabs the iron close to Burgermeister's wrist. But the big man holds on tight enough to cause Roberto to start to spill the heavy bike into the grass. Still grasping the bar, my brother springs from the seat and drives a knee into the other man's chest. They both go down in a tangle. The two wrestle for just a moment before Roberto flips him on his back with a judo throw. Burgermeister is discovering my brother's crazed strength. The other men are running toward them.

An explosion splits the air just as Roberto raises the tire iron over the man's face, ready to strike. The gunshot seems to rip the valley wide open, freezing time. The only move anyone makes is to jerk their heads at the sound. It had come from where Oso is still slamming against the rope, jerking my truck's four tires a few inches with each lunge.

My father stalks across the meadow with my .40 caliber Heckler & Koch held high. He must have found my keys and pulled it out of the glove box. "Get off him, Roberto."

My brother shakes his head as if amused, then climbs off Fast's enforcer.

Despite the gun in my father's hand, David Fast walks right up to him. "Put that gun away, mister," he demands, his voice out of breath. "It's over."

Behind him Burgermeister gets unsteadily to his feet with his eyes fixed on my brother.

My father complies. He uncocks my pistol with a snap of his thumb and slips the gun into a pocket of his baggy shorts. "You and your men leave. Now." His voice is crisp and sharp, a colonel's voice, used to having his orders obeyed. The force of his presence and his tone has all the men but Fast and Burgermeister walking toward their trucks. Roberto is righting his huge motorcycle, ignoring them all.

"Hold it!" Burgermeister shouts at them. Then to Fast he prods, "Tell him, Dave."

Fast looks slightly uncomfortable, as if his dignity is offended by Burgermeister's coarse presence, but he speaks with a firm voice. "This is my meadow. My valley. It will be by the end of the week, anyhow. We're not going anywhere."

Dad reaches into his pocket. For a moment I'm afraid he's going to bring the H&K back out—the colonel isn't used to being disobeyed. But instead he brings out the almost brick-sized shape of his satellite phone.

"If that's the way you want it, then I'm going to have to call the authorities. Let them know that you and your men assaulted a young man and woman."

Fast chuckles. "You go right ahead, mister. The girl and that fellow"—he points at me—"started it. Besides, the sheriff's a good friend of mine."

Dad doesn't even blink. "I mean the federal authorities. This is still National Forest land."

Still chuckling, but now to save face rather than out of amusement, Fast holds up his hands. I can see his face is red and that his thin lips twitch while trying to hold up his false good humor. "All right, all right. We'll leave you and the hippies to smoke pot and do whatever else you people do while working men are out there trying to make a living."

It's funny to hear my dad called a hippie. If I weren't hurting so much, I might laugh.

Then Fast calls out louder so that the entire meadow can hear him, even the Tribe members who watch from the trees, "But on Friday, you people better be out of here. I mean that. This will be my land by then."

Burgermeister adds in a booming voice, "My boys and me are going to do what we call a 'citizen's arrest' to anyone who's still here. For trespassing. And I hope no one *accidentally* resists."

As Fast and Burgermeister walk by where Roberto's crouching by his motorcycle and plucking grass and mud from the cowling, Burgermeister points at him. "You're gonna be mine, bitch."

For a long moment they stare at one another. Roberto slowly comes to his feet. A smile creeps onto his face, then slowly disappears. He's a lot smaller than the weight lifter, but as his smile fades, he looks just as mean.

"Roberto," my father says warningly.

Fast, too, tries to intervene. "Come on, Alf."

Burgermeister pauses before leaving and turns to me. "You too, Scarface."

SEVEN

As THE PICKUPS rumble down the valley, I walk over and hug Roberto. "Good timing, bro. As always." Just putting my arms around him gives me a jolt of his energy. It's like touching a nuclear bomb—you can't even imagine what it's capable of.

"Shit, *che.* What's the matter with you, letting those rednecks get you down? You should of just whipped out that shiny little tin badge of yours."

"My badge is no good here. I'm a cop in Wyoming, remember?"

"Oh yeah, I know to stay out of that fucking state," he laughs, squeezing me gently, then pushing me away. "Wouldn't want my little brother throwin' down on me or nothing."

I smile at him with the same combination of awe and fear that I've always felt around him. The awe comes from the fact that he's unwilling to accept anyone's limits and has no concern for any consequences. The fear is not for anyone's safety but his own. He's hurt a lot of people in his life—I'd recently looked up his criminal history on the FBI's national database and had seen a laundry list of assaults and batteries, many that I hadn't been aware of—but at least in his mind he's only hurt those who had it coming. Roberto doesn't tolerate cruelty or meanness.

During my college days we were once having lunch and a beer at an outdoor café in Boulder. Nearby, on the sidewalk, a local well-known television reporter was berating his girlfriend for something. The conversation between us stopped as we watched. I was wondering, *What should we do if it gets physical. Get the police? Intervene somehow between them? Try to reason with the couple?* When the chubby reporter raised his hand and brought it across the girl's face, I didn't even hear the sound of the slap because my brother had already launched himself out of his chair. The table crashed to the ground in a racket of breaking bottles, glasses, and plates. The reporter turned just in time to see my brother's grinning, predatory face coming at him from just inches away as Roberto's forehead crashed down on the bridge of his nose.

The result had been one of many assault convictions. It was an unprovoked attack on one of the community's most cherished citizens, according to the local paper and the girlfriend (who, of course, had reconciled with her boyfriend and denied that she'd ever been slapped). Due to the contradictory statements of the parties and witnesses, my brother pleaded the case down to a misdemeanor and a stipulated thirty-day sentence in the

Boulder County Jail. He had no regrets, would make no apology, he told the judge at the risk of having the plea refused and a felony mandated. He'd do it again if he ever saw the fat bastard hit a woman.

Although a slew of military physicians and psychiatrists had diagnosed him with dozens of different disorders throughout his childhood, everything from severe hyperactivity to a variety of antisocial neuroses, and he had been the guinea pig for a hundred types of medication, I think my mother was the only one who truly understood what was wrong with him. "*Destraillado,*" she'd said. Unleashed. "He lives in a world where he's totally free, totally unrestrained. Your father used to have a foot in that world, too," she'd told me. But Roberto was born with both feet over the line, like a spastic puppy that has slipped his collar. My brother acts on all the urges and impulses the rest of us are either too civilized or too afraid to express.

For the first time I notice that Oso is silent and has been ever since Dad fired that shot. I look toward the truck, worried that the rope has broken his neck or crushed his trachea. But he's standing rigid in the tall grass and is still straining against the rope. I walk quickly to him and rub his head while kneeling in the damp earth. He pushes his froth-covered snout against my chest. "I know you were trying to help, Oso. I should have turned you loose."

"Look at that thing!" Roberto says from behind me. "He looks like a goddamn bear."

Before my father or I can warn him, Roberto reaches out a hand. Oso gazes steadily up at my brother with his eyes narrowed to golden slits for a few seconds, his lips raised in a half-snarl. Then the black lips drop over the long, clenched fangs. He licks my brother's fingers with his rough tongue. I'm amazed. I expected Oso to take his hand off. Stepping back, I watch the two study one another. Oso's ears start to lie back in a smile. They seem to recognize each other, maybe as fellow wild beasts. Like wolf cubs from the same litter.

Roberto is movie star handsome but his face has a feral cast. Behind the sunglasses he almost always wears, he has our father's slanting, crystal blue eyes. But they're set wide like our mother's, and even in repose they burn with restless energy. Like dry ice, which will burn you if you touch it. No one looking at him would question the fact that he is a dangerous man. My features are like his but not quite as sharp and defined. More of our mother's high Pampas blood shows on his face, while mine is thick-nosed and heavy-browed thanks to our father's Celtic ancestry. He wears his tangled dark hair long, down to his shoulders. Mine is short and conventional.

I hear the snap of my glove box and the rattle of keys as Dad locks my gun away. He walks over to us, hesitates, and then throws an arm over Roberto's shoulder. "Hi, son." It's an awkward gesture, this half-hug, and appears even more awkward because it's my father who is performing it. Roberto pats my father's chest with his far hand, turning it into a sort of embrace.

"Dad" is all he says.

This brief, tender moment ends quickly. My father says just the wrong thing without meaning to. "I'm glad you're here, 'Berto. It's good to see you. I just wish you hadn't gotten involved in that brawl. You're still on parole, aren't you?"

Roberto's face remains impassive, but I think I see a tightening of the muscles along his jaw. I know from my recent conversation with his parole officer that he'll be under her supervision for years. His most recent conviction was for vandalism. The story I'd heard was that after a few days of being jerked around by the local telephone company (which is famous for bad service) about the installation of a line in his rented cabin, Roberto had borrowed a neighbor's chainsaw and cut down six miles of poles. Unfortunately, the destruction of communications equipment is a federal crime. With federal time.

I chime in before Roberto's almost nonexistent self-control is overridden. He looks on the verge of saying something that could ruin this whole trip. "When you guys are done playing grab-ass, would someone mind telling me if I need any stitches?"

"Same old Dad," Roberto mutters, releasing my father from his embrace.

My entire body stings from abrasions and rising bruises. I touch my scarred left cheek, probe gently, and decide my cheekbone has remained intact although my fingertips come away bloody. The old wound on my face has reopened. Some of the blood is running into my mouth—I spit out the coppery taste. So much for my hope of the scar one day fading. The other damage seems to consist of bruised ribs and numerous contusions that I know will all start to hurt like hell in a few minutes, once the adrenaline climbs back into my glands.

My father, who's had enough medical training in the Pararescue Corps to be a trauma surgeon, examines my face. I watch his eyes as he studies my cheek and notice that his blue eyes have faded to gray over the years, and that the whites surrounding them have become almost yellow. Deep creases that I'd never really noticed before fan out from the corners.

"You're lucky, Antonio," he says, turning toward his backpack in the rear of the open truck. "No stitches. Let me see where I put the Krazy Glue."

I groan and Roberto chuckles. Ever since the stuff first came out when we were kids, when that ridiculous commercial always played on TV of a man hanging from where his hard hat had been glued to a beam, my father had been experimenting with the stuff. On us. Our mother would shout at him that he was poisoning us. He'd argue that he'd read the ingredients and none of it was toxic. But Roberto and I had been wary, sometimes staying out all night to avoid getting what we called the "treatment" and praying our new wounds would clot. It burns like hell when dabbed on raw flesh. On his missions he claimed it saved a lot of space to dump the bandages and field dressings and just carry a tiny tube of the gunk. He also carried a few tampons—his way of plugging bullet wounds.

After rummaging through the first-aid kit he always carries in his pack, my father snaps a sterile glove over one hand. Then he squeezes some glue onto a gloved fingertip.

"Bend over," Roberto advises me.

Dad ignores him and smears the stuff on my cheek. The fumes and the sting make my left eye burn and water. He uses both hands to pinch my reopened scar together and holds it for about thirty seconds.

When he steps back, not only does the sting remain,

but my face feels unnaturally tight, as if I'd just had plastic surgery. "Thanks, Dad. I think."

In the meantime Roberto has wheeled the giant motorcycle next to my Land Cruiser. It's a type I've never seen before. A single word, *Indian,* is painted on the fuel tank. Dad and I admire it while Roberto explains some things about cc's and gear ratios that I don't understand while he picks dirt and grass out of the handlebars. Apparently the bike is more than forty years old and is something he's rebuilt himself. It has enormous wheel covers, a low-slung seat, and sounds as deep as Oso's growl when he starts it. My dad straddles it, looking strangely pleased. I'd never known he was interested in bikes. I've always thought of them as simply dangerous toys—I can easily understand the thrill that must come with the exposure and speed of such a machine, but all the uncontrollable elements of other traffic makes the risk seem not worth the pleasure.

I'm glad, though, that Roberto has found something other than soloing and drug abuse to occupy his attention. And motorcycle riding seems safe in comparison.

"Where's your gear?" my father asks, getting off the bike. All that is visible on the back of the motorcycle is the rolled leather jacket and a tightly bundled sleeping bag. Roberto lifts the top of a saddlebag and takes out a pair of climbing slippers and a bag of chalk. "That's all you brought? Not even a harness?" Dad either isn't aware of my brother's recent soloing exploits or he's refusing to acknowledge them.

"I've got an extra harness," I interrupt.

"Okay. What do you boys want to do? After all the excitement, I'm itching to get up on something."

"You guys climb," I say. "I think I'm going to go soak

in the hot spring." I want to wash out the blood I can feel hardening in my half-grown beard. And do something to ease the bruises that are already stiffening my muscles. Besides, they should spend some time alone together—I can't always be around to act as a mediator.

"You'd be better off in cold water," Dad advises. Roberto lifts his sunglasses to roll his blue eyes at me.

I shrug and start to walk to where the activists are camping. "See you in a few hours. Take whatever gear you need."

I also want to see if Cal's nose is busted. And I want to check on Kim.

EIGHT

THE ACTIVISTS' CAMP is tense in the aftermath of the brawl. The college kids and the retirees are gathered in small groups, talking animatedly and looking both angry and scared. Cal sits on a log holding a bloody rag over his nose. Sunny, who appears cheerful and proud that her boyfriend had been a part of the excitement, stands behind Cal and massages his shoulders. A few of Cal's metal-studded crowd surround them as if to offer some belated protection. Nearby, Kim is being engulfed by an older, concerned group of her own. Everyone stops talking and watches when I approach.

"Are you all right?" I ask Cal.

"Yeah, man. I guess. Shit, are you?" Speaking through the rag, his voice is high and nasal like he has a bad cold.

"Nothing's broken. But I'm not so sure about your nose. Let me take a look."

I squat painfully in the grass, inflamed joints creaking, as Cal lifts the rag from his face. There's drying blood all over his cheeks and mouth, and his eyes are both turning black. He winces when I run a thumb and finger down his nose from between his eyes, checking for a rough ridge under the skin that could indicate a serious break. I feel nothing but it could be because of all the swelling.

"You should probably get an X ray," I tell him, wiping my fingers on the grass.

"Nah, dude, I'm okay." He glances up at Sunny to make sure she acknowledges his stoicism. "Thanks for stepping in. You definitely got the worst of it."

"That's your brother?" Sunny asks, staring across the meadow at where Roberto kneels shirtless on the grass and wipes dirt from his bike. His bare torso is bronzed from the sun. Even at this distance he resembles a perfect anatomy specimen. You can read every flex of muscle as he moves his hands over the bike.

"Yeah. His name's Roberto."

"He's like . . . he's like a Greek god or something."

I say nothing but agree inwardly, thinking about just how much trouble those mischievous gods always seemed to get themselves into.

Sounding a little jealous and annoyed, Cal says to Sunny in his newly nasal voice, "Don't get too excited about that guy. He's not long for this world."

I look at him. He begins to turn red where he's not already bloody.

"What do you mean?" Sunny asks.

"Sorry, man," Cal says to me. "It's just that he's always in the climbing rags, soloing some impossible shit. Guy has a serious death wish." He shakes his head in wonder, and, I think, admiration. "He's fucking sick."

From the widely spaced trees beyond Cal and Sunny, Kim is walking toward us. Without a word I step up to meet her halfway. The taut skin on her face is streaked with red splotches—stains of anger. Even enraged, she looks beautiful. And my attraction to her is magnified when she works at a smile and it comes out almost shy. She's still wearing the transparent beer-stained shirt. Her dark hair is a sticky mess with grass and twigs poking out.

Coming up to me, she says, "I'm not sure whether to thank you or apologize, Anton. But I'm glad you were around."

I smile back and touch the stinging cut on my cheek. "I kind of wish I'd been somewhere else."

"We've been trying to decide if we should call the police, even though they aren't exactly friendly to our cause. Would your father get in any trouble for firing the gun?"

He probably wouldn't, at least not with the local authorities. There's nothing illegal about firing a gun on Forest Service land unless it's done recklessly. But if some sort of complaint is filed, it could make more problems for him with his superiors back at the Pentagon. Roberto, though, would be in serious trouble for having taken part in the brawl. No fighting is usually an explicit condition of any parole.

"I'd rather you didn't," I say. "My family can do without the hassle."

"All right. No cops. Fast is a friend of the sheriff's,

anyway. He's a volunteer deputy or something, if you can believe that."

For a moment neither of us says anything more. We simply look at each other. Then she raises a hand and gently touches my cheek just as I'd touched Cal's nose. There's a trace of electricity in her fingers, a far milder buzz than the jolt I'd felt when hugging my brother, but powerful nonetheless. *First contact,* I think. *Progress.*

"You need stitches." She drops her hand to her side and wipes a drop of blood on her jeans.

"It's okay. My dad Krazy Glued it." When her single eye widens, I explain, "It's an old Burns family remedy. Probably not a very good one, but it does the trick."

Kim laughs. "Krazy Glue! My God!" It's the first time I've heard this woman laugh. The sound is surprisingly light, like a small bird fluttering into the air. The angry red splotches start to fade from her face.

Emboldened by the laugh, I ask, "I was just going to soak in the spring, and I'd like to hear what you and Fast were fighting about. Want to come? You look like you could use a bath."

"Good idea," she says, and rubs a hand through her matted hair. "I'll get us both some cold tea and meet you there."

The hot spring is wonderfully deserted. The activists are too busy rehashing the fight to bother with taking advantage of the valley's amenities, even though they won't be available for public use much longer. It's quiet, too. Thicker stands of spruce and aspens border the small pools, forming a kind of screen. The trees block out the sound of the conversations taking place just a hundred yards away. The only noise is the trickle of the stream feeding into the pools and the rustling of an easy breeze through the aspen leaves.

The three bathing pools are bordered and split by tall boulders and the rotting logs of lightning-struck trees. Dad and I had sat in the highest pool yesterday afternoon. According to his decades-old memories, it's the warmest but also the most shallow, barely two feet deep. He'd said the two lower pools are cooler because the hot venting water has had more time to mix with the creek's snowmelt. Remembering too Dad's advice about cold water being more helpful to a bruised body than warm, I choose the lowest and deepest pool for my soaking. The water is the color of pennies.

Kim walks up as I sit on a boulder, groaning quietly from the pain in my ribs as I work to unstrap my sandals. In each hand she carries a dripping Mason jar with a liquid inside that's almost as dark as the stream. Nothing's ever looked so good to me as this woman bringing me something cool to drink.

"I make it myself. It's a restorative tea, which you look like you could use. I make it from herbs I grow in the garden at home, then brew it in the sun," she says, unscrewing the lid from the jar and putting the jar in my hand. It's cold—she must have gotten it from an ice chest. "My way of saying thanks."

"Cheers." I finish half the tea in one pull. It tastes as if it's been sweetened with honey.

Kim sets her own jar on a rock with a clank. She turns to one side and begins to unbutton her shirt. Trying not to stare, I get my sandals off, then drag my vest over my head. Again I feel a painful tweak in my ribs. It almost makes me gasp. My bruises and stiffening muscles ache. But I'm too distracted, checking Kim out, to really notice the pain.

She slips off her shirt to reveal a pale yellow sports bra. Turning away again so that her back's to me, she shimmies out of her jeans. Matching yellow bottoms. Her body is lean and tan. Long runner's muscles carve down her thighs and calves. Above them, she has narrow hips and a slender back faintly etched with muscle. If I had time, I could count the ribs. When she turns back in my direction, I see that her breasts are small and high beneath her bra.

She looks at me and catches me staring. I clumsily look away but not before I see her flush. I take another pull from the jar, draining it this time. She steps into the water with jerky steps and her hands held unnaturally rigid against her thighs. It's as if my ill-concealed leer has robbed her of her grace. I mentally kick myself, not for admiring, but for having gotten caught.

"Uh, I don't have a swimsuit," I hear myself say. "Actually, I'm not wearing any underwear either." Yesterday the activists had all been frolicking naked. I guess Kim is more modest than her followers.

"Don't worry," she says without looking at me. Her voice sounds a little strained. "I doubt you can show me anything uglier than your face right now." Then she gives me a quick laugh to show me she's only kidding.

"Ha-ha," I answer. Dropping my shorts, I step into the water. It's colder than I expect. It pushes the breath out from my lungs and raises goose bumps on my flesh. It makes me want to dance and shiver. I crouch down until my butt is on the gravelly bottom and the water is high on my chest and try to focus on relaxing my stiffening joints rather than the woman across from me, who's now acting oddly shy.

"So you're a famous climber, huh?" she asks after dunking her head, scrubbing it, and pushing the hair from her face and eye patch. "Sunny said Cal was gushing about meeting you last night."

"A few years ago I was kind of famous. It was a long time ago."

"It couldn't have been that long ago. What are you, twenty-two or twenty-three?"

"Twenty-seven. How old are you?"

"Didn't your parents teach you never to ask a question like that of an older woman?" She laughs again, sounding more relaxed but, like me, not yet quite at ease. "Well, I guess today you earned the right to ask some impertinent questions. I'm thirty-six."

Her body is a decade younger at least. I want to tell her so but can't think of a way of saying it without sounding too aggressive.

"You look athletic, too. Runner?" Her almost total lack of body fat, her thin calves and lean muscles, make it a good bet.

"You've got good eyes, Anton," she replies, making it clear that I'd been caught. "I used to do a lot of running. Lately it's been more hiking and yoga. This thing with the valley has got me a little too preoccupied to train."

"Speaking of eyes—what happened to yours?"

She flinches as if I'd slapped her.

Oh shit, I think. I expected it to be some ridiculous childhood accident that she laughs about now. But from the wounded look on her face I can tell it's something much more than that, something she certainly doesn't laugh about. I should have asked Sunny instead, made sure the injury wasn't private. But I'm not very good at restraining myself—in that regard, but to a far lesser degree, I have the same tendencies as my brother.

She touches the eye patch in the same painful, self-conscious way I've been probing my cheek. Then she folds her arms across her chest and settles lower in the water as if to hide herself beneath the nearly transparent liquid. It feels like she's gone from just a few feet away to miles. For a moment she doesn't answer, just looks down at the water. But then her eye locks on mine.

"It was pierced by a knife," she finally says. Her words hit my chin like a sharp jab. Then she swings the hook. "It happened right after I was sexually assaulted."

Fuck.

I turn away from her gaze and lean toward where a large boulder perches on the pool's bank. I pretend to beat my head against it. "I'm sorry for asking. I'm sorry it happened. Please believe me when I say that I had no fucking idea."

She doesn't laugh at my make-believe self-flagellation, but she does smile just a little, grimly, when I look her way again. "It's okay. You didn't know. And I'm dealing with it."

"It's not something you get over very easily," I say quietly as I settle back into the water.

She's staring at me, probably trying to see if I really believe that or if I think like so many men that rape is just something you can walk away from, like falling in a mud puddle. Wash it off and you'll be fine. I hold her good eye until she finally says, "You're right. It's not."

After a moment of staring back at me, Kim apparently decides to tell me about it. "It happened twelve years ago, when I was a law student at the University of Utah."

Despite the way my body has finally adjusted to the cold water, her story gives me a fresh chill. I'm no stranger to violence and the sick things people can do to one another, and I've heard and seen far worse, but hearing it from this proud, beautiful woman in her calm voice both enrages me and at the same time makes me feel helpless and weak.

A football star at the university asked her on a date. She accepted because the invitation was so strange, coming from a jock a few years younger and someone so different from her—Kim describes herself in those days as a "rabid activist for all causes," from the environment to gun control to protesting the U.S.'s interference in Latin America. A real hippie chick, she says, fifteen years too late. She snobbishly thought of the invitation to a fraternity party as something that would expand her consciousness and understanding of mainstream America. Sort of like a visit to a less intelligent, foreign culture. And she admits she was flattered by her date's popularity at the school, too.

But the date didn't go well. They'd argued before they even arrived at the party. And Kim drank too much wine at dinner. She continued drinking at the party and annoying her escort by quarreling with half the people there, yelling over the booming music. In hindsight, she suspects someone put something in one of her drinks. But in the subsequent police investigation it was never proven. They said she probably just drank too much.

She woke up somewhere in a room in the back of the fraternity house. It was the strobelike flash of a camera burning through her tightly shut eyes and the sound of drunken laughter that brought her out of her stupor. She lay still for a long time, too horrified to open her eyes, too scared to move. This had to be a nightmare. But it didn't stop. The laughter, the rough touch of hands—squeezing, prodding, slapping—and the camera's red flash through the veins in her eyelids didn't stop. When she finally opened them, she discovered that she was naked in a room with four young men. One of them was her date.

They probably hadn't *physically* raped her, according to the examining physicians at the hospital. There was no bruising and the rape kit showed no signs of semen. But that wasn't the point. At the very least they'd violated her with their eyes, their camera lens, and their laughter. There could have been no greater defilement of her pride.

Without her clothes, she staggered from the room and down a staircase. The party was still in full swing. Another girl took pity on her. She helped collect Kim's clothes and drove her home. Kim ran from the car, sobbing with rage, shame, and fear. She ran right into her apartment to vomit into the sink. As she lurched and heaved over the porcelain, she didn't notice the upturned knife in the drying rack.

Tears are rolling out of her remaining eye but her voice has no quaver in it. Despite her svelte and graceful exterior, there's a hardness to this woman. A tough, sturdy strength. There's a weakness to it, though. Deep underneath I get a sense of brittleness. As if it wouldn't take much of a fall for her to break. After holding herself together for twelve years, it seems that this thing with the valley might just be the straw that breaks the camel's back.

"Jesus, Kim. I'm sorry," I say uselessly.

In my head I'm taking the bloody knife back to that fraternity house. I'm carving up four young men. If I'd known her then, and if I were just a little more like Roberto, I would have taken more from them than just an eye.

I can't help but ask, "Did they get arrested?"

I'm praying that they did. Then at least she would be given some sense of closure. Some kind of justice. My face is aimed at the water between us but my vision is lifted up, trying to gauge the psychological damage. My hands are clenched under the water so tight that my fingertips might puncture my palms.

"No. The police said they couldn't prove that it happened, much less that it wasn't consensual. It was their word against mine. The school didn't even suspend them because *my date* had rich parents who gave the school a ton of money."

"Fuck," I say out loud. "That makes me feel really good about our justice system. What a fucking joke."

She shrugs, now looking far calmer than I feel. "They're always improving the laws, trying to make it work better. Like protecting witnesses and with rape shield laws and all that. After finishing law school, I worked to get what happened to me included in the elements of sexual assault. It's still not perfect, but our laws are getting closer to being an instrument of justice."

She can't really believe that. In my three years as a cop I've come to realize that criminal law is simply a weak attempt to disguise a world of anarchy, chaos, and unfairness. A world where the rich and the strong prosper and the weak suffer. It's a pretense, the idea that the laws are based on it being better to let ten guilty men go free than convict a single innocent man. Innocent men are still convicted, and the guilty, even when they are convicted, rarely pay what they should. And the so-called "search for the truth" of the trial process is totally ridiculous. Evidence is often inadmissible because it's "too prejudicial." The defendant has the right to remain silent or lie even when he knows the truth. The right to plead not guilty even when he *is* guilty, then to beg for forgiveness prior to sentencing. The right to challenge evidence even if it's both reliable and probative. And he has the right to counsel, who will counsel him not to confess, not to answer questions, who will blame the victims, and will do everything in his or her power to get the client off.

I close my eyes and slouch lower in the water. I make an effort to unclench my fists but it doesn't work.

"Glad you asked?"

She's smiling again, a sort of sad half-smile. She splashes water onto her face to wash away the tears.

"I'm sorry, Kim. Again."

"Hey, I don't want to be depressing. I shouldn't have even told you. It's just that you pretty much saved me in the meadow there, and I feel like I owe you for that. Believe me, it's not something I talk about much. So tell me, what do you do when you're not being a famous climber?" She's trying hard to lighten the mood.

"I'm a cop. A special agent for the Attorney General's Office in Wyoming. I mostly take down meth labs."

"Really?" She cocks her head. "What you were saying just a minute ago, about the law being a joke..."

Well, it doesn't sound like something a police officer would say."

"It's exactly what most cops I know would say. It's just a game."

"What about the scar on your face? Did that happen climbing or policing?"

I feel foolish, after having heard what happened to her. Earlier I'd played with the thought of how our disfigurements might bring us together. "Climbing," I say. "Just climbing."

"Was it worth it?"

"Yeah, I guess so. It was a good trip despite getting smacked in the face by a falling rock. I couldn't wait to do it again."

Kim smiles fully for the first time since we've gotten in the spring. "You're honest," she says, "too honest and intelligent to be so dumb." Then, after a minute, "I can't imagine why you guys do it. Risk your lives on the cliff for nothing. How is it worth it? Don't you get scared up there?"

I want to explain it to her but don't know how without sounding even dumber. I want to tell her about the joy that comes with the terror, and how it bursts into flame when the fear is conquered. The bigger the fear, the bigger the rush. The best rushes come more than a thousand feet off the deck, when you've got a hundred-and-fifty-foot rope-length of shitty gear connecting you to your partner and it feels as if Death is climbing just beneath you, grasping at your ankles. When your heart is pounding out a heavy-metal rhythm at a hundred and eighty beats a minute and your muscles are racked with lactic acid. When the easiest thing in the world would be to just let go. But you don't. You fight.

I don't say any of this, though. I'm realizing that I know nothing about fear compared to her. Nothing about the consequences I take such delight in cheating.

Instead I just say, "You ought to try it sometime, Kim."

She laughs this time. "No thanks. Not until hell freezes over."

Neither of us realizes that Satan is pulling on a pair of his warmest socks.

NINE

TONIGHT I DON'T go back over to join the activists' bonfire—playing the peacemaker between Dad and Roberto has to take priority. They'd apparently argued while climbing down in the canyon this afternoon. When they returned, my father's face was tight with a frown. Even Roberto's ever-present smile looked forced beneath his crystal blue eyes. But I couldn't seem to focus on our family's problems. Instead I watched the dark shapes of the activists moving before the flames from across the meadow, trying to spot Kim. While my brother and father talk loudly over the hiss of my stove with false amiability about past climbs, visions of Kim's tan skin, slim hips, and small breasts beneath the yellow fabric float through my mind. Foolishly, I know, I've convinced myself that I'm the one who can ease her pain.

"Remember that trip to Notchtop Spire?" Dad asks. "When you and Antonio dropped the rope?"

Roberto groans and laughs. We'd been very young at the time, just boys, thrilled to be allowed to climb with Dad up a moderately serious alpine route. We climbed all day with my father leading then belaying Roberto and me, who were tied ten feet apart at the end of the rope. He led us up to broad ledges before the real business began just below the spire's peak. Halfway up, a steady drizzle engulfed us. It took hours to reach the summit because Dad had to haul us most of the way. Finally, on the summit's tiny perch, he set up a rappel off the back side while Roberto and I readied the rope. A sudden bolt of lightning frightened us—we somehow managed to drop the rope too close to the edge. It slithered down the steep incline like an angry snake until it snagged on a flake of rock fifty feet below. Dad didn't berate us, but his eyes gave us a beating. He had to risk his life soloing down to the rope on the slick granite. We'd been scared shitless, thinking he was so disgusted he would leave without us. Or die. But he came back, the errant rope coiled neatly over his shoulder.

"How's the parole going?" Dad asks out of nowhere. His voice is as nonchalant as if he were asking Roberto how his motorcycle is running.

Roberto stares at him for a while before answering. There's no smile at all on his face now. "Fine."

"They still having you do UAs?" Dad means urine analysis to detect the presence of drugs in my brother's blood.

"Yep." The single word comes out hard.

"Are they coming back clean?"

"Yep," he answers after another pause, harder still.

How is that? I wonder and I know my father does too. But I'm desperately trying to think of a way to change the subject.

Then Roberto answers for us, smiling suddenly. "You know, I guess I don't hydrate enough or something. Sometimes I've got to bring my own piss in a bag. Or someone else's." He doesn't have to tell us this; he doesn't have to be honest about it. But I guess he wants to rub it in to see what Dad will do.

But the issue arouses my professional curiosity. I know that parolees are watched by their parole officer as they pee in the cup just so that they can't bring it in a bag. "Doesn't your PO watch?" I ask.

"Sure, she likes to watch. There and at her apartment sometimes later."

Without a word Dad pushes himself to his feet and stomps away into the dark.

It's still hours before dawn when I'm awakened by the sound of distant voices. I sit up in my sleeping bag and hear nylon rustling nearby as my brother and father do the same. Tiny sparks jump from where the fabric scrunches in the dry alpine air.

"What the fuck?" Roberto is saying.

The voices come from across the meadow at the activists' camp. There's what sounds like a small cheer from a group of the environmentalists. I slide out of my bag and see the shapes of people gathered in the darkness. A million stars illuminate the meadow in the moon's monthly absence. Feeling the chill air, I shiver and turn around three hundred and sixty degrees. Up high on the mountain, where the workers had been hammering and sawing two days before, flames are leaping like they're dancing above some enormous campfire. *The lodge,* I realize.

I tell Roberto and Dad there'd been some threats at the meeting the night before about burning down the structure Fast was building. Some hotheads—I don't say any names—didn't want to go along with Kim's legal strategy.

"Goddamn fanatics. Lunatics," my father says sadly.

"Way to go!" Roberto responds, shouting toward the activists' camp. He raises a clenched fist to the stars in a power salute.

I pull on a pair of jeans and the fleece jacket that I'd been using as a pillow. "I'll see if I can figure out what's up," I tell them.

"Stay here, Ant. It's not your fight. You're already too involved. You don't want any of this mess sticking to you."

I go anyway.

The activists' camp is obviously divided. I'd noticed that at the campfire meeting two nights ago. In the dim glow of the distant flames up on the mountain, I first recognize some of the young men and women from Cal's crowd. As a whole they seem younger and appear to have more metal studs in their ears, noses, and eyebrows than Kim's older and more conservative supporters. The silver piercings spark with orange in the reflected light. They're talking excitedly to one another, occasionally slapping hands.

The others, Kim's followers, are solemn and quiet. They remain in the trees at the meadow's edge. I see several of them shake their heads in the direction of the burning lodge.

I find Kim sitting alone in the dark on the trunk of a felled tree. She's watching the blaze, too, with her head lowered and her sleep-tangled hair covering the eye patch and most of her face.

"Hey."

She doesn't respond. She doesn't even look my way. Uninvited, I sit down next to her.

"Where's Cal?" I ask.

She shrugs. We sit in silence for a little while, listening to the chatter of Cal's friends. In the breeze coming off the mountain, I can smell burning wood and insulation. It's a chemical scent. I sniff the breeze for gasoline or some other accelerant, but we're too far away to pick up any indicators of arson.

"Asshole," she finally says. "He has no idea how this will look to the Forest Service. And in court. If there was ever any chance of convincing them to deny the swap, it's gone now."

There's something in her voice, though, beneath her words, that makes me look at her carefully. It's what I think might be a note of vindictive pleasure. Maybe even triumph.

TEN

FAR DOWN THE valley, where the Forest Service road winds up toward the meadow from the highway, there are flashing red and white lights but no sirens. Ten minutes later a fire engine noses into the meadow over the ruts in the rough road. The heavy machine moves barely faster than a crawl. Close behind it are two SUVs bearing the emblems of a sheriff's department. I'm not surprised to see them, as often state and county peace officers have jurisdiction in national forests by agreement with the federal government, which doesn't have the manpower to investigate all the crimes that occur on the millions of acres of federal land. Although I barely have a glimpse of them before they turn onto the newly cut access road that twists its way up Wild Fire Mountain to where the lodge is still burning, I'm able to follow their flashing lights all the way.

By the time the emergency vehicles reach the lodge, the flames are already starting to die down on their own accord. There probably isn't a lot for the fire truck to do but start an arson investigation. The remains of the building glow orange and red like molten lava in the predawn sky.

About a half hour after the emergency vehicles passed through the meadow, when the sun's first rays are curving around the mountains and into the valley, there's the roar of another engine coming up the road. I recognize Fast's gleaming black Suburban as it tears into the meadow with the horn blaring angrily. He keeps the sound up nearly all the way to the burnt-out lodge to ensure that the activists—his enemies—are aware of his displeasure.

It's full dawn by the time the emergency vehicles come back down the mountain. The fire truck disappears down toward the highway after bumping past us. The two police SUVs return behind it and they park not far from the activists' camp. It's light enough now that I can read the emblem on the trucks' doors. It's the emblem of the Tomichi County Sheriff's Department.

Having worked all over the state of Wyoming, I've gotten to know many types of rural county sheriffs. There are the Good Old Boys, the friendly slobs who are elected to office by nature of their good humor and their families' long-standing presence in the community. There are the Transplants, former senior officers in big cities who bring their knowledge and efficiency to pastoral states in order to escape bureaucracy and overwhelming amounts of senseless urban crime. There are the Flunkies, who are elected by the town's prominent families or businessmen in order to serve their self-interests. There are the Bad Boys, who seek the job as a power trip and love the authority it gives them to bully the county's weaker citizens. And then there are the Reachers, ambitious men who take the job and strive to be perfect at it in order to use it as a trampoline to higher office. All these characteristics are usually present to some degree, but usually one trait is most prominent.

The sheriff of this Colorado town is something new: a Caricature. If Hollywood were to come looking for someone new to play Wyatt Earp, then Sheriff Munik is already dressed for the role and working hard to be in character.

He is a tall, wiry man roughly my father's age. Tufts of salt-and-pepper hair curl from beneath his white Stetson. A wide and drooping cowboy's mustache makes his long face seem even longer. His eyes are steel gray and set close together, like a gunfighter's. Typical of a county sheriff, he doesn't wear a uniform—just boots, jeans, pearl-button shirt, and a blazer with leather hunting patches. But his job is obvious because of where his coat is hitched up over the revolver that's strapped to his hip. I almost smile when I see that the gun is an enormous old Colt .45. It completes the cowboy image.

Despite his corny appearance, my next impression is that he appears competent. When David Fast tears back into the meadow and springs from his truck—red-faced, cursing, and looking seriously pissed off—the sheriff strides over to him and pushes the developer back toward the open driver's door. I hear the sheriff say, "Davy, for your own damned good, sit down and stay put. I don't want you interfering while I talk to these folk."

It's interesting that Burgermeister remains in the

passenger seat. He too looks pissed, and the expression on his face is far more dangerous than Fast's, but he apparently wants nothing to do with the sheriff. I remember noting his jailhouse tattoos and bet he has a record. He's going to let his employer and partner handle this side of things.

Fast argues briefly but I can't hear what he's saying other than the occasional four-letter word. Finally, though, he pulls himself back behind the steering wheel and he slams the Suburban's door.

For a moment Burgermeister's eyes meet mine through the windshield. He glares at me. Used to receiving such treatment from the suspects I've arrested, I'm nevertheless surprised by the lethal potency of his gaze. It even makes me feel a little uncomfortable. Alf Burgermeister has a world-class stink eye. But I don't look away. The bruises I'd received at the hands and boots of him and his men seem to radiate heat beneath my skin. Just to be rude, I slowly smile and tap my raised knee to remind him of how I'd brought it up between his legs.

No one's kicking the Hacky Sack in the meadow as the sheriff and a deputy, a very short and chunky guy with the swagger of a teenager who has become a cop just to take revenge on the big people, start interviewing the environmentalists. The sheriff does the talking. He's not accusing anyone, but his tone makes it clear the activists are all likely suspects. I stand with the group around him trying to eavesdrop and at the same time trying to avoid being questioned. My father and brother are wiser and stay at our camp at the far end of the meadow.

While the sheriff gathers people's names and addresses, the small deputy writes them down with great difficulty. The pen looks ridiculously large in his stubby fingers. Making it even harder on himself, he wears fingerless leather gloves—also a trait I'm familiar with from my experiences with small-town law enforcement. The gloves are the insignia of the head-busters—cops who like to hit, who do it often enough that they need to wear the gloves to keep from splitting a knuckle on a suspect's head. Like the sheriff, it's an image thing, I guess. But it's hard to imagine this little guy doing much damage.

The sheriff asks if anyone left the campsites that evening. No one admits that they had, and no one mentions Cal's name. But I can see from the uneasy looks on some of the older activists' faces that they're likely to have a personal chat with Sheriff Munik the next time they go into town. Probably that very afternoon. At that point Cal will certainly be fingered as the perpetrator of the arson.

At one point, when the sheriff and his deputy are close to me, the horn blasts again from Fast's truck. Through the windshield I can see Burgermeister still glaring at me and Fast motioning to the sheriff. Munik shakes his head in irritation and again stalks over to the gleaming Suburban. Fast leans out the open window, pointing at me, and then jabs his index finger toward my father and brother across the meadow.

"What's your name, son?" the sheriff asks me when he returns.

I tell him my name and his deputy takes down my current address in Lander. Answering his questions, I explain that I'm in the valley to climb, and that I hadn't been with the activists the night before.

"What happened to your face?"

"It's a long story, Sheriff. I broke my cheekbone

climbing a few years ago, then I got in a little scuffle yesterday and it split open again."

"Tell me about the scuffle."

I explain what had happened after the demonstration in the meadow.

"You looking to press charges?"

I shake my head. "Not unless they are," I say, indicating where Fast and Burgermeister still glare from behind the windshield. "From my point of view, it isn't something anyone's likely to get convicted of."

"How'd you know what a fellow can get convicted of?"

"I'm a special agent with the AG's Office in Wyoming, sort of like your CBI guys here in Colorado."

Munik looks at me with fresh interest in his metallic eyes. "You're a cop?" His deputy pauses as he strains to finish a note on the pad and tilts his head up at me without smiling. I can sense a critical assessment from behind his sunglasses. Some cops are like that; they don't like an outsider stepping onto their turf.

"Technically, yeah. Mostly I deal with drug stuff."

The sheriff gestures with his hands at a scruffy young gathering of the activists, and says, "Too bad you're out of your jurisdiction, Agent. Bet you'd have your hands full with this crowd. Are those two, over there, with you?" He points at where Dad and Roberto are finishing their breakfast.

"My brother and father. As I'm sure Mr. Fast just told you, they were involved in that scuffle yesterday, too. Like me, they don't want to press charges."

Munik clears his throat. "Right now the three of you ought to be more worried about charges being filed against *you*." The pint-sized deputy beside him smirks at me from behind his wraparound shades.

The sheriff wants to talk to my family. As we walk over to them, my brother puts on his own mirrored sunglasses. With a frown, I remember having seen him wander into the forest a little earlier while I was hanging out in the activists' camp. He probably took a post-breakfast walk in order to give himself a start-me-up injection.

"You look familiar," the sheriff says to my brother after I've introduced them. "You been in any trouble in my county?"

Roberto smiles. "No, Wyatt, at least none you know about." My brother has obviously picked up on the same carefully cultivated resemblance. By the angry squint Munik gives him in return, I can tell he doesn't take it as a compliment. At least not coming from my brother's mocking mouth.

Roberto looks the short deputy over, taking in first his face, his fingerless gloves, his boots, and then his name tag. The aluminum tag on his breast reads "B. J. Timms." My brother is good at reading the vibe coming from people, and he clearly doesn't like the one he's getting from Deputy Timms.

"B. J.," my brother says, "what does that stand for? Blow job? You probably don't even need to kneel."

From behind the police officers, I shake my head frantically at Roberto, willing him to shut up. The officers stare at him in disbelief. Before the words take effect, my father interrupts, "You'll have to excuse my son, Sheriff. Deputy. He has a problem with his manners when speaking to authority."

The sheriff doesn't take his eyes off his own reflection

in Roberto's glasses. "Nothing a trip to the woodshed wouldn't fix, I'll bet."

I'm thankful that Roberto doesn't say anything further, though he does once again give the sheriff his sardonic grin. The sheriff lets it go by just shaking his head. Deputy B. J. Timms, on the other hand, appears to be in apoplectic shock. He's frozen in his boots and his face is turning a screaming red.

"Both my sons were here with me all night. I can vouch for them," Dad says.

The sheriff allows himself a chuckle. "But who can vouch for you? Your sons? That isn't exactly a sterling alibi, Mr. Burns." Again, Munik's tone isn't accusatory. It sounds to me like he's simply trying to convey the fact that at this point no one's above suspicion for having lit the fire.

But my father's face grows hard anyway. I don't imagine he's ever had his integrity called into question before.

"Sheriff, I'm a colonel in the United States Air Force. I can assure you that I'm not interested in any petty vandalism."

The Wyatt Earp look-alike doesn't respond except to grunt noncommittally. His eyes pick over my ancient Land Cruiser, the alert and menacing beast tied to the bumper, our unrolled sleeping bags, and Roberto's huge bike. I'm thankful that unlike many off-road trucks, mine doesn't have extra fuel containers mounted on the back. But despite the brawl with Fast and his men in the meadow, I don't really believe we can be suspects. After all, we'd pretty much won the fight. We have no need to seek revenge against the developer.

"Hell of a dog," he comments, "if that's what it is."

"I took possession of him after a raid on a meth lab," I tell him, feeling the need to reestablish that I'm a cop, too. "He was rumored to have eaten a missing informant."

That makes the sheriff chuckle again. "Looks like he could do it, all right."

Munik has to ask Deputy Timms twice to write down my father's and brother's addresses. The first time the deputy didn't respond to his command. His gleaming black boots were still rooted to the earth as he glared furiously up at my brother. He finally takes down their information like he had the others, but his tiny hands now have a noticeable quiver. As usual, Roberto hasn't made any friends.

The sheriff tells us, "Don't go anywhere for the next couple of days. I'll probably be wanting to talk with you gentlemen again."

"We plan on being here for two more days at most," Dad says. He wants to make it clear to the sheriff that he's not taking orders from anyone. Munik responds by giving my father a long gunfighter look and spitting some tobacco sideways onto the grass. Two bull elk, I think. Shit, three, with Roberto. And then me and the pint-sized deputy. It wouldn't take a whole lot to start another brawl right here. My brother had come close to doing that already.

Without another word Sheriff Munik walks back over to Fast's Suburban, followed by his sidekick. Even from this distance I can see the sheriff and the developer arguing hotly. Obviously Munik is unwilling to do what Fast wants. Fast probably wants us arrested. He finally slams his truck into gear and roars out of the meadow, tearing two long strips of grass and alpine flowers from the ground. I take the ferocity of his exit as a warning, or maybe a threat. It seems to say, "I'll be back."

Then the brake lights flash as Cal steps out of the trees just where the road begins its descent down the valley to the highway. Cal stares without expression at Fast's truck, but there's something arrogant, something victorious in the young man's posture. When he walks across the road, and when the sheriff's view of him is blocked by Fast's tinted windows, Cal takes a lighter from his pocket, grins, and lights the flame.

I expect Fast to run him over. Or at least for him and Burgermeister to get out and give chase. But they don't. They don't even get out to tell the sheriff what Cal has just done.

Fast only starts moving again when there's a light honk from the sheriff's SUV behind him.

ELEVEN

LATE THAT MORNING and later into the afternoon I climb with my father and brother down in the canyon. There's no talk about drugs or family disputes or any of our futures. Our conversations, when we have them, are only and carefully about climbing. Dad and I are full of bluff cheer. If Roberto is aware of the undercurrents and the occasional looks passing between us, he's sharp enough to appear oblivious.

We tell each other stories when we pause to rest. I have Roberto laughing, and even my father grinning, when I tell them about a time I'd taken Oso ice climbing last spring.

A friend and I snowshoed with Oso five miles into the Winds through more than two feet of fresh snow. It was hard going from the very start. Oso, who always insisted on leading the way on summer trails, was frustrated by the way his thick legs sank all the way into the powder. For a while he tried to swim shoulder-deep in the snow ahead of us. Then he figured out that if he followed in our tracks—walked where we had broken and compacted the snow—it would be a lot easier.

Only he was annoyed and impatient at not being in the lead. He walked behind me with his snout nearly up my ass. It seemed like every few steps he would place one of his fat paws on the heel of a snowshoe and send me sprawling face-first into the deep powder. Because of the heavy pack filled with ropes, screws, crampons, food, and other gear, I'd crash so deep into the soft stuff that it would take me long minutes of cursing and writhing to get back on my feet.

We kicked steps up a long couloir toward the base of our intended route. Where the real climbing would begin, when the angle turned steep and the snow changed to gray, rock-hard ice, I stomped a platform in the snow for Oso. I even put down an insulated pad for the ungrateful beast so he could wait for us in comfort. The sight of the three hundred and fifty feet of virgin ice above put me in a forgiving mood. Then we started climbing.

An hour later Randy and I were three hundred feet up the frozen waterfall, less than a pitch from the top, when we began to be pelted from above by spindrift, gravel, and plates of ice. I looked down for Oso, hoping he wasn't being bombarded, too. But he was gone. I looked up and was terrified to see the black end of his snout protruding over the top of the climb. He'd somehow managed to scramble up the steep talus to one side and now stood above us, triumphant at being first again, as we labored below on the frozen ribbon of ice.

I swore and shouted for him to stay away from the edge. The sound of my voice only excited him more. The beast sent a new barrage of ice and rock to assault us as he danced happily above. Randy took the lead, whacking his axes and kicking his crampons with amazing speed, trying to get to the top before the beast slid over the edge. He was just pulling over it when I heard a shout. I looked up to see a great black mass cartwheeling down the ice, out of the sky, right toward me.

Oso hit me square in the chest. The force of the blow was amazing. It blew the breath right out of my lungs. It ripped my hands from my ice tools and slammed the leashes against my wrists. For a few moments of agony I thought it had dislocated my shoulders. What was even more amazing was that the anchor I was suspended from—two ice screws drilled deep into the frozen water—didn't blow. Fighting to draw a breath, I managed to hold the massive dog in my lap. He twisted his head up to growl at me.

Randy yelled down that I was on belay and that he'd gotten a solid anchor around a tree. Now I had to figure out how to get out of this mess. Trying to ascend with more than a hundred and fifty pounds of squirming, snarling, snow-soaked dog flesh would be impossible, even after I rigged him a questionable harness out of a couple of slings. In the end Randy had to make a risky and unprotected down-climb to us so that he could lower us back to the platform three hundred feet below.

By the time we reached it, my calves, arms, and stomach muscles were screaming from holding the beast pinned between the ice and my hips. And my voice was hoarse from cursing.

As I tell the story the memory causes me to look down at where Oso now lounges in the shade by the river and swear anew at him. At least he'd finally learned to wait below.

Roberto tells stories of his own. But I seldom laugh at them and my father doesn't smile. His stories are just too wild, too scary, for those who know and love him. But the afternoon is still peaceful. A father and sons climbing together. Maybe for the last time. Definitely here for the last time, in this place that's about to be filled with cliff-side condominiums.

There's only one bad moment in an almost perfect day. It comes at about dusk, when the three of us are hurrying to finish one final climb to the canyon's rim before night falls. Roberto is leading the last pitch while Dad and I watch from the belay, a large ledge two hundred feet off the deck.

"Are we going to have the talk tonight?" I ask my father.

He shakes his head. "Tomorrow. Let's enjoy the rest of the day together before things get nasty."

I'm reminded again that tomorrow will be the last time he'll ever be able to climb here at the site of his glory days. His playground and my childhood Valhalla will soon be gone.

Waiting sounds like a good plan to me. I'm happy to put off "the talk" as long as possible. Dad and I have worked out a ridiculously hopeful strategy—he'll offer to pay for Roberto to enroll in an exclusive inpatient rehab center not far from my current assignment in Lander,

Wyoming. That way Roberto will be able to get out and climb with me on weekends.

Killing time, I ask my dad if he's aware of any caves or Indian ruins in the canyon.

"No," he answers, "but just because I haven't seen any doesn't mean they don't exist." He's intrigued by the possibility when I tell him of Cal's claims about finding an Indian ruin buried beneath rockfall somewhere in the valley region. He says he's never explored the lower walls farther down in the canyon. If we had more time, I'd like to wander around down there to see if I could find Cal's site. The idea of an unexplored cave exerts a magnetic force on me, like a black hole.

Far above us, Roberto grunts and curses his way up over a huge roof that juts more than 20 feet from the canyon's rim. It's the crux of the route, rated "5.12a" by the guidebook. In other words it's very, very hard. And it's just getting dark enough that finding foot- and handholds has to be difficult, especially on the roof's shadowed underside.

"How's it going?" I shout up as I feed out a little more line.

"Fucking grim, *che*," Roberto shouts back. Even though he's sixty feet above me, I can hear him gasping with exertion and the psychological stress that comes with tying in to the sharp end of the rope. I watch him pause to lick the blood from a split knuckle. His hands have been bleeding freely all day as we've climbed, and I wonder if the drugs he takes have caused him to become hemophilic. Looking down at my own bloody hands, I worry for a moment about AIDS. But surely he's smart enough to use clean needles.

I realize the rope is pulling out into space, away from the wall. It shouldn't. It should lie close, clipped through the protection Roberto has placed, even as he moves out from it on the underside of the roof. I study the wall above and realize Roberto hasn't placed any gear. Nothing. He's soloing again—the only good the rope is doing is that it will allow Dad and me to follow safely when he makes the rim, where he can belay us from above. If he makes the rim.

"He's not placing pro," I say quietly to my father, who's standing on the ledge next to me and staring out over his canyon.

He looks up sharply and sees as I had that the rope is free from the wall. "For God's sake, Roberto, put something in!" he hollers into a sky that's turning the color of a new pair of blue jeans.

My stomach tries to crawl up my throat when I see Roberto's feet kick out from under him, forcing all his weight onto his fingertips. His legs pedal in the air.

"Don't need it!" he yells down, panting hard. He folds his legs back up like the blade of a jackknife. They seem to find some invisible edges for the sticky rubber shoes to grip on the underside of the roof. With a slowness that's agonizing to watch from our position, he finally disappears over the roof's lip.

"Jesus Christ. Does he want to kill himself while we watch?" I say to my father. "What can he be thinking?"

When he doesn't respond, I turn my head to look at him. Despite the growing dark, I can see that his cheeks are shiny and wet. I quickly look away.

TWELVE

A FEW HOURS later I wake to hear a distant scream. Just when I've convinced myself that it was only a dream, and as I twist onto my side in the tight confines of my mummy bag to fall back asleep, Oso starts bellowing in my ear. I jerk as if I've been jabbed by a cattle prod. "Hey, hey. Easy boy. What is it?" The beast stops roaring at the sound of my voice but continues to growl at some faraway threat. I find the bag's zipper by my head and sit up.

In the starlight I can make out my father sitting next to me with his bald head cloaked beneath a balaclava. Roberto is groaning on the ground nearby, muttering, "What the fuck?" He had disappeared into the trees, heading toward the canyon, when Dad and I bedded down after dinner. He'd said he was going to howl at the moon for a while. And indeed we later heard a lonely

"Awwooo" reverberating off the canyon's walls. To shoot up or smoke something was the real reason. Oso had already woken us up once when Roberto staggered into the camp a couple of hours later.

"Did you hear that?" I ask them.

My father's head dips in a quick nod. Like Oso, he stares around the dark meadow intently.

"Yeah. I think that fucker just blew out my eardrums," Roberto says with his hands rubbing his ears.

"Not that. The scream."

Dad nods again, still listening. A few flashlights are blinking on and moving in the activists' camp across the meadow. Their beams swing around the open field and are snuffed by the night just a few hundred feet from their origins. I try to recollect the sound that had awakened me. It seemed like a short cry of pain cut off mid-scream. I wasn't sure how much of it had been a dream.

"It sounded pretty far away," Dad says, confirming what I'd thought.

Roberto groans again and flops back down in his bag. "Man, you can't get no sleep in this place!" In a few minutes he's snoring. Dad and I sit up a while longer, looking around, watching the flashlights click off one by one. Above us the sky is a deep, deep black. Thousands of stars are freckled across it. I'm reminded of how the ancient Greeks thought the night sky was like a great black cloth, veiling the sun, but full of tiny pinpricks.

"Nothing to do about it now," Dad says. He lies back down.

I'm about to do the same when Oso starts rumbling again. His head is pointed toward the center of the meadow, and I can make out a slim silhouette moving across the grass toward us. I recognize the smooth, efficient grace. It's Kim.

"Someone's coming," I say to Dad. "I'll talk to her." I try to quiet Oso again as I slip out of my bag and into my belay jacket. The figure stops a little ways away from our camp. I step barefoot into cold boots, leaving the laces undone, and shuffle across the grass to her. Oso follows at my side. He's no longer growling but is loudly snuffing at the air.

"Anton?"

"Yeah, Kim. What's up?"

"Did you hear it?"

"It sounded like a scream."

"I'm worried about Cal and Sunny. They're camping a ways down the canyon, away from everyone. I think it came from that direction."

I want to ask, *Why talk to me?* But I'm flattered she's come and don't want to put her off. Instead I say, "What can I do?"

"Well, you're a cop, right?"

"Right. In Wyoming, not Colorado." But she's made me feel important and sort of useful anyway. "Did it sound like Sunny?"

"I couldn't tell. Maybe."

"Do you have any reason to worry about her?"

She shrugs and hugs her arms across her chest as if to ward off the high-altitude chill. "I don't know. With the fire last night and all..."

I wait for her to say more but she doesn't. I know what she's thinking, though. Maybe Fast and his boys wanted a little payback. I remember Fast and Burgermeister intercepting Cal before the melee in the meadow.

I recall it looking like an angry exchange. Maybe Fast wanted to know about Indian ruins. Or maybe Cal was dumb enough to make some threats. And I remember how he'd stepped out of the trees this morning, as the developers were leaving with the sheriff, as if to say *Got you, dude.*

"Okay, let's go check on them. Let me get a light."

She follows me back to camp, where I dig a headlamp out of my climbing pack and explain to my father what we're doing. Feeling the chill on my bare legs, I also pull on a pair of gray fleece pants.

"Want me to come?" he asks.

I look his way in surprise—he'd been very clear earlier that he wanted nothing to do with the activists. He's worried about me, I realize. I'm too touched to respond right away.

"No, it's nothing," Kim answers for me, probably very aware of my father's disdain for her activities. "I'm just being paranoid, I'm sure." While she's distracted, talking to him and looking down into the star-filled V of the valley, I unlock the glove box and slip the reassuring weight of my H&K into a jacket pocket. Just in case.

THIRTEEN

WE HIKE IN the dark on the rugged Forest Service road. Far in the distance I think I can hear an engine gearing down the road toward Durango. The head- and taillights are either turned off or the forest obscures them. If the lights are turned off, it would explain the high-revving engine sound—they'd be downshifting to avoid braking and flashing the taillights. It's even possible, though, that I'm simply hearing the sound of a truck miles away where the valley road meets the highway. I ask Kim if she hears it, too, but she just shakes her head as she plays her flashlight over the screen of trees to the right. She tells me there's an old logging track into the woods somewhere around here and that's where Cal and Sunny are camped. Up high on the valley's side where the track dead-ends.

The night is otherwise silent but for the gentle sweep

of a breeze against the trees' upper branches and the pulse of crickets. Overhead, the stars cast enough light on the ground to make hazy shadows. Oso sniffs along beside us, no longer growling but looking alert with his ears bunched forward.

We find the old track. It's barely more than a trail, just a skinny break in the forest to the right of the road. There's the odor of exhaust fumes in the air. To me it smells like diesel, like many of the trucks Fast and his friends had driven into the meadow for their counter-protest two days ago.

"Kill the light," I say quietly.

She flips the beam off and stares at me in the dark. I stand still and silent for a few minutes, letting my eyes adjust to the night. Something feels wrong. Dangerous.

From a few hundred yards away and up the valley's side, where the track seems to lead, I hear the faint jangle of keys. Then a door slam and the whine of a four-cylinder engine revving way too high.

"Let's get into the trees," I say quickly. "We don't know if that's the screamer or the screamee."

Kim slips off the road and disappears into the forest. I hurry after her, grabbing Oso's collar and pulling him along.

Headlights slash through the straight trunks of lodge-pole pines as a car comes slamming down the old logging track. The axles bang again and again over deep ruts. Branches screech against the paint. From where we crouch in the trees I take the pistol out of my pocket and point it at the ground between my legs. With the other hand I keep a tight grip on Oso's collar. After only a few seconds a small white car bounds past us.

Suddenly Kim is leaping out after it. She's yelling, "Sunny! Sunny!" But the car hits the Forest Service road with a crashing slide and keeps slamming west toward Durango.

"Was she alone?" I ask, running after Kim as the taillights disappear around a corner but the motor's noise still tears through the night.

"I... I think so. I just caught a glimpse of her. She looked like she was crying. And there was something dark on her face. Like blood."

Kim's standing in the middle of the Forest Service road now, one hand still half raised toward the sound of the engine. It's more than a mile back to the meadow, back to our cars, so there's no point in trying to go after Sunny. I put a hand on Kim's arm and gently pull it down to her side.

"Come on. Let's see what she was running from."

We hike up the old logging road. It runs almost straight up the steep, forested hillside. We walk slowly, not using our flashlights at my insistence and letting our vision get used to the dark again. I don't have to tell her to avoid making noise. Oso keeps a shoulder against my hip, for once obeying my command to heel.

"I think their camp is somewhere up there," Kim whispers, and points ahead.

As we've climbed, the track has turned into little more than an overgrown trail that's been almost entirely reclaimed by the wilderness. At various places diseased or lightning-struck trees have fallen across it, rotted to mushy kindling, then crushed under the recent passage of wheels. Heavy bushes press against the sides, fighting for the light the narrow track provides in the daytime. Young aspen saplings rise right in the very center of the road to take advantage of the same light and one day soon block it out. Splintered bark is as white as bone in the night where the undercarriage of a car has bent the saplings until they snapped.

The forest here seems denser than that which surrounds the meadow. The trees are closer together and, weirdly, the underbrush too is thicker. It takes me a moment to realize that the hillside probably faces south, therefore getting a lot of light to justify the heavy growth. The smell of decaying vegetation is also stronger here. It smells a little like the mushroom bin at the health food store.

"Why would she be driving like that? And the screaming earlier . . ." Kim talks quietly, more to herself than me. She sounds worried but not necessarily scared. It seems like the forest is a comfortable place for her. I like that—that she could be out in these cloying woods so late at night, with a stranger, and still not be too frightened. So many people I've known find the woods menacing. If it hadn't been for the scream earlier, and if it hadn't been for the wild-eyed girl behind the wheel of an out-of-control car, I'd probably be trying to figure out a way to kiss her.

"Maybe she and Cal got high or drunk or something . . . every time I came up here to visit them they were baked out of their minds. I never should have introduced her to Cal. But he wouldn't hurt her—he's not that kind."

Up ahead in the dark I see some yellow fabric. Part of a tent? Laundry? I touch Kim's arm to make her stop. Then I touch her lips with a finger to keep her quiet. I push Oso's collar into her hand and whisper for him to sit, to stay.

As I move very slowly, trying to avoid the worst of the twigs and the leaves in the dark, I think of the possibilities. Maybe Sunny and Cal had a fight and she split. That seems most likely. Maybe I'll just find Cal drunk and pissed. Still, some sixth sense makes me stealthy and causes me to once again take the gun out of my pocket. I don't want a surprised and stoned ecoterrorist to split my head with an ax.

The yellow is a part of a tent. The nylon rain fly. It looks like someone's half wadded it and tossed it over a leaning tree. And as I get closer I can see clothing and pots and sleeping bags messily scattered about a small clearing. There's an unpleasant odor, too. I'm still for a minute, sniffing the air, and thinking that I'm spending too much time around that dog. Then I recognize the faint, coppery smell of blood. It's laced with the heavier scent of voided bowels. That's when I see the foot.

I'm almost tempted to ignore it because it seems so out of place in the cool, quiet night. So ugly, bare and extending from under a bush. I stare at it long enough to be sure that it's what I think it is and to be sure it's not going anywhere. My eyes make out the whiteness of a calf through the thin broken branches, then a thigh, and another foot to one side. Cal must be really wasted to crash naked under a bush, I think wishfully, already knowing that's not the case.

I scan around the dark woods three hundred and sixty degrees, listening for any sound other than Oso's panting thirty or forty feet behind me. Nothing. With my free hand I take the headlamp out of a pocket and hold it in my palm. I take a deep breath. Then I turn the switch.

The body under the bush is chest-down. One leg straight, the other folded. As best as I can tell through the leaves, the hands are wrapped loosely around the bush's knotty trunk. It's a skinny young man's frame, naked and tattooed and streaked with blood. There's no doubt in my mind it's Cal when I angle the light to illuminate a patch of short, bleached hair and the light reflects off the metal studs he'd pierced through his ears and face. His head appears swollen and lumpy, like a rotten fruit. It's turned to the side. His jaw looks as if it's come unhinged. His lips are pulled back in a surprisingly gentle smile. Even violent death will do that to you, make you look as if you might have enjoyed it. It's one of the Grim Reaper's dirtiest tricks. Thankfully, the one eye that's visible is puffed shut.

As I reach my hand into the bush to touch the carotid artery on his neck, I can't help but feel an unreasonable fear that the corpse might suddenly turn and bite me. I consider for a moment reaching for the wrist instead. I shake my head, willing away the irrational fear. With two fingers I finally touch the lukewarm skin of his throat and the sticky blood that covers it. As I press just a little for a pulse, Cal's skin sinks beneath my touch like warm wax. No muscular resistance. And no pulse.

"Did you find anything?" Kim hisses in my direction.

"No. Stay there. Don't move."

I switch off the headlamp in my palm and put it back in my pocket. I put away the gun, too. Standing still, now blind in the night, I wonder if I should say a prayer over Cal's corpse. I hope he believed in more than I do. I hope he was expecting something to follow this instead of just rotting away under a bush. The problem for me is that I don't have faith in much. People never seem to get what they have coming—good or bad—and there's an ungodly amount of cruelty and pain in the world. But at times like this it would be nice to believe in something.

"Anton?" Kim says. She sounds far away.

I walk back to where she waits on the narrow track. Oso is straining at his collar and she's having trouble holding him. The beast is still wild enough to get excited at the smell of death.

Kim's good eye is wide in the night. I can see the white all the way around her single dark sphere. She senses something, too. I take Oso's collar with one hand and take her arm with the other. "Come on," I tell her, pulling her back down the track.

She tries to tear free of my grip. "Let go of me! What is it? What did you find?"

I don't let go. "A crime scene. Cal's dead."

FOURTEEN

KIM AND I hurry up the road back toward the meadow. The night is totally different now. Before it had been comforting in its starlit silence. Now it feels oppressive, full of ominous shadows. The crickets' rhythm sounds mocking and evil, like the heavy breathing of a horror movie killer. I can't get the image of Cal's bloody smile out of my mind. I find myself looking back over my shoulder on several occasions. Oso trudges along beside us and I'm glad I brought him. He can handle any murderous phantoms hiding in the black trees.

Kim speaks just once. The two words are plaintive, almost desperate, coming from her dazed-looking face. "How? Who?"

"I don't know. But I'm guessing Fast or his friend. Maybe both of them."

Sometime during the rapid march in the dark Kim

takes my hand. Or maybe I take hers. Her grip is tight and sweaty. Despite the circumstances, the touch of her skin gives me that almost electric tingle once again.

It takes us ten or fifteen minutes to return to the meadow. Some of Kim's friends are still awake, huddled in a small group near the tents and cars. They shine their flashlights in our faces. Our night vision destroyed, both Kim and I immediately stumble over clumps of grass. I snap, "Turn those things off." The lights go out.

One of them calls out to Kim, "Was it Sunny? Is she all right?"

Kim says nothing. She doesn't even look over at her friends.

I say, "We'll be over in a few minutes. We'll talk about it then." I don't want anyone messing with what will shortly be an official crime scene, and I don't want anyone driving to town to look for Sunny. Tire treads on the logging track or the Forest Service road might be obscured. The local police need to check it out first.

My father is waiting for us in the dark across the meadow at my family's camp. He sits as still as a Buddha on a camp chair, watching us kick through the dew-wet grass. His sleeping bag is pulled up over his legs and lap. Next to him is the long black shape of my brother on the ground in his own bag.

"Someone's been killed," I tell my father.

Roberto sits up. "Holy shit, *che.* What the fuck happened?"

"Was it one of your friends?" Dad asks Kim. His voice is surprisingly gentle.

Kim lets go of my hand, and then she puts both hands to her face. Her silhouette begins to shudder with soundless sobs. The numbness she'd exhibited with me on our panicked hike back up the road is finally shaking loose. Sometimes it takes something unexpected, like a small kindness from a stranger, to make the reality and grief really sink in.

"Yeah," I answer for her, speaking fast. "A guy named Cal. We saw his girlfriend tearing down the road, looking like she might have been beaten too. We don't know what happened, but I doubt she killed him. I might've heard some other car going down the road ahead of her. I can't say for sure."

While I punch my car key into my truck's glove box, my father stands and lets his sleeping bag spill into a black puddle at his feet. He puts an arm around Kim. "I'm sorry," he tells her quietly. Kim folds into him. I'm astounded that anyone would look to my brusque father for comfort. After all, he'd been rude to her the two times they'd met. I guess that makes the gentleness on his behalf all the more touching. My brother is watching, too. It's too dark to make out the expression on his face.

I get my cell phone out of the glove box and turn it on. I'm relieved that the batteries are fine, but the lit-up screen tells me that there's no signal. To the west the broad massif of Wild Fire Peak blots out the stars. I consider a run to the summit with the phone and wonder how long it would take. Forty-five minutes? Then I look at the hill to the north, the one with the crumbly red cliff in its center that I'd seen Cal and Sunny rappelling just a few days ago, and consider it too. It's much closer and might be high enough to catch a signal. Just before I leave to jog up it, I remember my dad's satellite phone. I borrow it without asking.

I dial 911. The Sheriff's Department in a county

to the north answers and then transfers me to Tomichi County. A sleepy dispatcher says the same thing as Roberto when I tell him someone has been murdered up in Wild Fire Valley. "Holy shit!" Tomichi County must not have many murders. For some reason, I picture how that will sound at the killer's trial, when the tape is played—my own voice oddly calm, stating that I want to report a murder in the valley, then the dispatcher half shouting a "Holy shit!" The jury will probably chuckle. The dispatcher puts me on hold; he excitedly explains that he'd better wake up and then patch in Sheriff Munik.

"Burns, right?" the sheriff drawls when he comes on the line. His voice isn't particularly sleepy for a man who had been up most of the previous night dealing with an arson investigation.

"Yes, sir," I say, knowing we're still being recorded.

"They call you Wyoming guys special agents or something, right?"

"That's right."

"I thought only those FBI assholes did that. What does 'special' mean? That you guys are retarded or something?" The jury will laugh at that, too. The sheriff must only be half-awake.

"Sheriff," I say officially, "about an hour ago I heard what sounded like a scream down-valley from where I'm camping near the base of Wild Fire Peak in the San Juan National Forest. I hiked down there with a woman named Kim Walsh, who knew a couple who were camping in that direction. She saw a female with what might have been blood on her face driving toward town in a small white car, like a Ford Escort—I couldn't read the plates. Then up at their camp we found the body of a young male. He looked like he'd been beaten to death." I want to add that I don't think the girl could have done it, but don't say that. My cop instincts tell me that if it turns out Sunny really had killed Cal, then my recorded opinion would be something her defense attorneys would jump all over.

The sheriff is quiet on the other end. I wonder if he's gone back to sleep. But then over the hiss of the satellite connection I hear what sounds like a zipper shutting. "I'm on my way, *Special Agent.* This better not be bullshit. I'm getting tired of running up into that valley in the middle of the night."

"I'll meet you at the turnoff to the camp," I say. "You'll want to park down the road a little when you see my headlights, so you don't drive over any evidence."

There's another long silence. "You special agents are just like the Feds. Always trying to tell us ignorant country cornpones how to do our jobs." He hangs up. The defense lawyers will have a lot of fun with that. I can picture the sheriff being cross-examined: *"So you admit to being an ignorant country cornpone?"*

Once my father has released Kim from that odd, comforting embrace, I drive her across the meadow to the activists' camp. Dad rides uncomfortably in the backseat with Oso while Roberto stays behind, sleeping off whatever he'd smoked or injected earlier in the night. We leave Kim in the hands of her friends. Before we drive down the Forest Service road, I ask them all to stay in the meadow. There's nothing they can do. Someone wants to drive down to look for Sunny, but I explain about tire tracks and that they would just be turned around by the sheriff anyway. Someone else asks if I'm sure Cal is dead. I think about the mangled face, the naked body sticky with blood, and the placid skin. "Pretty damned sure," I tell them. My tone leaves no opening for argument.

Dad and I wait for the sheriff in my truck down near the turnoff for the old logging track. Neither of us says much, but I can guess what my father is thinking: *I told you not to get involved.*

While we wait I think about Sunny, how she'd looked so at home the day I'd met her when she bravely rubbed Oso's chest. She'd been like a forest sprite, a part of the meadow. I think about Cal, trying to be so cool, embarrassed that I'd seen him rappelling off a rotten cliff instead of climbing in the canyon. I think about the feel of Kim's hand in mine on our hurried return to the meadow. I think about what she'd said to me before she'd gotten out of the car at the activists' camp.

"It's my fault. My fault, Anton. I got them both into this."

I told her the obvious. That it's no one's fault but the killer's. That no one could foresee something like this. But she shook her head and bent forward as if she'd been punched in the stomach.

"No. You don't understand. I got them into this. This whole thing with the valley...I pushed Fast too hard... made him have to go and hire that goddamned pit bull.... And then Cal found that cave he says is such a secret." Her breath and words came in short bursts. "Sunny just told me that he'd taken her there...and that it was unreal, like something out of a dream....Cal was going to send some photos of it to the Forest Service manager... to try and get them to reconsider approving the land exchange....But he didn't want to tell anyone where it was... because he was worried Fast would get there first and dynamite it or something.... Or that the Forest Service would keep him from exploring it... send in their own people... turn it into a tourist trap."

She covered her face with her hands and rocked back and forth. "I started all of it.... And then I let it happen."

The lights that come flashing up the valley on the Forest Service road are blue and red. They reflect off the forest and up the slope on each side of the road. I can hear the drone of several engines, not unlike what I thought I'd heard earlier in the evening just before we'd found Cal's corpse. Only the rumble grows closer rather than the other way around. It's weird, seeing those flashing lights approach but without the screams of their sirens. As they get closer I can hear their axles scraping over the deep ruts.

There are two cars from the Tomichi County Sheriff's Office, one a regular patrol car and the other the sheriff's big SUV, plus an ambulance that follows a moment behind. Their tires crunch on the dirt and rocks. When the caravan is about a hundred feet from us, I flash my brights at them twice, then flick my headlights off. The first car, the SUV, stops in the middle of the road. The tall figure of Sheriff Munik gets out. In the headlights of the cars behind him, I see him wave for them to park and come on.

The short, fat silhouette of Deputy B. J. Timms is unpleasantly obvious.

"Special Agent Burns," the sheriff says to me as I squint into the blaze of light, "I hope you approve of where we parked. If you have any other suggestions, please keep them to yourself. Now, where's this body?"

I point at the narrow cutoff to the side of the road. "Up there, about two hundred yards."

Munik sweeps his long Maglite at the trees as three deputies come up behind him. "Do you know the deceased?"

"I met him the other day. His name's Cal something. And the girl we saw tearing out of here is named Sunny. She is . . . was his girlfriend."

"You know anything about their relationship? Or where they're from?"

I shake my head. "No. I'd just met them three nights ago. Then Cal was the one who got busted in the nose by one of David Fast's men the next day. The woman who found the body with me, Kim Walsh, I think she knows them both pretty well. She should be able to tell you their full names and all that."

The sheriff plays the light over the ground at our feet. It looks like a hard-packed mixture of dirt, rock, and pine needles. It's unlikely they'll find much in the way of tread marks or footprints unless the ground is softer up the logging track. Then he shines the light through the windshield of my truck.

"Who's that?"

"My father."

"Ah, the colonel. And where's the rest of the family this evening?"

"My brother's up at our camp. The woman who found the body with me is camped up there, too."

Sheriff Munik gives me a long look, but I can't see his eyes because of the headlights blinding me. "Tell me, Burns, what are an Air Force colonel, a felon, and a Wyoming cop doing hanging out with a bunch of ecoterrorists?" Obviously he'd taken the time to run my brother's name through the computers.

"We came here to climb and that's it. And I think most of those people up there would resent you calling them terrorists. From what I've seen of your friend Fast and his men, they're the ones trying to cause a little terror."

Neither of us speaks for a moment. Then Munik calls for one of his deputies to bring the crime scene equipment. "If you'd be so kind, *Special Agent*..." He gestures at the narrow track.

I lead them through the thick forest foliage to one side of the track so we don't walk over any evidence. And I take a small pleasure in letting branches snap back in the sheriff's face. It's not that I don't like him—from what little I've seen he seems competent enough at his job—but I want to pay him back for all the mocking "Special Agent" stuff. I'm actually sort of impressed that he hadn't arrested anyone or busted any heads in the meadow yesterday just to satisfy his town's leading citizen, who'd been watching from his Suburban. Too many small-town sheriffs in Wyoming would do just that.

Behind me the flashlights cut back and forth through the trees. When I spot the yellow rain fly, I say, "He's right up there. Under a bush, just past the yellow." I have no desire to take a second look.

I wait behind while the sheriff and the two deputies who must be his crime scene technicians push their way forward through the brush.

I hear the sheriff's voice, which is for once very quiet. "Damn" is all he says.

Back down on the road, I wait in my Land Cruiser with my father and Oso. Sheriff Munik confers with his men a little ways away. They're probably deciding to wait for dawn, I explain to my father. They don't want to risk missing or contaminating anything. Beside me my father grunts.

Just as I make a jaw-popping yawn, realizing how hungry and tired I am, the sheriff walks up flanked by a deputy on each side. His face is grim.

"Agent Burns, come with me please." He gestures for me to follow him back to his SUV. Maybe he's changed his mind about getting my opinion after all. In my mind I try to put together my suspicions about Fast and Burgermeister. The sheriff gets in the driver's side, I get in the passenger seat, and the short deputy slides into the rear with a notepad and pen in his tiny hands.

"I checked up on you, you know," the sheriff begins. "You've got quite a reputation up in Wyoming. Not a very good one, I'm afraid. Three years as a special agent and already you've been suspended twice."

I'm tempted to explain that the first time it had been the normal suspension-with-pay following any officer-involved shooting. And the second time I'd hit a cop who had it coming. But I say nothing. It would only come out defensive and self-serving.

"For a drug agent you sure seem to cause a lot of ruckus. Always thought you guys were supposed to stay behind the scenes."

Again I don't comment.

"Your brother has even more of a reputation. Or should I say record?"

I stay quiet. Deputy B. J. Timms laughs in the seat behind me. It comes out high-pitched and mean.

Munik turns to frown at him, then says, "Tell me about tonight."

I tell him everything again while the deputy scratches his pen against paper. I tell him about thinking I'd heard a woman's scream, then Oso's barking, and Kim asking me to go with her to check on her friends. As best I can, I describe Sunny's car as it came bouncing down the trail and add that Kim can describe it a lot better, that she might even know the license number.

The sheriff listens without asking any questions. I take this as a compliment on my professional description of the events leading up to the discovery of Cal's body, until he asks, "And where was your brother, the felon, during all this?"

"My brother had nothing to do with this, Sheriff. He was asleep next to me when I heard the scream."

"You sure about that, son?" In the glow of the green dashboard lights, I can see he's smiling slightly. It's a sad, compassionate smile, offering me another shot at telling the truth.

A warm heat floods through me. I'm tired and hungry and I don't need this shit. "Listen, Sheriff, and listen carefully. *He was right next to me.*" I turn to the scribbling deputy behind me. "Did you get that down?" Timms glares back at me.

"Never left, huh?" the sheriff asks.

I think about Roberto's disappearance down the

canyon earlier in the night and debate whether to tell the sheriff about that. It can't hurt, as it was far earlier and Dad and I had heard him howling in the canyon, not in the broader valley. Anyway, I bet that his next move is to talk to my father alone, who will probably tell him that. Besides, the truth will set you free. Right?

"My brother hiked down the canyon to be alone for a while just after dinner. He was back well before I heard the scream."

"You're sure?"

"Yes. I'm sure. I told you—my brother has nothing to do with this. You should be looking at David Fast and his hired gun. A guy named Burgermeister."

The sheriff turns and looks at the deputy in the backseat. Then he looks back at me. "Here's a thought for you, Special Agent. Your brother might have been next to you when you heard that scream, but that doesn't prove he wasn't down here earlier. Maybe the girl came up later, found her guy's body, and started screaming then."

I stare at him, openmouthed. I want to explain that Roberto would never hurt someone who'd done nothing to offend him, but know it will sound stupid since the sheriff's already commented on my brother's long record.

Instead all I say is "Bullshit."

He sighs. "Stay here a minute, Agent." The sheriff then does what I predicted. He gets out and walks up to talk to my father, who's still sitting in the front of my truck. In the headlights of the police SUV, I see my father's face turn hard and cold with anger.

I pull at the door handle and start to get out.

"He tol' you to stay put," Deputy B. J. Timms says from the backseat. They are the first words I've heard him utter. Like his laugh, his voice is oddly high-pitched. It's no wonder he seldom speaks.

"Fuck off, Blow Job."

As soon as I step out, the deputy's getting out, too. He's shouting at the sheriff, "Hey, Sheriff, the guy won't stay. Want me to cuff him?"

Munik turns and watches me stomp up to him and my father.

"Burns," he says wearily, "you can either do as I tell you and stay put or I'm going to cuff you for obstruction. And, Colonel, I'm afraid the same goes for you."

Things are moving too fast for me. There have been times, in fistfights, on climbs, and in my one gunfight, when the world seems to fade into slow motion and I feel that I'm the only one moving at regular speed. In the gunfight I had thought I could almost see the bullets coming. That I had time to get out of the way. But that isn't happening now. I can't even get a mental grasp on what the sheriff's saying to his deputies, punctuating his words with short, brusque hand motions. And it's probably for the best that I don't notice the weight of the pistol in my jacket pocket.

A couple of deputies get into the sheriff's SUV and pull it forward. They slow when they approach my truck and turn out their lights. Deputy Timms is ordered out by the sheriff before he climbs in. Timms argues to come along, surely remembering how Roberto had insulted him the day before, but the sheriff gives another indication of competence by refusing to take him. "Cool down," he says. Then the SUV rumbles up toward the meadow, as they go to interrogate my brother about a crime he hasn't committed.

Timms and the other remaining deputy watch us from positions behind my truck and closer to the meadow. Both of them have their thumbs hooked on their gun belts. The pint-sized cop smiles at me, daring me to disobey the sheriff's orders, and I have to restrain myself from saying or doing something. I won't be able to do anyone any good if I get arrested for interfering.

"What's Roberto going to do when those fools wake him up?" Dad asks me, getting out of my Land Cruiser and looking up the valley. The white shape of the sheriff's blacked-out SUV creeps around a bend, disappearing toward the meadow.

"I don't know."

FIFTEEN

AROUND US THE night is close to fading. Birds start to wake and call to one another in the predawn darkness. The crickets have finally abandoned their nightly rhythm. My truck creaks every now and then when Oso shifts his weight to lean out a new window. Muted rock music plays from the cab of the ambulance where the two paramedics wait to "bag and tag." To keep from worrying about my brother and how he'll react when he's awakened by a gang of country cops, I think about Cal. How the caver in his mud-stained clothes had been so amped with life on the two occasions I'd met him. How he'd acted with foolish courage when he'd leapt on the back of one of Kim's assailants during the fight in the meadow. And how now he's just a piece of evidence for the coroner and his staff to cut up and try to decipher. Like a puzzle.

The two deputies talk in low voices, sometimes

laughing as they keep an eye on us. I'm inclined to glare at Deputy Timms but know it won't do any good. I'm desperate to do something, anything, but I'm utterly powerless here. It's a constricting feeling akin to claustrophobia. Like I'm being squeezed into a very small place. With clenched hands I stand beside my father in the road. We're both silent and unmoving, both listening intently to the end of the night. We hear no shouts, no sounds of violence, and, thankfully, no gunshots coming from the direction of the meadow. But I remember that the meadow is far enough away that I'd barely heard the scream.

"I think we're going to have to change our strategy," Dad says to me.

I cock my head at him, not knowing what he's talking about.

"Talking's not doing any good. It might dry him out, to spend a few days locked up. Until they find out who really killed that boy."

"Jesus, Dad," I snap.

The thought of Roberto back in a cell makes me feel a cold chill. And it adds weight to the claustrophobic feeling that's pressing down on me. From what little I'd heard about the federal time he did, it almost killed him. His sentence was extended twice because of fights he'd gotten into there. He almost never talked about it but I know it took a permanent toll on his psyche. It had upped the ante on his excesses—the soloing had begun in earnest when he was released. The one time I'd visited him at the medium-security facility outside Denver, he'd been like a caged mountain lion. Pacing, snapping at the bars, slowly burning himself up with his own energy.

In a calmer voice I add, "I think he needs to make his own decisions, not have them forced on him."

My father grunts and turns away again to look up the valley. Over it the stars are fading as the sky turns from black to a pinkish gray.

It's perhaps twenty minutes before a pair of headlights starts heading back down the valley toward us from the meadow. And it's maybe five minutes after that before we can hear off-road tires crunching on the rocky road. Every few seconds the SUV's engine noise is punctuated by a heavy thump. As they drive slowly past us and into the light made by the ambulance's high beams, I realize the cause of the periodic thump. Roberto is sprawled in what amounts to a cage at the very rear of the big SUV. His hands are pinned behind his back and his shackled bare feet are slamming into the reinforced glass of the rear window.

The truck stops beyond us, close to the patrol car and the waiting ambulance. Sheriff Munik steps out. He slaps the hood twice after closing the door behind him. Then the truck pulls away and heads down-valley, creeping past the other vehicles. The Wyatt Earp look-alike gives us a brief look and hesitates before walking toward us. His coat looks rumpled. One sleeve is half torn off. When he gets closer I notice a trickle of blood running from one of his ears.

"I apologize for having tried to be helpful earlier," I tell the sheriff as I advance to meet him. "I mistook you for a competent peace officer."

"Now, son—" Munik says.

"You've arrested an innocent man while Fast or Burgermeister or whoever really killed Cal is covering their tracks. This is bullshit." I'm up in his face but the sheriff doesn't move away. The brim of his big Stetson almost hangs over my forehead. The two deputies who'd been assigned to watch us quickly flank their boss, waiting for a signal to drag me down. B. J. Timms slides his nightstick from his gun belt with the low hiss of wood on leather. I have enough sense to keep my hands at my sides and swing only from the mouth.

"Simmer down," the sheriff says.

"What the hell do you think you're doing, Sheriff? You don't have probable cause to arrest him. You don't have shit. My brother is going to sue the hell out of your county, and if he's lucky, even you personally." Law enforcement officers are generally immune from lawsuits unless it can be shown that they were acting in bad faith, but right now I'm angry enough to believe we can prove it.

"Step back, son." The sheriff says it quietly but his tone is hard. He's not going to take much more. And that's fine with me—I want something to happen. But I need him or his sidekick to be the one to start it.

I begin to say more but my father takes my arms with an iron grip and pulls me back. From behind us I can hear Oso growling from inside my truck.

"Antonio, shut up," Dad says.

Then to the sheriff: "My son is right. You've arrested the wrong man. Roberto was asleep beside us when we heard the scream."

Munik rubs his chin with the back of a hand. "Well, sir, you may or may not be right about that. The scream might have come when that girl they saw flying down the road found her friend beat to death. Or you might be wrong about the timing. I'm not going to call you a liar, but contrary to what your other hothead son is saying, we've got more than enough PC." He means probable cause to make an arrest.

"One, your boy Roberto just fought with me and another officer when we tried to ask some questions. As the *special agent* here can probably tell you, that in itself can be evidence of guilt. Two, he's got a history as long as my arm for assaults and vandalism. Three, he's got dried blood on his hands, and I'm betting it's that boy's blood." He gestures up the hill to where Cal's body is decomposing. "And four, both you and the special agent here admit he took off for a few hours sometime earlier in the evening. That adds up to a hell of a lot of evidence, General, and it doesn't look good."

"Colonel," my father corrects, but the sheriff knows that.

"The blood's from climbing," I snap. "His hands got torn up climbing yesterday afternoon. Look at my hands, look at my father's."

"Son, you trying to get yourself arrested, too?"

A phone chirps twice. The sound it makes is unnatural in this place with the primitive emotions in the air. The sheriff, my father, and I all slap our pockets with the annoying habit of a cellular culture. For a moment I think it's Roberto, somehow calling me, but then I remember that my phone is locked in the glove box of my truck and that Roberto is halfway to Tomichi already, trussed like a turkey in the back of the sheriff's SUV.

It turns out to be my father's satellite phone. He lets go of my arms and walks a little ways up the road.

"Look, Sheriff, this is bullshit," I say, trying hard now to keep both the anger and the pleading out of my voice.

"Test the blood. Find the girl. You're going to be apologizing when all this is sorted out."

Munik shakes his head almost sadly. He turns and walks down toward the patrol car and ambulance.

Deputy Timms snorts at me. "I've got a prediction of my own." He closes his eyes for a second and holds a finger pointed to his temple as if he's receiving a vision. "I see your brother apologizing to a jury, begging them not to give him a ride on Old Sparky. And I see you up there pleading with him."

Without thinking, I step forward again, but he anticipates my move. He has his nightstick held parallel to the ground, an end in each hand. With the rounded edge he shoves me hard in the stomach.

"Try it," the deputy murmurs up at me, correctly reading the look in my eyes.

I swallow my anger. Turning my back, I spit on the road to rid my mouth of the bile that has crawled up my throat. *It will only make things worse.*

"Thought so," I hear Timms say. "He's a pussy." His partner laughs.

"And I guess you only like dicks, Blow Job," I tell him.

From where he's taking an evidence kit out of the trunk of the patrol car, the sheriff shouts at us, "Now you and the general clear on out of here, unless you want to get yourselves arrested for obstruction. Go on back up to your camp—this road's closed for the next hour or two. I don't want anyone but my men fooling around with the crime scene."

"You hear that?" the pint-sized deputy says from behind me. Then he imitates his boss by saying, "We'll let you know if we need any help, *Special Agent* Burns."

* * *

When my father walks back, pushing his phone back into a pocket, his face is as expressionless as ever. But I notice an even greater rigidity in his steps and in the way he drives the heels of his hiking boots into the ground. I'd been too angry and worried about my brother to care much who was calling him. Now, I realize, it must be something important if someone's willing to interrupt what's left of Dad's vacation with a five-thirty A.M. phone call.

"We've been ordered back to the meadow," I say.

My father doesn't reply as we get in my truck with Oso. I maneuver the truck back and forth on the narrow Forest Service road, trying to turn around. The whole time, Deputy Timms stands close, his burnished wood weapon still in his hand. It takes four or five shifts between first gear and reverse while spinning the steering wheel before I get the truck pointed back up-valley. I pop the clutch and press the gas pedal a little too hard, sending a small spray of dirt onto the deputy's boots and uniform trousers. In the rearview mirror, I see him giving me the finger.

Up ahead the sun is finally rising over Wild Fire Peak, putting an end to this nightmarish night. But the day is not looking like it's going to be any better.

"You look like you got some more bad news," I say.

He looks straight ahead and grunts once in acknowledgment. How much worse could it be than having your drug-addict son arrested for a crime he didn't commit?

"Was it Mom?"

Dad exhales loudly in what could be a sigh. There's a long pause before he answers. "No, Antonio, it wasn't your mother. It was work—they're calling me back.

There's a situation in Bosnia. It hasn't been released on the news yet, but a helicopter crashed behind Serbian lines with four Americans aboard. They want me at my desk today, and maybe on my way to the Balkans tonight."

The truck bounces over a series of ruts, filling the interior with the sounds of metallic rattling. In the backseat Oso sneezes in the dust that's coming in the open windows. I realize I'm gripping the wheel with unnecessary tightness. I look over at my father's rigid face.

"Did you tell them you've got a situation right here?"

He pauses again before answering. "No, son, I didn't. Your brother's safe enough for a few days. Safer, anyway, than on the loose." And we both know it won't do any good to tell his superiors about this new family problem; it would only result in another black mark in his official file.

But even understanding that, a new anger warms my blood. *Roberto needs you here. I need you here. Whatever happened to all those years of preaching that family comes before all else? That we Burnses need to stick together, support one another through hard times?* It is a concept he'd drilled into us as children, the same as he'd drilled us to always double-check our knots. In these last few years we've all been forgetting to do what's necessary to keep each other alive. And there's no time we've needed one another like right now.

"So you're going?"

"I've got to."

I don't look his way again as we pull into the meadow.

SIXTEEN

THE TOMICHI COUNTY Courthouse is a rambling three-story brick building that looks as if it's been added to as the county has grown. At both ends of the main building are single-story prefabricated additions of cheap wood painted white. According to a sign near the complex's front, it houses a multitude of city and county offices as well as the courts and the county jail. When I circle the block looking for a parking space, I notice a small recreation area on the other side with a bent, netless basketball hoop that's surrounded by several chain-link fences topped with razor wire. I wince when I see that sad hoop and the cracked and weedy asphalt around it. I can't stand the thought of my brother being in such a place. I've got to get him out.

Feeling irate and exhausted and a little bit scared, I find a parking spot to one side of the main building and walk bleary-eyed to the big glass doors at the front. According to my watch it's eleven o'clock. Neither my father nor I had even tried to sleep. As dawn came, and while the deputies were still messing around with my brother's enormous motorcycle and its saddlebags, looking for a potential murder weapon and other evidence, Dad and I brewed oatmeal and coffee. We didn't speak much. I was gorged with recriminations I wanted to snarl at him for leaving Roberto and me. And I imagine he was probably feeling a fair amount of guilt, which was all right with me. I could tell he was also angry.

When he threw out the last of the coffee from the pot, he flung it far out over the grass in the direction of the searching deputies. It splashed close to their boots. They started to challenge him on it but were unable to hold his silent, cold glare. My brother must have hidden his drug stash in the woods because the deputies left without any signs of excitement.

I dropped my father off at the Tomichi airport before heading for the courthouse. From there he would catch a feeder flight to Denver and then on to Washington, D.C. He could be in Bosnia by the end of the day. Or stuck at his desk at the Pentagon. Both places a thousand or more miles away. His phone had rung incessantly, so much so that he had to plug it into my truck's adapter.

Our parting conversation hadn't gone any better than when he'd first told me he had to leave.

"Whatever you do, Ant, don't bail him out," he said to me.

"What are you talking about? Of course I'm going to bail him out."

He shook his head and stared out at the other people

unloading at the airport's curb. "They're going to set it high, you know. Because of his history."

I shrugged. "I've got the money that Papa left me." I was referring to a generous trust that my mother's father, a prominent rancher in Argentina, had left Roberto and me upon his death a couple of years ago. It's something I never touched.

"Think about it, son. A condition of any bail will be no further crimes, no drug use, those sorts of things. You know that better than me."

In Wyoming, suspects on bail are monitored by something called "Court Services." Defendants with histories of drug or alcohol abuse are required to take weekly urine tests. If they "drop a hot UA," their bond is revoked. If they miss an appointment, their bond is revoked. If they get in a fight, their bond is revoked. And the bail money is forfeit. I suspect Colorado employs the same monitoring system. There's no doubt it won't take Roberto long to run afoul of it.

"I'll think about it." I knew he was right but didn't want to admit it. All I could focus on was how pissed I was that he was leaving us and flying back to Washington. A part of me knew he had no choice, that he must obey his orders, but I couldn't help feeling like he was abandoning Roberto just when he needed Dad the most. Dad's past lectures about family loyalty played over and over again in my head.

Bullshit.

The security guards in the courthouse lobby eye me suspiciously when I come in. I remember that my face is still lumpy from the beating I took in the meadow. When I touch my cheek self-consciously, I feel a heavy growth of whiskers from more than two weeks now without shaving. And although I'm wearing the nicest clothes I could find amid the climbing gear in the back of my truck, the rent-a-cops don't seem to regard sandals, grass-stained jeans, and a recently unwadded flannel shirt as the sort of clothes a law-abiding citizen would wear to court. I flip open my wallet and flash my Wyoming badge at them as I walk through the metal detector without stopping, ignoring its shriek. They don't call me back.

According to a map on the lobby wall, there are only two courtrooms in the building. The rest of it is a warren of city and county offices, including the sheriff's and the district attorney's. When I ask an elderly clerk where first appearances are made, she looks me up and down for a long moment. Without speaking she points at a large pair of wooden doors just off the lobby.

I look through a small window in one of the doors before going through. Inside the courtroom my brother sits in the jury box. He's dressed in orange coveralls, as are the four other men he's chained to. The coveralls resemble hospital scrubs but for the color and the stenciled legend, "County Jail," stamped on the chest. The clothes are stretched tight across his shoulders and biceps. A thin young man with a ponytail and a polyester suit is whispering to the five chained men while frantically scribbling notes on a legal pad. I guess that he's the public defender, or, as cops and their clients alike often call them, the "public pretender." The only other people in the courtroom are two overweight deputies who stand guard at each end of the jury box.

Everyone looks up at me when I come in through the swinging doors. Roberto smiles broadly. "*Che,*" he calls to me, "nice of you to come, bro. How long till you can get me the fuck out of here?"

As I walk into the well of the court, I study my brother's face. His skin appears sallow and tight after just four or so hours of captivity. The lines on his face are deeper. One eyebrow is bruised and swollen. His hair hangs in lanky strands around his face. He looks awful.

"I don't know, Roberto. Depends on what the judge says."

Then the nearer of the two overweight deputies says to me, "Step away from the prisoners, mister. Everyone but the lawyers has to stay in the gallery."

Trying to be affable, I show him my badge. "It's okay. I'm a cop."

He squints at my badge from ten feet away. "Not here you aren't. And we've already been warned about you—you're the brother. Now get back."

I try to keep a hot rush of blood from coming into my face. "Look, my brother's in here on a bullshit charge. I'd just like a few minutes to talk to him. I'd really appreciate it if—"

"Get back now, asshole."

Before I can respond Roberto rises from his seat. The handcuffs that link him to the men on each side raise their arms with him. He twists his head to look at the deputy. Although his mouth is smiling, his eyes are not. Nor are his words. "Don't talk to my little bro like that, you fat fuck." From the eyes and the tone, I know Roberto is on the verge of stepping over the edge again and doing something really self-destructive. The anger I've been feeling choking up on me drops like a bad meal to my belly and is replaced by a helpless concern.

Both deputies have started moving across the back row of the jury box toward him. The one who hadn't spoken to me has his radio to his lips. He's saying something, perhaps calling for reinforcements. The public defender backs away.

"Sit down, Roberto! Shut up," I say to him. "Don't make this worse. Please."

The deputy who'd called me an asshole slips what looks like a electric razor out of a leather holster. A stun gun. The prisoners around Roberto are grinning nervously at the deputy, unsure what to do, and unsure whether they'll feel it through the chains if Roberto is zapped.

"Please, bro."

With another smile and a short toss of his head at the approaching deputy, Roberto turns and sits.

The deputy stands behind him with his stun gun in his hand. It's half-raised and ready to descend on the back of my brother's unprotected neck.

I speak quickly to the guards, "You touch him with that and you're finished. He's a witness"—I point at the public defender—"and he can see that Roberto's not resisting in any way."

The deputy with the stun gun looks at the young attorney, who has stopped beside me and is bravely staring back, although the pages of his legal pad flutter in his trembling hands. The deputy then looks at the other orange-clad prisoners, several of whom are twisted in their seats watching him, too.

The guard with the radio says to him, "Don't do it, Joe."

He backs off to where he'd been standing at one end

of the jury box when I first walked in. "One more remark like that and I'll take your head off," he says to Roberto.

My brother ignores him. Instead he smiles at me with what he intends to be an innocent schoolboy's grin.

I sit on a hard wooden spectator bench. The ponytailed attorney cautiously steps back up to the jury box's rail and begins whispering again to the prisoners and writing on his legal pad while the deputy with the stun gun and I exchange glares.

After a few moments the public defender comes over and introduces himself as Tony Allison. I immediately peg him as a True Believer, one of the defense attorneys who are certain that the criminal justice system is one of evil repression and that cops and prosecutors are its satanic minions. And for the first time in my life I'm feeling a little bit of the same.

In Wyoming, public defenders and defense attorneys in general are my professional enemies. They'll do anything to try to get their clients off on whatever charges I have filed against them. Even when they know I have played by the rules, they will try to trip me up on the witness stand to make me look dishonest. They'll call me a liar to the judge or the jury even when it's they who are doing the lying. But despite that, there are a few attorneys in Wyoming I like, even admire. They are the True Believers, the ones who are utterly convinced that every client is a scapegoat to society's woes. I have the same pity for them that I have for all other True Believers—fundamentalist Christians, militant environmental activists, and the men and women who are devoted to climbing and nothing else. It isn't just pity, but also a little bit of envy in that they can always be so certain they are right.

With the True Believing defense attorneys on my cases in Wyoming, I take it as a challenge to uproot the foundations of their faith. Like many other cops I know, I go out of my way to show them just how fair and honest and nice I can be. One had even paid me what I considered a high compliment. "I hate it when you're the investigating officer on one of my guys, Burns," he'd said. "Give me a scumbag cop any day."

Tony Allison, with his cheap suit, long hair, and wispy beard, has the look of a True Believer. He's probably fresh out of law school, where he undoubtedly spent three years being indoctrinated by radical professors about the terrible injustices of the criminal justice system. And now I like him for it, because in this case I agree.

"Mr. Burns, I'm not likely to handle anything but the preliminary stages of your brother's case," he says a little shyly. "Although I'll probably get to sit second-chair. With a murder charge and all, my office will bring in someone with more experience for the hearings and trial. And that's only if your brother qualifies." He means that the Public Defender's Office will only represent him if there's no way for Roberto to borrow, beg, or steal the money to pay for his own lawyer.

While my grandfather's trust had been released to me, Papa had wisely put conditions on my brother's before he passed away. My father and mother have to cosign for any release of funds. I don't mention any of this to Allison, though. If I can clear my brother's name quickly, it will never come to a trial, and for the time being I'm happy to have this eager young lawyer representing him.

"He'll qualify," I say, knowing it's unlikely Roberto will ever even mention the trust because he'd been so offended by its terms. "What exactly are they charging him with?"

Allison shows me the affidavit for the warrantless arrest of my brother. The statement is brief, and signed by both the sheriff and the district attorney. It alleges that Roberto Burns, a man with a long history of violent behavior, fought and tried to flee when first approached by the sheriff and two deputies in close proximity to a murder scene in Wild Fire Valley. It continues to read that he had blood on his hands, and that his brother and father, Antonio Burns and USAF Colonel Leonard Burns, had both made admissions that the defendant had been away from their campsite for several hours near the time of the murder.

My face reddens when I see my name on the paper. I've incriminated my own brother.

Allison notices my mortification. He points at my printed name. "That doesn't help, you know."

"I know." I explain that he'd been right there in the camp, though, when we'd heard the scream. I also tell him that I didn't have any choice but to tell the sheriff about Roberto's absence earlier because I knew the sheriff would ask my father the same question, and that my father wouldn't lie.

"You don't have to talk to anyone, Mr. Burns. You and your father don't have to tell them anything."

"I know. I know." I shouldn't have cooperated with the sheriff. But I didn't know they were going to finger my brother at the time. And for the three years I've been a cop, I've been outraged every time a citizen has refused to cooperate with me. *We're all just after the truth, right?* I think bitterly. But the worst part is I don't really think the sheriff is consciously trying to frame my brother. If I'd been in his oversized cowboy boots, I probably would have done the same thing based on the evidence at hand.

"The blood's going to be a problem, isn't it?" Allison asks.

I realize he thinks my brother did it. And why not? Ninety-nine percent of his clients are guilty.

"No, the blood is what's going to exonerate him. He didn't do it, Tony. We were rock climbing yesterday. His hands got cut up. How long does it take to check the blood around here?"

He looks at me kindly but disbelieving, used to hearing protestations of innocence from a client's relatives. "Well, they have to send the samples to the state lab in Grand Junction. And that's once they get a sample from the victim's autopsy. A couple of days to a week. But it really doesn't matter, because even if the blood on his hands doesn't match, they'll still hold him until the preliminary hearing, which could be weeks or even months away. Because he resisted, and because of his record."

I sink back on the hard wooden pew. The thought of my brother in jail for weeks to months brings back that claustrophobic pressure I'd felt earlier. Trying to gather my thoughts, I explain to the lawyer about the argument I'd seen Fast have with Cal prior to the brawl in the meadow. I tell him about Cal getting punched in the nose and the fire he'd almost certainly lit at the structure Fast was building on Wild Fire Peak. And I tell him that Fast had to have a good idea it was Cal who'd done it, the way Cal had strode defiantly out of the trees flicking his lighter just as Fast was leaving the meadow. "Fast has all the motive in the world to kill this guy. My brother has none."

Allison doesn't look convinced. "Look, Mr. Burns, I know you're a cop, and that I probably don't need to tell you this, but motive doesn't mean anything. It's not an element of any crime. The only people who care about motive are jurors, and believe me, the state will think of some motive to tell them in a year or so when this thing goes to trial."

He looks around the still-empty gallery before he continues in almost a whisper, "And, well, if you're going to accuse David Fast as an alternative suspect, you'd better have some serious weight behind you. That guy practically runs this town. He and his family have been around here for like a hundred years."

I tell the young public defender, "I'm going to find the girl. Sunny, the one who we saw driving away from Cal's camp like a bat out of hell. She should be able to tell us who the real perp is."

Allison nods, looking distracted. He is nervously watching people come into the courtroom behind us. Undoubtedly this is turning into the biggest case he's ever seen. "Sure. That would be a good idea." After a second he adds, "Listen, Mr. Burns, I'd better start getting ready for the arraignment. It looks like it won't be long before the judge comes out."

"What's the judge like?"

"She's a real...witch." He'd been about to say something stronger but had thought better of it.

SEVENTEEN

THE ARRAIGNMENT DOESN'T go well.

It begins with several local reporters coming into the courtroom with their pads and pens, then swells with a swarm of curious spectators. Apparently word has gotten around. Murder has to be rare in a small town like Tomichi, and everyone wants to check out my brother, the supposed killer. There are local lawyers in their suits, ranchers in their jeans and pearl-button shirts, retirees in their jogging suits, and other assorted townspeople. In just minutes the gallery is full. Latecomers stand against the wall at the very rear of the courtroom. A clerk occasionally peeks out of a small door behind the judge's bench. I guess she's giving her honor updates on the size of the crowd and letting the anticipation build. Across the rail in front of me, that divides the gallery from the courtroom's well, Tony Allison takes advantage of every spare second to scribble furiously on his pad.

The clerk finally shouts into the room, "All rise!" Everyone shuffles to their feet, including the prisoners (with some prodding from the deputies guarding them), as a pale, bony woman takes the bench.

I would guess the judge to be in her mid-forties. She's not a pleasant-looking woman. Allison's description of her as a "witch" had been right on. Her pockmarked face is pinched and pale; her nose is slightly hooked. All she needs to complete the image is a pointed black hat to wear over her robes. She has obviously just finished brushing her thin blonde hair—it's artfully draped over the shoulders of the robe in what appears to be a failed attempt at a halo effect. Upon seating herself in an enormous raised chair, she nods to her clerk, who announces that everyone can sit.

Judge Carver makes no remark on the size of the crowd in her courtroom. She simply begins by calling the cases of the other prisoners chained next to my brother. Without exception, they all have either Spanish or Indian names. One by one they're unhooked from the others in the jury box by the overweight deputy with the stun gun. The deputy recuffs the prisoners' wrists behind their backs, then leads them to a podium between the prosecution and defense tables.

The prisoners stand there, hunched and startled by the size of the crowd behind them, as the judge reads to them the indictments, their rights as defendants, and requests that they formally make a plea of guilty or not guilty. The charges against these men are mostly petty—drunk driving, disorderly conduct, possession of marijuana, and that sort of thing.

After a quick whispered conference with Public

Defender Allison, the plea is inevitably not guilty. A short bond hearing occurs next, where the prosecutor exaggerates the seriousness of the charges and expounds on each defendant's prior record. For the four prisoners who stand at the podium before my brother's case is called, bail is never set higher than a thousand dollars. But it might as well be a million by the dejected looks on the men's faces.

Each case is a dilemma for Allison. He has to know that all of these men will eventually be offered pleas to reduced charges, with a sentence of time served, probation, and a fine. His problem is that the wheels of justice turn slowly, and that it could be a few weeks before the prosecutor studies the case and comes around to make the offer. In the meantime these indigent men will sit in jail, lose their jobs if they have them, and maybe even their wives and families. Yet Allison can do nothing to speed it up. If he were to advise them to plead guilty now to whatever charges the prosecutors have written up in the indictments, Allison could be disbarred from the practice of law even though the men would end up serving much less time in jail. Legal ethics require him to wait for the prosecutors to at least give him the discovery (witness statements, alcohol test results, etc.), to analyze each petty case, and to take a case to trial months from now if he thinks he can beat the charges or show that the police gathered the evidence illegally. Like so many other aspects of life, in the legal system, the poor get screwed.

No one in the gallery, however, is paying any attention to the mini-drama of each case the judge calls. They're all waiting for the magic words—"The People v. Roberto Burns." The spectators around me whisper to one another as they stare at my brother in the jury box. A couple of women in the pew behind me giggle as they compare him to various movie stars.

"He looks kinda like Tom Cruise with long hair. He's too good-looking to be in prison," one of them whispers. "Maybe I can talk the judge into bailing him right into my bedroom."

"You mean *balling* him," her friend giggles.

The center of attention, Roberto sits slumped in his chair in the jury box. His eyes are half-closed, hiding the spectacular azure color of his irises. He doesn't appear interested in what's going on with the other prisoners. Every now and then he glances my way, lifts his lids, and rolls his eyes. One time the women behind me catch him doing this and titter, "Did you see his eyes? My God!" I have to restrain myself from turning and telling them to shut the fuck up.

The judge slowly works her way through the lesser cases before calling my brother's. She takes the time to lecture or berate some of the defendants, and sounds like that annoying radio talk-show host, Dr. Laura. The judge is clearly showboating for the packed courtroom.

"The People v. Roberto Burns!" she finally calls out when she can delay no longer.

All the whispering in the gallery is cut off as if every vocal cord in the room were suddenly severed with a knife. All eyes are on my brother, studying him when he rolls to his feet and throws his broad shoulders back in an abbreviated stretch. I can hear the rattle and clank of the handcuffs and leg irons as Roberto is led to the podium. Even chained, he moves with a predatory grace.

"Tony Allison of the Public Defender's Office appearing for the defendant, Judge," Allison says for the record, just as he had with each of the previous cases. But there is a new tension in his voice. He's feeling the excitement, too.

"Roger Acosta for the People, your honor," the Tomichi County DA says, stepping in front of the younger deputy prosecutor who handled the other cases. The DA wants this one for himself. He is an older man, small and perfectly groomed. He wears his thinning hair in a long sweep over the dome of his head. His suit is an expensive double-breasted blue, cut so as to make his prominent belly look prosperous and respectable. The folded white square of a silk handkerchief peeks from his breast pocket.

Allison says, "Your honor, I expect that this might take longer than the other cases. Would it be possible to have Mr. Burns's handcuffs removed?"

Hearing that, I like the young man even more.

"The prisoner will remained chained, Mr. Allison. You know the policies of this court."

And I like the judge even less.

The judge begins by reading out the charges against my brother. As we do in Wyoming, the Colorado DA has only charged him initially with the most easily provable charges—manslaughter and resisting arrest. They will save the bigger charges, like murder, until they have enough evidence to explain the intent requirement. They are allowed to add charges almost right up until the day of trial.

Roberto stands at the podium, still handcuffed and with the young public defender at his side, as the judge explains the full elements of manslaughter in strict legal terminology that must be utterly incomprehensible to most defendants.

"A person commits manslaughter, Mr. Burns, if such

person recklessly causes the death of another person or such person intentionally causes or aids another person to commit suicide. 'Recklessly' is defined as a person consciously disregarding a substantial and unjustifiable risk that a result will occur or that a circumstance exists. 'To aid' includes knowingly to give or lend money or extend credit to be used for, or to make possible or available, or to further the activity thus aided—"

"Are you saying I lent this guy some money to beat himself to death?" Roberto interrupts, making his voice slow and stupid with a strong south-of-the-border accent. He's mocking the small town and the court. The prisoners watching him from the jury box snicker.

The judge looks up from the fat book she's been reading from. She glowers at my brother. "Hold your tongue until I'm finished, young man."

Roberto shakes his head, acting perplexed, while the judge continues reading. "Manslaughter is a class 4 felony," the judge concludes, giving Roberto another hard look over her reading glasses. "If convicted, you may be incarcerated for one to twelve years in the Colorado Bureau of Prisons and fined up to $500,000. Now, Mr. Burns, do you have any questions?"

"Yeah, I do. What the hell are you talking about? I didn't do none of that stuff." He's still talking like some illiterate farmhand.

Snickering again erupts from the prisoners. Even some of the spectators around me chuckle. I want to lean over the rail and tell Roberto to shut up. I know he understands all this and is just being a clown, but I keep still. The judge bangs the gavel on her desk. "There will be no swearing in my courtroom! You apologize, young man."

Roberto looks around at the crowd behind him, wide-eyed and startled. "Shit, I'm sorry, Judge. But I didn't know 'hell' was a curse word. Those preachers say it all the time, don't they?"

The public defender steps over to Roberto and hisses something at him.

Judge Carver stares at my brother nastily, intending to intimidate him. Her pale face is red and pinched with anger. My brother just smiles back. After more earnest hissing on the part of the public defender, which Roberto listens to with a cocked head, unwilling to break the judge's stare until he's conquered it, Allison says, "Your honor, my client, Mr. Burns, apologizes for any inappropriate language. He understands the charge against him."

"You do?"

"Well . . ." Roberto smiles.

The public defender again quickly answers for him, "He does, your honor."

Speaking with exaggerated slowness and simplicity, as if talking to an idiot, the judge tells Roberto, "I am now going to explain your rights as a defendant to you. Do you understand what I'm saying?"

"I guess."

"You have a right to an attorney, Mr. Burns. That means a lawyer. One will be provided for you if you cannot afford to hire your own."

"*Bueno*," Roberto says, "I need some help with my taxes and shit like that."

The judge pretends to ignore him but her face turns an even darker shade. The book she's reading from trembles in her hands.

"You have a right to a trial on the charge or charges

against you. You are presumed innocent until proven guilty—"

"Hold on, Judge. If I'm innocent, what am I doing in cuffs? Why you got me in your jail?"

"Because the police and the prosecutor say you committed a crime—"

"But you just said I'm innocent."

"Mr. Allison, control your client," she snaps, slapping the legal book down onto the bench. "Mr. Burns, from now on you direct your questions to your attorney or else I'll have you gagged."

"But—" Roberto is still playing the wide-eyed role.

"Mr. Burns, I won't tolerate any more of your impertinence! Now let's move on to the issue of bail. Your attorney can explain your rights to you some other time."

Allison pulls Roberto over to the defense table and pushes him down in a chair.

I see a bit of genius in what my brother's doing by antagonizing the judge. He's trying to screw up the court record, so that even if he is someday convicted, an appeals court years down the road can consider whether or not he was properly advised of his rights. The law requires the judge to get him to acknowledge his rights on the record, something she's clearly failing to do. If all of this weren't so unbelievable, I might be proud of him.

The district attorney stands and folds his hands behind his back. He speaks from behind the prosecution's table, wisely not going near either the podium or my brother, who sits just a few feet away from it. "Your honor, Roberto Burns is a felon. In 1995 he was convicted in federal court of felony vandalism and the defacement of public property. I'm told by the authorities in Durango that he's a well-known drug addict down there and has been arrested innumerable times for crimes including possession of narcotics, assault, disorderly conduct, and resisting arrest. Last night he beat a young man to death and may have injured a young woman as well."

"Bullshit," Roberto interjects.

"The woman is still missing, but was last seen with blood on her face fleeing the scene. Mr. Burns tried to fight with officers who approached him for questioning. They had to use considerable force in detaining him. Subsequently, a large amount of blood was discovered on Mr. Burns's hands and clothes. As you're aware, your honor, the charge against him is quite serious and my office anticipates filing a charge of murder in the first degree once the investigation is fully under way. We also anticipate filing an arson charge for the destruction of property in the same general area on the previous evening. I believe Mr. Burns is a danger to both himself and the community. I also believe he is a flight risk—I'm told he has family in Argentina. I ask that bond, if any at all is granted in this case, be set at a half million dollars. Cash only."

The judge turns to the young public defender. "Do you have anything to say, Mr. Allison?"

"Your honor," he answers, his face flushed by the force of the judge's disdainful tone. "Well, I, uh, a half million dollars is ridiculous—"

"So are the fucking charges," Roberto prompts him, now back in his normal voice.

"Yes, as are the charges, your honor." Allison picks up his legal pad and starts reading. "My client and I are convinced that as soon as more investigation is conducted, Mr. Burns will be exonerated. He shouldn't have to sit in jail until that happens. There is absolutely no evidence that I'm aware of that even ties Mr. Burns to this crime other than that he was camping with a group of people a mile or so away from where the young man was found dead." Up on the bench the judge is writing something, not paying attention, but the public defender continues on.

"The blood was on his hands because he'd been rock climbing yesterday. Frequently, I'm told, climbing results in scratches on the hands. He—"

The judge bangs the gavel. "Thank you, Mr. Allison. Bond is set at five hundred thousand dollars. Cash only. I'm setting a preliminary hearing in ninety days. My clerk will give you the exact date later today." She turns to the deputies guarding the prisoners. "You may take them away."

Allison stands gaping like a hooked fish as he turns his legal pad in his hands. Not only is the judge ignoring his arguments, she's not even deigning to hear them.

I expect an explosion from Roberto but he just shrugs in front of me. I'm relieved until he stands up. He's worked his pants down until the orange suit is most of the way down his butt. And he's not wearing anything underneath. Up on the bench, the judge is rising out of her big chair and pulling her reading glasses from her face, readying to disappear through the hidden door that leads to her chambers. She half turns when she hears the laughter that's rolling out of the gallery.

In the jury box now, Roberto is bent over, as if picking up something from the floor. His bare ass is pointed at the judge.

EIGHTEEN

"HEY! YOU CAN'T go in there!"

I don't even flinch at the desk officer's shout as I stride through the Sheriff's Department lobby, through the low swinging doors that lead behind the counter, and into the interior hallway beyond. Small offices line the walls on each side of me. The walls are covered with stapled sheaves of papers, wanted posters, and assorted flyers. Just seconds before, the desk officer had looked me over and told me the sheriff was too busy to see me.

"Hey!" the desk officer shouts again, her voice fading behind me.

From the cluttered offices I pass, men and women with startled expressions rise up behind their desks. The fact that many of them hold sandwiches in their hands reminds me that it's lunchtime and that my own stomach is rumbling. More people are beginning to call out in alarm.

I'm thankful that among them I don't see pint-sized deputy B. J. Timms with his gloves, boots, and wrap-around sunglasses. He'd probably shoot me on sight.

"Hey!"

"Stop!"

One young officer has seen too many cop movies. He shouts, "Freeze, motherfucker!"

I ignore them all. I'm heading for the office at the end of the hall. It's the only office directly facing the length of the hallway, and it's located at what I guess is a corner of the building. Before making this intrusive dash I'd tightly tucked my shirt into my jeans so that no one would think I was carrying a weapon.

A hand grips my arm from behind just as my intuition proves correct regarding the location of the sheriff's personal office. Aroused by the shouts, Sheriff Munik's lanky frame fills the doorway at the end of the hall. It's the first time I've seen him without his white Stetson, and I notice that his head is totally bald but for where the long tufts of gray hair stick out from the sides of his head. He'll have to get a toupee if he wants to play Wyatt Earp indoors. The sleeves of his shirt are rolled above the elbows to reveal long, knotty forearms.

"I need five minutes, Sheriff," I say as I try to jerk free from the hand on my arm. "Just five minutes, and I'll start with an apology."

I keep my eyes on his as more hands grab at me, attempting to pull me back. I try to twist free while being careful not to appear so aggressive that someone will decide to brain me with a nightstick or fill my face with pepper spray.

"Down on the ground!" someone's yelling from behind me. It's probably the young cop who has seen too many movies.

The sheriff just stares back at me with his cold gray eyes. They're the same color and hardness as the pearl buttons on his shirt. The only move he makes is to raise one hand to his chin, where he rubs the stubble of another sleepless night between his thumb and forefinger.

The mass of the deputies, the office staff, and whoever else is joining in the dog-pile on my back is beginning to drag me down. My legs can't support all the grappling weight. My knees bang onto the thin carpet, and then I catch myself with my palms. I'm embarrassed to realize that I'm now on my knees, like a beggar, and may soon be prostrate. When I barged through the lobby I'd hoped my entrance would be a little more dignified than this. I keep my head arched up so as not to lose the sheriff's gaze and so that I can implore him with my eyes.

The voices behind and on top of me are a single, shouting clamor. I can barely hear what Munik says when I finally see his lips move.

"Let him up."

The dog-pile either doesn't hear or pays no attention. They keep piling on, collapsing me under their weight. I shout to the ears closest to my mouth, "He said to let me up. Now get off!" but to no avail. Their weight and someone's fist hammering at my locked elbows spills me face-first onto the carpet.

"That's enough," the sheriff says, louder this time. "Let him go."

I twist my head to look up at him from between the legs of a pair of uniform pants. The corners of his mouth are raised in a faint smile.

Once the swarm above me has disentangled themselves, I get to my feet and try to stand up straight. My bruised ribs ache from where someone has been kneeling on them.

"You've got five minutes," Munik tells me, the smile having disappeared. Then he adds, as if I didn't already know, "I've got a murder case to build." He waves me into his office. At the entry I pause to hold the doorknob. The sheriff, now seated behind his desk, nods his permission for me to shut the door in the faces of my new friends in the hallway. I give them a flat look and resist the urge to mouth *Fuck you very much* before the latch clicks shut.

"Sit down," he orders, pointing at a leather visitor's chair.

His office is about what you would expect of a small-town sheriff. There is a scarred wooden desk that's fairly clean of papers and other debris (a testament to a low crime rate), a glass-walled gun case full of rifles and shotguns, a coatrack from which a sweat-stained bulletproof vest hangs on a hook next to his white Stetson and tan sport coat, and the two battered leather chairs facing the desk. On the two walls without windows are a couple of dead animal heads. Trophies, like the framed photographs beneath them that show the sheriff with his arm around people I assume are important. There are also two large windows behind the desk. One looks out onto the courthouse lawn and the other looks east. In the distance I can see the pyramid-shaped summit of Wild Fire Peak. Grateful that he hadn't ordered me to be thrown out into the street, or worse, thrown in jail with my brother, I sink into one of the leather chairs.

Munik is looking at me with what seems to be a

forced frown. I suspect that he's still working to suppress the grin I'd glimpsed on his face just a minute earlier. I recall all his "Special Agent" cracks from earlier in the morning and assume that he had enjoyed watching me be taken to the carpet out in the hallway. I've felt a mild animosity between us from the very first day we met, up in the meadow just following the burning of the lodge.

From what I can tell, Sheriff Munik seems like a fairly competent, rigid, by-the-book–type elected official. A plodder. And probably a decent man, but not too bright. In contrast, I tend to project a rebellious, smart-ass attitude. It's reinforced by the Roberto-like things I can't help but do, such as forcing my way into the office of the man who had just arrested my brother. This attitude of mine works well when I'm undercover, dealing with drug dealers and other scumbags, but often serves me badly in the eyes of my superiors at the Wyoming AG's office and with the county law enforcement officers I often work with. What Sheriff Munik and I have is a conflict of personalities. Usually I take a little pleasure in tweaking men and women like him, but right now I can't afford that kind of fun.

"Let's hear that apology," the sheriff says.

I take a deep breath and slowly let it out. This is hard because of my bruised ribs. The words are even harder.

"I'm sorry I got in your face this morning." As much as it pains me, I also admit, "If I were in your shoes at the time, I would have probably done the same thing. You've got a body that's been beaten to death up in the mountains and you've got a, as you said earlier, a 'violent felon' up there too that no one can account for, at least for part of the night. And then, when you go to talk to him, you find him with bloody hands and an attitude."

Across the desk from me, Munik isn't gloating or even nodding as I say this, but his eyes lose some of their cold flintiness.

"But, Sheriff, with all due respect, that doesn't mean you've got the right man. When you get the blood results back you're going to see that the blood is all Roberto's. And while you're building a case against my brother, trying to think up some reason you can sell to a jury about why he might have killed that boy, the real killer just has more time to cover his tracks."

"I don't need a motive, son. Last time I looked, 'motive' wasn't one of the elements of murder."

"That's true, but you need one if the DA's going to get a jury to convict. And he won't have one. Because not only is there no reason Roberto would have done this, there's the simple truth that he didn't do it. Have you talked to the girl yet? Sunny?"

His eyes take on a new alertness when I mention her name. Attempting to conceal it, he turns his wooden chair to one side with a loud creak of unoiled metal-on-metal and glances out the window toward Wild Fire Peak. I wait for him to say something.

But when he speaks it's not about Sunny.

"I know about you, son," the sheriff tells me, still looking out the window. "I made another call up to Wyoming this morning and heard you've been suspended for assaulting an officer. Before that, it was for shooting some guy in the ass. You and your family seem to have a thing about guns and fighting with cops."

I close my eyes and will my voice to remain steady.

"I'm suspended right now for hitting a cop who was torturing a dog. My dog. Before that, two years ago, I was suspended with pay, pending a standard officer-involved-shooting investigation," I say, and then add with a sigh, "and that guy was a dealer who shot at me first, Sheriff." God only knows what he's heard from my office. There are some people in the senior administration there who would love to make trouble for me.

"Heard you were a smart-ass about it, too. Kind of like you've been with me." He turns back to me with the faint smile back on his mouth.

"Sheriff, I don't know what you heard, but that shooting was ruled justifiable. And this thing I'm suspended for now will never be charged. If you don't believe me, call my immediate boss at the AG's Office. His name is Ross McGee."

"That's who I talked to."

I exhale in relief. While Ross might have taken a great deal of delight in retelling the stories of my suspensions to this Colorado sheriff, I'm sure in the end he would put a positive spin on it.

"He says you're a good cop," Munik grudgingly admits. "That's why I'm talking to you right now. As a professional courtesy and that's it."

His admission gives me my chance. "Then let me help you, Sheriff. I'll be honest with you about my brother, and I'll tell you some more reasons why you should be looking at David Fast and his enforcer, a guy named Alf Burgermeister. Sunny must have told you my brother had nothing to do with it."

The sheriff leans back, causing the chair's metal springs to screech again in protest. He puts his leathery hands behind his head. "First of all, son, I don't need you helping me with anything, especially when it's your brother I'm investigating. And second, you'd better be awfully careful about accusing a man like David Fast in this town. Third, no one's talked to the girl yet because we can't find her. What I want to know is where she's at."

He says it like I should know. I lean forward, keeping the distance between us even and wanting him to know I'm sincere. "Sheriff, I have no idea where she is. But if you haven't talked to her, then the first thing I'm going to do is find her."

He assesses me for a few moments, then apparently decides to give me a little information. "After we got her name and address from your friend Ms. Walsh, we checked her apartment. Someone had kicked her door in."

Shit. "Was the place trashed?" I want to know if there'd been a struggle or if the place had been ransacked during a search.

"Yep. Someone was looking for something. And we got this"—he holds up a rough tracing of a shoe print—"from her door. Just for fun, Agent Burns, let's see the soles of your feet."

Shaking my head in disbelief that he would suspect me of trying to intimidate a witness or worse, I grip the arms of the chair and lift both my feet toward him. The sheriff leans forward again to study the soles. After a moment he lifts his eyes back to mine. His look is so intense, so hard, that I pull one foot over my knee and twist it up so that I can see for myself. The sandal's sole is worn almost smooth—it's nothing like the pattern on the paper he'd shown me.

"Got you," he says, giving me his first real smile.

I'm not amused. "Have you checked where Fast was last night, and early this morning?"

Munik rests his elbows on the desk and gives me another one of his long looks, this one for real, while the smile fades. "Son, you don't seem to understand the way this town works. You just can't go around accusing a man like David Fast of things you've got no evidence he actually did. Now, I wouldn't go so far as to say Dave runs this town, but he sure comes close. If you were to look at public records about campaign contributions, you'd see that he's the number one benefactor for everything from the school board to the mayor. In fact, you'd see that he was also numero uno when it came to ponying up for my last campaign. The DA's, too."

Money and politics and justice. The three should never mix but they always do.

The look of distaste I give him causes him to raise his hands in defense. His drawl becomes crisp. "He doesn't own me—if that's what you're thinking, then you can get the hell out of my office right this minute. But I ain't gonna go accusing him without having me some hard evidence first. I know he made a deal with the devil when he brought in that guy Burgermeister—he's a hard-time con with a NCIC sheet even longer than your brother's. I knew that would cause some trouble. But right now all I got is a bunch of stuff all pointing at your brother."

I slump down in the chair, trying to digest what he's telling me. I really don't give a shit if Fast is the town's most prominent citizen—all I care about is getting my brother out of jail. But it would be awfully nice if I could implicate Fast in Cal's death. I'd liked Cal, appreciated that he'd talked me up to Kim as a once-famous climber, and know that if it can be shown that Fast had something to do with Cal's murder it would certainly queer the development of Wild Fire Valley. And that would earn me some bonus points with Kim.

I tell the sheriff about the argument I'd seen Fast and Burgermeister have with Cal before the brawl two days ago in the meadow. With a silent apology to Cal's ghost, I even go so far as to tell the sheriff that Cal had boasted that he was going to burn down the lodge Fast was building on the peak.

"Would have appreciated you telling me that a couple of days ago," he responds. "Might have saved us a lot of trouble."

I agree. "It might have saved Cal's life."

"Only if your brother's not the one who beat him to death."

I don't want to argue. The sheriff already knows all the reasons I believe Roberto didn't have anything to do with Cal's death. Feeling even guiltier, I also violate Kim's confidence in order to tell the sheriff about the ruin and the cave Cal had supposedly found and was in the process of revealing in some secretive way to the Forest Service. I explain that according to Kim Walsh, Cal believed the caves were such a valuable resource to the valley that their acknowledged existence would halt the exchange.

"Sounds like a fairy tale, or a joke," Munik says when I finish. "Cal's Bad Caverns," he chuckles, shaking his head.

I think about the fact that someone kicked in the door to Sunny's apartment and searched the place. And I recall Kim telling me that Sunny said Cal had taken her to see the caves two days before. Even if she hadn't seen Cal killed, she is the only person alive now who knows just where Cal's caves are. And someone isn't taking it as a joke.

"They're looking for her, Sheriff. She witnessed the murder and she knows where the Indian ruin is. Either one will screw up the whole deal for Fast and Burgermeister."

"Then why didn't she come here?" Munik says skeptically, meaning to his office.

"Because she'd helped Cal burn down the lodge. If she came to you, then she'd have to tell you the whole story and get arrested for arson."

"You got to be kidding me, Burns."

I ignore his tone. "What are you doing to find her?"

He sighs. "There's not a lot we can do other than check around town for her and put out a Colorado BOLO on her car." He means Be On the Lookout. It would only do any good if she were stopped in Colorado for some sort of traffic infraction or other crime. "We found an old address in her apartment. We're going to follow that up with a call to the locals there."

"Where?"

"Sorry, son. You don't need to know that. I'm pretty sure you're clean, except for being a little naive and imaginative. But I'm not taking any chances."

I start to get angry again but decide to just let it go. I'll get nowhere by pushing it. "What about Fast? Will you look into him?"

"I'm going to tell you this only so you aren't pestering the man. I tried to call him this morning, just as a courtesy, see, to let him know someone'd been whacked up on what's about to become his land. His secretary said Dave's out of town and has been since yesterday afternoon. She said he was up on the family property in White River, and that he couldn't be reached there even by cell phone. She'll have him call or stop by when he gets back. Now, don't you worry, Agent, I'll make sure he had nothing to do with this. And I'll check on the con, too, that fellow Burgermeister, and I'll check out any alibi he gives me. Now, stay out of it and let me do my job. All right?"

It would be a waste of time to argue about his assumption that Fast couldn't be involved. I swallow the words. The sheriff's not going to help. If anyone's going to look for evidence against Fast, if anyone's going to clear Roberto, it's got to be me.

NINETEEN

COMING OUT OF the courthouse, I jog down the steps and start to cut across the courthouse lawn when I hear my name half shouted from across the broad field of well-tended grass. Kim is stiffly running toward me, her usual fluid runner's grace absent. She no longer looks like the proud, tough woman I'd first been attracted to. Now she looks more like a frightened young girl. As she comes closer I can see that her single good eye is bloodshot and that her cheeks are swollen from crying. Her hard exterior has cracked; her spirit appears in danger of shattering.

When she's just a few feet away I start to ask, "What's wrong?" but the words never leave my mouth. So much is wrong for both of us. What else could go wrong?

"I can't find Sunny!" she blurts out.

After a second's hesitation, remembering the way

she'd stiff-armed me with her eyes when I tried to comfort her once before, I put my hands on her shoulders, then slide them around her neck in a quick platonic hug. "I know," I tell her. "The police can't find her either."

She doesn't immediately pull away from my embrace. Her torso is small and hot against mine, her fists clenching handfuls of material at the back of my shirt. Despite the circumstances, my attraction to her returns. Magnifies.

"What's happened to her, Anton? I went to her apartment and there was a cop in the living room. He said someone had broken down her door."

"I heard."

Everyone wants to find Sunny. Kim wants to make sure her friend is all right. I need to find her because she's the only one who can decisively exonerate my brother. The police want her so that she can further implicate him. And David Fast and Alf Burgermeister, if they are Cal's killers, must find her to shut her up before she can point the finger at them.

And there's also the fact that she may be the only one who knows where the entrance to Cal's Bad Cavern is, if it exists at all. I remember what Kim had told me the night of the Tribe's meeting around the campfire, about how Cal believed that the cave was important enough that it could keep the Forest Service from approving the land swap. Maybe that's why Cal was beaten to death rather than just shot or stabbed—because he wouldn't tell them where the entrance is. The developers might have tortured him to get him to talk.

Kim takes a step away, then looks up at me with slightly quavering lips. She speaks in a rush. "I've been looking everywhere, trying to find you and Leonard. I was about to drive up to the valley again when I saw your car over there. I was writing a note to leave on your windshield but your dog acted like it was going to come through it after me."

"He wouldn't hurt you," I say, not entirely sure. Oso isn't tolerant of people coming around the truck when I'm not in sight to grant them permission. "I was about to go looking for you. My dad had to go back to his job in Washington, and I need your help to find Sunny. She's the only one who can get my brother out of jail."

"What about the police? The officer in Sunny's apartment said they were doing all they can to find her." In a way I'm relieved that she doesn't question further where and why my father has gone. It would be embarrassing to my sense of family pride, having to to admit out loud that he's abandoned his sons.

"I just talked to the sheriff. There's not all that much they can do." I explain that they're looking for her around town and about the BOLO. "You two were friends, right? If something scared her real bad last night, where would she run to?"

Kim's face regains some composure. The question, the requirement that she do some thinking, seems to calm her. "To my house, I guess. But I've already checked there." She looks down at the grass. "Lately we haven't been as close as we used to be. At one time we were really close. I guess I was a sort of a mentor to her or something."

"Do you know where she lived before she came to Tomichi?"

"With her family in Arizona. She's only nineteen, you know."

"Where in Arizona?"

"A place called Page. It's on the shore of Lake Powell."

A bit of her old toughness creeps back into her voice when she says the lake's name. I recall that many environmentalists continue to be horrified by the lake's existence. Its creation, due to the building of an immense dam back in the fifties, had destroyed thousands of pristine desert canyons. Edward Abbey had vilified the huge new body of water in *The Monkey Wrench Gang.*

"Do you think she might have gone back there?"

Kim shakes her head. "I don't know. She didn't talk about it all that much, except for about how she liked to get away from everyone out on the lake. She had some secret place there she liked to escape to. Her parents weren't abusive, but it sounded like they were pretty neglectful. And she had some boyfriend who liked to knock her around. I don't know if she's stayed in touch with any friends there, but maybe she's out on the water."

"How far is Page?"

"It's a seven- or eight-hour drive. If you're going to look for her there—"

"I'm going."

"—then I'm coming with you." She finally looks up at me again, determination now on her face. With one hand she pushes back her tangled hair and reveals the eye patch. "When do we leave?"

I'm tempted to say *Right now*, but restrain myself. "Give me half an hour. There's something I've got to do first." For more reasons than one I'm glad she's willing to come along. And I'm feeling unusually lonesome, with my father gone, my brother in jail, and everything a mess.

Then there's the thing I have to do first, something I

definitely don't want to do. But I feel obligated to let my brother know that I'm not going to bail him out with the money in my trust. Dad had been right—he's safer in there. For the time being, anyway. Maybe a few days in jail will dry him out to the point where he's ready to get some treatment. But if it's too long he's going to burn himself up with his own energy.

TWENTY

AN ELDERLY DEPUTY, too old and crabby for street work, makes me wait while he finishes his cigarette. With a palsied hand he leafs through a faded copy of the *Sports Illustrated* Swimsuit Edition as he smokes. Normally I would be amused to see that libido still exists even at his age and condition, but all the stress and sleeplessness have left me irritable. And I'm in a hurry to get on the road—I need to find Sunny before Fast and Burgermeister do.

"Can you suck that thing down any faster?" I hear myself say. I immediately regret the words. Antagonizing the jailer will only result in him prolonging my wait. And I don't need any more trouble with the Sheriff's Office.

The older man's hand freezes from where it had been turning a page. He looks up at me slowly, his eyes tight in what's supposed to be a menacing squint. Instead of intimidating, the effect is pathetic. The deputy is long past being able to intimidate anyone.

"Sorry," I force myself to say. "I don't mean to be rude. I'm just in a hurry." I'd left Kim on the street outside by my truck. Thinking it might be a good idea for her and Oso to get to know one another before an eight-hour drive, I'd let the beast out to urinate on the courthouse trees. Kim nervously held the old piece of climbing rope I used as a leash. For a few moments, at least, her mind was occupied by thoughts of her own safety instead of concern for her friend.

The deputy inhales deeply on his cigarette and blows the smoke out of his nose, looking like an elderly bull. Then he slaps the magazine shut, takes the soggy butt out of his mouth, and flicks the cigarette past me and out the open door behind my back. The whole time he keeps up the sad glare.

"All right," he finally says, deciding he has me thoroughly cowed. "Let's go."

He leads me through two steel doors and into a closet-sized room. Above a waist-high counter dividing the room is a sheet of bulletproof glass. On each side of the counter are heavy black telephones. The walls are freshly painted but the glass on my side is smeared with finger and lips prints—a silent testimony to the longing that occurs for the men and women in the jail. Bare concrete makes the floor. There are two plastic chairs on my side of the window and a single metal stool on the other. The stool looks as if it's bolted to the concrete.

The deputy leaves me alone and disappears back out into the corridor. I wait alone for five minutes until the steel door on the other side of the glass swings open. Two burly young guards plus the elderly deputy escort my brother into the visitors' room. He's shuffling in leg irons. All three jailers watch him warily, the same way Kim had watched Oso when I'd left them outside. They take the handcuffs off his wrists. One of them says something warningly to him but the window is thick enough to obscure all sound on the other side. Roberto glances back with a smile and a shrug.

Once seated on the stool on the other side of the two-inch-thick glass, Roberto appears calm and bemused except for his eyes. They are red and bleary, hot and angry. On his head is what looks like a broad-brimmed hat made of tissue paper. It takes me a minute to realize it's a sanitary toilet bowl cover.

"*Che*, what's up?" he asks when we each pick up the phones on our respective sides of the window.

"Roberto. What the hell is that on your head?"

He grins again. "Urban cowboy hat. My new look."

I shake my head and say, "It looks like you're having fun."

"There's some cool guys in here. Bunch of Indians. We've been having a little party while waiting for you to get me the fuck out of here. It's the only way to pass the time, bro. I learned that in the pen. You wouldn't believe the sweet shit they've got in this place." He lifts his index finger and thumb, which are touching, to his lips and rolls back his eyes. "It's like a fucking wild powwow in—"

I tap the phone sharply on the glass to interrupt him, then point at the phone. I know of plenty of jails in Wyoming that tap the phones. It would just make things worse if he's caught with contraband.

"Yeah, yeah," he says, catching my drift but either

not taking it seriously or not caring. "This whole thing's bullshit, you know. There's no reason to stress about it."

"They're charging you with arson and murder, Roberto. And whatever else they can think up. You'd better stress about it."

He laughs. "What evidence? Why would I fucking do it? I just showed up in this county two days ago. All the sheriff, that Wyatt Earp–looking wanna-be with the pole up his ass, all he's got on me is that I'm a felon. Their whole case will get kicked at the prelim, *che,* if not before. Shit, you should know that—you do this stuff for a living. And then I bet I can sue the bastards for false arrest and imprisonment."

I'm more disturbed by Roberto's legal acumen than impressed. From all his prior trials and the time spent in the federal pen, he'd acquired the usual perp's knowledge of the legal process. Often it is just enough to make them dangerous to themselves. They take seriously the "innocent until proven guilty" line and always seem to be puzzled when they are held in jail until a jury convicts them. Since becoming a cop and learning that juries cannot be counted on to convict the guilty, I'd usually been pleased when a suspect was made to rot behind bars until the jury kicked him or her loose. Now I'm not so sure.

"The judge liked the case enough to set bail at five hundred thousand dollars, Roberto."

"That's because the DA fed her a bunch of shit about me being a danger to the community, not because the case is any good. I'm innocent, bro. So you gonna get me the fuck out of here or what?"

"It's five hundred thousand dollars, Roberto."

"Why are you harping on that? You've got it in the

trust Grandpa left us—just have the bank wire it north. All you need is ten percent, fifty thousand, for the bail bondsman. Right?"

"No bondsman will touch you. *You* should know that. Besides, I called around after the arraignment this morning."

He snatches the tissue paper hat off his head and wads it into a ball. The amused look is gone. "Why the fuck not?"

"Because you're an addict, bro."

"You told them that?"

"No. The cops did. Or the DA."

He slams the phone on the counter surface before him. He does it hard enough that the sound makes me wince and jerk the receiver away from my head. I expect the phone to shatter in his hand but it doesn't. I also expect a guard to check on us but no one appears. Probably another cigarette break. Through the window he glares at me. His eyes seem hot enough to melt the glass.

After a long minute he picks up the phone again. It still works. "Then you put it up, Anton. The whole thing. You know I'd do it for you." My name is funny coming from his mouth. I've only rarely heard him call me anything but *bro* or *che,* which is roughly the Argentinean equivalent of *dude*.

I shake my head. "I can't."

He stands quickly and leans toward the glass until his forehead is pressed against it. His bright blue eyes are blazing. They look like the hottest part of a candle's flame. He's not threatening me—I know he'd never hurt me, and it's just his natural reaction to get in someone's face when they're giving him news he doesn't want to hear.

But still I find myself leaning back in the plastic chair. I'm not exactly scared of him; it's more a fear of what he'll do to himself.

"*Why the fuck—*" His breath steams the window, obscuring his mouth.

"Roberto, listen. If I were to bail you out, then you'd have to stay sober, take urine tests and all that until the charges are dropped. And even when the charges are dropped, they can take the money and charge you with violating bond conditions. Put you right back in here even though the original case was bullshit. Violation of bond conditions is a mandatory minimum one-year sentence."

With a bit of shame I remember how I'd once used that against a suspect when I couldn't prove a heroin distribution charge beyond a reasonable doubt. After I'd arrested him on the weak charge, I'd arranged with the DA up in Wyoming to set a low bond so the guy would be able to get out, knowing he was addicted and that he'd violate the "no drugs or alcohol" conditions of the bond within hours. Then I'd followed him to a shooting gallery, picked him up when he came out, had him pee in a cup, and locked him away on new, solid charges. The original distribution charges were dropped. He was convicted of violating his bond conditions and sentenced to the mandatory one year.

"You're safest where you are right now until I can get the case dismissed. I'm working on that right—"

"Where's Dad?" he demands, his voice as hot as his eyes.

I hesitate for a moment and look away. Then quietly I tell him the truth. "He split. He got called back to Washington, 'Berto. Some emergency in the Balkans or something."

I expect him to explode, to rip the counter off the window and try to put the stool through the glass. But he doesn't. Roberto looks at me for a moment, then takes the phone from his ear and places it gently in its cradle. He lifts his forehead off the glass. Then he turns and stands by the steel door, facing it after knocking, with his back to me.

"Roberto!" I shout into my phone. I crack it three times against the glass. My brother doesn't turn around.

"Roberto!" I shout again as the steel door on the other side of the glass swings open. The same three deputies pull him roughly into the corridor on the other side. He never looks back at me.

Out in the sunlight, I'm nearly reeling with the shame of my perceived betrayal. As far as he knows, I've abandoned him, too, just like our father had. And despite all his reckless energy, all his uncontrollable urges, Roberto is intensely sensitive. I remember the time he'd shown up in the Tetons one summer when I was guiding there. He tore into my camp on the Grand's Lower Saddle like a tortured demon trying to claw his way back into heaven. His girlfriend since our childhood on Grandfather's ranch in Argentina—the only serious girlfriend he'd ever had—had just sent him a letter. She loved him, it said, but he had no future. He would die young. He would break her heart. So she was cutting all ties and moving to Spain. Roberto borrowed some climbing gear, showed me a mind-blowing stash of acid, and then disappeared into granite spires. It was a month before he came out, a month that I spent snapping at clients and fighting waking nightmares of him falling through the sky. When he reappeared he was just a stinking shell—burned down to nothing but muscle and bone.

I've abandoned him in a way he would never abandon me. If it were me in jail on some bullshit charge and he couldn't post the bond, then he'd just bust the place wide open and drag me out. But I can't do it. Unlike Roberto, my actions are restricted by the fear of consequences. Walking back across the courthouse lawn toward where Kim and Oso wait on the grass near my truck, I think about how betrayed, how hurt, how unloved he must feel, sitting all alone in a concrete cell.

I make a promise to myself: I'm going to make it up to him.

PART TWO

JUSTICE TRAVELS WITH A LEADEN HEEL, BUT STRIKES WITH AN IRON HAND.

—JEREMIAH S. BLACK,

FORMER U.S. ATTORNEY GENERAL, 1876

TWENTY-ONE

THE TRUCK IS humming with speed, shaking a little as the recently replaced engine pushes the rusting frame faster than it wants to go. But my foot remains heavy on the accelerator. Outside, the nighttime desert seems devoid of obstacles and the road is ruler-straight, encouraging even greater velocity. One of the few benefits of my job is that an "accidental" flash of my badge when removing my driver's license makes me immune from speeding tickets in most states. I make a mental note to recall that fact the next time Dad and I argue about the job—that is, if I ever speak to him again.

The bright stars illuminate a strange desert landscape all around us. Odd towers of sandstone are occasionally silhouetted in the sky. The earth is bright red in the glow of the headlights on the sides of the road. If it weren't for the shrubs and chaparral, it would appear to be an almost

Martian landscape. I've heard of some legendary climbs in the area—the Moonlight Buttress, Shiprock, Castleton Tower, the Totem Pole, and Spider Rock—but have never been on them, having always preferred a more alpine environment.

Kim's been silent beside me for over an hour now, ever since surprising me with the selection of a Nirvana CD from the kit on the floorboard. Behind us Oso is grumpy, displeased by his backseat position. He's unhappier still that I refuse to roll down the window so he can hang his head out into the night. At ninety-five miles per hour, a moth or a bee could take an eye out. Every few minutes he smacks the window with a heavy paw to register his complaint, then scrapes his claws down the glass and over the plastic armrest.

"Tell me about Sunny. How well do you know her?" I ask.

We've been driving without speaking and my mind has been wandering. I've realized that it must mean something, Kim knowing the address of Sunny's parents. Despite the more than a decade-and-a-half difference in their ages, they'd seemed close when I first met them in the meadow. But the other times I saw them together Sunny seemed closer to Cal, who was clearly Kim's rival for the leadership of the Wild Fire Tribe.

"She was my friend."

Kim's not looking at me, instead staring out the passenger window at the dark desert beyond. I wait for her to say more and she complies.

"Like me, she volunteered at a battered women's clinic in town. She looks up to me, I guess. She thinks I've got it all together." She says this last part with a disbelieving shake of her head.

"How about Cal? Was he a friend, too?"

"No, not really. Just Sunny. She met Cal through me, though, when I got her involved in all this."

Kim finally turns to look at me. There is guilt in her voice.

"Cal's been a part of the Wild Fire Tribe from the start, ever since the development was proposed and I started organizing. He is—was—kind of a weird kid, like he was wrapped too tight. He helped me recruit a lot of other students in the Tribe. He and I got along okay. I liked him—but he always wanted to make a more direct, more antagonistic challenge to the developers. He never had a lot of patience for the legal process. And once he found that Indian cave he was always talking about, well, he just got weirder. Wrapped tighter, you know. I think he was conflicted between wanting to have it all for himself and wanting to preserve it and the valley, too. Anyway, once those two hooked up, Sunny and I stopped hanging around together. At least, we weren't friends like we'd been before."

"Did you disapprove of Sunny going out with him?"

"Something like that."

Kim looks away again and I think I catch a flicker of irritation in the way she moves her head.

It's obvious she doesn't want to talk about it. Unsure if it's because of my too-personal questions or something else, I turn up the volume on the CD player. In a minute I turn it back down to ask, "What can you tell me about David Fast and his sidekick, Alf Burgermeister?"

Kim sighs. Apparently this, too, is a topic she doesn't want to discuss. But she answers my question.

"David Fast's family has been in Tomichi for more than a hundred years. He's thirty-five years old, born and bred locally, attended my alma mater, the University of Utah, on a football scholarship, although he certainly could have afforded to go to school anywhere. The family had a lot of money back then." She turns to me. "Like I told you before, he's an arrogant prick who has led a charmed life. So far."

There's a tight strain of anger in her voice. I wonder if it's due to her personal dislike for the man or a general dislike for anyone who's led a charmed life. For a moment I wonder if my own life appears charmed to her. It shouldn't, not after she's met my brother and seen what happened to him.

"I say 'so far' because the ranching and timber industries have taken a lot of hits lately. And Fast has been spending what his parents left him on shiny trucks and a new house. He had to mortgage everything in order to buy the White River land, which he planned to use all along for blackmailing the Forest Service into the exchange for Wild Fire Valley. And he had to borrow more from people in town. I guess about half the important businesspeople in Tomichi are investors. And more than half of the city council. If the exchange doesn't go through, he'll lose *everything*. That's what makes him so dangerous."

Kim's emphasis on him losing everything is strong. I glance at her and see she's looking out the windshield. There's a faint smile on her mouth as she contemplates the thought.

"What about Burgermeister?"

"He's the guy they call Rent-a-Riot. Alf Burgermeister considers himself a consultant, but really he's just hired muscle for antienvironmental groups all over the country. To find clients he holds clinics on how to harass the environmentalists into leaving your projects alone. He's quite effective—you heard the stories the other night. The Feds think he was the one who planted a pipe bomb in the car of an Earth Firster a few years back. But they can't prove it. Anyway, Fast brought him in when we began to protest the development at the public hearings held by the Forest Service."

I remember the jailhouse Aryan tattoos I'd seen on his arms. I'm willing to bet he has a prison record for something serious. I'm also willing to bet his interests aren't limited to just antagonizing environmentalists.

"And Sheriff Munik? What do you know about him?"

Kim shrugs. "He's a friend of Fast's family. A distant cousin, too, or something like that. People say he's clean, but you never know. When all the harassment started a few months ago, when Burgermeister came to town, I had a lot of talks with the sheriff. He said he talked to Fast and told him to cut it out. He probably did, too, because the harassment slowed a little for a while. Of course then it got worse as Fast got more desperate. Sheriff Munik wasn't exactly proactive in finding out who was doing it—he certainly never made any arrests. When I asked him to come keep an eye on things during the rally the other day, he refused. I have the feeling that in a pinch, though, he'd probably do the right thing. Reluctantly."

Her assessment is pretty much the same as mine. I don't bother asking her opinion of Deputy B. J. Timms—

I know my brother correctly pegged him as an asshole at first sight.

"Let me ask *you* something," Kim says. "Tell me about Leonard, your father. What happened to him? How come he isn't here with us?"

"Do you mean trying to find Sunny or supporting the Tribe against Fast?" I reply, trying to be a little evasive.

"Both."

It's my turn to sigh at an unpleasant subject. "He won't openly support the Tribe because he can't. He's an officer in the Air Force, and to get involved in a political action, particularly an environmental action, would just cause trouble with his superiors." Even though it sounds like I'm understanding, I'm not. The people I admire most are those willing to throw away everything for a righteous cause. And my father, with his history in the valley, certainly should have a cause in saving the valley. I don't mention what he'd told me that first day in the meadow, after Kim had tried to recruit him with me—that he believes it's hopeless and therefore not worth fighting for.

"As for why he's not with us now—well, he had a major falling-out with my brother a few years ago. It had to do with some trouble Roberto got in and the effect it had on Dad's career." My voice sounds bitter even though I try to speak evenly. "He got a call from his work this morning, right after Roberto was arrested. And he flew back to Washington. I guess he decided his career was more important."

I glance over at Kim to see if she's noticed the anger in my voice. She's looking back at me.

"I'm sorry," she says simply.

She looks like she's on the verge of asking more, so I say quickly, "We should be in Page at about seven in the morning. I'd like to get a room and take a shower."

"Let's see Sunny's parents first, and hope she's there."

"How about you go see them while I clean up?" My eyes are bleary from staring at the dotted white lines on the road and half-blind from the occasional stab of on-coming headlights. I rub the nearly two weeks' worth of growth on my face and stroke the long scar on my cheek. "I don't think I'm exactly presentable. And I don't think I'll be too sensible."

After a moment Kim reaches over and touches my arm. Her irritation is gone—her voice is now just tired and sad. "Please come," she says. "You can take a quick shower before we go."

I feel that same electric tingle running through my skin.

"Are you sure? You'd be better off on your own. Sunny doesn't even really know me."

"I'll need you there" is all she'll say.

She drops her hand from my forearm and plumps a jacket against the window as a pillow for her head. In minutes she's asleep. With the music low, I try to think about anything but Cal's battered body and my brother burning himself up alone in a cell. Surprisingly, it's not impossible. My thoughts keep focusing on the woman at my side.

The sun's been up for an hour already when the narrow two-lane highway releases us onto the turnoff for Page. A high-pitched whine has been coming from the tires for so long that the deeper hum of a slower speed sounds strange. The truck's reduced momentum makes Oso stand up in the rear seat and shake out his coat in the small space. The rattle of his collar in turn wakes Kim. At some point during the night, when the truck wound down into some canyons whose gentle turns had made it difficult for her to keep her head upright against the passenger window, Kim had put the jacket in my lap and then laid her head on it.

"Do you mind?" she'd mumbled.

I was surprised and pleased by the intimacy. "Not at all." That action alone had removed any risk of me falling asleep behind the wheel.

"We're here," I tell her when she sits up and rubs her single eye with a knuckle. "I'll find a motel so we can get cleaned up."

Using the rearview mirror, Kim combs her short black hair in place over her bad eye with her fingers, while I assess the handful of motels that are scattered down the main street. One is a Best Western with a sign that reads, "Pets Welcome," so I choose it. Out of concern that Oso may not be the kind of pet they have in mind, I park the truck just out of sight of the office's window. "Be right back," I tell Kim and the beast.

Inside the office an elderly woman with bluish hair and too-tan skin looks me over. I smile as disarmingly as I can and tell her by way of explanation as I touch my face, "Car accident."

"Ouch. It must have been a bad one," she says kindly.

"It was. Do you have a room for two people and a dog? Nonsmoking?" Coming in the door, I'd considered asking for two rooms but determined double beds would suffice. With my lap still warm from Kim's head, I'm a little hopeful that one of the beds will go unused.

"What kind of dog, sir?"

"Oh, he's sort of a Lab mix," I lie. There's nothing even vaguely Labrador-like about Oso.

She tells me the only pet room available has a single king-sized bed. I take it reluctantly, wishing I'd brought Kim with me into the office so she wouldn't think I'd planned it this way. The matronly woman explains the rates and that I have to pay for two nights as check-in isn't until three in the afternoon. Even though we might not be here even one night, I'm too tired and too uncomfortable about the single bed to argue.

The room is in the back of the building, overlooking a swimming pool. Despite the early hour the pool is already swarming with kids and watchful mothers. Their husbands and fathers are probably out powerboating or fishing on the lake. When I lead Oso to the room's door on the short leash, the children are suddenly silent, awed. One young mother even stands and steps in front of her child as if to protect him from the sight of such an intimidating beast. My battered appearance probably doesn't help, nor does Kim's eye patch. I try my disarming smile again and say to her, "He's harmless, really," before hurrying Oso into the room. It didn't look like she'd believed me.

The room is large, spacious, and clean. As promised, there is an enormous bed as well as a long couch beneath the window. I toss a duffel bag onto the bed. Oso immediately shambles into the bathroom to drink from the toilet, but I call him back. Kim drops her small backpack on the bed beside the duffel. She gives my dusty bag a curious glance.

Looking up, she sees me watching her in the bathroom mirror as I fill Oso's bowl with water. She gives me an awkward smile. "In your dreams, kid," she says, and then picks back up her pack and tosses it on the couch. "You're paying, so I'll take the couch."

I laugh. "Hey, I'm a gentleman. I always defer to my elders. I'll take the couch tonight, if we're still here."

Her smile fades, replaced by a look of concern. "Do you think we're going to find her here?"

"I don't know. You know her a lot better than me. I'm just wondering if Fast and Burgermeister are here, looking for her, too. If they are, then it should confirm that they killed Cal."

"What will we do if we see him? I'd like to let Oso tear his lungs out." The fierceness in Kim, what I'd seen that first time I'd met her in the meadow, makes a brief appearance. And I'm glad to see it. Her spirit is getting stronger. Just twenty-four hours earlier she'd appeared on the edge of a total breakdown. As much as I'd been touched by her grief, shock, and sorrow, I feel more comfortable with her when she's acting tough. It makes me feel less guilty for wanting to kiss her every time I look at her damaged face. I wonder if I'll ever get her mind on other things so that I have the chance. I wonder if she'll kiss back.

"I don't know. Try and look inconspicuous, I guess. Follow him and see what he does. Call and tell Sheriff Munik, too."

"Yeah, we'll be real inconspicuous," she allows herself to joke. "A scar-faced man, a one-eyed woman, and a freaking bear."

TWENTY-TWO

A SHOWER LATER we're back on the road. I get my first glimpse of the huge man-made body of water when we turn off Lake Powell Boulevard and onto a smaller street that leads into the residential neighborhoods. The water is a brilliant blue beneath red and white sandstone cliffs. Islands, really massive buttes, rise directly out of the water. The lake's surface is alive with the wakes of powerboats, Jet Skis, and the leaping acrobatics of water-skiers. From staring at a map in the motel room while Kim showered, I know that what I'm glimpsing is only the tiniest portion of the lake. It winds and twists through hundreds of sheer canyons for two thousand miles of shoreline. The climbing potential here is astounding. The thought of being belayed from the deck of a boat makes the corners of my lips raise a fraction in an involuntary grin. It gives new meaning to the climber's term for falling—"decking out."

Beside me, Kim seems less pleased with the view. She barely gives it a glance. Instead she flips restlessly through her address book, staring at it for a moment, then at the street map we'd torn out of the motel's phone book, then at me, then out the window at the signs on each corner, and then starting all over again with the book. Every now and then she tells me to turn right or left.

"Are you all right? You seem tense."

She starts at my words and puts the book back in the nylon bag she uses as her purse. "I'm worried about Sunny, is all. What if she's hurt? She must be scared out of her mind."

I simply hope she's here, that she's alive, but don't say that.

Kim's nervousness increases as we navigate the streets of Page toward the home of Sunny's parents. Even for a cheap, plastic town like Page, this neighborhood isn't a good one. It's a mix of beat-up trailers and small, prefabricated cottages with crumbling porches and dry, weedy lawns. The yards are decorated with beer cans and cigarette butts instead of the gnomes and flamingos closer to the main part of town. Cars in a state of either regeneration or deterioration are propped up on driveways. Pickups with huge tires and American muscle cars seem to be the vehicles of choice around here. Young white men and women hang out in groups on tobacco-stained sidewalks. A majority of the men wear a haircut known as the mullet: long in back, short on the sides and top. The women have a style all their own: frizzy hair with the bangs ironed straight up, sometimes almost six inches, as if in imitation of a steeply cresting wave. Tattoos seem popular, too. I wonder for a moment if it's the neighborhood that has

Kim so upset, but realize it's not unlike certain parts on the outskirts of Tomichi. Only the view down some streets to the blue water of Lake Powell would make me prefer this town over the ugliest of neighborhoods I've seen in third-world countries.

The temperature outside the truck is visible in the blurry waves of heat rising off the asphalt as we pull up in front of the address. This particular lawn is better cared for than most of the others on the street, well watered and neatly cut. But the house itself is a perfect representative for the neighborhood: part trailer and part stucco. It appears to have begun as a large mobile home that's been added onto with discounted materials of varying generations. The porch is lined with a variety of potted cacti.

We leave Oso in the car with the engine on and the air conditioner blasting. I'm not concerned about some young mullet-head stealing it—not with Oso inside. Kim pauses at the start of a crumbling concrete walkway.

"Why don't you go to the door alone, Anton? They might have heard some things about me from Sunny, things they might not like. I think I'd really prefer to stay in the car," she says. Her voice is quiet and sounds somehow small.

"With my face looking like this? They'd call the police." At the motel I'd done my best to make myself as presentable as possible, putting on a clean T-shirt with my single pair of jeans. I'd also shaved for the first time in almost a month, revealing a pale and generous length of Celtic jaw beneath darkly tanned Latin cheekbones. The two-toned effect is probably more disconcerting than it had been with the beard. The mirror showed that my eyes are still purple with bruising and the scar on my left cheek is red and vivid. It's a colorful look.

"I think we'd be better off if you did this alone," I tell her. "What could they have heard about you—that you're an environmentalist?" That makes some sense. People in towns like this usually don't join the Sierra Club or the Audubon Society. "Besides, you said you don't even know them."

"But they might know me."

"Kim, how about giving me a hint as to what you're so worried about."

She opens her mouth, looking as though she might, but it's too late. The front door to the modified trailer swings open and an older man wearing the neighborhood uniform of a dirty tank top and Bermuda shorts steps out onto the porch. He's chicken-necked and skinny but for a grossly protruding belly. In one hand he holds a can of beer; in the other is a stubby cigar. The screen door slaps shut behind him. Even though it's still morning, the man is already swaying on his feet. "Help you?" he asks, his voice and stance more aggressive than the words.

Kim doesn't speak or move, so I smile as innocently as possible and ask, "Mr. Hansen?"

"Never met him."

I remember Kim saying that Sunny's mother had remarried. "Are you Sunny Hansen's stepfather?"

"Depends. Who the hell are you?"

"This is Kim Walsh, and my name's Antonio Burns. We're trying to find—" but he isn't listening to me. He's staring at Kim with his mouth writhing somewhere between a frown and a smirk.

"The lesbian lawyer," he says slowly, the nasty smirk

winning out. "What do you want, girl? My Sunny run off and leave you for some man?"

I look at Kim, finally understanding her reluctance to come here. Finally understanding a lot of things. My desire for her goes from hopeful to hopeless in less than a second, and I feel a flush of anger at the man who has so crudely revealed her secret.

Kim, on the other hand, appears to be composing herself. The man's aggressiveness brings her out of the embarrassed trance she has been in since we left the motel. I realize that she's a lot like me in other ways than just liking women—she's learning to be stronger in the face of adversity.

"Mr. Villanova, is Sunny here?" she asks coolly while moving up the walkway.

Sunny's stepfather is still leering at her unpleasantly. "I thought you lesbians were supposed to be all butch-looking or something. Like clomping around in motorcycle boots with a man's haircut."

"No, sir. We're not all like that." And Kim clearly isn't. "Look, Sunny's a friend of mine and I need to talk to her. Is she here?"

The stepfather remains standing in front of the door, making no move to invite us in. He takes another swig from his beer and puts out the cigar in one of the cactus pots. "Girl, I'll tell you the same thing I told everyone else who's come poking around for her today. Sunny was here sometime real late last night, then she took off again real early in the morning. Don't know where to. Don't know if I'd tell you even if I knew."

Kim lets out a sigh of relief. Sunny's here, somewhere. And I'm pleased we're on the right track, that at least

Sunny's alive, but concerned that someone else has been looking for her. "Who else came by asking about her?"

He looks at me for the first time since I'd said Kim's name. "Who'd you say you are? Some queer? Another 'friend' of Sunny's?"

I smile, but not as nicely as before. "Nope. My name's Antonio Burns. I'm a special agent with the Attorney General's Office in Wyoming."

"Then let's see some ID, cowboy."

Stepping up the creaking porch stairs, I hold my wallet open just two inches in front of his face for a moment. Then I snap it shut.

"I know what the lesbo wants with Sunny," he says with another leer toward Kim, "but what the hell does a Wyoming cop want with my girl? Far as I know, she's never even been to that goddamn state. You trying to get in my girl's pants, too?"

I can see why Sunny chose to live in Colorado rather than Arizona. I'm surprised she didn't leave the country. With a stepdad like this guy, it's a miracle she made it out of here at all.

"Wyoming," Mr. Villanova says to himself as he takes another swig from the beer can he grips in one fist. "Where the men are men and the sheep are scared."

"I'm sort of involved, helping out, on a Colorado case," I say evenly. I want to lie as little as possible out of habit, knowing it could tangle me up later with Sheriff Munik if I try to make it sound too much like I'm here in an official capacity.

"Maybe you should explain that to the Colorado boys. When they came by this morning, they didn't say nothing about getting any sheep-friendly help."

"Who came by?" I'm amazed that Sheriff Munik would send deputies all the way to Arizona when he could just call and request some assistance from the local police.

"Just a couple of Colorado pigs." He sucks down more of the beer.

"The Colorado cops, were they in uniform?"

"Nah, but one of 'em had a badge kinda like yours. Wanted to know if she'd been by, just like you."

"What did you tell them?"

"That she came barging in at like three in the morning, all weepy about something. Wouldn't tell me what it was about and her momma's off in Vegas. I went back to bed, then the little bitch stole my boat this morning. I found my trailer down at the ramp." His eyes become a little unfocused. "Goddamn that girl, I just paid that thing off. A twenty-seven-foot Sea Ray, brand-new 350 Mercs. Was going to call the police myself, but figured since the law was already after her I wouldn't bother."

"Tell me what the Colorado guys looked like."

"What do you care? I thought you was working with them."

"Just tell me, Mr. Villanova," I say, trying to keep the exasperation out of my voice. I have a strong urge to put my hands around his scrawny neck.

He looks quickly at my face, correctly gauges the threat there, then stares down at his beer.

"One of 'em stayed in the car, some big black yuppie-mobile—a Suburban—and another guy pounded on the door. Guy at the door was dressed like he's a rich bastard. Acted like it, too. Probably on the take, like all you—" He pauses, looks again at my face, and decides not to pursue the thought. "Had a badge. I didn't get much of a look at the guy in the truck—I only saw that he was as bald as a bowling ball, 'cept for some funny sideburns."

Fast and Burgermeister, no doubt. I need to call Sheriff Munik and let him know that his benefactor isn't on his property in the White River National Forest as his secretary had claimed.

Kim asks from behind me, "Where would she have gone in your boat, Mr. Villanova?"

The man leers at her again and holds up his beer can in the direction of Lake Powell. "The frigging Arctic Ocean. Where do you think, girl?"

"Where in the lake?" I ask, not smiling at all now as I step up onto the porch, deliberately invading his space.

He yanks open the screen door and half staggers inside. He tries to close the flimsy door but I catch it first. "Hey! What the hell? You can't—"

"Where in the lake?" I ask again, giving him my hardest look from my swollen eyes.

"Get the hell off my property! I'll call the police!"

"Go ahead. I expect they'll be more happy to listen to me than to you," I say. "And I bet it'll take them a while to get here." From the disparaging way he referred to the police earlier, and the fact that he's drunk at nine o'clock in the morning, I have a feeling he's not too friendly with the local force. "Now, where in the lake, *sir*?" I grab his wrist and pull him back out onto the porch.

"I swear I don't know." He tries to tug his wrist away from my grasp. I hold it tight for a moment, letting him feel the grip that comes from years of hanging by one's fingertips, then let it go. "But you can tell her if she brings back my boat in one piece, she won't be in any trouble.

Not with me, anyways." He steps back inside and tries again to close the screen door. I let him.

"Tell me the names of some of her friends around here."

Mr. Villanova is more confident again, now that he's back inside his home. His watery eyes twitch and I can tell he's trying to decide whether to be mad or scared. He evidently chooses cooperation along with the risk of a little more impertinence. "Ask Freddy Kruge," he finally says. "He was her boyfriend before that dyke came along." He points the beer can at Kim with an angry shake, saying, "Now get the hell off my property before I call the police!" and then he quickly slams the interior door.

TWENTY-THREE

WE GET BACK in the car and drive to a local coffee shop on Lake Powell Boulevard. From a vinyl booth with a window, Kim orders orange juice and dry toast, which explains her slim, athletic figure. I request coffee, pancakes, eggs, and bacon. Although Kim appears more confident now, no longer in the agitated trance that had affected her earlier in the morning, she still sits across from me unsmiling and preoccupied. I'm sure she must be enormously relieved that Sunny is unhurt. And maybe also relieved that the secret regarding their relationship is no longer a secret.

"We're off to a good start, Kim. At least we know she's okay. At least she wasn't physically hurt. Even her drunken, scumbag stepfather would have noticed if she was injured."

She plays with the utensils in front of her, not looking at me. "Now it's her emotional state I'm worried about."

I nod. I'm worried about that, too, but not nearly as much as I'm worried about David Fast and Burgermeister finding her first. Neither of us speaks while I fill my coffee cup to the brim with sugar and cream.

"I didn't know you were gay." The words just slip out.

"Does it matter?"

"No, not really. But since we're working and traveling together, I'd like to know a little about you."

She finally looks up at me. Her thin lips are tight with something like exasperation. "I'm not *gay,* okay? I'm into people. If I'm attracted to someone, then I'm attracted to someone. Subject closed. Don't bust my balls, Anton."

"Weird. A lesbian with balls."

She doesn't want to, but she smiles. "That's right, kid. Big balls."

I think about the way she let me hug her outside the courthouse yesterday. The way she'd pressed herself against me—chest, hips, and thighs—making it a full-body hug. And the way she'd touched my arm during the night and then laid her head in my lap. I wonder if I'm one of those people she could be attracted to. We're both staring out the window, watching the street. Mid-morning now, it's jammed with the pickups and muscle cars of the locals as well as tourists in motor homes and Cadillacs.

"So how do we find her?" Kim asks. "We know she's in a Sea Ray with Mercs, right, whatever those are. Do you know what one looks like?"

I shake my head. "I don't know anything about boats. Just that we need one to find her. And we need a clue where to look."

My knowledge of Lake Powell extends to having read *The Monkey Wrench Gang* years before and the brief glance at the map and tourist information in the motel room. What I know is that Lake Powell, with its innumerable canyons, islands, and inlets, has more shoreline than the entire western coast of the United States. Almost two thousand miles of it. According to the Visitors' Guide, the geography of the water-filled canyons includes natural arches, Indian ruins, and hidden slot canyons. The lake was artificially formed in 1956, when the Colorado River was dammed at Glen Canyon, just a couple of miles to the west. Someday I'll have to come back here and climb.

"We'll find this Freddy Kruge and ask him if she has a hangout somewhere, or if he knows anyone who might know of a hangout. Did she ever mention that guy's name to you?"

"Yep. He's an ex-boyfriend who liked to smack her around. I only remember his name because it was so unusual. Freddy Kruge. She called him Freddy Krueger, like the evil character in those horror movies." She stares at my bacon with distaste. "You're the cop. How do we find him?"

The waitress walks over and refills my coffee cup. She does it with a flirtatious smile and I'm flattered to receive such a gesture in my current condition. She's a pretty Indian girl; her face is full and round yet her body is still slender despite working in a greasy diner. She wears a halter top under a baggy pair of overalls. When she leans over the table, I can't help but notice a pair of black panties down the side of the denim.

Turning to Kim, she asks, "Would you like more juice, ma'am?"

"Please," Kim says with a smile of her own, then, "And please don't call me ma'am. I'm not his mother."

I laugh, catch a half-chewed piece of bacon in my throat, and spend a minute alternatively coughing and drinking water while my eyes leak tears. It's the first time I've heard Kim make something akin to a joke. The suddenness of it has surprised me.

When I'm recovered and the pretty waitress has come back with more orange juice for Kim, I ask her, "Do you know a guy named Freddy Kruge?"

The girl frowns. "You mean Freddy Krueger, that freak. Yeah, I know him. Everybody does. He works down at the Lube Monkey. Whatcha want to see him for?"

"I just want to hit him with a few questions."

"You ought to hit him with your fist." She gives me a good look. "You look like you could do it. The guy's an asshole." She's embarrassed by the use of the obscenity and colors slightly, looking away.

"How about Sunny Hansen? Do you know her?" I ask, hoping to get even luckier. But the girl shakes her head.

"Not really. I know who she is, but she was a couple of years ahead of me in high school. She used to date Krueger before she left for college in Colorado. God, I hope I can get out of this place someday, too."

After leaving her a large tip, we follow the girl's directions to the Lube Monkey just a couple of blocks away. Taking the waitress's word for it, I assume Freddy's going to be an asshole and decide it's time to take Oso for a walk. Even outside the building I can smell the odor of marijuana wafting through the open garage door. The three of us walk into the garage together, ourselves as motley a trio as the three young men we find inside. They're all marked by grease, acne, and spotty facial hair. But they have one redeeming quality—they stare at the beast with admiration.

"Check that out!" one exclaims to the other two, coming forward and hesitating before reaching out to pet Oso. "He friendly?"

"Not really," I tell him.

"Cool." He draws back his hand. "What do you need? Oil change?"

I see a grimy patch on his shirt that reads "Fred." Pulling out my wallet and giving him a flash of the badge, I ask, "Are you Freddy Kruge?"

"Uh, no," he says, then looks down to where I'm pointing at the name on his shirt. "Shit." His two pals catch on and snicker at him before moving away, closer to the open garage door. It's clear none of them are strangers to the police. "What are you after me for, man?" Fred whines at us. "I'm not saying nothing, not till I get lawyered up."

"Actually, I just want to ask you some questions. Tell me what I need to know and I won't mention that pot you just smoked to your PO," I say, guessing that he has a probation officer.

He grins at me, suddenly eager to please. "Shoot, man."

"Outside."

Freddy Kruge follows us out to some browning grass on the side of the building. His eagerness has me a little suspicious—I worry that he might try to run. But I look at the baggy pants he wears halfway down his ass and figure he won't get far without being tripped up on his own clothing. Besides, Oso keeps his yellow eyes fixed on the young man. There's a predatory gleam in those eyes, as if he'd like nothing better than to chase a man down like a fleeing deer and rip out his hamstrings.

Fred keeps his distance from the beast and watches him warily but admiringly. Although the hair on the top of his head is close-cropped and the sides are shaved white, a long ponytail of glossy black hair hangs over one of his shoulders. On his upper lip and chin a few straggly dark hairs dangle in a pathetic attempt at a goatee. I can't picture the Sunny I'd met, the girl with the blonde dread-locks and free spirit, having anything to do with a punk like this. But I can picture her all too well with Kim—I push the thought from my mind.

As I study Fred he rolls an empty soda can under his Doc Martens while Kim leans against a scraggly tree, content again to let me do most of the talking. From my experience dealing with lawyers, knowing when to be quiet is a rare and valuable trait among them.

"When was the last time you saw Sunny Hansen?" I ask.

"Sunny?" he looks surprised. "Look, man, I don't know what that bitch told you, but I never touched her. And I haven't even seen her in like two years. Isn't there a statue of limitation or something on whatever bullshit she said I did?"

I've always wondered just what a "statue" of limitation, as all the suspects I've met refer to the statute of limitations, might look like—maybe something like Fred?—but I don't let a smile come to my mouth.

"You haven't heard about her being back in town lately?"

"Hell no. When she split, she split for good. She always thought she was too good for this place. I hear her folks are still around, though."

"How long did you date her?"

"Year, maybe two."

"You guys ever go out on the lake together?"

"Sure. All the time. She used to like kicking around in the canyons, you know. She was crazy about that shit. Why you want to know?"

"Don't worry about it." I want to think of some excuse so that he really doesn't worry about it, but can't think of anything plausible. "Any canyons in particular?"

"Don't know. Maybe out around Last Chance Bay or somewheres. She dug it back in there. C'mon, tell me. Why are you looking for her, dude?"

Kim helps me out by saying, "We're trying to serve a subpoena on her, Freddy. She's a witness in a federal case. You see her, you stay as far away from her as you can get. If we hear you were near her or went looking for her, then there's going to be some assault and battery charges filed against you, young man. And I can promise you that your probation will be revoked like *that*." She snaps her fingers in front of her eye patch while fixing him with an angry gaze. "You'll find yourself in the state pen. You understand?"

"Yeah, I got it." His eyes are sullen but he smiles at us again, displaying dirty and uneven teeth. Then he crushes the can beneath his boot.

TWENTY-FOUR

THE MARINA IS a gridlike tangle of piers and boats that is set just off the lake's shore. Unlike other marinas I've seen, this one is relatively clean. The water here is a translucent green and without any rainbow-colored slicks of oil. Very little trash floats in it. But the air is littered with the roar of revving engines. All around us people mill aboard the powerboats, fishing barges, Jet Skis, and enormous houseboats. Cutting through the engine noise are the sounds of laughter and the excited chatter from the tourists. Just up a hill from the water, we stand in line outside an adobe building to rent a boat. While we wait, I keep looking around, trying to spot Fast and Burgermeister among the shouting people.

To get to the marina, we had driven a few miles west of Page and crossed a hanging bridge above the Glen Canyon Dam. Kim had rolled down her window and leaned out, imitating Oso. I'd wondered if she would spit or curse at the dam that had created the lake and caused so much devastation to the surrounding environment. She didn't. She just stared at the towering canyon walls beneath the dam. And I couldn't help but imagine climbing them.

Before we left town, while Kim ran into a supermarket to purchase groceries for what I expected would be a long day's search of the lake, I had called Sheriff Munik in Tomichi from my cell phone.

It took him a long time to answer the call. I'd assumed that as the brother of a prime murder suspect, I wasn't too high on his list of important callers. After letting me spend ten minutes waiting on hold, he finally picked up the phone.

"What do you want today, *Special Agent* Burns?"

"Guess where I am right now, Sheriff."

There was a sigh on the other end of the line. After a moment he said, "Arizona, I take it."

"Yeah, I'm in Page, where Sunny Hansen's family still lives. And I'm not the only one here. David Fast and his hired muscle are around, too, asking about Sunny."

He didn't respond. I could picture him rubbing the stubble on his chin between his thumb and forefinger.

"His secretary lied to you when she told you that your friend and benefactor was on his property up in White River."

Still no response.

"According to Sunny's father, Fast is flashing a Tomichi County badge and asking around for her."

Finally the sheriff spoke just one word. "Shit."

I was feeling paranoid—wondering how Fast had found out so quickly that Sunny's family was in Page. Had the sheriff told him? Was I wrong to trust Munik? After all, I knew that not only was Fast his biggest campaign contributor, but I also remembered Kim telling me that the sheriff had been a longtime friend of Fast's family. It was possible, though, even likely, that Fast had been the one who had kicked in Sunny's door, and that in her apartment somewhere he had found out that she was from Page.

"How about dropping those charges against my brother, Sheriff? We now know who really did it."

The sheriff laughed, but there wasn't a lot of confidence in it. "I don't know any such thing, son. We're still waiting on the blood test from the stuff we scraped off his hands. Anyways, maybe Dave's trying to do me a favor and find the prime witness to a murder case. Maybe he's just trying to find out more about that mythical cave you told me about."

"He doesn't need to impersonate a peace officer to do that." Why was the sheriff trying to bullshit me about this?

"Look, son, just about every businessman in this town has a badge. My campaign manager gives 'em out like popcorn at election time. Sheriff's Volunteer Reserve, they're called."

After another few moments of silence, he asked, "You found that girl yet?"

"Not yet. But I've got a good lead."

"You find her, you bring her to me. I'll listen to what she has to say. I suspect you aren't going to like it, though. She's going to say it was your brother. In the meantime, stay the hell away from David Fast. One thing I can promise you, son, is that when I see him I'm going to rip him a new asshole for interfering like this without my permission."

"I'm kind of hoping him you'll arrest him for murder, Sheriff," I said, letting the sarcasm come out strong in my voice.

"You bring me some evidence and I might just do that."

Before Kim came out of the grocery store, I'd taken my .40 caliber H&K out of the glove box and slipped it into a hip pack.

The man at the rental dock is reluctant to let a dog on board one of his boats. Kim again comes up with the solution—a one-hundred-dollar nonrefundable deposit, in other words a bribe, to get him to look the other way. Oso is even more reluctant about the boat than the man had been. He plants all four paws solidly on the dock and struggles against me when I lean on his collar with all my weight. Kim finally bribes him, too. With the slices of turkey I had asked her to pick up for my lunch. Now I'll be forced to share the cheese and bread Kim has gotten for herself.

The boat is small and almost square. It is entirely open-decked but for where a blue canopy covers the windscreen and steering wheel. An oil-stained engine is mounted at the rear, its propeller tilted out of the water.

The rental attendant is curious about why we don't want to rent and take along a water ski or a towed surfboard. "Don't you even got swimsuits?" he asks. Before Kim or I can answer, he thinks he figures it out for himself. He winks at me and says, "Oh yeah, good sightseeing in them canyons. Skinny-dipping too."

Kim blushes, then glares at me with her good eye when she sees me wink back at the man.

I look around at the other people waiting to rent a boat or a Jet Ski. They are obviously tourists, with their swimsuits, plastic bags of beer, and suntan lotion. "You have any other people renting today who *don't* look like the rest of this crowd?"

"Yep, two uptight guys in cowboy boots. Said they were going fishing, but they didn't have no poles, no gear. Only a duffel bag with what looked like a rifle inside. Going target shooting, I guess. Friends of yours?"

"Sort of. Was one of them a big ugly guy with a shaved head and sideburns? The other neat, going gray?"

"Yessir. That was them all right. Acted like they were in a big hurry to get out on the water." He chuckles and shakes his head. "Gonna catch themselves a lot of fish with that gun."

He advises us to stay away from where the water is green or brown, as that's the indication of shallow water. Dark blue water means deep water. "You rip the bottom out of the boat, you're going to be in a damn sight of trouble. And you'll have to pay for the damage, too."

At my request he points out a Sea Ray so we know what one looks like. The one we see parked nearby is long and low, a good deal bigger than our little ski boat. Two huge motors are bolted to its stern. I don't doubt that it is very, very fast. According to the attendant, it also has a decent-sized cabin below the front deck. He tells us you can live aboard one of those for days.

After a quick lesson in how to drive the ski boat, we're under way.

I observe the no-wake restriction around the marina area and ease the boat slowly and carefully out into the lake while Kim studies the map we'd purchased. Once past the limiting signs, it feels good to push the throttle forward, to feel the boat leap up and plane on the lake's surface, and to leave the heat and the stench of gasoline behind. The roar of the single engine drowns out the shouts and laughter of the other boaters. Oso stands on the foredeck or the bow or whatever it's called and hunches low when we bounce across small waves. His lips lift from his long white teeth and begin to flap in the wind. I think he might be enjoying it, too.

The surrounding landscape is almost devoid of vegetation. The blue water twists between bordering cliffs of red sandstone. For just a few feet above the water, the cliffs are a chalky white up to what I guess is the high-water mark. It's as if the lake's water has leached all the color out of the rock it touches. Far ahead the land's relief increases dramatically, where the low cliffs rise up in multiple steps until they tower hundreds of feet above the lake's surface.

Next to me, Kim flattens the map on the dashboard beneath the windscreen. Despite the protective glass, the map flutters violently at the edges. A quick glimpse of the laminated chart's center between her spread fingers shows we are headed toward an area where the lake reaches out in all directions like a spider's legs. The multitude of canyons to the left, the area Freddy Kruge had called Last Chance Bay, is about thirty miles east of us.

All around us are sailboats, houseboats, powerboats, Jet Skis, and leaping water-skiers. We're moving swiftly among them, sending out a two-foot wake. The Jet Skiers and water-skiers chase us, catching air on the V fanning out behind us, while the houseboaters occasionally shake their fists or middle fingers. I can't wait to be away from them all. For a while a low-slung speedboat runs alongside us, as if we're in a race. It's nearly twice our length and its deck is crowded with young women in bikinis. They wave to us until the pilot, apparently the only man on board, shoves the throttle forward and nearly swamps us with an incredible burst of speed. I guess we lose.

"How do you want to do this?" Kim shouts in my ear. The crowd is thinning as we get farther away from the marina.

"Let's start with the first canyons, the ones to the south, and work our way north." I'm beginning to get concerned, just now truly aware of the gigantic scope of the lake. Still studying the map at my side, Kim confirms my trepidation.

"It's going to take forever—each canyon has like a hundred side-canyons within it. Even the side-canyons have side-canyons."

For more than an hour we bounce our way eastward. The scenery around us grows more spectacular with each passing mile. The cliffs rise higher, some of them hundreds of feet straight out of the water, and the stone is an even darker red. Almost crimson. There are island buttes, too, standing tall in the center of the channel. Sometimes our passage is only a few hundred yards across and other times it's miles wide.

When we pass a long, sharp peninsula on our left, I know we're getting close to the canyon turnoff. Kim points out an island butte a short distance ahead—Gregory Butte. It marks the turnoff for Last Chance Bay. I nudge the steering wheel left and we sweep to the north.

The bay is about a mile wide. It's hard to visually tell where it ends because of the way it writhes northward, but according to the map the bay forks into two smaller canyons about forty miles up. I curse when I see all the tiny ravines peeling off on each side of the bay. The words are swallowed by the engine's roar, and they were in Spanish anyway, but Kim understandingly nods beside me. By shouted agreement we start with the small canyons and sub-canyons to the right, saving the ones on the left for the return trip.

I slide the boat through the twisting canyons with a growing confidence in my handling of the machine. I keep my eyes on the water—trying to stay where it's deep blue—as well as on the other boats and the cliffs while Kim searches for Sunny's Sea Ray. The initial canyons are well populated with houseboats and Jet Skis. Drunken college students jump from their decks and some nearby low cliffs, barking at Oso as we zoom past. And Kim earns more than one wolf whistle despite her eye patch after she sheds her shirt. She stands next to me with her feet braced wide and wearing only an orange sports bra over her worn-out jeans. After one particularly drawn-out whistle, I think I hear her make a noise. I turn to glance at her and see she's smiling.

Taking a chance, for just a moment I take my eyes off the cliffs, water, and boats to give her a longer look. I make my own low whistle. It pays off—she laughs out loud and slugs my arm with her bony knuckles. Progress, I think. Maybe.

After more than an hour of racing through the maze of water-filled canyons, I spot a small, deserted beach. I circle back around to it and answer Kim's quizzical look with one word: "Lunch." For a long time my stomach's been growling and my bare feet ache from where the big motor's vibrations have been rattling up my legs.

Unsure if it's safe or acceptable to nose the boat up onto the sand, I let it drift to a stop about ten yards from the shore. Kim drops what we guess is supposed to be the anchor—a nylon rope tied around a bucket filled with concrete—into the water. She ties the free end around a metallic T screwed onto the boat's deck.

Shimmying out of her jeans, she quickly dives overboard. For a moment I'm actually breathless at the sight of her tan, slim figure curving through the air and entering the water almost without a splash. Almost without a sound.

An instant later the sound of scrabbling claws gets my attention. I turn my head just in time to see Oso launching himself after her. He, however, is far from splashless. The beast hits the water with a loud smack and a high wave. "Cannonball!" I yell as Kim comes up for air just in time to meet Oso's tsunami.

In seconds I'm following Oso's example, having hastily stripped off my own clothes down to my boxer shorts, and I cannonball perilously close to Kim's head. It's a delight to see her laugh again. For a few minutes she and I paddle around one another in the cool water, occasionally splashing, as Oso circles like some ridiculous, hairy shark. He has a dead-serious expression on his face. His rubbery lips float wide on either side of his mouth as he steadily huffs and snorts at the water. We can't stop laughing at him. It takes all my will to keep from pulling Kim's slick body to mine.

For the next few minutes all my worries and frustration are forgotten. For the first time in more than twenty-four hours, the image of my brother slowly combusting in a jail cell is out of my head.

Too soon the frivolity ends. Kim walks up onto the beach with my eyes stuck to her backside. When she turns and sits in the sand, with her legs tight together and pulled up against her chest, I haul myself halfway into the boat and pull out the small Styrofoam ice chest into which she'd packed our lunches. Or what was left of mine, anyway, after Oso's sliced-turkey bribe.

Oso paddles gravely beside me as I swim to the beach with our lunches held high.

I'm self-conscious about being half-naked in her presence. My thin cotton boxers cling transparently to my thighs. Self-consciousness is an emotion I'm not used to feeling. I sit down next to her after handing over the cooler. She hands me back a bottle of apple juice, a banana, and two slices of bread—all that's left of my portion. For herself she takes out a thin plastic bag full of thick pita bread and a plastic container of garlic hummus. Seeing me eyeing her food with desire, or at least she supposes it's the food I'm desiring, she smiles and offers to share.

"Tell me some more about yourself," I say, determined to take advantage of her light mood. And while I chew I need something to focus on other than her slender, well-muscled shoulder, the delicate ribs of her back, and the small weight of her breasts beneath the thin top. All I really know about her is that she was once terribly degraded, that she loves Wild Fire Valley, and that she hates David Fast. "Where were you born? Raised? And all that."

Her story starts out slow, but gathers details as she becomes more involved in the telling. "I grew up in L.A.," she says, frowning. "The Valley, not the beach. I escaped from there as soon as I could, which meant boarding school in France. After that I went to Yale for a year but I couldn't stand all those uptight Ivy Leaguers, pretending to be so concerned and involved and smart about everything but only really caring about getting trashed at parties for four years before they could go work at Daddy's firm. So I blew out of there, too, and spent a year on a sort of commune in Oregon. Yes, Anton, a real commune, the kind we had about the time you were born—"

I interrupt to protest that she's at most ten years older than me, so she must have been about twelve at the time, but she ignores me.

"Then I went to Berkeley to get a degree in environmental science. I loved that place—the coast, the groves, the hills. But it was just too populated; there wasn't any space where you could really lose yourself. And anyways, the people there were kind of like the people at Yale; they acted concerned and dedicated to saving the world but they were more concerned about image than sacrifice."

While she talks I edge my sandy foot away from me until my calf rests over her toes, barely touching. She doesn't withdraw her foot, nor does she comment on the contact.

"I went to law school at Utah, where I got joint masters in law and environmental science," she continues, not referring to the awful thing that happened there. "Then I moved to Tomichi and did whatever kind of legal work I could find—land stuff, representing domestic violence victims, even some divorces. And then that asshole David Fast worked up his scam...." She's frowning, but then forces a smile and looks over her shoulder at me. She lifts her toes beneath my calf but doesn't remove them. "Sorry. You already know about that."

I'm about to ask why she'd chosen Tomichi as her home. But before I can get the words out she says, "Let's hear your story, Agent Burns."

So I tell her. "I was raised all over the place. A typical military brat. The first time I ever lived in the U.S. for more than a few months at a time was when I started college at Boulder. I felt almost like a foreigner in my own country." My father and mother had met when he was briefly stationed in Argentina, fresh from the trials of Vietnam. Mom was still basking in the glory of having competed in the 1972 Olympics as a distance runner; although she didn't medal, she was a bit of a hometown hero. But she'd been happy to follow him to different bases all over the world. Her own country, and that of my grandfather, was just beginning to deteriorate into what would be known as the Dirty War.

"How did you end up a cop in a place like Wyoming?"

I shrug. "I spent my college summers guiding and climbing in the Tetons when I wasn't working in Alaska. I fell in love with the place. But I didn't want to be a guide anymore—I didn't want to spend my life dragging rich businessmen and their families up the Grand. The AG's Office has a nice vacation schedule. And being a cop, a state agent investigating drug crimes, seemed like the natural thing to do, since I'd been watching what the stuff did to my brother. Plus, it's exciting. I feel like a little kid, getting to carry a gun and badge and all that. Like cops and robbers."

After a few minutes of inhaling the scent of the sun on her skin, I take advantage of her momentary openness and ask, "How did you and Sunny hook up?"

Kim sighs. She looks at the boat and the canyon wall beyond as she relates the story of their brief love affair.

Sunny had been a volunteer at the battered women's shelter where Kim sometimes worked. On her very first day there, Sunny stayed late to talk with Kim. For such a seemingly vivacious girl, she didn't seem to have a lot of friends. Kim learned that she had a darker side, that she'd been abused by a series of boyfriends—she thought Sunny probably looked to her as a source of strength. And Kim was attracted to her youth and wounded beauty. Sunny took the first step in turning their friendship physical, and Kim went along at first out of fear of the hurt she'd cause if she rejected the girl as much as out of her own attraction.

But she knew it wouldn't last. Sunny was looking for a strong mother-figure more than a lover. And Kim could see that the girl was hopelessly straight. Just a few days before my father and I had arrived in the meadow, Sunny hooked up with Cal during the Tribe's weeklong vigil there. From the moment they'd met earlier in the summer at a Tribe meeting, Kim knew Sunny would end up leaving her for Cal. And she even encouraged it, knowing that as impulsive as Cal was, as weird as he was about the Indian cave he'd discovered, he'd never dream of abusing her.

We feed the remnants of our lunch to Oso and pack the debris back in the cooler. Swimming back out to the boat, I feel her palm touch the small of my back as I boost the cooler into the boat. I thrill at the touch.

Getting Oso into the boat proves to be a large problem. Weighted by his heavy wet coat, he's unable to pull himself onto the slippery ski step at the stern. It takes several tries to perfect a technique that works. Kim stands dripping wet in her improvised bikini, laughing and tugging on Oso's leather collar, while I furiously tread water and boost from behind. As a thank-you the beast showers Kim with a full-body shake.

Just when I crawl into the boat, we hear the rumble of another motor coming down the canyon branch. Kim modestly pulls on her T-shirt.

The boat is a rented ski craft very much like ours. Two hard-faced men in sunglasses stand behind the windscreen. They motor by us slowly, not waving or even smiling. But their eyes are fixed on us. Burgermeister's scalp is turning pink in the sun. Next to him David Fast handles the boat's controls.

"Anton!" Kim hisses. I don't respond.

Just as they pass us, Fast's hand drops down on the throttle. The boat idles forward a few feet farther then churns backward in reverse. The sunlight is suddenly brighter; the sounds magnified. I can feel every beat of my heart and every pulse of blood through my veins. I pick up my hip pack, unzip it, and slip my hand in to touch the hard plastic grip of the H&K while not taking my eyes off the men in the boat.

At least they haven't found Sunny yet. I wonder how they know to look in the same places we're looking.

Fast stares back at me as Burgermeister bends down so that his hands are out of view. Then he stands upright again, swinging a long-barreled shotgun up in his hands, its twin muzzles pointing for now at the sky.

"Anton!" Kim hisses again.

Some animal sense has alerted Oso to the threat. He stands on our bow with his legs spread wide and his eyes narrowed to golden slits. His lips are pulled high above his teeth; the fangs look like a steel trap about to be sprung. The wet black hair is raised around his chest and shoulders but is plastered tight to his belly, making him look like some monster out of a medieval painting.

"Get ready to hit the deck," I say to Kim over the drone of Fast's engine and the increasing roar coming from my dog's throat. Out of the corner of my eye I can see her frozen beside me. I remember the way she'd seemed to fall apart before when in Fast's presence and pray she doesn't now.

Fast steers the boat so that it backs up beside us, just forty or fifty feet away. An easy and deadly distance with a shotgun; not so good for a pistol. Not good at all. I see both men's sunglasses move slightly as they scan our boat and then the small beach, probably looking for the blonde mop of Sunny's dreadlocks. Fast's lips part as he says something to Burgermeister. The big man says something back and smiles wickedly at us—the shotgun starts to swing down in our direction.

To my eyes the arc of the double barrels descends toward us in slow motion. My hand feels as quick as lightning as I bring the sleek automatic up from my side. Just like in the meadow, a part of me can't believe that these men would want to kill us. *Over a piece of land.* Yet the set of Burgermeister's face is convincing.

Seeing my gun, Fast turns to his partner in alarm. He seems to notice the shotgun for the first time. He puts up an arm to push the barrels away, but Burgermeister shoves him back with a meaty arm.

This is going to happen. I can almost picture the pellets blowing at me from down those long iron rods. They'll come in an expanding pattern, at this distance maybe the size of a truck's tire. I can almost hear them tearing through the air, followed by a blast of sound I'll never hear.

But it's a rebel yell that echoes off the canyon walls. It hasn't come from either of them, nor from us. Nosing into the slot canyon is an enormous houseboat. A naked young man, as beefy as a professional wrestler, has catapulted himself off the boat's second story while screaming. He hits the water with the agonizing smack of a belly flop. A pounding rhythm of reggae music builds in volume. The boat's top and lower decks are filled with college students, a beer can in every hand.

Before the students notice us, Burgermeister bends and tucks the gun back down somewhere out of sight. Fast shoves the throttle forward while turning the wheel. Their ski boat lurches forward in a tight U-turn. Burgermeister never stops staring at us. Still grinning, and shaking his head at our luck.

"Fuck you!" Kim shouts at them.

I'm relieved she hasn't gone comatose on me again, but I'm not necessarily pleased that she wants to antagonize these men who'd been about to murder us. And who just a day and a half earlier had been brutal enough to beat a young man to death.

Fast turns his head at the words. He yells something back. It takes me a minute to register what he's said over all the noise now flooding the small canyon. Beside me Kim makes a noise of either terror or fury—it's hard to tell because the side of her face toward me is the one mostly covered by her eye patch and tangled black hair.

He'd shouted, "It's been twelve years, girl! For God's sake, let it go!"

TWENTY-FIVE

WHEN KIM FINALLY looks my way, her single eye sears right through me. She's silent, but pain and fury comes out of her like a gale-force wind. It almost rocks me back on my heels. I feel as if I'm seeing her unmasked for the first time. Another layer peeled away. Meanwhile, the houseboat continues into the canyon, blasting its reggae beat.

It has no effect on me that Kim has lied. That she probably doesn't give a shit about the valley and Wild Fire Peak. That her vendetta is about far more than preserving the environment. What it's really about is visiting devastation on the man who'd humiliated her twelve years ago. Ripping from him the things he holds most dear. Kim wants to take his money, his professional reputation, his livelihood. She wants to leave him naked and humiliated, just as he'd done to her. That's what the war over the valley is really about. And Kim's using the law as her weapon of vengeance.

As a sworn law enforcement officer, I know all too well the sad truth that the law seldom results in justice. And at this moment, my blood heaving in my veins from the anticipated impact of pellets, I don't give a fuck about the law. *They were going to kill us. Just like Cal.*

I grab the anchor's yellow nylon cord and rip the can of cement up out of the water so hard and so fast that it cracks against the hull, undoubtedly leaving a deep ding in the bottom of the fiberglass. When I spin to storm back behind the wheel, ready to slam the throttle forward and chase down the smug bastards with my gun in my hand, my bare shoulder crashes against Kim's wet shirt with an audible smack. She staggers and nearly falls out of the boat. It's only then I that perceive she's been shouting my name.

"Goddamn it, Anton!" she yells when I clutch her upper arm to keep her from falling overboard. "Cut it out!" Rebalanced, she snatches her arm from my grasp. "This is about me, not you! It's mine! Don't try to take it from me!"

I stare at her, bewildered by the anger that's directed at *me*. Her normally tan cheekbones are flushed scarlet; her single coffee-colored eye burns. She glares up at me from just inches away. Raising a hand with her fingers balled into a fist, she shakes it beneath my jaw as if she might hit me. "Don't take it away from me!"

I look away. The houseboat party has frozen just a hundred feet from us and the beach. Although the music still pumps, the kids on the decks are staring at us with open mouths. There are no more cheerful whoops or leaps from the upper decks, no more bursts of laughter. All conversations have ceased. I pick up my T-shirt and drop it over the pistol, which lies in plain view on a padded cushion. I don't think they've seen it, just as I don't think they saw Burgermeister leveling the shotgun in our direction. All they see is a maimed couple arguing and some great black gargoyle perched on the bow.

What am I doing wrong? I ask myself. I only want to kill the men who would have killed us if the houseboat hadn't chugged into the canyon. If I don't kill them first, then they'll eventually try again. It's a simple matter of self-preservation, even if they are armed with a shotgun and I only have a small pistol. But even as I put these thoughts together in my head, I realize that they're not entirely honest. What chance do I have against them and their long gun? The truth is that I'm gorged with the longing for blood and vengeance—I want to kill David Fast for what he did to her a dozen years ago, for causing Kim a lifetime of pain. I want to kill Burgermeister for almost killing her just now—and me. Somewhere in my mind I can see Roberto's face grinning at me—God, how he'd love to see me acting just like him, dealing out justice with my own hands.

But he'd also understand what Kim is saying. She wants to destroy this man on her own, not have me do it for her. And she wants to do it her way. It's a personal war between the two of them. A sort of blood feud. I'm nothing to Fast and Burgermeister, just some cop far out of his jurisdiction who happens to be the brother of a man wrongly charged for a murder they committed. And a man who is helping their enemy because I'm infatuated with her hot intensity.

I close my eyes and try to swallow the anger.

When I open them, she's still watching me from just inches away. The deep flush across her cheeks is already dissipating.

"*I'm* going to ruin him, Anton, you chauvinistic pig. And I'm going to do it the right way." When she sees the skepticism in my eyes, she adds with her lips turning up just the tiniest bit at the corners, "I'm going to bring all his bad deeds back to bite him in the ass. And even better than I'd dreamed, once we find Sunny. He's going to be more than ruined. He's going to prison on a fucking *murder charge*."

She turns to the spectators on the houseboat and waves cheerfully.

The shadows have grown long in this small side canyon. We wait within sight of the houseboat for almost two hours, needing the protection of witnesses in case Fast and Burgermeister come back for us. The party on board has tentatively resumed. While we drift a little ways away, the big boat noses up on the sand where we had shared our lunch. The kids run on the beach, chasing one another and throwing sand and beer, but they manage at the same time to keep a wary, almost sober, eye on us.

Kim and I, in turn, watch the main part of the bay. Fast and his enforcer had turned north to either continue searching for Sunny or to wait for us to come out into an isolated ambush. Now, as the shadows are lengthening across the water and the sun is just a bright light somewhere beyond the cliffs to the west, we see their white boat cruise slowly past us in the outer bay. Sunny is not on the boat. Kim and I both breathe a sigh of relief—

they haven't found her. Through our sunglasses, Burgermeister and I give each other the stink eye from a distance of several hundred yards. I can tell from the grudging way they are heading south, back toward the main channel, that they're calling it a day. Almost out of view, I see their boat's stern drop suddenly with acceleration. Foam churns into the air at a height of several feet. In a minute they disappear around the peninsula.

"So what's the plan?" I say, turning to Kim. She's standing in our boat's bow with one hand resting on Oso's head. She's like a fierce pirate, in her eye patch and with the beast at her side. A not-so-subtle change has taken place in our relationship and in our mission. She's completely in charge now.

"We keep looking. She's got to be out here somewhere."

I point at where Fast's wake is rolling lazily toward us. "They had the right idea, you know. It's going to be cold out here tonight and we don't have any gear." Already the air is noticeably cooler. I know from all the camping I've done in a similar climate, on my grandfather's ranch on the high pampas of Argentina, just how cold the desert can get at night.

"We'll deal," she replies.

"Aye aye, *Capitán*."

We leave our friends on the houseboat, who had unwittingly saved our lives, and motor back into the bay. I try to fix their position in my mind so I can find them again in the dark—if it gets too cold we can come back and beg some blankets and food. I swing the wheel to the north. We begin to cruise the next canyon and its sub-canyons, with Kim occasionally calling Sunny's name in an almost singsong voice.

By eight o'clock the sky is turning from the last, deepest shades of blue to what will soon be undeniably black. The first stars are already making an appearance. I'm thinking that we had better find a place to camp, but I don't want to be the first to say it. The boat's hull has already scraped submerged rock twice because I can no longer distinguish the green and brown of shallow water from the safety of the blue. It's also getting seriously cold. In the shade of the canyon walls our cotton clothes had never completely dried. They're still damp from when we used them to towel off after our lunchtime swim hours ago. Goose bumps cover my skin.

Kim's calls out suddenly, "Hold it!"

We're in a narrow ravine, the water just thirty feet wide between two hundred-foot walls. The cliffs are so vertical that they appear to lean over us from each side. Only a narrow strip of navy sky seems to hold them apart.

"Back up," she orders.

I nudge the throttle down and the boat churns over its own wake with a small bump. Kim is pointing at a black shadow on the left cliff wall. Peering at it, I can see that the black shape is more than just a water-blackened concavity on the north-facing wall. It's really a cavelike opening. Although its upper edge is curved down, the opening is about the size of a single-car garage door, ten feet wide and just seven or eight feet off the water.

"It's probably just a hollow in the rock, but let's check it out." Kim says.

I nose the boat toward it, telling Kim to get my headlamp out of the hip pack. She digs her hands into the pocket at the small of my back. I can feel her fingers fumbling there.

"It's the thing that's not shaped like a gun," I tell her, trying to be helpful.

Finding it, she flashes her small white teeth at me in the dark before twisting the plastic cover and blinding me. Then she holds the beam of light out to illuminate the black shape beside us as she steps back up onto the bow of the boat. I think I see another, more distant flash of white through the blackness but I can't be sure. I'm still seeing dancing ghosts from having had the beam aimed directly into my eyes.

I maneuver the boat closer to the cave. Kim has to duck when the bow slips a few feet under its roof.

"This thing's not a cave but an arch," Kim says excitedly, one hand reaching up to touch the rock above her head.

"Watch the sides—push us off if we get close," I instruct her as I turn into the hole. We inch twenty feet farther and around a slight bend before the roof slides away.

It's a tiny lagoon set among sheer walls. Amazing—I wish we were here in the daytime and that I had a camera. In the last of the fading light, I can see the walls are a deep copper while the water is the color of coal. The cove briefly widens to the width of an Olympic swimming pool before the walls close into a tapered slot too tight for a boat. It's shaped like a bullet, with the cave or arch as its flat rear and the slot ahead as its point. That gap is the only other possible exit, if it is an exit, and you would have to swim it.

The starlit sky is just a ribbon above our heads, impossibly distant in the gloom. Floating in the center of the widest part of the lagoon is a long, low-slung boat that looks exactly like the Sea Ray that had been pointed out to us at the marina. There are no lights aboard and there are no sounds.

I cut the engine with a turn of the key and we drift slowly toward the bigger boat. Oso stands braced on the bow like a fearsome Viking masthead.

No one appears when Kim shouts out "Hello." The hatch that leads into the small cabin is open and there's a towel spread on the rear decking next to a can of diet Coke. Tangled clumps of blonde hair float in the water just feet from the side. A pair of scissors lies on a cushion.

The two boats come together with a gentle bump. With our nylon anchor's line in one hand, Kim stretches a leg across onto the Sea Ray's stern. She straddles the two boats while fastening the line around a cleat on each boat.

"Sunny?" she asks quietly, stepping all the way onto the bigger boat. I rotate my hip pack around my waist so that my gun is within easy reach.

There's no answer.

Kim's expression matches the worried feeling in the pit of my stomach. I follow Kim onto the rear deck of the Sea Ray, intending to save Kim from the sight of any residual evil that might be on the boat. Maybe Fast and Burgermeister had found her first—maybe they'd tortured the location of the cave out of her before killing her. Maybe that's why she hadn't been aboard their boat when we had seen them heading back toward Page.

The silence is eerie, particularly with the evidence on deck that someone had been there so recently. I step in front of Kim before she can enter the cabin, and jump down the two steep steps. From behind me, she shines the headlamp over my shoulder. In its weak glow the cabin appears empty.

Climbing back up onto the deck, we both scan the black water around the boat. I can't see anything—there's only the gentle slap of our wake on vertical rock. The water looks ominous, though. Deep enough to conceal a body in its dark embrace.

"Sunny!" Kim shouts this time. The word bounces off the walls.

"Kim?" a voice calls out tentatively from somewhere above us. All three of us, Oso included, stare at the night sky. "Kim!" the voice calls again, more certain and desperate now.

Finally I make out the silhouette of a head and waving arms high up on a cliff. I point it out to Kim, who calls back, "Sunny! Sunny! Are you all right?" She shines the light up in that direction, but at that distance the beam is swallowed by the night.

"I'm fine. Hang on." The silhouette disappears. A few moments later there comes the sound of pebbles plunking down into the water.

Sunny appears at the lowest part of the walls that surround the cove, thirty or more feet above the lake. She's faintly spotlit now by the headlamp Kim aims and she's waving at us once again. The light plays over her pale skin. The natty dreadlocks have been cut away—her blonde hair is now short and sleek. I guess she's hoping to disguise herself. She's wearing nothing but a pair of river sandals, which she kicks off into the water. Then she jumps in, feetfirst and holding her breasts, far less composed and graceful than Kim's earlier dive by the beach.

The responding wavelets of water spread and rebound off the walls of the tiny cove.

After collecting her floating sandals, she pulls herself halfway up on the swim step of the Sea Ray and then hooks a heel on the platform. I look away at Kim as Sunny comes out of the water. I can feel more than see the enormous relief on her face. Oso is not so polite. He's poised on the edge of the ski boat, sniffing the air and straining to lick the wet skin on Sunny's back.

"Kim!" Sunny says again, grasping at her friend and resoaking the front of Kim's jeans and shirt. "How… How…How did you find me?" Before Kim can answer, Sunny takes a deep, gasping breath and begins bawling.

Trying not to intrude, I put the towel over Sunny's shoulder. Stepping past them and back onto our rented ski boat, I grab Oso's collar and drag him to the boat's cockpit. I huddle with him there in the evening cold while Kim tries to comfort the distraught girl. I listen to Kim's placating murmuring and Sunny's sobs. The blonde girl babbles something about how she'd been meditating on top of the cliff, something about praying to the she-god for guidance and protection. My stomach growls—I realize it's been several hours since Kim had shared her meager lunch with me on the beach.

After a while the crying stops. I step up onto the forward deck and see them huddled together on the cushions in the bigger boat's stern. "It's good to see you, Sunny," I say to let them know I'm there. "I'm glad you're okay."

They both look at me like they've forgotten I exist. In a way I feel a little jealous at the way Kim has her slim arms wrapped around the blonde girl's torso. She's wrapped her naked body in the big towel that had been lying on the deck. Sunny says politely, in a little girl's voice, "Anton. Thank you. Thanks for bringing her here."

I nod. Oso makes a sudden leap, breaking my grasp on his leather collar, and lunges onto the other boat. Before I can try to call him back, he nuzzles up to the two girls, licking as they pet him. I'm amazed. I never knew the beast could respond to other people like that. The women laugh as his rough tongue sandpapers their skin. His stump of a tail swings like a broken windshield wiper set on high.

"You come over, too," Kim calls. "I bet Sunny's got some food on this thing."

"Yes. I do." Her voice is stronger now. "I've got enough for all of us. Him too," she says, knuckling Oso's head. Sunny breaks free from Kim's embrace and ducks into the cabin.

"Everything all right?" I quietly ask Kim.

She shrugs but smiles a little in the darkness. "I think so. But I don't know the story yet." Her single eye looks wet and I realize she's been crying, too.

Sunny comes out wearing a Colorado Mountain College sweatshirt and a pair a baggy shorts. She's rubbing the towel over her shorn hair. "Come on inside. There's enough room for everybody."

It doesn't look like it from the outside, but the boat's cabin is actually quite large. Large enough to stand with my head bent just a little. Sunny flicks a hidden switch, making dim electric lights flicker on. There's a miniature kitchen—a galley, I think—along the rear wall and two long benches extending toward the bow. A table is bolted to the floor in the center. All the way at the front there's another low cushioned area that is about the size of a small bed. Blankets and clothes are scattered around the interior. Oso stays on deck but lies with his head thrust into the cabin above the steps.

Kim starts opening the cabinets that line the cabin's sides and pulling things out while Sunny primes and ignites the galley's tiny two-burner stove. They keep bumping into each other. Kim finally tells Sunny to sit down. She obeys, pulling the towel off her head and curling her legs up under her on the bench seat next to me. Soon Kim has a kettle heating water on one burner, the other covered with a pot of simmering Campbell's vegetable and rice soup. She catches my frown at the start of a meager-looking dinner and tosses me a can of pork and beans.

"I'll heat that up for you in a minute, Anton. Let me get some soup in Sunny first."

Oso's drool runs down the small fiberglass steps to our feet.

Sunny nudges my arm. "Your brother didn't do it," she says. When I turn to her it looks like she's about to start crying again. "Kim told me they arrested him."

I put my hand on hers. "I know. Fast did, didn't he? With Burgermeister?"

She nods, tries to gulp down a sob, and says, "That motherfucker. That sick motherfucker."

Kim turns, concerned, from the stove as Sunny begins to break down again. Feeling self-conscious, I put my arm around the sobbing girl and pull her to me. Kim nods at me, approving, then goes back to stirring the soup.

"I've got to get my brother out of jail and put those two in," I tell her. I want her mad like Kim instead of weepy, grieving, and scared. "Help me nail them, Sunny.

Tell us what happened so that we can make them pay for it."

Her sobs start to slow. She's still shivering, but warming me as she hunches half on my lap. Kim says, "Anton's a cop. In Wyoming, but he's still a cop. He knows what to do." I wonder why she appears to be relinquishing command to me.

She slides a plastic bowl of steaming soup on the table in front of us, then starts opening the can of pork and beans for me. While doing it she gives me a look and a small shake of her head that I think means that Sunny doesn't know that Fast is the man who'd been responsible for her humiliation and had indirectly taken her eye twelve years ago. I'm a tiny bit pleased that I'm the only one who understands Kim's vendetta.

After a minute Sunny pulls away from me. She ignores the soup except to blow on it a couple of times before she starts talking. Then she tells us what happened. She tells us everything, more than I really need to know, starting from the first time she'd met Cal. It's as much an explanation to Kim, whom she had left for Cal, as it is the testimony we'll need to spring my brother from the Tomichi County jail. And to put David Fast and Alf Burgermeister in his place.

TWENTY-SIX

IN THE LIGHT of the candle lantern suspended from the tent's roof, Cal's bare chest was flushed a deep pink. They sat across from one another, lotus-style, both naked on the tangle of sleeping bags and clothes. Cal spun the ball of his lighter beneath his thumb in order to light the joint he held pinched in his other hand. They were both still breathing hard from the efforts of their lovemaking.

She watched him as the end of the joint flared orange and he sucked in the sweetly pungent smoke. His eyes were closed. The flesh around them was purple from the fight the day before. His skinny muscles were tight and shiny from exertion. The Chinese symbols tattooed on his shoulders and arms looked glossy. She took the joint from him and put it between her lips.

"What was it like, between you and Kim?" Cal asked, his voice just a croak as he held in the smoke.

Sunny didn't answer as she took a hit for herself. She wished Cal would stop asking about that. She was still feeling guilty enough about leaving Kim. Her older friend hadn't done anything to make her feel guilty, but there was guilt there nonetheless. She'd felt it since she first met Cal at a Tribe meeting, and it had steadily increased throughout their flirtation until it peaked just a few days before, at the start of the Vigil for the Valley, when she finally moved her sleeping bag out of Kim's tent and into Cal's.

There were other things she wanted to talk about. She wanted to talk about the fire they'd started the night before, after Cal siphoned a gallon of gas out of her Escort's tank and then led her on a midnight hike to the partially built lodge halfway up Wild Fire Peak. She'd stood guard while he splashed the gas against the foundations and then spun his lighter. When the flames raced around the structure, far faster than she could have imagined, they ran laughing down off the mountain and through the woods on one side of the meadow.

"That will teach him to fuck with me," Cal had said, trying to sound like a man. But his voice shook when he said it and she knew he was still just a boy. And that he'd been as scared as she was.

She wanted to talk about the cave, too. Even after seeing it with her own eyes, it was hard to believe that the tiny hole in the cliff face could lead to such unbelievable sights. Just the day before, he'd taken her there for the first time, telling her she was the only person besides him who had ever seen it. Telling her the cave would save the valley if he could ever get the Forest Service to agree to his conditions for revealing it.

Holding in the smoke, she remembered shivering with excitement when she crawled from hot sunlight into the cool black air. It smelled earthy and damp and ancient. Powerful, too, like a secret holy temple. She'd stood there alone for a moment trying to make out the shapes she could only dimly perceive. Outside on the small ledge, Cal pulled and coiled the rope so that no one would spot them, before wriggling through the hole after her. Then he switched on the flashlight and made her gasp.

It was a small, congested village of brick huts. Sunny stood on the slight rise of jumbled stone by the entrance and was able to look out over the twenty or more huts crammed into the cavern. Narrow avenues ran between them, so narrow that she could touch the huts on each side if she were to lift her elbows. The walls were constructed of large red bricks, the same color as the cliff outside. Aged wooden poles extended from the highest points on the walls at two-foot intervals, but some were missing and others broken. For the first time in her life she felt history like a physical force. She could almost hear voices calling quietly in a strange language, babies crying, grains being hammered to wheat in stone bowls, and bare feet slapping at the dusty floor.

Stepping around the huts and low walls, Cal warned her to be careful of the delicate structures as he led her toward the back of the chamber. The cave magnified everything, making each faint noise sound weighted and deep. She could hear her own delighted but whispered exclamations as if coming back to her from a distance, a faint trickle of water, and the sound of their own breathing. The only other noise was a low, faraway moan.

"Wind," Cal explained. "There's a connection somewhere, another way out." Sunny could feel just the slightest breeze. She knew from listening to his stories about caving that establishing a "connection" was a caver's ultimate goal.

Cal played the flashlight over a large depression on the ground. It was a cylindrical pit, almost twenty feet deep and with nearly vertical walls. At the bottom of the pit was a black hole. He held the light steady on it. It was where the moan of wind came from.

"I think it's called a *kiva.* They used it to pray or something. You ain't seen nothing yet, not till you've been down there."

She couldn't get the questions out fast enough. How had he found this place? How old was it? What had happened to the people who lived here? What was down the hole? How much had he explored? Would it really save the valley? Cal put his arms around her and warmed her with his body's heat as he told her about finding it while teaching himself to rappel, how he'd moved a big flake of rock on the narrow ledge while looking for a place to set an anchor. About how he hadn't explored very far, just down into the hole and into an enormous chamber beyond where passages led off in all directions. And about how *hell yes* this place would save the valley, if he could only get those buttheads in the Forest Service to agree to his conditions of secrecy and come see it for themselves.

That was the first time she'd made love to him, when he'd given her this extraordinary visual gift. With his hands rubbing over her to keep her warm, she'd stripped off her own clothes right there and lain down on a low wall beneath the vaulted stone ceiling.

Sunny let out the smoke while Cal took another hit for himself. She decided to once again ignore his question about what it had been like to make love with another woman. "When are you going to take me back in the cave?" she wanted to know.

"Tomorrow," he croaked. "We'll bring some waterproof clothes and I'll take you down into the hole."

Sunny closed her eyes, imagining slipping down a rope into that wet, dark hole. It would be like going back to the womb, entering the safety and security of the Earth Mother. The thought made her smile.

In the distance she could hear an engine on the road that led up into the meadow. Strangely, the noise went away all at once instead of fading on up the road. It was as if the car had stopped by the old logging track that led up the hillside to their camp. The only sound now was the pulse of the crickets. It eradicated all but the nearest sounds for an instant, then made the night totally quiet in the next. She wondered if it could be Kim or one of the other activists but dismissed the thought. Everyone had been at the campfire meeting just an hour before, and the car had definitely come *up* the road, not *down*. Maybe it was those climbers, the two wild-looking sons and the grumpy old man, the ones who had fought the developer in the meadow the day before.

"You hear that?" she asked Cal.

He shook his head. He was still sitting in the lotus position across from her, but he'd twisted around to get out his Walkman and two sets of headphones. Looking down and trying to hear the engine, she noticed that Cal's penis was at half-mast and rising.

She thought she heard a faraway snick. The noise came again, more certain now. It sounded like a car door being bumped shut with a hip. Cal held out a set of headphones to her. A Phish song began to play from the tiny speakers.

"Turn it off. Someone's coming." She could hear the rustle of pine needles and the snap of small twigs as someone, maybe two people, began walking up the narrow track. Cal shrugged and pushed the Stop button.

"Who is it?" he asked, as if she would know. Then he answered his own question with a shrug. "Probably some of the dudes, coming to beg for weed."

The footsteps grew louder until she could hear them even when the crickets intervened. She could also hear heavy breathing caused by the exertion of hiking up the hill. Two people, it sounded like. Men. Big men. She extended her legs out from where they were folded beneath her and slipped on her panties.

Finding her top in the dim glow from the suspended candle lantern, Sunny pulled it over her head when a man's voice said from outside the tent, "Cal? You in there?"

It was a man's voice, deep and confident. She recognized it but the pot had hazed her brain just enough so that she couldn't place it.

"Yeah," Cal answered. From the puzzlement in his voice she could tell he couldn't place it either. She could picture the speaker standing outside the tent, staring at the yellow and blue nylon panels illuminated by the flickering lantern within.

There was a long moment of silence except for the crickets. Sunny lifted the elastic of the halter top over her breasts, then looked at Cal's face as she hurriedly tied the strings behind her neck. He was looking right back at her, his eyes growing wide and scared.

"We were hoping to find you, *dude,*" a harsher voice said; the last part was a mocking imitation of Cal's habitual overuse of the word.

Then the top of the tent crashed down. The candle lantern exploded, spraying hot wax onto her thighs and stomach. Everything went dark. The flexible poles snapped the tent's roof back up for a moment before she felt a rough hand through the nylon rip them away. The fabric sank over her head. Sunny screamed but the sound was cut short when something hard, like a baseball bat or a steel bar, smashed into the side of her head.

"Jesus, Alf! Take it easy!" the first voice yelled.

Savage blows continued to rain onto the collapsed tent. One caught her on the shin. Another in the ribs. The pain was like a hot knife stuck in her flesh. She was delirious with fear—she couldn't even draw her breath for another scream. Kicking out wildly at the suffocating nylon, she struggled to pull a sleeping bag out from under her to cushion the force of the repeated strikes. One of her feet struck Cal, who felt very still, as if he were not fighting at all.

"That's enough! That's enough, goddamn it!"

Then the blows stopped. She wanted to beg, to plead. But her lungs just wouldn't draw air. She could feel a fluid warm on her face—either blood or tears. Outside, just feet away, came the rough laughter of a man who was winded from the exertion of beating the tent as if it were a piñata. Sunny tried to lie as still as Cal and struggled to keep from gasping for air. She struggled to remember a prayer she'd learned in Sunday school as a little girl.

"They're playing possum. Let's drag 'em out," the panting voice said.

"Jesus, Alf. Jesus."

A pair of hands skittered over Sunny's calf, plucking at the tent's fabric.

"Help me find the goddamn zipper, Dave," Alf said, his voice as flat as an old grave.

The hands passed over her leg again. She wished she could scream but the air just wouldn't come into her lungs. And then she wished she were dead, wished that she would be spared any further horror. Death couldn't be far off—her heart felt like it was going to explode.

"I'm gonna cut it open and let the critters out."

There was a snapping noise. The blade of a Buck knife locking into place. Then a slow ripping sound from down where the hands again skittered over her legs like a pair of tarantulas. Sunny felt cool air on her leg. A hairy forearm brushed her knee.

"Let's see who we got here."

She felt the arm reaching past one of her calves. Then it came back and stroked her skin. The hand slithered up her thigh and paused between her legs, patting her lightly, before moving on. "You stay right there, honey. Keep playing possum. I'll get back to you in a minute." And suddenly everything was sliding—sleeping bags, Ensolite pads, tent, and their tangled bodies—as Cal's unmoving form was dragged out by the ankles.

"How you doing, Cal? *Dude?*"

Cal's body came free from the jumble. Sunny could

hear him being dragged in the dirt and leaves a few feet away. Her lungs were finally starting to work, but it was at the beat of a hummingbird's wings. She lay as still as she could, with her head and torso still under the tent.

"Wake up, boy. We got some stuff to talk about." There was the sound of a loud slap. "I think you're just *dying* to tell me where I can find that cave of yours, right?" Another slap. "Shit, Dave, check this guy out. He's doing the best possum job I've ever seen." Then a laugh. "Help me out. Grab his nuts and squeeze."

"No way. You do it. That's the kind of shit I pay you for."

After a brief pause, Alf chuckled. "Fucking-A. This sucker's already dead."

Then there was a longer silence. A suffocating void of sound.

"Damn it!" the one called Dave—Sunny now recognized the voice of David Fast—said in appalled fury. "Damn it, Alf! You were swinging too hard! I told you to be careful, not to kill him."

"Cool it. Get the girl."

"You get her. Damn it! You killed this kid!"

"No, Dave, we killed him. Don't forget that 'we' part now. You're in this as deep as me, pal. But you'll forget all about it when we got a cool few mil in our pockets. We're gonna make me rich and save your ass."

"Jesus. Jesus."

The air finally came into Sunny's lungs. It came in a big, whooping moan, like something a dying elk would make. Even though the sound was her own, it scared her as much as if it had come from one of the men. But it also brought her out of her cringing stupor. She kicked her legs and thrust the tent from over her head. Moving faster than she'd ever moved before, she leapt to her feet and began running. She ran totally blind and far too fast, crashing off trees, being whipped by branches, stumbling and rolling and sobbing. Behind her she could hear the heavy footsteps of pursuit.

"That way!"

"Get her!"

She thrashed her way deep into a thicket. Suddenly the ground dropped away as she was falling. Then rolling through more bushes. She came to a stop deep in foliage. It held her in a tight, scratchy embrace. The footsteps kept crashing somewhere above and behind, but now she didn't move. All she wanted to do was scream. The air for it was finally there. She wanted to let the terror out with a cutting intensity. She held it in, though, some still-rational part of her brain telling her it would only lead them to her.

So she held it in. Not moving a muscle, she lay in the bushes as if she were dead like Cal. Tears ran down her face but she made no move to wipe them away. The voices and searching noises continued for what seemed an eternity. She was deaf to them, too full of terror and grief to let anything else intrude into her senses. After a while the noises stopped.

TWENTY-SEVEN

"DIDN'T YOU SEE us? We ran out onto the road when you came down the track." Kim sits on the other side of Sunny now, cushioning her between us.

Sunny shakes her head and a tear splashes against my arm. "I didn't see anything. It was like I was in a fog. I just knew I had to get out of there. Oh God, when I crawled back and saw Cal, the way they'd stuffed him under a bush..." Her voice dissolves in a fresh wave of tears. I wait for them to slow before speaking, picturing my own vision of Cal's battered flesh.

"Why didn't you go to the police, Sunny?"

The blonde girl turns her wet face up to me. Thick water is dripping out of her eyes and nostrils. "How could I? Fast is friends with the sheriff—Kim told me so—and I'd help set fire to the lodge." She pulls away from me and leans harder against Kim, wrapping herself in Kim's strong, thin arms.

After waiting a while longer, I try another, easier question. "Where's the cave?"

Sunny's voice is muffled by Kim's shoulder. "It's on that red cliff. Above the meadow."

I remember my first morning in the valley, climbing on the hot granite with my father. When we hiked back in toward the meadow for lunch, I thought I saw two climbers rappelling down the cliff. I remember wondering why anyone would bother with that crumbly red clay when there was such fine granite down in the canyon. And I remember that night, when Sunny had introduced me to Cal, and I asked him if he was the one I'd seen rappelling. He looked away, refusing to confirm that it had been him. I took it for embarrassment, not secrecy.

Kim strokes her friend's freshly shorn hair. I assume she's cut it off either to disguise herself or as some way of attempting to rid herself of the memories. Becoming a new person in a new life. Maybe she doesn't understand that the old one's not done with her yet.

Above Sunny's quivering head Kim and I stare at each other. I'm happy, or at least enormously relieved, despite the horrible story she's just told us. Once Sunny tells it to the sheriff and district attorney, after I somehow arrange for her to get immunity on the arson charges, they will have no choice but to let Roberto out of jail.

Kim is thinking in the same direction, but she's looking at it from a different angle. Holding the sobbing girl, she says, "Sunny, we're going to put those men in jail for the rest of their lives. They're going to pay for what they did to Cal. And we're going to save the valley, too. Okay?

Cal didn't die in vain. Remember that. He was a soldier for a rightous cause, just as you are." She's still not admitting to her friend that Cal had died serving another cause as well. Vengeance.

Staring at her, I see that Kim's mouth is grim but her single eye is blazing. I guess what she's feeling is vindication. Although it had cost Cal his life, her vendetta against Fast is turning out better than she could ever have hoped. Not only will he be ruined financially, but he'll spend the rest of his life in a cell. Maybe he'll even get injected. His charmed life is over.

Sunny's testimony is the kind of evidence that it will be hard for any prosecutor to screw up. Even if she hadn't seen the men's faces, she'd heard them call one another by name. There's no way a jury could believe she would make it up or lie about it. Innocence and sincerity radiate from her. She is utterly without guile.

And the valley will be saved. It will remain public land, open for my father, brother, and me to return and climb there again. The Forest Service won't exchange land with a killer. It won't matter that it could take months for David Fast and Alf Burgermeister to be brought to trial. Just the charges against them should be enough for the deal to be put on hold. We can also assure the denial of the swap by telling the government the location of Cal's cave and the Indian ruins. If it's everything Sunny has said it is, and if it's as extensive as Cal claimed, that alone will be cause enough for the Forest Service to reject Fast's development scheme.

"First, we've got to make it back," I tell them both. "In the morning Fast and his buddy will be out here again, looking for us all."

Sunny's body jumps in Kim's arms with a small spasm of fear.

"Let's go back now," Kim says.

"No, let's wait a few hours. For all we know, they're waiting at the marina. They'll be less likely to be looking for us in the middle of the night." They'll probably be sleeping in shifts if they're there at all. The one that's awake will be watching the docks and hopefully not my truck. We can beach the boat somewhere else and I can go for the vehicle. Had Fast or Burgermeister paid any attention to it the time I'd seen them in the meadow? I guess we'll find out.

Those two men have earned my respect as well as my strong desire to see them both dead. It takes a special kind of monster to beat another human to death. A bullet from a distance is one thing—the contusions I'd seen on Cal's body are something else entirely. Somehow much more personal. And Fast is just as much a monster as the one who'd swung the club. He'd brought the monstrous act about.

Kim says something about me needing sleep. Only now do I recall that I hadn't slept at all the night before, and only a few hours the night before that. I shrug in weary agreement. She and Sunny spread blankets on the wide cushioned space by the front of the cabin. It's relatively warm inside from the three of our bodies and the dissipating heat of the propane stove. I try in vain to coax Oso into the cabin before setting the alarm on my watch for two-thirty A.M.

Sleeping with two beautiful women at the same time is supposed to be every man's fantasy. But I'm more than a little uncomfortable. From everything Kim and Sunny have said, it sounds like their relationship is over. The way Sunny has clung to Kim all evening, though, makes me wonder. I don't feel any jealousy—just resignation to the fact that Kim isn't likely to choose me over this innocent blonde nymph. I sure as hell wouldn't. Some of the happiness I'd felt at finding Sunny and the irrefutable evidence she will give to exonerate my brother is diminished. But the relief is still there.

I step over Oso and out onto the deck. I want to give them a few minutes alone together. In the night air I stare up at the black walls surrounding us before I kneel on the swim step to splash cold water on my face. Although there isn't any moon, the stars in the narrow strip of sky are bright enough to cast faint shadows. I sit for a while on the deck and rub the beast's hips.

That Kim cares for Sunny is obvious. After all, she'd come all this way with me to find her. She didn't cry with relief when we succeeded just because Sunny will help her get her revenge on David Fast. I also think of my father and the plain fact that he's not here. He'd given his career priority over a son in jail on bullshit charges. I remember again all those lectures on family loyalty that I'd endured as a child. How we should be willing to sacrifice ourselves for one another. How it was like his cherished Pararescue motto—"So that others may live." And where is he now?

Back in the cabin, both Sunny and Kim are wrapped burrito-like in individual blankets. They lie with their sides touching. Sunny's face is half-hidden behind the wool but I can see that her tear-swollen eyes are shut. She looks asleep. Kim's single eye, however, is bright and wide.

"You okay, Anton?" she asks. Her voice is unusually soft.

I just nod. There's a third blanket that I wrap around my shoulders. I find the switch for the electric lights and turn them off. Oso yawns in the darkness outside. His head still hangs above the steps of the small cabin door. Feeling as tired as I can ever remember, I slump down on one of the bench seats near Kim's head.

Kim's eye remains open. It's a tiny spark of reflected starlight, glinting up at me. I wonder what she's thinking. Is there some new message I'm supposed to be receiving by telepathy? I don't have to wonder for long. It turns out she's reading my thoughts.

"You've learned a lot about me today," she whispers. "Not all of it good. Are we still friends?"

"I'm definitely your friend, Kim," I answer, wishing it were more.

She stretches a hand out of the blanket and finds one of mine. The glint disappears as she closes her eye. The hand doesn't draw back.

TWENTY-EIGHT

I WAKE TO the smallest sound. It takes me a minute to realize where I am and what I'm doing. My neck aches because of the way it's propped forward by the cabin wall. It feels like I've been sitting in an airplane seat for far too long. Kim's hand is still in mine, warm and charged with the tingle of electricity that I have felt every time I've touched her. I glance at the iridescent wands on my watch and see that it's one-thirty in the morning. Then the small sound comes again, louder now—I realize it's the ID tags on Oso's collar. They clatter lightly when he jerks his head.

His ebony coat is streaked with silver in the starlight. He's sprawled on the rear deck outside the open cabin doorway with his paws hanging over the first step. Except for twisting his head to the boat's rear, the beast hasn't moved since I'd fallen asleep. Now he's staring off into the darkness beyond the rented ski boat tied behind us.

His ears are all the way forward. A gentle huffing sound comes from his nostrils and I watch him tilt and raise his head to better test the air. A rumble begins faintly in his chest, then steadily becomes louder.

Letting go of Kim's hand, I use the table to pull myself to my feet. The boat rocks a little from my movement. To my left, Sunny and Kim are motionless and breathing deeply. Even though I suspect the beast is growling at some leaping fish or bathing bird, I touch the hip pack on my belly to make sure my gun is there.

It's not. I rub my face, annoyed at myself, remembering that I had taken it off and left it under the steering wheel on the floor of the ski boat. As upset and scared as Sunny had been when we'd found her, I'd thought it was a good idea to leave the gun out of her sight and reach. That was an early rule I'd learned at the police academy and a good one: *Keep your weapon away from emotionally disturbed people.* But now the night seems more menacing than it had earlier, when Kim and I were so pleased with our good fortune in finding Sunny.

Growling louder, Oso lumbers to his feet. As he moves the boat rolls again, but this time with more force than could be caused simply by his weight. And it continues to roll back and forth even after the big dog has stopped moving. I hear another rumbling sound that, like his growl, is also growing louder. The sound seems to pulsate off the narrow canyon walls.

"Anton?" It's Kim's voice, slurred by sleep. "Is it time to go?"

"Hang on."

I step around the table to the cabin's half-sized doorway. Behind me there are rustling sounds as Kim or Sunny squirms beneath the blankets on the vinyl mattress in the forward area. Pulling myself through the small doorway and out into the night, the first thing I see is Oso standing by the stern. His growl has increased to a low roar. His black lips are raised and his clenched white teeth are the size of small daggers. His legs are slightly crouched. He stares at something in the night beyond the smaller ski boat.

I'm just unfolding to full height on the Sea Ray's deck when I see the ski boat suddenly shove toward us on its short tether. I have just enough time to brace a hand on the cabin roof before the two boats come together with a soft, jarring crunch.

Sunny screams from inside the cabin. I strain with my eyes to see what had caused the smaller boat to bang into us. And what I see makes my heart drop down to my gut.

In the dim starlight, I make out several things in a split second. First, that a third boat has entered the tiny cove. Second, that it's a small white ski boat just like the one Kim and I had rented. Third, that there are the figures of two men on board. Fourth, that one of them is extraordinarily big and bald and that he has the long shape of a shotgun cradled in his arms. He's staggering from the deliberate collision.

My brain begins racing at full speed, every flashing thought telling me just how incredibly stupid I've been. I never thought that Fast and Burgermeister would be tenacious enough to look for us in the dark. And I never thought that they would be lucky enough to actually find us. But then it must have been a simple thing for them to circle back after rounding the promontory and fooling us into thinking they were heading back for the marina. It would have been so easy for them to hide under the shadows of some outcropping below a cliff and watch to see which canyons we explored. And from which we failed to return. *Stupid. Stupid. Stupid.* I deserved to die for my stupidity. But not Sunny and Kim.

With a quick scrabble of claws on fiberglass decking, Oso releases from his crouch like a missile from a silo. He shoots out into the darkness, a thundering black blur arcing in the night. He comes down running on the bow of the ski boat tied behind us. He moves though the open hull in a single lunge and is once again arcing through the air toward the two men in the third boat. Then the night is split open by a blinding flash of light and a sound that blows all the air from the narrow cove. Oso skids off the deck of the third boat—I see him cartwheel sideways and crash into the black water.

That strange, familiar feeling comes over me. The feeling that comes on the rock, when I'm high off the ground and run-out far above any protection. When the rope is no longer a lifeline but just a dead, swinging weight. Time slows. Sensations magnify. The night becomes brighter, more focused. My body feels like a tightly coiled spring. It's the noradrenaline squeezing from my nerve endings, firing into my blood and brain.

I don't feel my flesh tear and I realize in another split second that the shotgun blast hadn't been pointed at me. Its double barrels were aimed at the flying beast. And he'd been hit. Without ducking, without thinking or even flinching backwards, I launch myself over the side into the water just as the shotgun fires again.

The cold shocks me, as if the blast and the sudden radiance and Sunny's scream hadn't done that already. But for a moment it blessedly swallows all the noise except for the throb of the engine. And it allows me just an instant to think. *Oso*. He's somewhere in the water. He'd been shot in the side at close range—he'd cartwheeled off the deck as if he'd been punched by the night. *The fuckers*. My blood seems to rear up from where it had dropped so low with the initial fright.

Underwater, I twist around and kick until I can feel the hard fiberglass of the Sea Ray over my head. I pause there, feeling the convex shape of the hull, and trying to orient myself as my lungs begin to struggle against the need for air. *Get it together, Anton*. Fast's boat is in front of me. The boat Sunny and I had rented is tied bow-to-stern with the Sea Ray, between it and Fast's. And Oso had splashed into the water somewhere over to the left. So I start kicking to the left with my eyes open wide against the blackness.

Pausing before surfacing far out from the side of the Sea Ray, I try to will my lungs to relax. I don't want to come up loud and gasping. I blow out the remaining air while still under water. Then I raise my head slowly, trying to somehow see before my eyes break the surface.

The beam of a powerful flashlight is fixed on the water just a few yards away. Focused on my dog. Oso's eyes are colored a demonic red in the white light, but they are the only thing intimidating about him as he splashes in a wounded dog-paddle, huffing and coughing and still trying to growl. It hits me like a blow, seeing my great beast rendered hurt and helpless. It also stokes the fire in my chest.

"Don't worry about the fucking dog, Dave," a man's voice says from the darkness behind the flashlight beam.

It's Burgermeister's voice, deep as a bass drum. I remember him threatening Roberto and me that day in the meadow, after Dad had prevented my brother from braining the big man with his own tire iron. "It can't get up on the boat. It'll drown or bleed out in a minute. Shine the light over there. Look for Scarface. I want to make sure he's dead before we fetch the cunts."

I try to keep my thoughts from focusing on a single-minded desire to make them pay—I need to concentrate on somehow getting Oso and Sunny and Kim out of harm's way first.

"I don't see him," says the man who started all this twelve years ago, when he'd humiliated Kim, taking her pride and causing her to lose the eye. Fast's voice sounds dull and tired. From what Sunny had said, I know Fast never expected things would go this far. He didn't want to be a killer. But I feel no sympathy.

The light swings away to the other side, leaving Oso grunting in the darkness.

"I think I nailed him, right as he went over," the man called Rent-a-Riot tells his partner.

"I don't see any body. Or any blood," Fast responds.

Now the light passes over the back of the Sea Ray. A piece of the cabin's rear wall is a mess of splintered wood. Right where I'd been standing.

"Forget him. I nailed him. Blew his ass right off the boat."

"A body should float."

"Not a dead one. Not in fresh water, anyway. They sink for a few hours until they fill up with gas. Then they come up."

"How long's it take one to gas up?"

"Shit, Dave, I don't know. Don't worry 'bout it."

I breaststroke silently through the water. The big dog is surprised when I grab his collar. He twists his head violently to the side with the speed of a rattlesnake's strike and sinks his teeth into my forearm. The beast is capable of snapping through bone, but he doesn't. He smells my scent before biting down all the way. I grit my teeth and hiss, "Oso." The pressure fades until it releases all together. I begin sidestroking, pulling the beast behind me, toward where I hope is the narrow gap at the far end of the cove. I remember Sunny telling us it was by swimming up the gap that she'd been able to climb the cliff.

Behind me I hear Burgermeister's voice booming off the walls. "You girls come on up out of there. Come up with your hands over your heads and you won't get shot." The light is still on the back of the Sea Ray.

With my forward hand I touch cool rock. I swim to the side for ten feet until I reach what feels like a corner. The gap. I edge into it, still tugging Oso behind me, not knowing where the gap goes but praying it leads to dry land. In the darkness behind me I can hear Sunny crying and Kim's scared voice calling, "Anton? Anton!" I have to will myself not to go back. At least not until Oso is safe from drowning.

"I'm afraid he got his head blown clean off," Burgermeister explains with a hoarse laugh. Then the voices fade out behind me.

At what I guess is about fifty feet into the gap, my knees touch sand. The gap here is no more than five feet wide and the high walls block out all the starlight. Climbing to my feet, I pull Oso toward what feels like a narrow, sandy shelf. Oso tries to walk up on his own but one of his hind legs collapses under him and he staggers in the shallow water. It takes both my hands on the dog's collar to drag his waterlogged mass up onto the sand. I don't have time to check his wounds but I do take just a second to whisper, "I'll be back, Oso. Wait here. Stay. Stay, damn it," and I rap his muzzle with the palm of my hand.

After stripping off my wet shirt, jeans, and shoes, I soundlessly reenter the cold water. I pray to a god I don't believe in that for once the contrary beast will listen. I pray for Sunny and Kim to have strength and courage. I pray for a lot of other things, too, like for my gun to be somehow within reach over the side of the ski boat. That's an unlikely wish, though. I recall that the sides of the ski boat are high and that I placed the gun well out of both sight and reach below the steering column in the center of the boat.

Breaststroking hard, my hands brush both walls most of the way back out of the gap. When I'm close to the cove again, some of the starlight returns. The wider walls ahead allow it to illuminate the three boats there. Fast has nosed his boat up to the Sea Ray's stern, right next to my rental boat. His isn't tied to anything, though, and it seems to drift a few feet away from the others as I watch. Somehow they've gotten Kim and Sunny aboard it.

The two women are huddled beside each other on the stern bench seat. Sunny has her face buried in her hands. Burgermeister stands near the steering wheel. He has the shotgun in one hand and the flashlight in the other. Its beam is pointed toward the women's faces. In the refracted light I see Fast standing there, too, with a pistol pointed loosely at the deck.

Closer still, I can hear Kim talking over Sunny's sobs

and the drone of the idling engine. Her voice is low and brittle. "You aren't going to get away with this, you motherfucker," she says without much outrage, as if she's in shock. She's speaking to Fast alone and ignoring the greater danger. "The Forest Service knows about the cave. The sheriff knows you killed Cal. He knows you're stalking Sunny here in the lake. He's going to know what you did to Anton. It's all over." For just a moment I'm proud of her as I swim and listen to her valiant bluffing.

But the bluff is going nowhere. "Unfortunately for you, Miss Walsh, you're full of shit. The sheriff is a friend of mine, and he's got nothing to tie me to Cal's death. And all the Forest Service knows is that some whacked-out kid keeps sending them cheap photos of a ruin that could be anywhere. They think it's something you hippies made up just to keep me from making a living." Then he says, more softly, "You should've let it go, Kim. You should've let it go twelve years ago. It was just a stupid prank. No one got hurt, at least no one was supposed to. What happened to you later was an accident. I never even touched you, girl."

"Just like what you did to Cal was an accident?"

Fast shakes his head but doesn't reply.

Kim stares at him for a second, trying to keep up the pretense that she's in control, then I see her bow her head. *Don't give up, Kim,* I think. *I'm coming.* I stroke closer, ready to duck beneath the surface if the light swings my way. But it doesn't. Instead it moves down from Kim's face to play over her shirt. Burgermeister makes it swirl around where her breasts push against the fabric of her damp T-shirt. Then it drops to her crotch and pauses there before disappearing from my view as it slides over her legs.

"He may not have touched you," Burgermeister says, laughing, "but *I* sure as hell am."

The light rises back up but Kim doesn't raise her head to meet it.

Fast says almost sadly, "You brought it on yourself, you know. Haunting me all these years around town. Trying to stir up trouble."

Burgermeister steps forward, his oversized mass rocking the boat. With the muzzle of the gun, he probes between Sunny's arms and presses the barrels into the sweatshirt covering her chest. "That's soft," he says. "And don't that gun feel hard?" He takes one of Sunny's unresisting hands and pulls it against his pants. "Just like me."

Sunny makes another noise. This time it's more of a whimper. Then he turns the twin barrels to Kim. My breath begins to hiss from my lips and I have to struggle to contain it.

Kim looks up and my heart sinks. There's no defiance in her good eye. No hope. Only terror.

Her face slides out of my view as I kick closer to the side of the vacant ski boat.

"We don't need to do that, Alf," Fast says.

"Shut up, Dave! You can blow yourself for all I care. Me, I'm gonna have some fun."

"Not here, not now." Fast tries to put him off. "There's too much to do."

Burgermeister grunts and the flashlight sweeps out over the water. "All right. I don't like it that Scarface and his dog have disappeared. We need to get these sweet little bitches up to the valley so they can show us that fucking cave. After we dynamite it, we'll have all the time in the world."

The flashlight keeps playing in random patterns over the water and the canyon's walls. It searches on my side of their boat now, but I'm protected from view by the hull's overhang at the bow end.

"What about the boats, Alf? How are we going to make sure no one finds them?"

The light shifts to the Sea Ray and my rental. "I'm gonna blow some holes in the bottoms. They'll go down quick enough. I wish I knew where that scar-faced bastard is, though. I don't want that ugly fucker floating up for a few days."

I'm glad he's worried about me. The way I'm feeling, he'd better be worried.

The boat rocks and the bow dips down as Alf moves forward. "He's got to be on the bottom with his ugly dog. The boats'll land right on top of them. Just watch the cunts, Dave."

Treading water, I slide down the vacant ski boat's side to about where the steering wheel should be. I've got to move fast—I can hear Rent-a-Riot ramming more shells into the shotgun. I look up at the boat's rail and realize that I'll have to pull myself all the way out of the water to reach the gun under the steering wheel. I risk discovery by backing a little ways away for a better view. That's when I notice the windscreen. I'd forgotten about it. A windscreen wraps around the boat's side to protect the driver from spray. There's no way I can get over that without the shotgun blowing a very large hole in me. I might as well have left the gun in my truck. *Stupid.*

As if to punctuate the realization, a shotgun blast explodes in the night. I flinch and almost shout—there's no time to dive. My ears ring, deafened. But when my head doesn't blow apart, I figure out that the shot had been aimed into the floor of the ski boat. Burgermeister is just doing as he'd said and sinking the boats by shooting the bottoms out.

I dive, then swim underwater until I feel the hull of Fast's ski boat above my hands. I slide my hands down to the straight edge of the stern careful to avoid the churning propellor, then slowly raise my head out of the water, my cheek pressed close to the fiberglass. Another explosion rips and flashes in the night. The ignition of the compressed gasses light up the canyon wall like a lightning strike. Very cautiously, I lift myself high enough so that I can see Fast standing by the stern, in front of Kim and Sunny. His head is turned away—he appears momentarily entranced by the sinking of the boats. In one hand he holds the small gun that's still pointed at the deck. With the other hand he's aiming the flashlight on the two boats in order to assist his partner. I can't see Burgermeister but I assume he's still on the bow. It feels like it, anyway, due to the way the swim step is lifted a few inches out of the water.

The idling motor just inches from my hip keeps the men from hearing a faint splash as I pull myself higher with one hand on the rear rail and a knee on the step. I reach in and grab Kim's wrist. Over the ringing in my ears from the shotgun blasts, I hear a sharp intake of breath. But she is able to stifle whatever shout had almost risen in her throat. Her face jerks toward mine. Her single eye is huge. I know I must look like some sort of monster, sliding suddenly out of the black water like a giant eel, my hair plastered to my head and with the vivid scar on my face. Fast is still turned away.

I point toward the gap in the canyon wall with my free hand. Then I nod my head at Sunny before twice making a fist and opening it to show her all five fingers twice. Ten seconds. Kim's eye is still huge and wide. Her mouth flinches. *What?* I make the motions again and whisper, "Ten seconds. Count now." Then she gives me a quick, short nod. She whispers in Sunny's ear, then looks back at me.

Fast's head is turning back, swinging the flashlight with it. He's aiming the beam high, so I'm able to slip lower in the water and closer to the hull where he can't see me.

Burgermeister apparently looks over, too. "Looking for your boyfriend, honey? He'll probably float on up in a few hours. I can guarantee you he's dead—I don't miss."

Alf is a moron, I think. He only grazed Oso and missed me entirely.

Counting the seconds off in my head, I slide around the rear corner of the boat to where Fast had been standing. *Nine. Eight. Seven.* Treading water with my feet whirling like eggbeaters, I touch the side of the rail with my fingertips. At *Two* I grab the rail. Then with the power of the noradrenaline shrieking in my blood, I lunge up out of the water and reach for Fast.

The fingers of one hand get a handful of shirt. The others find his belt. He cries out, "Alf!" as he drops both the gun and the flashlight. The surprise makes his legs fall out from under him. I try with all my strength to wrestle his greater mass out of the boat. But I have no leverage—

my hips are on the rail and my feet are kicking in the air over the water. And Fast's legs are entangled beneath the steering wheel as he tears at my fingers and beats at my face. Burgermeister is standing on the bow, whirling, the shotgun swinging around with him.

"Go! Go!" I yell at Kim and Sunny.

The command is unnecessary for Kim. She's already in a dive, arcing her body over the stern to my side. I barely hear the splash. But Sunny doesn't move. She doesn't even flinch. As Fast and I fight, as Burgermeister leans over the side and aims the shotgun at my waist and legs from an angle that won't hit his partner, she just sits huddled and sobbing. I shove Fast away, using his weight to propel me back into the black water, and take a huge, sucking breath.

TWENTY-NINE

THE WATER'S SURFACE over my head explodes with a thunderous crash. I look up and see an orange flash of light before everything again turns black. Swimming away from the boat in an upside-down breaststroke, I watch the flashlight's beam probe the water. I feel a fresh rush of fear when it plays over my chest—the surface explodes with another flash—but the shotgun pellets ricochet off the water. There's the relatively quieter crack of shots fired from Fast's pistol. I roll, change directions, and dive deeper where the depth will diffuse the light to better hide me.

I somehow find Kim in that strange, cold world. A passing wave of pressure brushing against one of my legs alerts me to another swimmer's presence. In the shifting glow of Fast's flashlight, I can make out just a slender shadow and a billow of hair. I reach up, grab what appears to be an ankle, and feel a hand clasp around my wrist. I pull her to me for a moment, finding her jean-clad hips with my hands. Then I push her away in the direction of the gap. I feel a fluttering, fading caress on my chest from the force of her kicks.

I wait a while longer ten feet below the surface and hope to feel the presence of a second swimming body. I wait until my lungs scream for air and the darkness begins to leap and spark at the edges of my vision. Sunny's not coming. She might even be dead. More shotgun blasts splash the surface not far from me, and the flashlight continues to search the water. When I can't last any longer, I kick until I'm under the Sea Ray's white hull. I feel my way up to the bow, my lips almost kissing the fiberglass, and take three long, quiet breaths before diving deep again and kicking off in the direction of the gap.

Kim is waiting for me there, treading water just inside the narrow walls. She's breathing loudly, loud enough for me to fear that the men in the boat will hear her over the low rumble of the idling engine. But it sounds as if they are too busy arguing now to notice us just fifty feet away. I am almost sorry they've stopped shooting—I'd allowed myself to hope that a ricochet would catch one of them in the chest. The beam of the flashlight dances madly off the canyon's walls but never comes to rest on the skinny fissure.

"Where's Sunny?" she whispers.

"She didn't jump." I'm breathing too fast and too loud myself.

I edge back around the corner of rock and look in the direction of the voices. The flashlight beam cuts over the two other boats—my rental and the Sea Ray. Both of them are sinking tail-end first. I can hear the gurgling water through the shattered hulls. The weight of their rear-mounted engines is dragging them down. When the light flashes across the stern of Fast's boat, for just a moment Sunny is illuminated on the rear bench seat. She is still hunched there, holding herself and staring at the deck.

"I'm sorry, Kim. There's nothing we can do. She didn't jump," I say when I'm safely back inside the gap. "Come on."

I swim up into the narrow throat of rock. Kim follows close behind me. My snapping feet graze her chest with each kick as we move away from the engine noise, the gurgling, and the raised voices. My hands touch the sheer sandstone walls on each side.

Behind us there is another shotgun blast.

I don't feel Kim with my feet, so I stop and turn. I hear her say too loud, "Sunny!"

Grabbing her shoulder to prevent her from swimming back out into the cove, I whisper, "She's okay. They're just finishing off the boats."

"No—"

"They can't shoot her, Kim. Not yet. They need her to find the cave."

She struggles against my grip for a moment until her mind digests my words. They'll need her alive to find the tiny, hidden hole in the cliff wall that Sunny had described. Then Kim begins swimming behind me once again. After a few strokes the engine roars louder. Because of the echoes off the walls, it sounds like a hundred boats are racing their motors. My fingers brush sand. Solid ground.

I hurriedly splash up to where I'd left Oso on the powdery sand. The beast is still there, lying on one side and panting heavily. A deep growl is steady from his chest. I suspect he's in shock. When I stroke his muzzle he takes my hand in his jaws for a moment. He squeezes it gently, letting me know he's in pain.

The engine noise gets quieter, fading in the distance. But I can still feel its pulsing vibration reverberating off the canyon walls. I kneel beside my dog and feel his haunches for wounds while Kim splashes out of the water.

"What's wrong with him? Is he shot?" she asks, breathing hard from the cold swim.

"I don't know yet. I think so."

My hand comes away from Oso's right hip feeling warm and sticky. "Yeah, he was shot."

"Let me feel."

Together we explore every bit of fur on Oso's body. The beast is compliant, not whimpering and just barely growling. But he continues to pant as if he's just run miles through the woods. The only wound we can find is an absent piece of his right hamstring. The chunk that's missing feels to be about the size of a tennis ball. He's lucky to have been so close to the shotgun when he was hit—more than ten feet away and the pellets would have spread wide enough to blow off his entire rear end.

"Shit," I still say, feeling the amount of sticky wet stuff spilling into the sand from beneath my dog's leg. "It's bad, but I don't think he's bleeding out." Some of the blood feels reassuringly clumpy, as if it's coagulating, but I can't be certain it's not just mixing with the powdery sand.

Kim pulls off her wet T-shirt and squeezes it over the wound. Then she dips the shirt back into the water and does it again. I hope the dripping water will wash out the sand. After several washings she shoves the shirt into my hands. I squash it into a tight ball and press it into the wound. This finally draws a low whimper of pain from Oso.

"I need something to tie it off with. Go in the water and see if you can find my pants." I vaguely remember having kicked them off after leaving Oso here.

She splashes around for a moment, then says, "Take mine." In the darkness I can see Kim's gray form writhing in an odd dance as she struggles out of her wet jeans. I take them and tie them tightly around the dog's leg to hold the shirt packed in the wound.

"Is he going to be okay?"

"I think so. The wound's already starting to clot. But there are probably pellets still in the leg, so infection is the real danger. And I'm worried there might me some serious damage to his tendons or bone. I need to get him to a vet." I wonder for a moment if Kim's one of those people to whom a dog is just another animal. To such a person it would sound strange to be so worried about a gunshot dog when your friend has been kidnapped and is probably being assaulted as we speak. But Kim is crouched by the beast's head, gently massaging his ears. When he groans she gently shushes him, her voice more tender than I've ever heard it.

"He's really hurting."

"He's tough," I tell her. "Before I adopted him he'd been neglected, starved, tortured, and maced. He's probably just pissed. He'll want a piece of those two." And so do I.

After rubbing his chest and murmuring in Spanish about what a *buen viejo perro* he is, I finally sit up. For the first time I notice how cold I am. The water that's still beaded on my naked skin feels like it might turn to ice.

My teeth are making rapid clicking sounds. I reach out an arm and put it around Kim's shoulders, noticing that she is also shaking uncontrollably, still wet in just her underwear. I pull her to me.

"Curl up with Oso. You know, spoon him. Use each other's warmth. I'm going to see if I can find a way out of here. Or some sort of shelter. We're going to get hypothermic if we stay here." I sense more than see Kim nod beside me.

I march away from the water like a zombie, holding my hands outstretched before me and stepping high with my feet so that I won't break a toe on any unseen rocks. In the dim starlight that reaches into the gap, I can see only the two dark walls on either side, close enough so that if I stretch my arms to the sides I can feel them both, and the strip of sky above. I remember Sunny saying something about there being a place where you could climb out but it being too hard to climb back down. That was why she'd jumped in the lake from above when she'd recognized us in the late afternoon.

The canyon twists and turns several times but heads for the most part in the same direction. I keep my eyes on the sky, looking for where the line of stars might open or branch. I guess I walk for several hundred yards on the mercifully smooth floor without seeing any change before I give up and turn back. We will have to wait for more light before we can find Sunny's climb. My brain only then remembers that this is wild land—I remember the map showing nothing but canyons and buttes for miles and miles. Even if we find a way to climb out, it's unlikely it will lead anywhere. Our best chance of finding help is on the lake.

As I near the place where I'd left Oso and Kim curled on the sand, I can still hear tiny waves spilling on the sand at the water's edge. It worries me for a moment. I don't know if the water's disturbance is due to wind on the lake or the reflection of the speedboat's wake off the canyon walls. Conceivably, they could come back. But a boat won't fit in the gap and I don't think they'd take the trouble to swim in. I worry about it, though, to keep from worrying about what they're doing to Sunny. It's easier that way.

"Kim?" I call, my voice barely louder than a whisper.

"Here," she answers, almost at my feet.

I stare at the ground and in a moment am able to make out the dark shape of Oso prostrate on the sand and the lighter shadow of Kim beside him. Her arms are wrapped around his chest. She is pressed against the big dog's back.

Kneeling, I put my hand on Oso's head. The dog flinches at the touch, then snuffs at my scent. A hot, dry tongue rasps against my palm. "Easy, Oso. Easy." He continues to growl.

"What's the plan?"

"We have to wait for light—I can't find a way out. When it gets light I'll swim for help." I try to recall the beach where we'd had lunch. Hopefully the kids in the houseboat will still be there.

I touch Kim's bare shoulder. Her skin jerks and twitches like Oso's had. She is shivering violently. I consider getting her back in the water, which is surely a lot warmer than the nighttime desert air, but I know it will suck the heat from our cores much quicker than the air and leave us hypothermic in minutes. So I lie down beside her. I curl myself against her body, pressing my own half-frozen flesh hard against hers. One arm I slip under her head, then Oso's. The other I put across her chest. Unable to stop myself, I put my lips against the back of her neck and blow gently, letting the warmth of my lungs seep into her skin.

"What are you doing?"

"Warming you up."

And suddenly, despite it all, she laughs. But within seconds that laugh turns heartbreakingly cheerless. She begins to sniffle.

"I did it again. I let it happen. No, I made it happen. And I didn't even fight for her. Oh God, Anton."

"You waited for your chance and you got the hell out of there. There was nothing else you could do."

"No, I ran. I ran and left a friend. I'll never forgive myself."

"You did the only thing you could. They had guns—you didn't. And we'll get Sunny back."

"How? They'll take her back to the valley, make her show them the cave, and then they'll kill her."

"We've got some time. It will take them most of the night just to find their way back to the marina. And then they'll have an eight-hour drive to Tomichi. They won't dare march her around the valley in the daylight because someone might see them. So we have until tomorrow night. If we don't freeze to death tonight." I scoot closer, fitting my bare legs tight against hers, my hips to her buttocks, my chest to her back. I don't mention and try not to think about what Sunny will have to endure until then. It would probably be better if they killed her outright.

THIRTY

I CAN SENSE the sun's heat above the gap's high walls but feel none of it. The night's deep chill lingers on the canyon floor. A slight breeze magnifies it. It's frustrating to think that just a hundred feet over our heads the desert sun is probably beginning to bake the rust-colored earth. Sandwiched between Oso and me, Kim still shivers in her sleep as my stomach clenches with hunger and cold. It has been a long night.

I peel myself away from her curved back and climb unsteadily to my feet. My body feels worse than if I'd abused it by drinking tequila all night. Sand is plastered to my skin from where I'd scooped it half over me in a vain effort to stay warm. Standing, I feel a heavy ache in one shoulder and one hip. My left forearm is black, blue, and yellow, but otherwise unmarred. Oso's teeth had not punctured the flesh when I'd surprised him in the water right after he was shot. I try to stretch as I take in our surroundings.

The shallow water a few feet away is very still and very green. It turns to deep blue about fifty feet out where the walls open up into the tiny hidden cove. The gap itself is only five feet wide; the walls are close to a hundred feet high. In the other direction, the gap is floored with fine-grained sand. It stretches back a hundred yards or so before twisting out of view. I can see my footprints from the night before, when I'd staggered between the walls in a hopeless search for some shelter.

I swing my arms in circles and again try to ignore the rumbling in my stomach. And the way the cold seems to have clenched all my muscles into tight fists. At my feet, Kim and Oso, still spooning, are showing signs of life. Kim moves her head and coughs sand into the fur at the back of Oso's neck. The beast rumbles, flexing his forward claws. The homemade bandage of Kim's T-shirt and jeans looks crusty with a mixture of dried blood and sand.

Kim's back, butt, and legs are naked. Sometime during the night I'd persuaded her to take off her wet underwear and bra. Cotton doesn't dry easily and wet clothes just make you colder. I'd taken off my own shorts. The undergarments, now almost dry, lay spread on the sand in front of Oso's head. I pull on my shorts before Kim looks around so as not to make too obvious a certain embarrassing stiffness. Despite the night's terror and fury, the feel of her bare skin against mine is something I suspect will be branded in my mind for a long time to come.

My attraction to her had already made itself more than evident in the dark some hours ago. As I held her, trying to both give and receive life-saving heat, my independent-minded limb swelled up between her naked thighs. "Anton, what are you doing?" she asked not exactly in alarm, but not in rapt pleasure either.

"Nothing. It's a natural reaction"—I breathed against her neck—"caused by the cold." I thought about mentioning that she was having an apparent reaction to it as well—right where my left hand cupped one of her small breasts—but decided against it. Other than the feel of her skin, my only other comfort in the night was the sensation of that pointed nipple in my palm.

She made a noise, almost a cough. "I'm glad to know it's the cold and not me that gives you a hard-on." I thought she moved her hips just slightly, pushing them back harder into me.

"Well, I might've lied about the cold part," I whispered carefully, as if my voice might wake Oso. It was a pointless concern—the beast was surely awake. I felt his head twitch beneath my right hand each time I spoke. I knew his eyes were wide with discomfort—both from his wounds and from having Kim wrapped around him, and me, in turn, wrapped around her. "Actually, I've been climbing in Alaska for weeks at a time without a hard-on. It's you. Only you, Kim."

I waited without moving for her response. It took a long time in coming—but the tension took away all thoughts of my wounded dog, my caged brother, a kidnapped girl, and the brutal desert cold. While I waited I continued to blow gently onto the back of her neck with my lips just a fraction of an inch away. For a moment I sensed that we were on the edge of a cliff, ready to tumble off in one another's arms.

But then she pulled us back by saying, "I can't deal

with this right now, Anton. I really can't. You're a wonderful man, unbelievable in some ways. But there's just too much going on."

"I'm going for help," I tell her, my first words of the day. She's still curled tightly against Oso's broad back. Her face remains buried in his coat and all I can see of it is her sand-encrusted eye patch beneath the tangle of dirty black hair. I drape her sports bra and underwear over her side. Turning my shoulder to her, I squat beside Oso's head. The beast tries to get to his feet but I put a hand on his shoulder to keep him down. "Easy, boy. Stay." I'm afraid that if he gets to his feet the wound will split open and start bleeding again.

"How does he look?" Kim asks through his fur and her own hair.

"Better. He's not in shock anymore, and that was the real danger last night. Now it's just infection and tendon damage that I'm worried about." My stomach clenches again. "We need food."

I hear the snap of elastic as Kim tugs the sports bra into place. When I turn to see her face for the first time this morning, she looks down shyly. It's surprising to see this beautiful, self-assured woman acting timid—almost as if she were the one who had made a fool of herself last night instead of me. Neither of us mentions it.

I dip my foot into the water, then jerk it out. After a night of teeth-chattering cold, the water feels like it should be skimmed with a layer of ice. In reality it's probably almost sixty-five degrees. But the thought of immersing myself in it and having to swim is appalling. Like all breeds of fear, I know it's best to confront it immediately, without hesitation. I look at Kim, still huddled and shivering in her bra and panties, and I look at Oso panting and bloody, and I think of Sunny and Roberto. Then, with a gasp, I march into the water.

"I'll be back in an hour, I hope. It should warm up before then."

"Be careful," Kim calls after me.

God, the water is cold. It takes all my will not to dance uncontrollably in the shallows. When I lunge headfirst into the gap, the cold rips the breath from my lungs. My calves try to cramp in rigid protest. I crawl-stroke hard down the gap and into the small cove, hoping the exertion will at some point warm me.

The cove has none of the menace from the night before except for where the air-filled bow of Sunny's Sea Ray points out of the water like the white tip of an iceberg. And where a single red shotgun shell floats nearby. The top of the west wall shimmers red and gold in the morning sunlight. I pause, treading water, to look around for a moment. The place would be perfect for a postcard picture if the cold and the night's terror didn't still have its grip on me. Deep-blue water, a sign of great depth, causes me to give up any hope of diving for my gun.

I swim through the low arch leading to the subcanyon, and up that toward the bay. The steady stroke is finally beginning to warm me, but it's tiring, too—it's been years since I've done any serious swimming. The muscles in my shoulders and back burn as if I were on a long climb. I welcome the lactic acid's heat. After ten minutes I try to rest by floating on my back, but it's not much of a rest because I keep sinking. I remember that fresh water is far less buoyant than the salt water I swam in as a child. So I forget about resting and just swim on.

Coming out into the bay, I'm disappointed to neither hear nor see any sign of other boats. It's too early for the sightseers to be out. There's just a flock of white birds that spins and dives in formation far out over the water. I turn to the south, my right, and crawl on toward the canyon with the houseboat on the beach.

I'm almost to the canyon when I hear a hollow pumping sound. For some reason it brings back memories of high school and college. I wonder if the cold is making me delirious. Then I latch onto a memory and pinpoint the sound—it's the heaving of someone's stomach after a night of excess. The gut-wrenching sound is actually welcome to me. Turning the canyon's corner, I find the big houseboat with two speedboats tied to the side. A beefy young man with sleep-tussled hair is leaning over the boat's second-story rail. He's spasming with a long series of the forceful contractions. I head toward the closest end of the beach, wanting to approach on foot rather than like a thief from the water. And I'd rather not swim through his vomit.

The sand feels good under my feet. I stagger on it as I come out of the water, my legs having turned to wet noodles. They're too tired from the swim to respond to the ordinary demands of walking upright. I feel like I'm drunk myself—my mind and limbs are so numb with cold. And like something out of an alcoholic daze, what appears on the beach is beyond surreal.

Three topless girls are sunbathing just a few yards away. They stare at me in horror as I trip and splash face-first into knee-deep water. "Oh my God!" one of them says.

Back on my feet, I stumble toward them. One girl springs to her feet with the agility of a startled deer and sprints on board the enormous boat. The other two fumble with their swimsuit tops before standing awkwardly, unsure if they too should flee.

"There's been an accident," I say to them, trying hard to look as inoffensive as possible in my clinging underwear. "I need help."

During the long swim I had decided to tell no one here at the lake about the shooting and kidnapping. To do so would mean hours spent with the local police and whatever federal agency had jurisdiction over a national recreation area such as Lake Powell. It is imperative that we get back to Tomichi as fast as possible, where we can enlist Sheriff Munik's help in finding Sunny. If he refuses, I'll go to the FBI, the Forest Service, or anyone else who will listen.

The girls evidently decide I'm harmless despite my scarred face and lack of clothes. One of them tilts her sunglasses down on her nose and looks me over. "You're the guy who was with the woman and the dog, right?" Apparently having been seen in the company of a beautiful woman and a dog gives me some credibility.

"That's one badass dog," the other says. "Was he hurt?"

"My friend and my dog are okay, although my dog cut his leg pretty badly in the crash. But our boat sank. Can somebody here give us a ride back to the marina? I've got to get my dog to a vet."

The girls look at one another and at the speedboats. "Sure," the one with the sunglasses tells me. "It sounds like fun. It's getting kind of boring here anyway, just listening to the guys puke."

They explain to their friends on the houseboat what they're doing while I sit on the sand, warming in the sun. Even though I can feel its hot touch on my skin, the shivering won't stop. The young men on board glare at me suspiciously but they are too hungover to argue much. I borrow a pair of shorts and a T-shirt for Kim, and even manage to beg a box full of granola bars. I'm out of luck, though, when I ask for water. "It's all gone," one of the girls tells me cheerfully. "All we've got left is beer."

I can't hold back a smile. "Then I guess that will have to do."

By speedboat it takes the two girls, named Candy and Amber, sorority sisters at UNLV and indistinguishable from one another, only ten minutes to take me under the arch and into the cove. Delighted by the hidden wonder, one of the girls pulls out a camera and starts snapping pictures. They wait in the hidden cove with the big engine idling while I swim up the gap to retrieve Kim and Oso.

Kim is still trembling violently in the slot's perpetual shade when I come out of the water. She's kneeling beside Oso, massaging his fur.

"How's he doing?" I ask.

"He started growling and tried to stand up when he heard the boat," Kim reports, proud of her patient's spirit. "You found help, I take it."

"Wait till you meet our rescuers."

Together we ferry Oso out into the cove. The girls chatter like concerned birds as they struggle with us to lift Oso's mass into the boat. They apparently fall in love with the wounded dog at first sight, feeding him half a box of granola bars before I ask them to stop. One of the girls gives Kim the clothes I'd borrowed along with a beer. She looks at the proffered can in amazement until I explain the lack of drinking water.

The improvised bandage on Oso's hind leg smears the white vinyl cushions with blood, but the girls are thankfully more concerned about the dog than the damage. He's bleeding again from the swim. As we motor back out into the bay, I use the medical skills my father had taught me and the boat's first-aid kit to cleanse and rebandage the wound. In the daylight the damage to his haunch looks even more severe than it had felt the night before. The shotgun blast tore away more than two inches of muscle along the back of his leg. I'm not certain what the permanent damage will be—he'll probably have a limp at the very least—but I'm pretty sure he's not in danger of dying. Better news is that the wound appears to be clotting well despite the fresh soaking. I think it won't do much more harm if we wait to get back to Tomichi before taking him to a vet. Kim tells me that she's friends with the woman who runs the animal hospital there. It will save time and save me from having to explain to an Arizona vet just how my dog managed to get shot.

The speedboat creeps back under the arch and into the canyon and then into the bay beyond. I ask if we can pick up the pace a little. "You bet!" one of the girls tells me. She shoves the throttle forward and the twin engines dig deep in the water. Twin plumes explode from behind the propellers as the boat rears like a panicked horse.

We're getting out into the main channel when I'm struck by the whole surreal scene. Just eight hours ago, someone was trying very hard to kill me, my dog was wounded, and a friend had been kidnapped; meanwhile, my brother self-immolates in jail and another young man sleeps on a stainless steel bed in a coroner's cutting room. And here I am being taxied at high speed by two college girls in bikinis and a one-eyed woman I'm infatuated with, amid the lake's equally spectacular scenery. I sip my second beer and shake my head. *This can't be real.*

"Having fun?" Kim asks with a tired smile.

I raise my beer to her and the two girls in the cockpit. "I wish Roberto could see the hell I'm enduring to get him out of jail."

THIRTY-ONE

IF FAST AND Burgermeister had been a little smarter, they would have punctured the tires of my truck. That had been my greatest fear on the forty-minute boat ride back to the marina—it would have cost us hours. But my aged Land Cruiser is intact except for the rust holes above the fenders. Candy and Amber help us load Oso into the backseat while a throng of tourists gape from the docks. They appear more interested in the three straining women than in the wounded dog.

After we thank Oso's new girlfriends, I get in the driver's seat and start the engine with the Hide-A-Key. Kim sits in back with Oso's big head cradled in her lap. We pass the boat rental office without a glance. Before we're even out of town, I'm punching numbers into my cell phone.

"Tomichi County Sheriff's Office. Can I help you?"

The voice is that of the desk clerk I'd run past in my impulsive yet successful attempt to see the sheriff. I remember arguing with her over the speaker outside the lobby before she finally buzzed me in to supposedly leave my card. It's hard for me to believe that it had just been two days before.

"My name is Special Agent Antonio Burns. I need to speak with Sheriff Munik immediately," I say in an official tone, hoping she won't remember my voice or my name.

There's a long silence on the other end of the line. *Shit.*

"Please," I try. Outside the car, I see that we're dropping from a high plain down into a red canyon. Mesquite pines and chaparral flash green as we speed through the otherwise Martian landscape.

"You got me in a lot of trouble, mister, running past me like you did. I hope you app—"

"Listen, I'm very sorry. But this is an emergency and I need to talk to the sheriff right now!"

"Then call 911." She hangs up on me.

"Fuck!"

Behind me I hear Oso growl in response to the shouted obscenity. I stab the redial button on the cell phone and then cut her off when she begins the same practiced greeting. The speedometer's wand is steadily rising.

"I can't call 911. I'm in Arizona. I swear, lady, this is an emergency!"

"Then you should call your local law enforcement agency. Have a nice day, Agent Burns." She hangs up on me again.

My jaw is clenched hard enough to make my teeth

ache. In my free hand I lift the phone, trying to decide whether to resist the urge to smash it on the dashboard. "Easy, Anton. Slow down," Kim says from behind me. She reaches forward and plucks the phone from my hand.

This time, when the desk officer answers, Kim says sweetly, "Hi, Doris. This is Kim Walsh. Is Sheriff Munik in?" She hands the phone back to me while the call is being transferred. And she again reminds me that I'm driving way too fast.

When the sheriff comes on the line, I quickly explain that I'm with Kim Walsh in Arizona so that he too doesn't hang up on me. Then I tell him what had happened during the night and about Sunny's confirmation that David Fast and Alf Burgermeister were the killers. He listens in silence. It lasts even after I stop talking, long enough so that I start to wonder if the line has gone dead.

"Sheriff?"

"What have you been smoking, Burns?" he finally says.

I take the phone from my ear and stare at it for a second. I simply can't believe what I'm hearing. The anger starts to bubble up in my chest like a pot boiling over. My throat swells with the need to let out the steam. It takes all the will I possess to keep from expressing it.

"What are you saying?" I ask, my voice sounding unnaturally calm.

The sheriff chuckles. "Your brother confessed this morning. I just heard about it myself from a jailhouse snitch we had in a cell with him. According to our man, your brother said something about 'fucking up the kid for the girl.' I suppose he meant that Sunny Hansen."

"Bullshit!" There's nothing calm about my voice

now. The word comes out hot enough to scald the phone. In the backseat I hear Oso growl louder.

"Anton, slow down!" Kim shouts.

I turn the wheel hard around a corner. We're winding our way through a desert canyon fast enough for the wheels to moan at each curve.

Trying to regain control of both myself and the truck, I say, "Kim Walsh is with me. She can confirm everything I said. Your snitch is lying, Sheriff. And Sunny Hansen has been kidnapped and will be murdered soon, if she's not dead already."

Munik sighs. "Burns, it's well known that Ms. Walsh has it out for David Fast. She's been doing everything she can to put a stop to the development in Wild Fire Valley. The DA's even thinking about charging her as an accessory to the arson. Everyone, including me, figures she must have had a hand in it. Maybe she even talked your brother into it. So excuse me for not believing the brother of a murderer and an arson suspect. Now, if you don't mind, I've got a roadblock to maintain. The Forest Service approved the land exchange yesterday afternoon, so I guess that land isn't public anymore. The deeds will be passed over in a couple of days. And Dave called this morning and asked me to make sure no more of those damn hippies get up into the valley to do any more mischief. So you make sure I don't catch *you* trying to sneak up there. I'll be sure to keep my eye out for that girl, though. With her testimony the case against Roberto Burns will be bulletproof." He chuckles again as he hangs up the phone.

"What happened?" Kim asks immediately.

I don't answer right away. My hands grip the wheel

hard enough that my rock-scarred knuckles flare white. My teeth feel like they're about to explode in my mouth. My foot raises off the accelerator and I let the truck slow to a stop in the middle of the road. I try to concentrate on just breathing. The sun beats down on the roof, heating the truck, but I seem to lack the strength to turn on the air conditioner.

"Anton?"

I blow out a lungful of hot air and suck a new one in. "He doesn't believe me. Us, I mean. He says my brother confessed to killing Cal this morning and that you're now a suspect in the arson."

"Bullshit!" Kim says immediately, duplicating my reaction.

"He also said the government approved the swap yesterday. The deeds will be formally exchanged in a couple of days."

We sit in the middle of the road for several minutes. No other cars come by. A hundred feet ahead three ravens are picking at the fly-blown corpse of a coyote on the side of the road. I watch them jab at the meat with their sharp beaks and then glare at me. One of them caws in the direction of the truck. It sounds like an evil laugh.

"Give me the phone," Kim demands.

I hand it back. "Who are you going to call?"

In the rearview mirror she looks once again like a rampaging pirate. She's tied a blue bandana over her filthy hair. A few tendrils spill out over her face to partially mask the eye patch.

"The FBI."

I say tiredly, "The valley's no longer federal land, Kim. They don't have jurisdiction anymore."

"Kidnapping's a federal crime, isn't it?"

I shift through the gears as we start moving again. But it feels like we're going nowhere. It takes Kim half the drive back just to speak to an actual agent, who then refers her to the local U.S. Attorney. She's told that they'll look into it after they speak with the sheriff. The federal prosecutor is all too aware that one of our alleged kidnappers is the son of a former United States senator. If they feel the need is justified, they'll see about investigating further. In a skeptical tone he suggests we stay in touch.

"I guess it's time to get serious," I tell her as she hands me the phone. When I take it from her I notice that her hand is quivering, as if the night's cold and terror has returned to hold her in its icy grip. "We're going to have to take care of things ourselves." The law's not going to work for us. The anger has washed out of my system. Replacing it is a strange sense of calm. I feel like the rope's run out and there's no ledge on which to set up a belay. No safety. All that's left to do is to untie the knot and let the rope drop away.

Her face is now hidden from me—she's buried it in Oso's fur. Even though I can't see her expression, I know the pirate is gone now. The scared little girl is back.

I reach under the dashboard and take out the backup gun I keep hidden there. It's a flat little Beretta loaded with hollow-point .22 caliber bullets. Despite its size, it feels light and lethal in my hand. I lay it on the empty passenger seat.

"How?" comes the muffled reply.

"I'm going to unleash the dogs," I tell her, thinking of my mother's term for Roberto's lack of restraint. *Destraillado.*

PART THREE

THEY SOWED THE WIND,
AND THEY SHALL REAP
THE WHIRLWIND.

—HOSEA 8:7

EIGHTH CENTURY B.C.

THIRTY-TWO

"I'VE BAILED HIM out, Dad. I could use your help riding herd."

There's silence at the other end of the line. I can picture my father at some gleaming steel desk in the Pentagon. On the car radio on the long drive back to Tomichi, I'd heard more about trouble involving United States soldiers in the Balkans. Then there was a report about American tourists being gunned down in the desert outside Cairo. And more of the usual trouble in Iraq. I imagine him surrounded by ringing phones and frantic aides. I picture him with his eyes closed, maybe leaning back in some futuristic executive chair before multiple blinking computer screens, as amid the chaos he contemplates the fact that I've risked my inheritance, my brother's freedom, and possibly his life by springing Roberto from jail.

Instead of angrily assailing me with all the arguments

of why I should not be doing what I'm doing, he quietly says, "I can't do it right now, son. Things are going to hell here. Twelve UN soldiers were shot down in Bosnia. I may have to coordinate a rescue."

I feel a fresh rush of disappointment and betrayal. All those family loyalty lectures over the years were just so much bullshit. His career's not going anywhere—what better time to bag it than now, when Roberto and I need his help?

"Perhaps I should send your mother," he says quietly.

Suddenly the emotion is gone and I can't help but laugh. I picture my mother, the spicy Latin princess, facing up to Fast and Burgermeister and the sheriff and the Tomichi County DA. When aroused, she uses her tongue like a whip. And the Spanish she uses at such times is like a barb at its tip. I have no doubt that Mom could do some serious damage here in southwestern Colorado. But now's not the time. Having her around would only make Roberto more protective, unstable, and dangerous.

"Negative, Colonel. I'll take care of it." I'm anxious to get off the phone with him before I say something just to hurt him.

When I walk back into the coffee shop, I see that Roberto has finally managed to coax a laugh out of Kim. A waitress stands by the table, laughing too, and staring at my brother with big doe-eyes as he tells some story.

After the waitress takes our orders and walks away, Kim says, still smiling, "Roberto was telling me about the time you guys were climbing in the 'Towers of Pain'?" She looks at Roberto to see if she's gotten the name right.

My brother says, "Close enough. Accurate, too." She

means Torres del Paine in Patagonia, not far from our grandfather's ranch.

"And you guys were on the top of some pinnacle in a storm when you knocked over the stove and burned down the tent?"

"It didn't seem so funny at the time," I respond grumpily.

I'm amazed at the transformation that has taken place in Roberto's face and attitude. When I'd met him inside the jail an hour earlier, his skin was sallow and his jaw muscles were bunched tight at the corners of his face. He looked years older. A scowl hung from his bright blue eyes like a physical weight. The orange jail uniform seemed to somehow dim their color. But the moment we stepped outside, the moment the late summer sun laid its high-altitude warmth on him, all that dropped away. He stood in the fresh air on the courthouse grass and sucked deep breaths. He looked right again in his motorcycle boots, his heavy brown jeans, and the tight black T-shirt. Grinning, he crouched and dug his fingers into the dirt. He turned to me, looking like a phoenix raised from the ashes.

With that amazing quickness he'd always had, he seized my face in his dirty hands and kissed me on the mouth. "Thanks, bro," he said while I feigned violent nausea.

His energy has infused Kim, too. On the long, high-speed drive back to Tomichi she'd sat in back the whole way, cradling Oso's massive head in her lap. Her brief moment of fire, when she'd taken the phone from me and called the FBI, quickly flared out when the Feds made clear their reluctance and disbelief. After that she barely spoke. And she never met my eyes in the rearview mirror. I was on the cell phone every minute I could get a signal, feeling a new sense of purpose. I arranged a wire transfer of a half million dollars from Argentina to a Tomichi bank as bail for Roberto. Then I spent more than an hour trying to keep from driving off the road as I waited on hold for my father. And I called the animal hospital and asked Kim's friend to prepare to perform surgery on my gunshot dog.

When we arrived at the veterinarian's office, we were met with a rolling crash cart. It almost brought tears to my eyes that finally someone was doing something to help us. The confident woman doctor there assured me that Oso would be okay, but she would need to knock him out so that she could open up his leg and dig out any remaining pellets and hopefully reattach any damaged tendons. She had me stay with the beast until he was sedated.

"So how we gonna clear my good name, *che*?" Roberto asks now.

"Good name my ass." I take a sip of hot coffee. "We have to find Sunny—she's the only one who can truly clear you."

"Blonde chick, right? Hot-looking, with dreads? You know where she's at?"

"Not exactly." I explain our finding her on Lake Powell, then losing her. About Oso getting shot.

"I'd like to find the guys that did that." One thing Roberto doesn't tolerate is the mistreatment of women, children, or dogs.

"So would I," Kim chimes in. The ferocity is coming back. Roberto's self-assurance is infecting us both.

Roberto cocks a thumb at Kim, then says to me, "I dig this girl."

"So do I," I say pointedly, which makes him smile

and nod in understanding. He even winks. "Kim and I think they're taking her back to the valley. To lead Fast and his friend to the cave so they can dynamite it or something. Then they'll probably kill her."

Roberto's smile fades. "That's going to be a problem, *che.* A deputy I made friends with in the pound told me that Fast has gotten the pigs—no offense, Ant—to set a roadblock up there. They're going to arrest anyone going in there for trespassing. And believe me, bro, you don't want to be in that jail."

"Because he's a cop?" Kim asks. Everyone knows that convicts aren't especially kind to jailed police officers.

Roberto shakes his head. "No, 'cause last night a bunch of Burgermeister's redneck buddies got themselves arrested for drunkenness or some shit. Word I heard from my friend was that they refused to sign a PR bond." He means a Personal Recognizance bond, which is a type of bail for minor offenses that only requires a signature and a promise to appear or pay a fine. No cash. A PR bond is like a "get out of jail free" card. No one refuses to sign a PR bond. "My friend heard these boys were looking to stick a shank in me. Ant got me out of there just in time, before I had to seriously fuck them up."

That explains the confession Roberto supposedly made. Fast and Burgermeister had some of their men get themselves arrested. It would be so easy for one of them to claim he'd heard Roberto confess to killing Cal. After that, once the sheriff and the DA had no further doubt as to my brother's guilt, the men could kill him in a jailhouse fight. The case of Cal's murder would be forever closed.

I think about it for a minute and realize how the plan would be even better for the developers if Kim and I were to get arrested, too, going up into the valley to rescue Sunny. It's a pretty good plan for a meathead like Burgermeister and a newly baptized criminal like Fast to have come up with. I remind myself not to underestimate them.

"Is there another way into the valley?" I ask Kim. We could hike out of sight through the dense woods, but the meadow beneath Cal's red cliff is almost twenty miles up the Forest Service road. It would take at least a day. Maybe two. Sunny will be very dead by then, if she's not already.

Kim slouches in the booth and stares at the table. After a moment she looks up with a determined expression. "Yes, there is. A narrow-gauge train, an old mining relic, is used all summer to give sightseeing tours up a gorge just east of Wild Fire Peak. If we can get the conductor to stop and let us off, then maybe we can hike up the peak's back side and drop into the valley that way. I imagine it's a tough hike, though. The west face of the mountain is much more rugged than the east. I don't know if anyone's ever climbed it from that side."

"Let's do it," I say. Conquering the mountain should be the easy part.

Roberto's not concerned about the climb either. If it were all that hard, he would have heard of it and already soloed it.

"Cool. A train," my brother says instead. "I fucking love it. Just like *Butch Cassidy and the Sundance Kid.*" To Kim he says, "You can be Etta," and then to me, "I guess that makes me Butch, right, Sundance? The odd man out."

"Odd is right, Roberto."

THIRTY-THREE

ACCORDING TO THE stationmaster at the depot off Tomichi's main street, the next train is leaving in just thirty minutes. It's already smoking on the tracks. A huge black engine leads a series of open passenger cars. A plaque above the cashier's window informs us that an actual coal-fired locomotive powers the train. I pay for tickets. Then the three of us stand around the truck in the parking lot while I shove gear into packs and discuss what we'll need to bring.

"Guns," Roberto says.

"I'll bring my Beretta, but that's it. The last thing you need, bro, is a gun." I rattle off a list of groceries to Kim, who'll run to a grocery store just a few blocks away. Bread, pasta, oatmeal, candy bars, water bottles, peanut butter and jelly. Kim scribbles on a torn piece of paper.

"We need more guns," Roberto says again.

"Don't forget the peanut butter," I tell Kim the vegetarian, ignoring my brother. "We'll need the protein."

"Peanut butter and guns!" Roberto suddenly hollers. People walking nearby turn to stare. Even Kim looks alarmed at his outburst.

"Easy, Hayduke," I say to him. Then to Kim by way of explanation, "Now he's doing Edward Abbey."

"Monkey wrenchers. I've read it," she says, smiling.

Before she leaves for the store, I give her a pair of worn canvas pants to replace the borrowed shorts. Pulling my sweat-stiff fleece pants over my own legs, I explain that for the long hike, she'll need something to cover hers. I wish I had some boots that would fit her—her worn-out sneakers are unsuitable for backcountry travel, but there's no time to run out to her house. Roberto watches approvingly, along with the other male spectators in the parking lot, as she drops the shorts right there by the back of my truck and steps into the baggy pants.

When she runs for the store, I ask Roberto to sit down with me on my truck's tailgate. Despite the warm sunlight on the asphalt, the gentle breeze, the easy talk and laughter of the people passing by, I feel incredibly wound up. Like an alarm clock wired to a time bomb. It's the apprehension of facing Fast and Burgermeister as well as Roberto's energy that's making me feel this way. Ever since I'd gotten him out of the jail just over an hour earlier, it's as if some storm is building and churning within him. It crowds me. And it scares me. "We need to talk for a minute."

"Yeah, bro, I know. The chick's yours."

"You call her that again and she might punch your

lights out. No, I want to talk about what we're about to do. I want to make sure you don't freak out on me and do something crazy." Roberto frowns, pretending to be hurt. "We're just going to grab Sunny and run. That's it. No paybacks or anything. We'll let the law do the justice part once we've got the girl. It's what Kim's been fighting for all along. And it's still more her fight than ours." I don't tell him about how Fast had been one of the men who had humiliated Kim twelve years before, causing the loss of her eye. I don't need to stoke the fire already raging within him.

He laughs. "Yeah, right. Justice. 'The law shows her teeth, but dares not bite.' I read that somewhere. Some old poet."

"I'm serious, 'Berto. I'd leave you behind if I could."

But I can't. If Kim and I are going to confront Fast and Burgermeister and rescue Sunny, we need some of Roberto's madness. Unleashing it, though, has me as nervous as the danger to ourselves. I stifle my second thoughts—it's too late to change the plan now. I know that if I leave him alone and bored, he'll get into some serious trouble and wind up back in jail where more killers are waiting for him. And I'd lose a half million bucks.

"You never could leave me behind, little bro. I'm always a step ahead of you, you know. But don't worry. I'll behave." The grin he gives me along with another wink doesn't inspire much confidence.

Kim comes back just as the train's whistle shrieks twice and the conductor, dressed in an old-fashioned engineer's suit and cap, shouts, "All aboard!" Plastic shopping bags dangle from her wrists. Roberto and I shove them into climbing packs and the three of us hop up the steps into an open car just as the train starts to move.

Leaving the depot, the train chugs at a snail's pace. When I stop the conductor and demand to know the reason for the exasperating lack of speed, he informs me that for safety reasons the train can't go faster than ten miles an hour until we're outside of town. I can't believe how far the small town's suburbs stretch. Heading north, we pass the Forest Service entrance to Wild Fire Valley to our right. I don't see any patrol cars parked at the base, but it's hard to tell because of the trees that line the tracks beside us. If what the deputy had told Roberto is true, the sheriff's men will be out of sight and up the road somewhere, hoping to catch us stepping past a newly posted "No Trespassing" sign.

The northern valley we enter is broad at first. Ahead, though, through the black cloud of coal exhaust coming off the engine's furnace and the stinging ashes, I can see that it narrows and deepens. A river of turquoise water gurgles, rushes, and boils to one side. It takes a long, long time before we're past the last of the town's trailer parks and cute trackside cabins.

While Roberto paces through the cars, drawing the usual admiring glances from the women and nervous looks from the men, Kim stands on the car's east side staring at the yellow-leafed aspens on the steep hillside that divides us from Wild Fire Valley. On an impulse I step up behind her and put my arms around her waist. She cocks her head back a little, rolling her dirty hair into the side of my neck and jaw. Her taut buttocks feel good against my hips. I remember the warmth of her shivering, naked skin last night.

"It's beautiful," she says quietly.

"I wish we were doing this under different circumstances."

She sighs. "I haven't figured it out yet, Anton. What I'm going to do with you, I mean." Then she looks around. "There's people staring at us, wondering what the handsome young man is doing grinding on his mom."

I laugh. "You were a young mother, then. All of nine years old." I push my hips against her butt again.

"I feel and look years older."

"I hear having only one eye can affect depth perception," I say with my lips brushing her ear. "The only reason people are staring is because they're wondering how a scar-faced freak like me is lucky enough to get to grope a tragic beauty like you. Should we sneak into the bathroom or something? It looked big enough when I was in there earlier." She elbows me in the ribs.

Finally away from the town, the train starts picking up speed.

THIRTY-FOUR

WHEN THE CONDUCTOR comes by collecting tickets and pointing out landmarks to the tourists, Kim talks to him and explains that we want to go backpacking. She asks if he's willing to stop the train when we're near the back side of Wild Fire Peak. He's reluctant, but it's hard to say no to a beautiful one-eyed woman. And even harder with Roberto and me standing by her side, looking determined. He agrees to stop the train for just a few seconds near an old mining camp on the side of the river we've been following up-canyon. He advises us to be ready—we need to immediately leap off so that he can stay on schedule.

Roberto and I shrug our way into the two packs we'd brought while Kim laces her running shoes tight.

The train chugs to a halt in a grove of aspens near where the river boils with rapids. Up until this moment, I hadn't realized that we would have to cross the river. But instead of taking a chance and trying to convince the conductor to make yet another stop once the train passes over a bridge, I quickly climb off the train and am followed by Kim and my brother.

As soon as we hit the dirt the train starts rolling again. The conductor had been serious about only stopping for a few seconds. As the cars full of tourists pass by, they wave to us, as if we're embarking on some great and dangerous adventure. We are, but they can't possibly know that. In just a minute or two the train is only a distant wisp of black smoke drifting into the sky. The whistle blasts twice again in farewell.

"That's it. Wild Fire Peak." Kim points at a jagged summit that rises at the end of the valley like a shark's tooth. It must grow three thousand feet out of the valley's end, all of it either vertical granite, dirty ice-choked couloirs, or steep fields of talus. I would never have recognized it—from the meadow on the other side, the mountain slopes gently and the lower two-thirds are thickly forested.

I had hoped to find an easy pass leading to the other side, but there is a sawtooth ridge to both sides of the summit, just five or six hundred feet beneath it. We're going to have to climb the damn thing almost all the way to the top.

"Maybe this wasn't such a good idea," Kim says. "I forgot how imposing it is."

Although it definitely is imposing, I feel confident because of the lightweight ropes and harnesses I'd had the foresight to stuff in my pack. Once past the tree line, I think we can weave our way up on the slopes of talus and along some sharply angled ledges. I hadn't thought to bring axes and crampons, so the speediest and safest method of ascent up the couloirs isn't an option. Beside me Roberto smiles at the peak. From this side, it's his kind of mountain.

"It'll go all right," I tell her. "What I'm more worried about is the river."

"Let's swim it, bro."

That's something I really don't want to do. The water is moving fast enough to make even wading dangerous, and it looks more than a few feet deep. Besides, the river is pure glacial meltwater. It's probably not more than a few degrees above freezing—cold enough to seize the blood in our limbs and make us hypothermic within minutes. This is the real thing, not like the desert lake water that had caused my teeth to chatter all last night and this morning. For a minute I feel unbearably cold again, even though I'm standing in the mountain sunlight. I can't suppress a shiver.

I walk out to the top of the steep bank and look up and down the river, hoping to spot a shallower crossing. There's cable drooped across the river a little ways away. It appears to be strung between two pines on opposite shores.

"What's that?" I ask Kim.

"I don't know. Probably some sort of old mining thing, some sort of pulley line."

We hike down to it. The cable is nearly an inch thick. The end on our side of the river is wired high up in a pine, which has old boards nailed to the trunk, making a sort of ladder up to a rotting platform.

"It'll beat swimming," I tell them.

"Shit. I was looking forward to seeing your girlfriend naked. Or at least in a wet T-shirt."

Surprisingly, Kim laughs.

I drop my pack and pull out the two lightweight harnesses I'd brought. With some webbing, I tie a third.

Roberto ascends the ladder and without a second thought clips a short sling from his harness to the cable. He shoves off from the tree's trunk with a powerful thrust of his legs and shouts a yodel of delight. Sailing out over the river, he travels at an incredible speed until just past the river's center and the bottom of the cable's droop. Past that, the upward momentum causes him to slow. Near the top of the inverted arc, he grabs the cable with his hands before he starts to slide backwards.

"He makes it look fun," Kim says to me.

"Your turn."

She climbs up to the platform and clips the locking carabiner to the cable as I'd instructed, but then she hesitates. She looks dubiously at where the cable is tied to the tree. Then she stares out at the droop above the river. I realize that from her perspective, and lack of depth perception, it probably looks like the wire runs straight down into the thrashing rapids. She looks down at me and shakes her head. "I don't know if I can do it."

"You've just got to go for it."

"How about telling me something helpful, Anton?"

"Okay. Put your eye patch over your good eye."

She looks at me without even a trace of humor in her expression.

"Just trust me," I say, sincerely now. "You'll be fine. Trust me."

She nods twice, closes her eye, takes a breath, and

leaps. She doesn't give an exuberant shout like my brother, but I'm pleased that she doesn't scream in fear either. Rotating in slow circles, she shoots past the droop to where Roberto still hangs from the cable, holding himself in place with one hand. He snags the back of her harness with the other.

I wait until they've pulled their way to the platform on the other side, not wanting my added weight to bring the whole cable down. Once they're across, I make the ride, too, and do my best to imitate Roberto's wild cry of exaltation. It lacks his authenticity.

For two hours we hike fast up the rising depression toward tree line at the base of the naked rock. I'm impressed that Kim moves without complaint and without apparent effort. All that long-distance running must be worth something. By the time we emerge out from the last of the wind-twisted pines, all three of us are slick with sweat. I can smell the strong odor of sun and exertion rising off me. I lick Kim's bare shoulder to taste the salt. Looking back, she smiles at me and shakes her head.

At tree line—about twelve thousand feet—there's a cool wind. It's getting darker, too—the sun is sinking past the mountains on the other side of the river. In another hour or so it'll be full night. We pull back on shirts, then jackets, as we choose a likely route up broken ledges and steep slopes of talus to the ridge just left of the summit.

"We should probably start trying to be quiet," I tell them. "They may be holding Sunny in those trailers up by the burnt-out lodge—they'll hear us if we bang around too much. And we should fuel."

Stopping for food is the last thing I want to do. But we'll need energy and fluids in our systems for the remaining climb up to the ridge and then down into the valley. And for whatever comes after that. For all I know, Fast and his pals may have already forced Sunny to show them the cave. They may have already killed her. At least we haven't heard any blast of dynamite, the sound of which I'm sure would carry all over these mountains. Or a gunshot.

None of us sit as we swallow sticky hunks of PowerBars and gulp down a quart of water each. Sitting would just make it that much harder to stand. Belatedly, I remember that I should have told my father what we're doing in case something goes wrong. I take the cell phone from the hip pack I wear reversed on my waist and hit the power button. "No Service," the screen reads. Within five minutes we're moving again.

The scramble to the ridge starts with a field of talus that rises nearly five hundred feet to a low-angled slab. The individual stones composing the steep field are large and fairly stable. Roberto hops from one to the next like a mountain goat, his movements pure and unhesitating. Kim moves more haltingly at first, and I try to stay near her side so that I can put out a stabilizing arm if the need arises. But within a few minutes she's gotten the hang of it and is moving with her usual grace.

The smooth slab above us rises another two hundred or so feet. It's steep enough to require the use of both hands and feet, which we smear against the weather-polished granite, while feeling for any edge or wrinkle. I consider taking the time to put a rope around Kim and belay her to the top, but decide it would take too much time.

"Keep your butt high in the air," I advise her instead.

"It seems counterintuitive, but your feet will have more friction against the stone that way."

Just as she'd done on the cable across the river, Kim nods at me in a way that says, "Okay, I'm scared, but I trust you," and starts up. That look makes me feel guilty—I'm putting speed ahead of her safety. But often in the mountains speed *is* safety. Especially when considering Sunny's safety, and how every minute she remains in Fast's control puts her in greater danger.

I try to stay just behind Kim, thinking that if she slips maybe I can arrest the fall. In truth, if she slips she'll just kill us both. She doesn't, though, and ten minutes later we're on a good ledge at the base of a cliff.

Roberto has already scouted ahead. He says he's found an ascending ledge that he thinks goes all the way up to the ridgeline to one side of the summit. Unfortunately, it's too dark now to know for sure. We drink off another half-quart of water each then follow him up.

Roberto's ledge is frightening. It would be scary even in the daylight. Between two and four feet wide, it rises steeply and at the same time slopes down toward the cliff. If any one of us falls, we'll bounce off the wide spot far below where we'd rested, then grate down the two hundred feet of slab. It would be a very bad way to die. To make matters worse, the ledge is covered with small, round stones that feel as if they could easily roll under our feet like ball bearings.

Up ahead and above, I can see stars to the west through a keyhole-like slot in the ridge. When Kim and I are just fifty feet from it, we meet Roberto, who is scrambling back down.

"Doesn't go," he tells us. "There's some big fucking

cliff on the other side and I can't tell if the rope will reach."

What he means is that he can't be sure a rappel on my doubled ropes will reach solid ground on the valley side of the mountain. Long ago and many times, Dad had lectured us about how one of the most foolish things you can do is to rappel at night when you're unsure if the ropes are long enough to reach a ledge. If you make an error, you'll be stuck swinging at the knots on the rope's ends. There's no way we can check the distance with our flashlights because lights high up on the peak could easily be seen from down in Wild Fire Valley. And other than my small Beretta, surprise is our only weapon.

Roberto moves off our ledge to the left, gripping unseen holds on the cliff face with his hands and the toes of his boots. Within seconds he's slipped into the darkness. I try not to think of the void beneath him. I'm worried, although I know this is nothing compared to some of the things he's soloed. Still, all it takes is one loose handhold...

While we wait for him to find a better route, I once again take out my cell phone and punch a button to activate the night-light. There's finally a connection, but just barely. The signal reads one-by-four. I realize it must be ten o'clock on the East Coast and suspect my father will be at his desk unless he's already left for Bosnia or Egypt. When I direct-dial his office, the connection is maintained despite the hissing and scratching sounds coming over the receiver.

"Air Force. Colonel Burns," his perpetually calm voice answers.

"Dad. It's me."

"Anton, are you okay?"

"No problems so far, but I may get cut off because my signal's not too good."

"—barely hear you. Where are you, Ant?"

"High on Wild Fire Peak, headed for that red cliff above the meadow. Roberto's with me. And Kim Walsh. We're going after the girl. I just wanted you to know."

There's a few seconds of silence on the other end. I start to wonder if I've lost the signal when the colonel says very clearly, "Back off, Anton. Now. That's an order. You get the hell out of there and let the locals or the Feds handle this!" His voice is still calm, but his words are so short and clipped that after a lifetime of knowing him, I recognize that inside he's shouting.

"I can't do that, Dad. The local sheriff might be in on it, and the Feds don't believe us. In any event, the valley's been sealed off now. They closed the road. So we're going in through the back door. It's now or never. They're going to kill the girl, Dad, once she gives them what they want. Remember her? That pretty blonde in the meadow we met our first day there?" I want the image of the vibrant young girl in the skimpy top and too-short shorts to be in his head.

There's a long hiss of static. I hear only a few words of my father's reply, and understand just two. "I'm coming."

The scratching over the receiver fades to nothing but the hair is standing on my arms. Those two words send a thrill through me. *He's coming.* He's far too late of course, but still, he's coming. All those years of indoctrination about family loyalty at all costs—it had been the truth.

THIRTY-FIVE

ROBERTO PULLS HIMSELF back up on our precarious ledge. His teeth are like tiny white cubes in the night. "Found it," he says. "We've got to traverse down and to the left 'bout a hundred feet. No sweat."

"Kim's not a climber, 'Berto."

"Guess it's a good time for her to learn."

I dump the rope out of my pack then put together the small selection of gear I'd brought. Roberto wordlessly takes the gear while giving me a long, significant look. Then he takes one end of the rope and disappears once again.

"There's no time to do this right," I tell Kim, helping her back into her harness. "Just try and follow the rope to the left. Use whatever hand- and footholds you can. Roberto's going to set some pro along the way, so if you fall, you won't swing too far. But the trick is that you have to unclip the rope from any gear you pass. I'll be right behind you. Do you understand?"

She starts to nod, then shakes her head. So I run through it again.

"What about you?" she asks. "If I'm taking the rope, then what's going to protect you?"

"Don't worry. I can handle it."

"Why don't you tie in to the rope, too?"

"Because then if I fell, I'd pull you off. And both our weights might be too much for this skinny rope. And it might be too much for the shitty belays Roberto likes to set."

"Are you as good a climber as he is?"

"Actually, I'm better. Trust me one more time."

After a moment's hesitation, she too disappears into the darkness over the side of the ledge.

I pull on my backpack, tightening the chest and shoulder straps but leaving the waist loop undone. I don't want it to pull my shoulders down. For a moment I listen to Kim panting in the darkness just a few feet away. While the long hike up the mountain's side had been nothing for her exertion-wise, the fear now is causing her heart to race and her lungs to accelerate as if she were sprinting, even though she's only moving at a sloth's pace. The suck of gravity can do that to you. I feel my own pulse speed up a notch as I lower myself over the side after her.

The holds are good. I find fat flakes for my hands and feet. Below and to the left, I can hear Kim breathing like she's in a race. She's silhouetted by the starlight, just ten feet away. "I'm right behind you. You're doing fine."

"Shit. Shit. Shit."

"Remember the rope, Kim. If you fall, it will catch you."

Gamely she keeps moving down and left, following the rope into the night. I try to stay just ten or so feet behind her. The rocks are getting looser—we're getting to a rotten part of the wall, and it has me worried. One protruding flake Kim had just used as a handhold comes off in my hand. With a shiver, I put it back instead of dropping it. We keep moving.

"Anton!" Kim says. "What do I do?"

The part we're on has turned vertical and I'm afraid to look too hard at the holds she's gripping. Leaning back to look beyond her, I see that the cliff inverts. A part of the rotten wall has fallen away as if some gigantic ice cream scoop has gouged out a portion of the mountain. And the rope leads on into the night just above the scooped-out part. *Fucking Roberto,* I think unreasonably.

There's a sort of rim that the rope trails laterally across. A kind of huge upthrusting flake that must be solid or it would surely have fallen away with the rest of the face years ago.

"Okay, Kim, here's what you do."

There's white all the way around her single eye when I quietly explain that she needs to grip the edge with her hands, then hook her right heel up there, too. With the stronger muscles of her leg she can take some of the weight off her hands. "Just go across hand-over-hand, keeping as much weight as you can on that heel. You'll be fine."

"You're kidding." There's just a trace of delirious humor in her voice.

"No. Are you having fun yet?"

She spits out a short laugh. I realize that she's having

an epiphany of sorts, that she's feeling the bite of the Burns family's first drug. Noradrenaline. The depth of the void beneath us is incalculable in the night.

I cling to a couple of lousy holds and watch her make her way across. I have to struggle to keep from shouting out encouragement. And then shouting in fright when her heel slips off the edge.

For a sickening moment she's floating in space. Her hands alone battle gravity while her feet kick above the dragging weight of the darkness beneath her. She swings like a child from monkey bars, only there's no soft playground sand to catch her if she falls—only jagged rock, far below. I try to see if Roberto has managed to put in some protection nearby but all I can see is the thin purple line running on to the left and into the night, hanging free. Obviously he hadn't found any cracks to plug in gear.

If she comes off, she'll drop, picking up speed, until the rope catches on a distant piece of pro. That will jerk her to the left and slam her into the side of the scoop, wherever that is. I tense and pray, waiting for her to swing off into the night, already hearing the sound in my head of her body smashing against stone.

But once again Kim is game. She gets her right heel hooked back up on the edge with her hands. Her breath is coming now like a bellows. Then she starts moving away from me, until she slowly follows the rope into the blackness.

Ropeless and unprotected, I make the same moves. And as usual, I can't help but smile to myself as Death tugs at my free ankle. In my mind I kick him in his bony face.

Soon I've caught up to Kim again, who's scrambling

sideways on thankfully solid rock. After another twenty feet I can see Roberto's shadow taking in the rope from a starlit notch in the ridge. Kim and I both drop into a small platform in the notch with relief.

"Nice job," he tells me quietly as I step past him and study the valley on the other side. I think about how just a few days before, Wild Fire Valley had seemed like the glorious temple of my father's youth. Now it looks much more ominous, especially now that I know that Cal's tales of caves and Indian ruins are true. The valley has a dark and hidden life below the earth. It's a temple full of secrets, one that occasionally demands blood sacrifices to nurture its soil.

Roberto was right about this being a good passage across the ridge and down. A long field of large talus leads all the way down the west side of the mountain to tree line. We're looking out over the dark valley from somewhere near the peak's summit. From two thousand feet below us and a little to the right comes the distant hum of a gasoline-powered generator. I can see lights on in one of two white construction trailers parked near the burnt-out remains of Fast's mid-mountain lodge. A couple of trucks gleam in the moonlight nearby. One of them looks like Fast's black Suburban.

I hear no tortured screams, which I guess is a good thing, but I'd sure like to know if Sunny is alive.

"You see that?" Kim asks.

She and Roberto stand on either side of me. Like me, they're both staring down into the valley. I follow the outline of Kim's pointing arm to the treeless expanse of the meadow, and close to it, the darker shadow of the crumbly red cliff on the hill. A few flashlights wink among the trees near the hill's base.

"I saw Sunny and Cal rappelling down that cliff the first day I got here," I say. "That's it. The cave's somewhere on it."

The cliff is invisible in the night, but the flashlights appear to be slowly working their way up the hill from the side.

"Let's go," Roberto says.

He leads the way down Wild Fire Peak, hopping from one boulder to the next on the long talus field. He seems to float above the ground like a phantom. And Kim follows right behind him. She too is amazingly surefooted now in the night. As I descend after them, my pack's zippers jingle softly. I wish I'd had the forethought to tape them. While it had taken us hours to climb the peak's back side, it seems like just minutes until we're back below tree line.

We enter the dark pines and the bone-white trunks of aspen groves, skirting well clear of the trailers and the burnt-out lodge. At the point when we're closest to them, just a hundred or so yards away, I can hear country music playing from inside. And the sounds of rough laughter. I'm tempted to peek in the windows but I don't think Sunny will be there—she'll be where the flashlights are ascending the small hill, guiding them to Cal's Bad Cavern.

Roberto finds a hiking trail and we jog carefully down it, trying to plant our feet as softly as possible and not trip over exposed roots.

The meadow is eerily quiet and vacant. It's hard for me to believe that just days ago it was swelling with activity. The environmentalists have been forced to end their vigil by the approval of the land exchange. They probably would have left anyway—there's been too much violence and death around here. And there's about to be more.

The flashlights are above us now, moving through the trees toward the hill's summit. They're about eight hundred feet up the gently sloping hillside. I call a halt in the trees after we sprint across the meadow.

"Here's the plan," I tell them as we huddle together, all three of us panting lightly from our rapid descent. "The cave is somewhere on the cliff face, but it's hidden enough that they need Sunny to show it to them. So they're going to set up a rappel on the top, the way Cal and Sunny did. When they find it, they'll dynamite it." Probably with Sunny inside, but I don't say it because I don't want Kim thinking about it.

"So this is what we're going to do. I'm going to go up the hill alone. With my gun. You two wait about halfway down. The three of us going all the way up together would make too much noise.

"I'm going to sneak up on them and pull my gun. I'll shout when I've got whoever's up there covered. Then you'll come up. Roberto will take any weapons and throw them off the cliff. Kim will go immediately to Sunny. Then we'll disappear into the woods and hopefully not see those fuckers again outside of a jail or a courtroom."

"Give me the gun. Let me be the one to go up," Roberto says. "You crash through the trees like a fucking rhino, bro."

"No, it's got to be me. You're on bond, 'Berto. Can't have a weapon, remember?" Besides, I know that Roberto has even less faith in the legal system than I do. A part of me is afraid he'll just shoot them all and spare the courts any trouble.

"Why not capture them? Tie them up or something?" Kim asks.

"We'd never get them out of here. Remember, the sheriff's men, Fast's men, are blocking the only road into the valley. And there's no way the three of us can get a bunch of prisoners out the way we came in. We'll have to deal with them later."

Kim gives my hand a squeeze before I move off. Her fingers are trembling, but I can't tell whether it's with anger or fear.

THIRTY-SIX

THE FOREST FLOOR is covered with a thin layer of yellow aspen leaves. They crinkle beneath my boots as I make my way up the slope with my flat little Beretta in my hand. Worse, the bright fallen leaves reflect the moon and starlight, illuminating everything in the forest with a ghostly glow. As I creep closer to the top of the hill and ponder the very real possibility that I may be about to get shot—that I might get us all killed—I feel a twinge of regret that I hadn't given Roberto the gun. There's no doubt in my mind that he would be willing and able to use it against the men who are holding Sunny. That he's capable of pressing the .22 to a temple and pulling the trigger, which is the only sure way to end things with such a small gun. He certainly wouldn't have any of my or Kim's qualms about keeping them alive so we can bring them to justice.

Roberto has his own brand of justice. And although right now I'm inclined to agree with him, I'm still too much of a cop to turn my approval into up-close, very personal action.

Distant voices drift down in the night from the hill's summit. Men's voices. I hear Burgermeister issuing orders in his deep bass and Fast responding, but I can't make out the words. I grip the little gun tighter in my sweaty palm and check for the fifth time to be sure the safety is switched off.

Sunny's high voice is clear, cutting through the dense forest. "Please. Don't do this. Please."

The last word is cut off by the sharp slap of a hand striking flesh. "This better be the right place, bitch. I'm not coming up here twice," Burgermeister says.

As my pulse starts racing, I struggle to move slowly, quietly. I measure my breaths, inhaling and exhaling with a steady rhythm. I focus on moving like some night creature, like Roberto, a coyote on the hunt, gliding soundlessly through the trees. Stalking.

The flashlights are visible now through the foliage above and ahead of me. And the voices are louder. I move forward at irregular intervals, hoping that the crunch of leaves under my boots will seem innocuous in the night. I can smell the strong odor of a burning cigar wafting down on the late summer breeze. Just ahead, the forest ends near the hill's summit, which has been swept almost clean of trees by another season's harsher winds.

The two men stand near Sunny in the sparse clearing. In the glow of a flashlight, I can see the three figures gathered near a single bent shrub. Sunny is awkwardly pulling a climbing harness over her legs. Even in the dark I can see that her limbs are visibly shaking. But despite the sobbing and quivering, she puts on the harness with jerky, mechanical motions. Burgermeister's huge form is obvious. He's looping a rope around the shrub, setting up a rappel. A red ember burns in front of his face, giving his features an evil orange glow. In one hand he holds the flashlight. David Fast stands nearby. There's the shape of a gun in his hand.

I crouch behind some brush, scanning the clearing and finally spotting Burgermeister's twin-barreled shotgun propped against the shrub. It's within his easy reach, leaning on the same plant he's just finished tying the rope to. Staring at it, I think, *That's what he used to shoot my dog*. I let the memory of last night roll over me like a cold wave. The anger washes away my fear.

Sunny, in a harness now, lies collapsed on the grass. She's speaking to the earth, the sounds pleading but at the same time flat and weak. "Please. Don't make me go down there. Please. Don't destroy it. Please. I swear I won't tell anyone..." It sounds almost like a chant, a useless mantra, that she's been mumbling for hours.

The drone of her pleas makes it clear that her mind has all but fled from here. In the last forty-eight hours she's been beaten, seen her lover brutally murdered, been told her remaining friends had been shot, and probably been raped. Animals like Burgermeister would need to play with and torture their prey.

"You're right about one thing, honey," the big man's deep voice growls from behind his cigar. "You won't tell anyone about it."

"Let's just get this over with, Alf," Fast says tiredly.

Burgermeister reaches down and grabs Sunny by her

neck. He lifts her to her feet. "Get on down there. This had better not be some wild-goose chase." He pushes the rope through the belay device on her harness and shoves her toward the cliff.

Sweat is running into my eyes, stinging and burning. I wipe it away with my sleeve, then take three deep breaths. *Time to move.*

I come out of the trees and walk quietly toward them. The brilliance of each star in the sky above seems to intensify; the air seems full of sound and scent. I can feel every stone, blade of grass, and twig beneath my boots. The world condenses to just this place.

At the first sign they're aware of my presence, when Burgermeister's cigar jerks in my direction, I squeeze the trigger of the small Beretta. I hear the hammer fall on the bullet, the explosion of gases, and the .22 caliber projectile spinning out of the short barrel to slice through the night above the men's heads. A thunder strike breaks open the cloudless black sky like a sign from God.

"Federal agents!" I shout. "You're surrounded! Put down your guns!"

The two men leap as if they've been electrocuted. Sunny's small form remains heartbreakingly still.

Fast, with the pistol still in his hand, hesitates.

"Drop it! Now!" I scream at him. I fire a second shot just over his head. The pistol bounces on the soft earth at his feet.

"Who the fuck are you?" Burgermeister asks in his dead man's voice. There's not a trace of fear in it.

I can hear Kim and Roberto thrashing through the leaves as they run up the hill.

"Shut up. Move away from her."

"Sure thing, partner." And he shoves Sunny over the edge of the cliff.

She screams as she falls, her white arms windmilling in the air before she disappears from sight. A second later the shrub gives a violent jerk as the rope around it goes taut. Sunny's belay device had automatically stopped her fall.

"Watch the rope!" I shout as Kim and Roberto burst out of the trees. Then, without thinking, I aim the Beretta at Burgermeister's left thigh and pull the trigger. In my sensory-enhanced state, I think I hear the bullet smack flesh before the explosion echoes through the night. He goes down without a sound. I'm disappointed the tiny bullet didn't have the force to blow him over the edge, too.

"Where's Sunny?" Kim's shouting from behind me.

"She went over the cliff—but she's tied in. Check on her." My gun is pointed at Fast's chest now, my index finger tight on the trigger.

Kim runs to the edge. Roberto stalks up to where Burgermeister's massive form is curled on the ground. He's acting like he's dead. But I don't believe it—a single .22 caliber bullet wouldn't kill a man that size, even if I'd hit him in the chest. And my aim isn't that bad. His cigar smolders in the grass an inch from his lips.

"Remember me?" I hear Roberto ask him.

"Sunny!" Kim's yelling.

"Get out of my line of fire!" I yell at my brother.

Roberto's boot blasts into Burgermiester's face with lightning speed. Sparks and burning ash explode from the cigar. If it hadn't been for that and the big man's head snapping back, I wouldn't have even seen my brother's leg move.

"Cut it out, Roberto!" I shout. Then at Kim, "Do you see her?"

My brother has moved on until he's standing before Fast. I start to yell again, "Get out of my line—" but my command isn't finished before Roberto punches Fast in the face. Fast sags backwards into the grass, sitting down hard and holding his nose.

"There's a gun by his feet—kick it off the cliff," I tell my brother, hoping for once he'll listen. He doesn't. He bends and picks up the gun.

"Kim?" A small voice calls from the darkness beyond the cliff's edge.

"Sunny! It's me! How far down are you?"

"Oh, Kim!" comes the sobbing reply. "I can't tell. I don't know."

"Ask her if she can climb back up," I order.

Headlights flash on near the trailers and the burnt-out lodge halfway up Wild Fire Peak. Two different pairs. I can hear the roar of racing engines as they begin to bang and weave their way down the mountain. Toward the meadow. Fast's and Burgermeister's men must have been alerted by the gunfire. *Shit*.

"We've got to get the fuck out of here, bro," Roberto tells me.

Almost at my feet and still curled in a massive ball, Burgermeister grunts a painful curse. Finally his voice has some feeling in it. He's holding his thigh with both hands. "That's how my dog felt," I tell him. "You shot him in the leg, too."

I walk to the shrub with the rope tied to it. I feel the

knot—it's tied securely. And all three of us still have our harnesses on. I take Burgermeister's shotgun by the barrel and sling it out over the edge.

"We'll rap it. You go down first and get Sunny," I say to Roberto. "I'll hold them while you guys get to the ground. If the rope doesn't reach, we'll find a ledge or something and traverse from there." I have an image in my head of the three of us—four with Sunny—gliding silently down to the meadow and then disappearing into the forest. There's no other way. With more of Fast's men coming, there's no time to haul Sunny back up and run from here.

"Fuck holding them," Roberto advises. "Just shoot 'em."

I'm tempted. My brother adds, sliding back and forth the chamber on Fast's gun with a vicious snap, "If you don't, I will."

Kim shouts at us. "No! Remember, Anton! This is mine! I want to see that bastard taken down in court!"

"Fuck that, too." Roberto lifts the pistol so that it's pointed at Fast's forehead. Fast is kneeling just ten feet away, his hands still gripping his own face. "I'm afraid you don't get your day in court, buddy."

With my free hand I grab the gun, pulling it toward me instead of Fast. "No, 'Berto. She's right. This is hers. We do it her way." I don't add that if he shoots them he'll spend years, if not the rest of his life, in prison. They'll nail him for everything they can, even if it's only violating his probation. I don't say it because it won't do any good—Roberto has no concern for consequences.

There's a slight tug as Roberto thinks about pulling the gun away from me.

"I want to see him in court!" Kim shouts again. "I want to ruin him. In public!"

"Twelve years ago," I say softly, talking fast, "he got her so drunk that she passed out. Maybe drugged her, too. Then he and his buddies stripped off her clothes. They touched her, they took pictures. And later that night she lost her eye while retching in a sink. This is her deal, 'Berto. Her call."

Roberto lets go of the gun.

"You're wrong, you know," he tells Kim. "A rich shit like him can afford a different type of law. But like my little bro said, I guess it's your call."

I throw Fast's pistol over the cliff, too. I don't want it anywhere near us, where it might tempt my brother into changing his mind.

Roberto manages to twist the rope, taut with Sunny's weight, through his belay device. "How far down?" he asks me. When I tell him I don't know, he grins at me. We're both thinking the same thing—we're breaking one of Dad's cardinal rules. "Soon as our weight's off, you come down," he tells Kim. Then he disappears over the edge.

While I keep my gun pointed at Fast, and Burgermeister remains curled in a massive ball, Kim keeps a hand on the rope, waiting for it to go slack. I explain to her how to push it through her belay device. And how to brake the rope with one hand. It seems like minutes go by as the headlights bounce down the dirt road to the valley's floor and then across the meadow.

Finally Kim says, "It's slack!"

"Push it through," I tell her. "Remember to brake."

She jumps up and shoves the rope through the piece of metal hanging from the front of her harness. Then she backs to the cliff's edge. I hope Roberto thinks to give her a fireman's belay from below. If she starts an out-of-control slide, by pulling the free end of the rope tight he can lock it in her belay device.

"Go!" I say. With a final look at me, she disappears over the edge.

I realize that there's no way I can rappel fast enough to hit a ledge or the bottom before one of my captives can either cut or somehow destroy the rope. Looking at Fast and Burgermeister on the grass before me, I give serious thought to shooting them both. But I can't. Not just because of Kim's command, but also because I don't have my brother's wild streak. I can't just shoot them in cold blood.

Below the hill the trucks slow to a stop at the edge of the forest. In a few seconds Fast's friends will be running up the hill. I hear doors slamming shut.

Burgermeister apparently is thinking the same thing I am. "You're all dead. You know that, don't you, Scarface?" I'm sure he's sneering at me in the dark.

"Bite me." I touch the rope with my boot and feel some slack. Roberto, Sunny, and Kim are either on the ground or on a ledge. It isn't easy to do while holding the gun on both men, but I manage to get the rope through my own belay device.

"What makes you think I won't just shoot you now?" I ask.

" 'Cause you're a pussy. Just like her."

I fire a shot into the grass in front of him. Then I

point the gun at Fast and say, "Start running. And drag that piece of shit with you." I want them as far away from the ropes as possible to give me at least a fighting chance of making it down. I can hear men crashing through the trees. Fast doesn't move, so I fire another shot. He bends and grabs his wounded partner's shirt to start pulling. The bigger man shoves him away and climbs unsteadily to his feet. I guess I'd just winged him earlier.

"You're dead, fucker," Burgermeister says to me. He's evidently collected himself—his voice is once again devoid of any emotion.

The two of them take a few steps back. Burgermeister is limping, holding his thigh with both hands.

"Move!" I shout. I fire my last bullets into the ground at their feet.

Even as I drop over the edge, I can see men with flashlights coming out of the trees. The last thing I see before the dark red cliff obscures my vision is Burgermeister's smiling face in the beam of a flashlight. The light flashes on a blade in his hand.

THIRTY-SEVEN

I'M SLIDING DOWN the rope so fast that the skin of my left palm begins to slough off as the rope burns through it. At first there's no pain, only the sensation of flesh peeling off like hot wax. Then an agonizing jolt of pain rips up my arm. I bite back a scream as I continue to drop down the cliff's face but don't let go of the rope. My abseil into the darkness is nothing more than a barely controlled fall.

Three pickups are visible far below me and to one side, parked where the flat meadow's grass ends and the forested hillside begins. A few doors have been left open. The cabs appear empty. Their headlights blaze into the woods. For a moment I think maybe we can steal one. But then I notice in some of the refracted light that reaches the cliff that it's far bigger than I remembered. There's no way a regular-length climbing rope will reach the ground.

I pray either Roberto or the men above have tied a knot onto the end of the line, because I'm descending so fast that I'll just slide right off the end of the rope.

Suddenly it's no longer an issue. I really am falling. The rope is no longer searing through the belay device—it's clenched and locked in the raw muscle of my palm. Burgermeister has cut the rope.

I'm toppling backwards in the night, starting to turn in a slow back flip, and hoping I'll at least turn all the way around before I deck out—I don't want to hit headfirst. But then maybe it's better to die clean than risking fifty years in a wheelchair. Headfirst doesn't seem so bad after all. Some barely conscious instinct has my free right hand whipping the slack rope around my thigh as the wind roars in my ears with the approach of terminal velocity.

This is how I've always known I will die. My mother, in moments of anger when she raged at my father for the needs and skills he taught Roberto and me, had predicted it long ago. She told him this addiction would kill us all, that Death waited for us in the great voids beneath rock walls. And for so many years I've teased that ugly cloaked skeleton, letting him snatch at my ankles and laughing as I rudely kick at his face.

WHAM!

I'm jerked to a stop, then thrown into the cliff. My body hits it with such force that the air is torn from my lungs. I want to howl in pain but air won't come back to me. The pain almost takes away my consciousness, too. A horrendous throbbing is shooting up my arm from my burnt left hand, my spine and ribs feel as if they've shattered on the wall, my lungs won't work, and where the rope's wrapped around my thigh it feels as if my leg's being crushed by some impossible weight. And that weight starts increasing with tiny jerks.

It takes me a minute to draw a haggard breath and figure out what's going on. There's no doubt I'm still alive—death could not possibly hurt so much. I'm hanging upside down with the cut rope wrapped around my thigh and locked in my belay device. Something has caught the other end. A new pain, a kick to the stomach, makes me realize that the belay device, overheated from the wild rappel, is burning through my jacket and shirt and is pressing against the bare flesh of my stomach. The tiny tugs keep constricting around my leg—suddenly I'm aware that I'm being slowly dragged into the sky.

I want to call out, to ask who's doing the hauling, but there's not enough air. It can't be Fast and Burgermeister, as they'd been the ones who'd cut the top end of the rope. So it must be Roberto. He must have gotten to a ledge or something and tied in with the lower, free end. I'd like to help but even the smallest movement is far beyond me right now.

I moan uncontrollably with each new tug. Staring out over the dark valley, I see men running down the hill and out of the trees now, running toward the two trucks. Engines rev. I watch their headlights swing out, then in, coming closer to focus on the base of the cliff.

The sound that comes from my mouth is what I remember Roberto once describing, after I'd taken a mogul full in the chest in a youthful attempt to ski a double-black-diamond run at Jackson Hole without turning, as a moose-call. The headlights below bounce like crazed puppies until they're aimed somewhere beneath me. I hear men's voices shouting. Then handheld deer-spotting lights are turned up toward me and the air around me becomes like the Fourth of July—there are the stars in the sky, stars in my head, and a whole new light show of other violent flares and explosions. *They're shooting at me.* I recall that in my two previous gunfights I'd felt like Superman, able to dodge bullets. Now I just feel like some celestial black hole, pulling them toward me with a force stronger than gravity.

Hands grab at my clothing and drag me over a sharp edge that tears at my ribs. Kim's voice is loud in my ear but still sounds very far away. Too distant to comprehend. Even though I'm finally on a relatively flat surface, the pain doesn't ease. The grasping hands, the shouting voices, they pull me up and over what feels like a low staircase before I'm shoved into a dark hole and dumped into total blackness. The only light comes from the stars swirling in my head.

"You shot? Anton! You shot?" It's my brother's voice shouting at me now. His words echo off the darkness in such an odd way that I figure I'm in a cave. Cal's cave. Cal's Bad Cavern. I want to respond but nothing will come from my lips but that low moose-call. I don't know what my response would be anyway.

A single blazing eye—the cyclops beam of a headlamp—begins cutting at me like a laser while hands roughly tear the rope from around my thigh. Then my clothes are being dragged off. I try to sit up but am shoved back down.

"I'm all right," I finally manage to rasp. "I think."

"No, *che,* you're totally fucked up." But my brother chuckles at my attempt to speak. "He knocked you down, but he didn't knock you out!"

"Who?"

"The Grim fucking Reaper, bro. He can't keep you down."

My burnt hand rages again as someone pours water over it. And then over my stomach. Soon the actions of the hands moving over me become less frantic. They don't push me down now when I try to sit up. "What's the . . . damage?" I ask, my voice so weak it's almost imperceptible to my own ears, as I move my good right hand over my parts.

It's Kim who answers. "I'd bet on some broken ribs, Anton. Can you wiggle your toes?" I flop my feet around on the uneven ground when the cyclops beam focuses there. "Good. You've got burns on your leg and stomach. On your left hand, too. But I don't think you were shot."

"Where?" I croak.

"In the cave."

"Sunny?"

"She's here."

"Let me see the light." My breath is finally coming back.

Roberto, the cyclops, pulls the headlamp off his head and puts it in my good hand. "Are *you* guys all right?" I shine it at the faces around me. Roberto's grinning, looking like an action-flick movie star who's just filmed the climax. Kim is breathing hard, her face streaked with dirt and red with exertion. Her good eye is alight with something other than fear. Anger, or maybe victory. Sunny is huddled against her, sobbing with her face buried against Kim's neck. Steam comes from everyone's mouth in the cool air of the cave.

"We're okay," Kim says. "You're the only one who's

physically damaged." Sunny, however, is clearly an emotional wreck. Kim gently touches her fingertips to my forehead for a second and then drags them down across my face. The pleasure it gives me is as intense as a kiss.

I shine the light beyond them and then all around. It's not a cave but a cavern. There's just a single opening—the one they'd dragged me through, which is a mere slot in the wall. It's just a foot and a half wide and maybe three feet high. Through it I can see the stars and hear the occasional snap of a rifle. Roberto tells me not to shine it there, not to give them any more of a target than they already have. I play the beam over my head and see a broken ceiling thirty feet high. I gasp again, but not from pain, when I shine the light behind us.

The cavern appears to extend back almost a hundred feet. The entire area is covered with crumbling mud huts. The ones directly behind us are low and squat; the ones against the cavern's walls on each side rise to the ceiling like tiny three-story condos. The flat surfaces and the maze of low brick walls are covered with broken pottery and stones that have fallen from the ceiling. Once the rubble-strewn area near the tiny opening must have been a great, broad ledge, allowing sunlight into the south-facing ruin. A centuries-old rockfall must have buried the ledge and hidden the tiny village. All but for the window-sized slot. Looking around, I think that this is how Howard Carter must have felt when he found King Tut's tomb. All that's missing is the gold.

"Holy shit."

I can't tell if I say it or it's Roberto. Maybe we both say it at the same time. But it's what all of us are feeling—all but Sunny, who has seen it before and who is now too demented with the aftermath of her captivity to appreciate it. It seems unreal to find ourselves in a place like this—where people once slept, made love, raised children, cooked over wood fires, and hid from their enemies. Only we can't hide here for long. Our enemies are more advanced. And they know just where we are.

"Is there another way out?" I shine the light at the cringing girl, hoping to somehow pull her out of her private pain. I'm thinking of the hole in the floor of the kiva she'd said Cal had shown her. A kiva, if I remember correctly, is some sort of ceremonial pit that's purpose is debated by archaeologists. Sunny doesn't appear to hear me—she continues crying into Kim's shoulder. She doesn't answer until I ask again in a harder voice.

"I don't know. Cal and I . . . we didn't get a chance to explore it."

"We aren't going out that way for a while," Roberto says, jerking a thumb at the opening. Pops of gunfire come from beyond it.

"How long do you think they'll wait for us?" Kim asks.

"As long as it takes. They can starve us out if they want. Or come in after us."

THIRTY-EIGHT

MY WORDS PROVE prophetic. No sooner have they left my lips than the rifle fire dies away and a moment later we hear a rattle of small stones on the ledge outside the entrance. Kim tries to take the light from me but I turn it out. Roberto crawls toward the opening—his shadow blocking out the tiny strip of stars. Beyond him, I can hear the rasp of a rope against nylon, like a snake sliding into a sleeping bag.

I grope my way up onto my knees, gasping with the effort, and feel for my gun. But it's nowhere to be found. I remember that I'd emptied it anyway. So I crawl behind my brother to the tiny opening. In a few inches of space over his shoulder, I can see the small ledge outside. Roberto crouches at the opening—a trap-door spider lurking in his hole.

Boots softly touch down on the ledge. A man's silhouette, smaller than either Fast or Burgermeister, is backlit by the handheld lights aimed up from the meadow. The developer and Rent-a-Riot are too cowardly to do the dangerous, dirty work for themselves. I feel almost bad for the short silhouette until I see him slap a hand to his side and make out the form of a leather holster there.

Roberto eases out onto the ledge. The man sees or hears him and tugs frantically at the holster.

My brother steps right up to him. "Hi," I hear him say, the way he might greet an acquaintance on the street. Then he pushes the man in the chest and laughs as the short shadow windmills on the edge for a moment before slowly teetering out into the night. A primal scream tears through the air. It's cut off with a thump on the talus far below.

"Flatlander," Roberto says disdainfully as he leans over the edge. "Didn't tie his backup knots. Posers shouldn't climb."

The rifle fire starts up again with renewed fury. Roberto takes two quick steps back toward the opening, then dives through, hitting me with the force of a tackle. I try not to scream from the pain in my damaged ribs while he rolls off me, laughing.

"What happened?" Kim is shouting at us in the dark.

A bullet finds its way through the entrance and zips briefly around the ruins. After two or three ricochets it buries itself in a dried mud wall somewhere. All of us scurry away from the opening, tripping over the ancient steps on the cave's floor. Our feet kick through a litter pile of pottery shards and shattered stones.

"They sent a guy down on a rope," I explain, still

racked with a myriad of sharp aches. "Roberto took care of him."

"Fuckers won't try *that* again."

"What are we going to do?" Kim asks when we've all caught our breath. With the headlamp turned back on but shielded by our bodies, we're huddled behind the hut closest to the entrance. I struggle to get back in my clothes. My body is wet with sweat and already starting to chill. Each movement, each inhalation, sends knives of pain stabbing through my ribs.

"I talked to Dad on the cell, 'Berto. When we were up on the ridge. He said he's coming."

Roberto is utterly still for a minute. He just stares into my eyes. I realize it's the first time I think I've ever seen him not moving, not animated. But his eyes are indescribably bright, almost creating a pale blue luminosity of their own. "He said that?" he asks finally.

I nod.

"A lot of fucking help that'll be." But his eyes are still shining.

"Can he help us?" Kim asks.

I shrug. "I don't know. He'll do all he can. But first he has to catch a flight out, and with the sheriff blocking the road he won't be able to get up here. And even if he can convince the Forest Service or the FBI that there's been a kidnapping, it'll still take time to get warrants and all that. Days, at the least. We've got to get out of here on our own. Before they figure out they can just lower some dynamite onto the ledge and blow this place away."

Dad may not be able to rescue us, but the look on my brother's face tells me that for a few hours at least the family's esprit de corps has been saved.

The rifle fire aimed at the tiny opening continues sporadically. Only an occasional bullet makes its way into the cavern. It would take a very fortunate bullet to ricochet into one of us. And we've already received more than our fair share of bad luck.

While Roberto guards the opening with a daggerlike rock in one hand, just in case any more of Fast's men are foolish enough to try to rappel in, Kim, Sunny, and I explore with the single headlamp. We move huddled together within the radius of the tiny beam of light that I try to keep pointed at our feet.

The pueblo or cliff dwelling or whatever it is seems smaller once we start moving around. I doubt if more than ten families could have lived here. The rooms within the adobe huts we peek into are tiny, the openings so low that even the women have to bend in half to fit through the open doorways. Inside they're all fairly regular and square in shape. There are some raised areas that I guess were used for sleeping. Ancient smoke has blackened some of the walls. The floors are littered with chunks of fallen dried mud mixed with broken pots. Everywhere there are hardened mouse turds.

"If the government knew this place really exists," Kim tells me, her voice filled with wonder, "there's no way they would even consider the swap. They would have laughed in Fast's face."

A sense of history is almost palpable. I can picture the huts swarming with lithe-muscled men, women, and children. They must have been very adept climbers to make this their home. The ruin has to be more than five hundred years old. I remember reading somewhere that the Anasazi are believed to have disappeared long before the

Spaniards began marching up from the south, killing Indians, then perversely building Christian missions in their wake. And I remember some more recent, darker headlines about the Anasazi—some archaeologists suspect they weren't the peaceable farming culture everyone had always romanticized them as. The articles referred to signs of clan warfare and ritual cannibalism.

The higher huts along the sides are inaccessible. Piles of rotten wood beneath them indicate that once ladders had been used to reach the openings high above our heads. I could probably hack hand- and footholds into the dry mud walls, but know it's not worth the effort and destruction.

The only structure that's different from these huts is all the way in the back of the cavern. A low, crumbling wall of large bricks has been built in a circle just ten feet in diameter against the rear wall. Enclosed within the circle is a pit. I shine the light down and the three of us lean over the wall carefully so that it doesn't collapse.

"That's the kiva," Sunny tells us. "Cal was going to take me in it."

There's a broken floor twenty feet down, littered with the same fallen stones and pottery that we'd found in the huts. A trickle of water runs down the cavern's back wall and into the pit but doesn't pool at the bottom. Instead it runs right down through a small dark hole in the stones. The sound of falling water is barely perceptible from beyond the hole. I remember Sunny telling us about how Cal had been down there—how he'd reported that there were passages everywhere. And possibly a connection to the outside.

I scramble down into the pit—the sides are less than

vertical, with lots of holds in the rough bricks. At the bottom, I move carefully to the hole, unsure if the entire floor is going to collapse beneath my weight. There's a small pile of stones near the opening where the water runs through—I guess that Cal had placed them there when he enlarged the opening enough to slide in. I lean over it and point the flashlight down.

"What's down there?" Kim asks.

The beam of light traces the trickle of silver water as it falls without touching rock for what I guess is about fifty feet. It's hard to tell, though, as the light is reflected back at me off a pool of water at the bottom. It looks like another cavern below us, but there's no way to tell how big it is because the hole is so narrow and long before it appears to open up.

"An underground lake or something. Maybe another cavern like this one."

Roberto calls out, "Hey, Ant, you'd better hear this."

I scramble back up out of the pit and the three of us pick our way back to him. Outside the rifle fire has stopped and a man is yelling. It's Burgermeister's voice.

"...one hour it's all coming down. You don't believe me, ask the girl. She knows we got the juice. So if you come out now, we'll see if we can work something out. Otherwise, you'd better put your heads between your legs and kiss your stupid hippie asses goodbye."

"He's talking about the dynamite," Sunny tells us. "They had crates and crates of it not far from the trailers. They showed it to me."

"How are they going to get it in here?" Kim asks.

Roberto points at the opening. "All they got to do is

lower it onto the ledge outside. That would be enough to bring the whole face down. The cave, too."

"We can't go out there. They'll kill us no matter what he says." Sunny's voice is high and tinged with the onset of fresh hysterics.

Kim puts her arm around her friend and former lover. "Easy. We aren't going out. It'd be better to stay in here, dynamite and all. Right, Anton?"

I lean out the opening and see the trucks backing away from the talus field at the cliff's base. They turn and drive into the meadow and I think for a moment that we can rappel down and have a chance of disappearing into the woods. But then one of the trucks turns and once again aims its high beams on the cliff. I hear the distant sound of doors slamming and know the men are getting out with their rifles. They'd just been putting some distance between themselves and the imminent explosion. The other truck continues up Wild Fire Peak toward the trailers. It's probably been sent to fetch the dynamite.

If we give up and go down, even if they don't shoot us as we slide down the rope, I have no doubt we'll all be killed. Fast and Burgermeister have nothing to gain by letting us live—and everything to lose. We have nothing to bargain with. And Fast knows about Kim's hatred for him. I pick up the packs and sling a strap from each over my aching shoulders.

"Get the rope, 'Berto," I tell Roberto with more confidence than I feel. "We're going spelunking."

THIRTY-NINE

"WHAT ARE YOU talking about, spelunking?" Kim whispers to me. "Are we going down the hole in the kiva?" The dark and the long-sleeping age of the ruin obliges us to keep our voices down.

"Unless you want to try and reason with those guys."

With the rope gathered over one shoulder, Roberto climbs down into the pit. I hold the light for him while he examines the hole at its base. He comes back up and begins a search for a crack or a stone solid enough to serve as anchor for a rappel. After examining several large boulders that have long ago been dislodged from the cave's roof, he pushes his shoulder against the biggest. It doesn't budge. It's probably sat in the same spot for hundreds of years. He loops the middle of the rope over it and drops the ends into the pit. All four of us then scramble down to squat by the dark hole. I feed the rope's ends into the unknown space beyond.

"Who's first?" Roberto asks. "Step right up. Don't be shy."

"I'll go." It's my idea and my responsibility.

But I desperately don't want to go into that slender cavity. I can't imagine anyone doing it voluntarily. I wonder if Cal had lied to Sunny about his trip into the depths—no one could have the courage to do such a thing, especially not alone. But I remember his mud-stained Gore-Tex shells and realize that he'd been a braver man than me.

I wish for another way—maybe Fast will listen to reason. Maybe he'll find some way to restrain his murderous partner. And maybe Burgermeister will forgive the bullet I fired through his thigh. Maybe they'll both forgive my brother his brutal punch and kick and Kim her years in search of revenge. *Right.*

This isn't my element. I belong on high and wild rock faces, the swirling wind all around me, not in some black pit like this. Especially not without light. But I have no choice and I hand Kim the headlamp so that each of them has light to tie in with.

I shove a bight of rope through my belay device and straddle the hole. *Oh shit.* I do everything I can to spend my life out in the open, unrestrained by walls and gravity, and here I am about to slide into an unknown hole that's skinnier than my mummy bag. Belatedly, I realize I'm claustrophobic, terrified of tight, enclosed spaces. I remember the utter panic I'd felt as a child when I woke up in a sleeping bag for the first time. Even now, twenty years later, I still sleep with the zipper undone to my waist no matter how cold the night. I'm ready to change my mind, to take my chances on reasoning with the killers outside. Even if they just put a bullet through my head, it would be better than the terror that's gripping my chest. Better than being buried alive.

Then Kim kisses my check. Roberto's holding the light on my face and I'm embarrassed, thinking that they can all see just how scared I am. Kim must, because she kisses me again, this time on the lips. She even lightly touches her tongue against my teeth.

"We don't have much time," she reminds me when she pulls away.

Leaning away from the boulder that holds the middle of the rope above, I place one foot at a time into the hole. I start lowering myself. The cold trickle of water immediately soaks through my fleece pants and runs down into my boots. As I wiggle my hips into the tight cleft, I realize that this is what it really feels like to have Death's bony hand grabbing my ankle. And here there is no room for me to kick.

The slot is even tighter than I'd thought. I squirm desperately against the cold, wet rock to fit my shoulders through. I almost get stuck and for a moment I want to scream. I imagine my body jammed into this cold hole at the bottom of the kiva, blocking the trickle of water as it slowly fills. But then I drop another inch. I turn my head to slide all the way in.

The fissure is probably only ten feet long but it feels like it goes on forever. It feels like I'm in the throat of some gigantic snake. Suddenly I notice that my feet are swinging free. Then my hips. And finally I'm released from its muddy grasp. But what's around me isn't much more comforting.

I'm suspended in a chamber that is smaller and higher than the one above. But it's hard to tell all the details because the light Kim's shining down the hole is growing dim. In the pale, dispersed beam I can make out steep walls that are riddled with holes, hopefully one of which is a passage. Pointed shapes are hanging beside me, like hanged men or jagged teeth. More sharp spikes rise up from the floor on the dry sides of the pool below. Directly beneath me is the water, which I pray is shallow. It appears clear and cold. The bottom of the pool is full of flakes of white stone.

"Hurry it up, Ant."

My brother's voice echoes off the walls and I remember that the dynamite could go off anytime now. I forget my own terror and am overtaken by fear for my brother, the young girl, and my potential lover above. I drop down the now wet rope and splash into the frigid water.

To my relief it's only knee-deep. My feet crunch on the strange white stones as I jerk the rope out of my belay device. I splash my way through the water and step up onto dry ground. It's a small, flat limestone shelf that encircles the water. There I wrap my arms around myself, trying to control the shivering. The whole world goes black as either Kim or Sunny fits into the hole in the roof.

FORTY

WE STAND CLOSE together on the dry ledge beside the pond. Roberto holds the dripping ends of the rope, which trail from the ceiling fifty feet above.

"Should I pull it?" he asks.

I don't want him to. I know it's at least possible that we could reascend the rope using prusiks made out of the slings of nylon webbing in my pack. By pulling it, I feel as if he'll be cutting us off from light, even from air. But we have no choice. With an explosion imminent, we sure as shit aren't going back out that way. I raise my hands over my head and feel a faint breeze on the burnt skin of my palms. Somewhere, somehow, there's got to be another way out.

"Do you feel that?" I ask them. "There's just a tiny bit of wind. I think I can even smell it."

"Sorry. That was me," Roberto says, trying to amuse

us. For the millionth time I'm envious of his élan, of his total lack of fear. Not even a million tons of unstable earth over his head can suppress it.

We all hold our hands in the air, ignoring his comment. "I can feel it," Kim says.

"Me too," Sunny adds.

"Pull the rope," I tell my brother. "We might need it to find a way out."

While Kim holds the light on him, Roberto begins tugging on one end of rope. The rope doesn't shift. Putting all his weight on it, he ends up penduluming out over the pond. When he swings back toward us I grab on, too, and the rope gives a little until we splash down in the cold water. Kim shines the light at our feet, intending to help us maintain our footing on the brittle white stones, as we pull together.

Suddenly Sunny screams. Again and again. The terrified keening coming from her mouth seems to push the air from the cavern.

The light jerks up so that it's in our faces. "What?" I shout.

Sunny stops screaming, but she continues making noises like a wounded cat. Beside her, Kim tries to keep her feet on the dry shelf as Sunny tears at her clothes. They are both breathing so hard it sounds as if they might be running in place. Or fighting.

"What?" I shout again, trying to whirl around in the shallow water to see the new threat. But I'm blinded by the light that Kim still manages to hold aimed at my eyes.

"Bones," Sunny says, her voice now a ragged whisper. "Bones. You're standing on bones."

Kim slowly lowers the light from our faces until it's

once again illuminating our feet, knee-deep in the clear, icy water. I realize what all those flat-looking white stones are—the delicate rocks that had been breaking beneath my boots. I feel a shiver that comes from somewhere beyond simple cold and fear.

Roberto pushes up one of his jacket's sleeves. He reaches deep into the water and pulls out a human jaw. He holds it up and Kim keeps the light on it. It's a little brown but otherwise perfectly preserved. The teeth, what would have been the bottom set, are painfully uneven.

"Dude needed a dentist. Bad." Roberto drops the jaw back in the water with what seems like a disrespectful splash. "Don't worry," he tells Sunny. "He can't bite. Not with those fucked-up teeth."

"This must have been their cemetery," Kim says, calming somewhat. "They must have pushed the bodies through the bottom of the kiva."

I have another, even more unpleasant idea. Some of the bones clearly show the long nicks of blades. From where flesh had been peeled from the human bones. This was their trash bin—nothing more. I keep my thoughts to myself in the cavern's gloom.

When we go back to tugging on the rope, ignoring the bones crunching underfoot, the headlamp's beam starts to flicker and dim. I wade over to Kim and Sunny while Roberto finishes with the rope, which is sliding easier now. I take the zip-locked extra batteries from my soaking pack and put them on my lap with the headlamp. Then I dry my hands carefully on my shirt. The shirt is already crusting with blood and pus from the open burn on my belly. I have to do this just right—if I drop anything there is no doubt we'll die in the gloom surrounded by the spirits of the cannibalized dead. After warning everyone as to what I'm about to do, I twist off the light. It feels like once again I'm falling in the total blackness. It rears up over us like a breaking wave.

Either Kim or Sunny staggers beside me, probably feeling the same lurch in her stomach. Although my numb fingers shake with cold and tension, I manage to replace the batteries and twist the light on again. That narrow beam of light is Hope—our only weapon against the dark. Without it the blackness just swallows everything.

There's a long, gentle splash as the rope comes trailing down out of the ceiling. Our only known connection to the world outside has been cut.

I play the light over the cavern's walls, studying the deep holes there. The slight breeze seems to come from a tunnel-like opening near the shelf where we stand. The four of us move together over the broken floor, huddled close together within the radius of light I try to keep aimed at our feet. Sunny requires extra effort from both Kim and Roberto because she won't take her face out of Kim's jacket. She's willing to move her legs but she must be balanced with each step. I think we're all relieved to be away from the pond and the bones.

What appeared to be a tunnel soon becomes very un-tunnel-like. After thirty feet the passageway narrows to just a refrigerator-size slot and rises in a series of jumbled steps. From the ceiling more white stalactites hang like dripping fangs. We continue into the fissure, trying to follow Kim's exhortation not to touch them with our hands. She warns us that the oil on our skin could discolor them, but right now I'm more concerned for my life than about vandalizing some future tourist attraction. And I've already violated every environmental and archaeological precept by stomping through the bones. My jacket rasps against the smooth stone as I have to turn sideways to fit through one particularly narrow opening.

The slot ends abruptly in a barrel-shaped chamber. The floor is a punji pit of low, pointed stalagmites. I play my light over the walls, still thinking I feel a faint breeze. There's a noise, too, a sort of distant moan. Wind somewhere on wet rock.

Up near the room's ceiling, ten or so feet above us, is a small hole. I slip the headlamp over my head so that the elastic straps grip snugly. Finding small edges on the cool stone wall, I work my way up to it. I move cautiously, trying to keep three points of contact with the rock at all times. I'm terrified of falling the ridiculously short distance onto the points of a hundred tiny stalagmites. But I'm even more terrified of the blast that could come roaring through the caverns any minute.

"Give me a second. This might go," I whisper into the darkness over my shoulder.

The hole is tiny. It's just eighteen inches by one foot, barely big enough for a badger. But there definitely is a breeze coming from it. And on the wind I can smell the faintest scent of pine. Nothing has ever smelled so sweet.

"You're fucking high," Roberto tells me.

I explain the wind and the pine smell. Kim says she smells it, too, that it's worth a try. The three make themselves as comfortable as they can next to the wall beneath the hole while I shed my jacket and rub my hands together, trying to warm them. I'm going to have to take the light with me into the hole, and I don't have to warn them not to stumble over the stalagmites in the dark. It would be like falling on a bed of nails.

I grip the hole's edge with my fingers and hesitate. The light from my headlamp reveals nothing down the narrow canal but a sharp turn a few feet away. If it weren't for the breeze blowing through it, it would be impossible to believe it could lead anywhere. I can't shake the feeling that I'm going to get jammed in there. Stuck.

Don't do this! a voice shouts in my head. But I slither in anyway.

For eighty feet I belly-crawl on my elbows and knees with my head banging into every irregularity on the fissure's ceiling. Strapped to my forehead, the delicate headlamp takes most of the impacts. I pray it doesn't break. The floor is thankfully mud-covered and soft instead of carpeted with sharp protrusions. The path winds to the sides like a fallen S.

Imagine twenty coffins lying end-to-end. Kick each place where they touch, so that they don't quite fit together. Then drop a mountain on them. That's what the part I've already crawled through feels like.

And it gets worse. I'm forced to drop all the way flat onto my belly, wriggling forward with my arms extended like a diver's. The closeness of the stone walls, the millions of tons of rock and earth above and around me, begins to push in on me. It's more than a physical pressure that robs my limbs of movement and my chest of air. It seems to press in on my mind, squeezing away my intellect and my rational thoughts. Instead the pressure focuses itself in my brain and then expands outward exponentially. Even when I try to lie still and rest, my heart rate keeps accelerating. My lungs huff faster and faster but they still can't seem to draw enough air. I force myself to wriggle some more.

And it gets tighter still. I have to turn my head to one side and splay my feet flat. The fissure pinches my bruised ribs. I have an urge to roll over onto my back but can't. My shoulders can't roll more than an inch or two. It's probably for the best, though—for some reason the thought of exposing my belly like a whimpering dog to the pressure and weight of all that earth above seems even more terrifying. I gain just an inch at a time.

A horrible thought keeps tugging at the edges of my mind, threatening to rip away my sanity. *It's going to dead-end!* And there's no fucking way I can squirm out backwards. There's no way Roberto, so far behind me now, could ever get the leverage in this death trap to pull me out. I'm going to die, plugged in this foul, muddy hole. I'm going to die screaming and howling. I've never felt anything like the fear that crawls along with me.

My breath comes in fast, mad pants. I can feel a bubbly froth gathering on my lips. I try to will my body to calm but my pulse keeps increasing until it's throbbing at what seems the speed of a hummingbird's wings—and each new beat seems to swell me tighter in the hole. It takes all my strength and will to keep from losing my mind.

In my mind I shout at myself: *Anton, you conqueror of mountains, you cheater of Death, are you going to let a little fucking hole get the best of you? Are you going to lie down without a fight while it squeezes the life out of you? Coward! You're going to die crying and gibbering, and they're all going to die with you. Fight, you stupid son of a bitch! Fight!*

Only the thought of my brother and Sunny and Kim saves me from the ultimate freak-out. I concentrate on them, huddling together in the pressing blackness of the round room with its floor of pointed rock stakes. I gasp and heave, squirming forward another inch. And another. *Roberto. Kim. Sunny.* Their names go through my mind like a mantra of salvation.

The pressure eases on my ribs. For the first time in what seems like hours, my lungs are able to fill all the way with dusty air. I gasp at it desperately, restraining sobs, and ignoring the awful pain in my ribs that comes with each full inhalation. Lifting my head, I look up to see the hellish tunnel emptying into a small room. The beam of light from my headlamp traces through it, measuring, and although it's not much bigger than a closet, it seems to me to be big enough to hold the entire universe.

I worm out of my prison and crash onto the rubble-strewn floor chest-first. Sitting on the sharp stones with my knees pulled against my chest, I try to hold back tears of relief. The scent of pines is stronger now. High on one wall is a couple of inches of space that remains black even when I shine my headlamp there. I turn out the light for a moment and see stars.

For some time voices have been calling my name. They reverberate toward me from the terrible hole. Twisting the headlamp back on, I aim it into the fissure. "Come on," I shout back in a shaky voice. "It goes. No problem."

FORTY-ONE

"YOU EVER HEARD that expression, the 'bowels of the earth'?" Roberto asks as he wriggles last out of the hole.

"Yeah?"

"If these are the bowels, then what are we, crawling through them?"

"Anton," Kim says, "please tell your brother to shut up."

The small chamber is crowded with the four of us in it. All three of them came through the rock without apparent trauma. Even Sunny made hardly a sound as she squirmed out of the tunnel with Kim close at her heels. But the claustrophobia still has a hold on my chest, and I sweat heavily as I chip away at the dirt near the starlit opening with a softball-size rock. It's not the warm sweat that comes of exertion, but the sick, chilling sweat of lingering fear.

I'm grateful when Roberto pushes me out of the way and takes over with a rock of his own. I'm even more grateful when Kim, somehow sensing my unreleased panic, puts her arms around my waist and pulls me down to huddle between her and Sunny. Whenever Roberto pauses in his work, we can hear the chirp of crickets in the night outside.

"What time is it?" I ask, finally regaining some of my composure.

Kim pulls her jacket up over her wrist and illuminates it with the light. "Three in the morning, if this thing's still working. Those assholes must have been bluffing about the dynamite. They probably think they can starve or freeze us out, then 'discover' the cave in a few days or weeks when the deeds are exchanged and the swap can't be reversed."

It will be dawn in a few hours. If we're in the valley somewhere like I suspect—we can't be far—then we'll have to hustle to get far enough away to be safe from Fast and his pals.

Something we don't discuss is staying down in our hole throughout the coming day and until the night comes again. Sooner or later, Dad would come looking for us. We have enough food and water in the pack that we'd pulled through the hole using the rope, but I think everyone shares a little of my desperation to get out from under the earth.

Roberto's making a lot of noise as he pounds his handheld rock against the tiny opening in the wall. It can't be helped. The stone he's cutting through is the same crumbly sandstone that makes up the red cliff by the entrance to Cal's ruin. Every now and then he tosses over his shoulder a piece he has hacked free. I can see that the hole is slowly widening when I aim the headlamp's beam around him. It's now big enough for maybe a large rabbit.

"Can you see anything?" Sunny asks him. They're her first words since she screamed about the bones. I take it as a good sign.

Roberto turns to us, his face streaked with dirt and his black hair tangled and filthy, and grins. "You aren't gonna like this, kids, but it looks like another tunnel."

Fresh fear floods through me. I don't know if I can handle another coffin-crawl. And if we meet solid rock, we're doomed. There's no way in hell we'll have the strength to crawl back through the slot and find another passage.

"Just kidding. We're almost out."

I can't decide whether to punch or hug him. So I just lie limply in Kim's arms while Roberto goes back to work.

When he tells us he's finished, I slither out first. The night caresses my filthy face like a lover. The darkness of it is so different from that inside the cave. It seems to welcome me. *Come out, come out and play.* Overhead the sky is so filled with beautiful stars that just a glance at it makes me dizzy. There are several pine trees on the rocky slope where I stand, and I want to hug them all. Strangely, the crickets aren't chirping anymore.

I don't take the time to hug the trees or wonder where the crickets have gone. We need to get the hell out of here as quick as we can. I close my eyes and take one deep breath, then stoop to help pull Sunny out of the ground. And right behind her Kim and Roberto. It takes just seconds before we're ready to run.

I hear a sound behind me. A boot brushing through grass. Just as I turn, something strikes my ankle with enough force to kick my leg out from under me and send me sprawling in the grass. The blow may have even broken my ankle. I fall on my back, trying to stifle a shout of warning and pain. Looking up, I see a huge shadow blocking out the stars overhead.

"Is that how it felt, motherfucker?" Burgermeister repeats my last words to him in his dead man's voice. "Is *that* how it felt when I shot your dog?"

Two more shadows step up behind him. One big—Fast—and the other very small. A higher-pitched voice says, "You dumb hippies sure make a lot of noise."

FORTY-TWO

Sunny is curled in a fetal position in the grass. Burgermeister had knocked her down with a brutal shove when she was unable to kneel with the rest of us. She'd been too scared to follow his commands, totally paralyzed and unbelieving that she was suddenly back in the hands of her tormentors. The giant laughed at her. "Welcome home, honey," he said. "I knew you couldn't keep that sweet young ass of yours away from us. You had to come back for more, didn't you? Just like your friend Ms. Walsh, although it took her a little longer. Twelve years, right, Dave?"

Fast doesn't reply.

Everything is crystal clear in the night. Horrifyingly clear. We hadn't gone anywhere by crawling through the mountain. It had all been for nothing. All that darkness and terror. Above and behind us is the steep field of broken red stone that has shed off the cliff's face over thousands of years. I know that if I turned and looked, I could probably spot the ledge that holds the secret entrance to Cal's ruin just a hundred feet up. We're in a grove of widely spaced pines just yards from the meadow.

Fast and Burgermeister have a new friend with them. I guess that the others with the rifles have been sent away—Burgermeister is smart enough to limit the number of witnesses. Even in the dark the new man is vaguely familiar. He is short and stocky with a bristling haircut. I don't place him immediately because of the dark and the fact that he's not in uniform.

His name only comes to me when Roberto asks from where he's kneeling to my right, "Doing a little moonlighting, Blow Job?" It's Deputy B. J. Timms, the sheriff's half-pint sidekick.

He responds to my brother's question by raising an oversized automatic and pointing it between Roberto's eyes. I know he's about to shoot but then Burgermeister intervenes.

"He's mine," the big man says. He's standing behind my brother with the wicked silver gleam of a Buck knife in one hand. Without another word, he raises it high, then slams it down, butt-first, on the top of Roberto's head. In the sickening crunch, I can hear both the tear of skin and the impact of steel on bone. My mad, unstoppable brother collapses forward into the grass.

Timms's pistol wavers, then swings to the side until its thick barrel is pointed at me. It stays on my head while the deputy walks around to stand behind me. In a way I prefer him there—in my state of heightened awareness I don't want to see the muzzle flash before the bullet rips through my skull.

David Fast stands with his back to the meadow, facing Kim and me over Sunny's prostrate form. He's resting the barrel of his rifle in the girl's exposed ear. She shivers violently at his feet, pinned to the grass by the gun, and makes no sound. I think I know what she's feeling—she's suffered enough and just wants it over with. Escape and capture, escape and capture, escape and capture. She's probably praying for a bullet right now. I'm feeling a little of the same thing.

Burgermeister stands beside Fast. He grins at us with his big white teeth glowing in the dark. "Y'all sure make a lot of noise for people being hunted. You couldn't have made it any easier for us to find you, screaming and hammering away down in there. What did you expect, carrying on like that?"

None of us answer. I fight an urge to close my eyes.

"Just look what crawled out from under a rock," he laughs. "That cave must really be something for you to get all the way down here. I guess that's Dave's and my cave now. We decided not blow it up after all. Once the papers are all signed, it might make us a couple of extra bucks."

I'm on my knees facing them. Timms is right behind me with the muzzle of his pistol pressed against the back of my neck. I can smell his fetid breath blowing into my hair. My hands are on top of my head, inches from the gun, but it's jammed so hard into my neck that I know the deputy's finger must be tight on the trigger. I can't risk even a flinch.

Kim is to my left, kneeling too with her hands on her head, with one sharp elbow against the inside of one of mine. Roberto is to my right. He's facedown in the dirt and grass. Burgermeister steps over and kneels on his back. I can hear my brother struggling to breathe from under the big man's weight. I can't tell if he's conscious. The giant has the blade of the knife against the skin to one side of Roberto's neck. From the forced breathing, I know my brother is alive. For the moment.

"It's kind of funny," Burgermeister continues. "You all coming out of the ground like that. Funny 'cause you're going right back in, if you know what I mean. But I don't think you'll be coming back out this time."

I speak to Fast instead of his partner and my voice sounds surprisingly strong, full of an assuredness I certainly don't feel. "People know where we are. They're going to come looking for us." I'm thinking of my father and his last thrilling words to me. *I'm coming.* I remember telling him we were headed for the red cliff. At least he'll know where to dig.

Fast says nothing. He just stares down at Sunny, so Burgermeister replies for him. "They aren't going to look too hard, I bet. Not for a couple of squirrelly ecoterrorists and an escaped convict."

"They're going to look for me," I tell him. "I'm a cop."

"We know all about you, Special Agent Antonio Burns. We know you're suspended. For the second time, too. Tsk-tsk, boy. They're probably gonna figure you thought you were going to get seriously busted this time. Especially after having helped your brother jump bail, which is what they'll believe when he doesn't turn up. Nah, they aren't going to look too hard for you."

He's wrong. My immediate boss and my colleagues know the suspension is bullshit. But he wouldn't believe me if I told him that. I again try talking to Fast's quiet form. He still has the rifle barrel touching Sunny's head where it lies in the grass.

"It isn't going to work," I tell him, trying not to plead. "It isn't going to work in the end. You can't murder the four of us—five, including Cal—without paying a price. And it's not worth the cost of the land."

I've sensed a reluctance in him all along. A bit of remorse for what he'd done to Kim all those years ago. And a distaste for his partner's violent tactics. I feel a tiny glint of hope. I try to will his gun from where it points directly into Sunny's ear. I will him to lift it up until it's pointed at Burgermeister.

Fast looks back at me for a long moment. I think all of us, even Burgermeister, who is armed only with a knife now, hold our breaths.

"This should never have happened," Fast says slowly. "All this, because of a stupid prank and an accident twelve years ago. Jesus, Kim, I can't imagine what's going on in your head." His hands twitch on the rifle. Then he snuffs out my hope. "There's no going back now. I'd lose everything. I'm sorry, truly sorry, but you brought this on yourself, Kim."

"It's time for the four of you to say good night," Burgermeister rasps, laughing.

"Not yet, Alf," Timms says behind me, his nasty breath still blowing on me and the pistol's muzzle still screwed into the back of my neck. "You promised that I could have a little fun first."

"That's true," Burgermeister explains to Kim and me, as if making an apology of his own. "I did promise him that. And he's earned it. After all, that was his cousin you knocked off the cliff up there. And he's had his eye on you for a while, Ms. Walsh. I'll bet Dave can tell us that the honey is sweet. And I've been thinking I ought to have some fun with you, too. I'd like to see what I missed by not going to college."

"Fuck you," Kim spits. But at Fast, not Burgermeister.

Fast shakes his head mournfully. "Blame yourself, Kim. You've fucked yourself."

"Man, I sure do like my women feisty," Burgermeister says with another laugh. He gestures at Sunny's prostrate form. "Not like that one. She's like dead meat."

Beside me Kim makes a hissing noise with a sharp intake of breath.

"Hear that, bitch? I'm owed. I'm getting my piece, too." Timms has pulled the gun from my neck and reached around in front of Kim with both his gloved hands. His free hand grabs at one of her breasts while with the other he shoves the pistol down the front of her baggy pants. "Your one eye's gonna meet mine."

They're making a terrible mistake but they don't know it. Their threats strike a match in my chest. Before they'd said that about violating Kim once again, I'd almost been ready to let him put a bullet in my head without a fight. I was just too weary. But no one's going to touch Kim. Not that way. The match flares with a brilliant white heat, so fierce it's nearly an explosion. *That will not happen. Not without him paying whatever maximum price I'm able to charge.*

I look out past Fast at the night sky and try to exhale, to blow the searing flames from my throat. The fire goes out in an instant. It's like it had never even been there. Instead what I feel is a great emptiness, cool and calm and easy, filled with the night, the sky, the trees and mountains. I'm a part of it all. Something in my brain breaks loose with an enormous yawn that sucks the whole world in. I'm going to make a final struggle. It's better to die fighting than to surrender, to let the woman I maybe love be violated for a second time in her life. The cells of my body are going to begin their reentry into the elements that made me. And it's okay.

I have no strategy. And the way I'm feeling, that's okay, too. I'm beyond fear and pain and worry and guilt. I'm soaring into another place entirely.

The old Neil Young lyric floats through my head as I tense myself for a suicidal lunge to the side. *Better to burn out than to fade away*. Above me in the night sky is a leathery flutter like a giant bat's wings. *Weird,* I think. Since my childhood I'd pictured Death as the Grim Reaper—bony hands and a cloaked face and blazing red eyes reaching up beneath me on an alpine wall to snatch at my ankles. Weird that it's more like a winged Angel of Death coming out of the sky, like something out of a medieval painting, something that I never imagined before. Weird that after all the time I spent fighting him on the rock, he can just sweep in like this and grab me.

As I start to raise a knee in order to get a foot beneath me, I look up to catch a glimpse of the monster. I want to smile in his face. Give him the finger one last time. But there's nothing up there but a thousand tiny pinpricks of light and Death's vast black shape sweeping across them. No one notices me brace my right foot against the solid earth that's soon to hold my decomposing flesh. They're all staring at the sky, too. He must be coming for more than just me. That makes me smile.

I spin and lunge to the left, driving with all the power in my good leg. My shoulder smashes into Timms's ribs down low beneath his arm. I rip him off Kim's back and take him down hard into the dirt and the grass. My hands grasp at his face and throat, tearing flesh and hair, seeking the soft gelatinous meat of his eyes. He's screaming with his hands flailing on my wrists. I realize he's lost the pistol—it most have gotten tangled in Kim's pants with the initial impact when I knocked him off her.

In my strange, expanded state of mind the others are clear around me despite Deputy Timms's screams. Kim still kneels in the grass with both her hands down her pants. She's trying to untangle the gun. I want to tell her to forget it, to run, but the words are buried by all the other noise.

Fast is hollering before us. He's pulled the hunting rifle's barrel from Sunny's ear and is aiming it at Timms and me. But he's unable to get a clear shot with the off-duty deputy writhing before me. Maybe he's unwilling to pull the trigger. But it doesn't matter. The way I'm feeling, it will take more than a few bullets to stop me before I'm done. *You're next.*

Fast makes it easy, coming at me now quick across the grass. He's reversed the gun and is raising the butt to smash at my head. I whip Timms back and forth as my fingers tear at his throat and face. Fast strikes once and the hard wooden stock cracks off the deputy's forehead when I use it to parry the blow.

To the right, Burgermeister is also caught up in the battle's frenzy. He's reaching under my brother's throat with the long knife. But Roberto has managed to grab his wrist. Even on his face in the dirt, with one hand awkwardly twisted before him, his maniacal strength is slowing the big man's stroke.

Then the night is split wide open when Fast strikes a second time. In slow motion I watch the rifle butt swinging in a short jab toward my temple. It's like a flashbulb goes off in my face. Night becomes day. My fingers lose their grip on Timms's face and throat. I sit back on my ass, unable to lift my arms to ward off a second blow. My arms just won't work.

But Fast hesitates. Through the brilliant light I see the deputy slumped at his feet. He's not moving. Fast glances down at him, too, then reverses the rifle a second time so that its muzzle is aimed at my face. The black hole in the barrel looks huge. It pulls at my starred vision, seeming to drag my very being into it.

A new sound overwhelms all the screaming and hollering. It sounds like the earth is opening up beneath us. Dirt and mud and sticks tear through the air, stinging my face. The sound of automatic weapons, I realize with a sudden jolt, and I'm almost disappointed when Fast's gun wavers off my chest. Around me I see three orange flames coming from three different directions, converging on our deadly little battle, but shooting short into the grass and the small pine trees. Fast still has the gun pointed in my general direction as he looks around wildly.

It takes a few seconds before my eyes clear of the blinding light. Then I'm aware of three shadows, darker than the night, loping toward us. Behind one of them billows an even larger black shape. It takes me a minute to realize it's a parachute trailing behind the running shadow. And it takes a moment for me to recognize the shadow's steady lope. That hadn't been Death fluttering overhead. Just Dad.

My father is dressed entirely in black. Even his face

has been painted with charcoal or tar. The only things not black are a pair of slender white parentheses on each side of his irises. The two other shadows circle us to the sides with ugly short rifles gleaming in the starlight.

"Put down the weapons! Put down the weapons!" my father is shouting. Even shouting, his voice still has that odd authoritative calm. The sound of it makes my hair stand on end.

I look over at Roberto. Burgermeister has let go of the knife and is rising off my brother's back with his hands in the air. Roberto's still pressed facedown in the dirt but his head is turned toward me. He's looking at me, and I realize he's grinning. I grin back. *Unbelievable. He came through.*

With a single motion that's so quick it's just a blur, Roberto rolls over onto his back, sits up, and keeps rolling forward. The long knife flashes before him. He thrusts it upward with both hands as he drives ahead. His back blocks my view but the grating sound of steel on bone is unmistakable. The giant screams.

Roberto, soaked with blood, whips the knife out and whirls to his feet as Burgermeister collapses like an enormous lodgepole pine. My brother bends down and spits in his face. "How's it feel to be violated, *puta*?"

" 'Berto! No!" my father shouts, way too late.

In front of me Fast drops his rifle. I think he drops it more in horror than from my father's command. Deputy Timms moans on the grass, clutching his head and throat. My fingers had pulled the skin half off his face.

Kim has finally gotten the pistol out from her pants. She takes two steps forward and shoves the barrel into

Fast's open mouth. I hear teeth breaking. "On your knees," she hisses at him.

My father comes forward. His gun is no longer on Fast but now points at Roberto. And his oldest son is smiling back with his eyes just bright slits in the dark. The blood that covers his face makes him look as dark as Dad.

"Step back, 'Berto. Put down the knife." His voice is immeasurably sad. It's as if he knows Roberto has crossed a line, that he's stepped over the edge now and will never come back.

Roberto does as he's told. But while my father watches, he licks some blood from his knuckles.

Life finally returns to my limbs. I get to my feet and put my hands on Kim's shoulders. "It's over," I tell her. "You're finally going to get to see him in court." She's shaking as hard as Sunny, who still lies curled and silently sobbing in the grass. I'd been tempted to let her kill him, but something tells me that's not what she needs. She needs the Law to exact her Justice—it's what she's fought for all these years. For her, my brother's type of justice would make those years seem empty.

I slide my hand down to her wrist and pull the gun out of Fast's mouth. The asshole looks relieved. And he should be. My brother would gut him, too, if my father and his men weren't here. I might have done it myself, with my bare hands, if the blow to my head hadn't temporarily paralyzed my arms.

"Lie down," I say softly to Fast after I kick the rifle into the deep grass. He does it, even putting his hands behind his head without me having to tell him to.

"Now who's *fucked*?" Kim asks him.

FORTY-THREE

TEN MILES DOWN the bumpy Forest Service road, just a few miles from where it meets the highway, two Sheriff's Department SUVs block the road. Beyond them I see a third truck with the same colors and insignia parked between some pines to one side. There are three men standing together talking in the clean morning light as we drive the black Suburban down toward them. I recognize Sheriff Munik in his Stetson with the two young deputies. They look up, see Fast's truck, and wave. Roberto toots the horn as we approach. He's driving because my right ankle's so swollen and sore from Burgermeister's blow that I can barely weight it.

Even though he'd washed his face in the creek, a fresh line of bright red blood runs down my brother's face from the wound on top of his head.

The sheriff walks toward us when Roberto brakes to

a stop. One of the deputies gets in an SUV to move it out of the way. As the darkly tinted driver's window slides down, Munik is saying, "Boys were here all night and nobody tried..."

His voice dies away when he realizes that it's Roberto, not David Fast, in the driver's seat. And that I'm beside him.

"Tried what, asshole?" my brother asks.

The sheriff's smile flexes into a grimace. His right hand slaps the leather holster under his sport coat and comes up with the huge revolver. He points it at my brother's face.

"Hands in the air!" he screams through the open window at us.

Roberto and I comply, Roberto rather leisurely. The two deputies realize something's very wrong and come running toward the Suburban with their own guns out.

"Sheriff, you've made some big mistakes—stupid mistakes," I say evenly. "Don't compound them. Look in the backseat."

Gun extended, Munik steps to his left so that he can get a view behind Roberto's seat. His eyes widen, then narrow, as he takes in the sight of Fast's red face and the duct tape that's wound around his mouth and head. And Kim, sitting beside him, touching a gun to Fast's stomach.

"Sheriff!" one of the deputies says from behind Munik, as if the sheriff's attention were not already riveted to the backseat.

"We've made a citizen's arrest of David Fast for the kidnapping of Sunny Hansen and for the murder of Cal Watkins," I say in my official voice, loud enough for them all to hear. "His accomplices are being brought down by other citizens in a pickup that will be following in a few minutes. The bodies of two others are up in the meadow."

I'd asked my father to stay behind for a few minutes until I could get things straightened out at the police roadblock. He's going to come down five minutes from now, in one of the construction pickups with Fast's remaining men bound in the bed. Dad and the two parajumpers accompanying him had rounded up the men from the trailers beside the burnt-out lodge. Leaderless, Fast's employees wisely decided not to put up a fight.

The sheriff is only half listening behind the revolver. "Put down the gun, missy," he says to Kim.

"She's not going to put down the gun. And you better not call her 'missy' again," I say, unable to suppress a smile. "*You* put down *your* gun, Sheriff. Your men, too. If you're thinking about trying to save your benefactor, forget it. There are U.S. soldiers—my father's men, Special Forces—in the trees on both sides of the road. They have you in their rifle sights." I'm exaggerating, but my smile makes the lie believable. I feel absolutely bulletproof right now. With my brother and Dad nearby, nothing can stop me.

While the deputies look around and lower their guns, Munik focuses on me with both his eyes and the long barrel of his revolver. I can almost see the wheels turning in his brain, trying to figure out if he can kill us and save Fast and make it plausible. Trying to figure out just how implicated he is already. Trying to figure out what kind of a cop he is. I decide to help him before he makes the wrong choice.

"We don't have anything on you, Sheriff. Just that you've been a little too helpful to Mr. Fast in protecting what he mistakenly believes is his property. You're going to lose some pride but that's it. Now put down the gun before you get yourself killed."

The wheels turn for a moment longer. Then he slowly nods. The gun lowers to his side until it's pointing at the ground. He hitches it up into the holster at his belt as his men do the same.

"Now, what's this kidnapping about?" he asks carefully.

Sheriff Munik argues to take custody of David Fast and his surviving employees, but I insist that we be the ones who will deliver them to the jail. I'm not going to risk Fast somehow "escaping." Once the pickup comes up behind us, with Dad and Sunny in the front and two camouflaged soldiers in the back with their side arms pointed at Fast's trussed men, we drive in a slow procession to the courthouse complex in the center of town. While we drive, Kim borrows Fast's cell phone from the console between the front seats and calls reporter friends in both Tomichi and Denver. She wants to ensure that the sheriff and the DA don't try to pull any tricks. The press will provide a little extra insurance.

She also calls the hospital, arranging for an ambulance to meet us in order to take Sunny for an examination and to submit to a rape kit. And she tries to get Roberto and me to agree to go with the girl. I'm convinced, though, that my ankle is just sprained, not broken. And I know from experience that nothing can be done for my ribs. Besides, I have too much still to do. Roberto refuses, too. He says his head's too hard to break.

When we arrive at the courthouse, a television camera from the local station and a small crowd are already waiting for us. They shoot both video and still images as the town's leading citizen, the son of a former United States senator, is led into the jail.

"Come on in, Agent Burns," Roger Acosta, the Tomichi County district attorney, tells me, waving me into a pale blue chair opposite his desk in the office.

He'd been waiting in the jail when our small caravan pulled up. The sheriff must have alerted him to the situation on the radio. Fast glared at the man whose campaign he had funded when he was led past with his mouth still taped shut. The prosecutor shook his head sadly in response, causing Fast's face to turn redder. He briefly struggled with the two uncertain deputies escorting him, who were obviously embarrassed to have a man of Fast's prominence in their custody. I reached in and shoved Fast's bulky shoulder, bouncing him off a wall, teaching him the new manners he would need to learn in prison. The DA intervened then by taking my arm and making quieting noises at Fast. Then he asked me to meet him upstairs, in his office, and I said I'd come after borrowing a crutch from the jail infirmary and seeing David Fast put in a cell.

I try to keep my face neutral as I hobble into the comfortable office. A variety of emotions are stirring inside me and I'm too exhausted to be able to judge which of them I should display. I slouch in the big chair, laying the crutch on the floor beside me. I'm unconcerned that the dirt and blood caked on my clothes must be staining the chair beneath me.

"Well," the DA says, "I'm assuming you've got some evidence to back up these citizen's arrests you've made?"

"I do."

"Can you summarize it for me, Agent?"

I explain that Fast and Burgermeister had killed Cal while trying to learn the location of the Indian ruin he'd found, which could foul up the land exchange, and to retaliate for the burning of Fast's lodge. Sunny will identify him and his now deceased employee, Alf "Rent-a-Riot" Burgermeister, as well as testify to her kidnapping from the lake and subsequent rape. My father, his two men, my brother, Kim, and I will all testify that Fast, Burgermeister, and Timms then tried to murder us all at the foot of the red cliff. Roberto stabbed Burgermeister in self-defense, I tell him, knowing the others will back me up. While I talk, the DA leans forward on his desk, propping himself upright with his elbows and resting his chin on his clasped hands.

He doesn't say anything when I finish. His eyes have drifted to the wall behind me. I guess he's considering the evidence, wondering how it will sound in court and perhaps trying to figure out how he'll be implicated in all this.

"You should know the sheriff had a role in all of it," I say. "He ignored evidence that Fast was Cal's killer. He arrested my brother based just on his criminal history." I don't mention that the DA was a part of that, too. "He didn't try very hard to find Sunny, the only witness to the murder. He ignored me when I tried to get his help in rescuing her. Then he blocked the road up into the valley for Fast."

"Can you prove anything against him?"

"Probably not. Just ignorance and stupidity."

The DA nods, unable to keep from looking a little relieved. If the sheriff's safe, then he probably is as well.

"You say this girl Sunny can ID everyone? She can identify the killers of that boy in the valley?"

"Yes."

"Can all of you give statements this morning?"

"Yes, all of us except Sunny, who's at the hospital right now. But we need some food and coffee first."

"All right then," he says with an unconvincing sigh. "Let's get it over with." He starts to stand behind his desk.

I don't move. "I want the charges against my brother dismissed now. And his bond released."

"All in good time, Agent Burns. All in good time."

I lean forward, ignoring the pain in my stomach and ribs. "Do you want me to go down there and tell those reporters that David Fast was your number one campaign contributor? About how you are as culpable as the sheriff in at the very least turning a blind eye to all the evidence pointing at Fast instead of my brother?"

The DA sits back down in his chair. He shakes his head sadly. "That's unnecessary, Agent. All that will come out anyway when a special prosecutor is appointed. You can trust me to do the right thing."

"I'd rather you just do it."

He shakes his head again but turns to the computer. He taps at the keyboard, prints out a piece of paper, and fills in some blanks on it. He signs it and passes it to me. It's a Motion to Dismiss case number 97CF2343, *The People v. Roberto Burns.* "You can take it down to the judge for her signature while we start interviewing your family and friends. I'll call the clerk and tell them to expect you."

The rest of the morning passes in an exhausted daze.

With the exception of Sunny, who remains at the hospital undergoing the indignity and new violation of a rape kit, the rest of us crowd into the sealed-off lobby of the

District Attorney's Office. One by one we're called in to give videotaped interviews. True to his word, the DA has called in a prosecutor from another county to act as an impartial witness and later, when appointed by the court, a special prosecutor in the case against David Fast.

Kim commandeers the receptionist's phone. She dials and speaks fervently but I'm too tired to pay much attention to what's being said. The two PJs who'd flown across the country and then jumped into the meadow with my father sleep on the floor with practiced ease. They'd been embarrassed by my profuse thanks earlier. They shrugged it off, making my throat swell by saying they would follow my father anywhere. Even into a court-martial. I never say thank you to my dad, but he knows how I feel. Saying it out loud would just cheapen the emotion. He nods back at me whenever I look into his hard blue eyes.

I overhear him being berated by some general in Washington. The voice over the big satellite phone is loud and clear. Dad in all likelihood will be court-martialed. Perhaps even charged criminally for leaving his post and disobeying orders. But he absorbs the abuse without expression or comment. He knew what the consequences would be when he talked a friendly Air Force pilot into flying him across the country and making the parachute drop into the valley. The only defense he strives to present is for the two men who'd volunteered to come with him. Dad makes it clear that he alone is responsible. Both his sons and his men would expect nothing less. The voice on the other end in turn makes it clear that my father's career is officially over.

At one point Dad and Roberto step out into the hall for a private talk.

It's a long, long time before they return. The whole time, I'd been listening for the sound of yelling, but it never comes. When they come back, Roberto is smiling sheepishly. His mad eyes are still lit up with something—I can't tell if it's that he'd found his hidden stash in the woods or if it's from the blow to his head or if it's the stupor of a blood lust satisfied. Whatever it is, it seems to have put him in a gentle trance.

He sits on the couch next to me. "I guess I'm coming to visit you for a while in Wyoming," he says. "Where the men are men and the sheep are scared."

I laugh at the old joke. "What the hell, bro?" but I realize now what his strange look means.

He knows Dad had ultimately been willing to sacrifice everything for us. Those old lectures about family loyalty—they were true in the long run. Now it is Roberto's turn to make a sacrifice. He's agreed to come back with me to Wyoming, to attend that rehab center near Jackson Hole that Dad had mentioned a week ago. I'll need to arrange it with the parole office in Durango, but that should be easy. Suddenly everything feels easy.

Roberto shakes his head. "*Che,*" he says softly, "I can't fucking *believe* the old man came through."

Kim comes out of her interview with the prosecutors positively glowing. Her filthy hair is covered with the blue bandana again except for the tendrils she's pulled free to cover her eye patch. Her face and clothes are smudged with streaks of dried mud, but she's never looked more beautiful. She's never looked younger or stronger.

"This is it," she tells me. "They're going to arraign him in two hours."

The excitement has overridden her exhaustion. Her single brown eye is shining with the thrill of vindication. This is when Fast starts paying for what he did to her all those years ago, paying in the way she always intended—with the law as the instrument of justice that will bring him to his knees. I don't want to tell her how from my perspective, a cop's perspective, the law seldom results in justice. A bit of the euphoria I'd felt on learning of Roberto's promise drains away.

"I can't wait to see the look on the bastard's face when the judge reads the charges and sets bail."

"Let's hope he can't make it," I say. For a lawyer, Kim certainly doesn't have a lawyer's usual cynicism. I guess she hasn't had much exposure to the criminal process. Maybe she doesn't realize yet that the rich and famous get special treatment. Unlike the masses, for instance, they don't have to spend time in jail while waiting for their trial to start.

"Ha! I talked to the Forest Service supervisor and I told them where the Anasazi ruin is and that it's everything Cal had claimed and more—they've put the exchange of deeds on hold. Then I called friends at a couple of banks, too. With the swap a nonevent, they're going to seize the assets he put up for the loans. Every dollar David Fast's ever made is going down the drain. He won't be able to make a ten-dollar bail."

Instead of sharing her elation, I think about all the sad, angry years Kim's spent here in Tomichi, waiting for the chance to start her vendetta. To get her revenge. All the years living in the same town with the man who humiliated her and caused the loss of her eye. All the years of waiting for something like this. I hope it's been worth it. Fast is unlikely to serve more than a few years in prison. The average homicide defendant receives only about six years—eligible for parole in two. And Fast, because of no prior convictions, and because the wealthy and famous, even when their money is gone, get special consideration, will likely do even less. And that's if he's convicted at all. Look at O.J. Simpson and all the other rich and famous defendants. Justice isn't the same for them.

"Remember what you said to me about the law, in the hot spring after the fight? You said it's a joke. Well, have a little faith, Anton. It may not be perfect, but it's going to work."

I nod without enthusiasm.

"You'll come with me, won't you? To the arraignment?"

"Of course," I tell her, masking my reluctance. What I really want to do is sleep with my arms around her the way we had in the canyon by the lake, but without the cold and the fear. I wish that coffee-colored eye would shine for me instead of with the sparkle of her vendetta's culmination.

Kim's friend the veterinarian is more than happy to see us when we come to pick up Oso at noon. Even from outside the building, in the parking lot, I'd been able to hear him bellowing. The outraged roars grow louder as she leads us through the lobby, where her other clients grasp their terrified pets close to their chests, and then into a kennel. Oso stands in a large cage near the gate. He's swaying on his feet from the sedatives they've given him in pieces of meat shoved through the fence. A nylon muzzle strains to contain his jaws as he thunders. His left hind leg is heavily bandaged and he holds it in the air, close to his stomach.

Because of the drugs, he doesn't recognize me at first. I put my fingers through the chain link and then jerk them back when he attempts to snap at them. The sound is like a bear trap slamming shut. "Easy, boy, it's me. C'mon, Oso, it's me."

Finally quiet, he tilts his massive head to one side, staring at me through glassy yellow eyes. Then he snuffs at my fingers. His tongue is dry and rough when it emerges from the muzzle to lick them. And the stumpy tail begins to swing.

"Get this thing out of here before he ruins my business," the vet tells us. She's already explained that she removed thirteen shotgun pellets and miscellaneous metal fragments from his hip and leg. Several of them had been buried deep in the bone. He'll recover, but it will take a few weeks of rest. And he's likely to be a little cranky during that time, she says with a nervous laugh.

Kim pays the bill with my credit card while I sit on the cage's concrete floor and rub Oso's chest. Not surprisingly, we're asked to leave by a rear door. After we get Oso into the backseat, Kim forgets about my bad ankle and starts to climb into the passenger seat. The anticipation of seeing Fast at the defendant's table has blocked out all of her other thoughts.

"Do you mind driving again?" I ask her. "I would have Oso do it, but if people see him behind the wheel, they might think *road rage.*"

Kim laughs and apologizes for her forgetfulness. We switch seats. With growing excitement, she drives us back to the courthouse for the arraignment.

FORTY-FOUR

DAVID FAST SHUFFLES into the courtroom with the other prisoners for the afternoon's arraignments. But unlike the five other men in orange jumpsuits, he wears slacks, a coat, and an open-collared shirt. His short, graying hair is combed and moussed. He isn't even chained to the orange-clad men, although he is handcuffed. Despite the damage evident on his tan face—a swollen mouth from where Kim had broken his front teeth with the barrel of his own pistol and the black eye from Roberto's blow just hours before—he looks surprisingly unaffected. He still maintains his arrogant posture.

There is a low murmuring from the packed gallery all around me. The room is full to the bursting point. A few of them are probably reporters, as they have notepads balanced on their knees, but the rest appear to be regular citizens who have come to stare at the wonder of the town's favorite son in chains.

I take some satisfaction from that.

Beside me Kim squeezes my hand and waves at her reporter friend from the Denver TV station. Earlier the judge had refused to allow the reporters to bring either video or still cameras into the courtroom—not because she hadn't wanted the publicity, but because there simply wasn't room. When we walked into the building, we'd seen the cameramen smoking cigarettes and fuming in the street near the media vans.

As the prisoners take their seats in the jury box, with the same overweight and overage deputies guarding them by standing at each end, I turn and look at Kim. Her good eye gleams back at me. With Fast indicted, the swap is history and her valley is free. She squeezes my hand again. Vindication.

Judge Carver bangs her gavel for silence. She has her thin blonde hair artfully arranged over her robes like a halo, just as she had at my brother's arraignment. But all that gold hair can't keep her from looking like a bad-tempered witch. She points the gavel at the gallery. "I won't have any outbursts," she warns us. Then she has her bailiff call up the first case: *The People v. David Fast.* This time the judge is going to let the less important cases wait.

The gavel bangs again as the murmuring resumes when Fast approaches the podium in the courtroom's well. "I've warned you!" the judge says. "I won't hesitate to clear this court." She's showing none of the pleasure at the attention that she'd exhibited at my brother's arraignment.

Fast is flanked by two lawyers—one a dignified middle-aged man and the other a pretty young woman. Both are dressed in expensive suits, indicating they'd probably hopped the short flight from Denver just hours ago. Local lawyers wouldn't dare to dress this nice for fear of alienating the locals—all potential jurors. I recognize the man as Morris Cash (known by cops as Mo' Cash), one of the most famous defense attorneys in the West. He's the type of attorney who will do anything and say anything to win his illustrious clients an acquittal. His appearance causes a sick feeling in my stomach—Cash wins some unwinnable cases. He'd been a primary consultant for O.J. Simpson's "Dream Team." But then I perk up a little, remembering that Fast is bankrupt now that the swap has been nixed. Cash, once he finds out, surely won't be doing any pro bono work.

"Your honor," Cash says before the judge begins. "My client has already been advised of the charges against him and he is aware additional charges might be added. He has also been advised of his rights and has signed a form to that effect. We would like to waive any formal reading of the charges and simply proceed to the matter of bail."

The judge smiles and nods now, obviously flattered by Cash's efficiency and his presence in her courtroom. "Certainly, Mr. Cash. Let's—"

Fast has been whispering in Cash's ear and Cash interrupts the judge. "One more thing, your honor. I expect the hearing to be somewhat lengthy, as I believe my client has been the subject of an environmentalist conspiracy and that he is the victim here, not the perpetrator. I'd like to request that my client be freed of his restraints for the duration of the hearing, if not forever," he says with a chuckle. "I believe that you've known Mr. Fast and his family for a long time and understand that he certainly presents no danger."

The judge is still smiling. "The Court *has* known Mr. Fast a long time. He and his family have been an important part of this community for almost a hundred years. I have no problem with giving him that small courtesy. Any objection, Mr. Prosecutor?" she asks Acosta.

"No objection, your honor." The DA gives me an apologetic look as I glare back.

You didn't give my brother that courtesy.

"What?" Kim whispers beside me. I realize I'm gripping her hand way too hard.

"They made my brother stand there in handcuffs when he was arraigned," I hiss back at her.

"Deputy, please remove the restraints," Judge Carver says from the bench.

A fat deputy moves quickly out of the jury box with a key in his hand. He unhooks the handcuffs, then kneels to remove the ankle restraints. For me it's a shameful and telling image—a uniformed officer kneeling before the defendant. Kim's still looking at me. I guess she is trying to understand what I'd said, and maybe finally becoming aware that David Fast will receive some very special treatment.

With the handcuffs off, Fast stretches his arms behind the podium. Then he rolls his shoulders and head. He turns to look at the crowd behind him, his eyes scanning the full courtroom, and pausing for a moment on Kim before moving on to me. I give him my hardest stare and restrain myself from mouthing Kim's words, *Fuck you.*

He has a cocky look on his face that makes me want to come over the low dividing wall and into the well. "No, fuck *you,*" I read in his eyes. He grins at me, showing his newly broken teeth. Then suddenly he's moving.

With an almost casual speed, like a hurried pedestrian, he parts the short swinging gate that divides the well from the gallery and strides up the aisle and out of the courtroom. No one else moves. We're all frozen in shock. I look to the judge and see her mouth open, the gavel raised hesitantly in her hand. The attorneys, prosecutor Acosta included, stare over their shoulders. I jump to my feet just as the courtroom door swings shut with a whoosh. Then all hell breaks loose.

Everyone is on their feet. In just seconds, murmured questions become shouts and the judge beats her gavel. I fight my way through the other spectators in my row as one of the jailhouse deputies runs up the aisle after Fast—the other staying to guard the remaining prisoners. Using my crutch as a club, shoving people back onto the hard wooden bench and others over the low wall in front of us, I reach the aisle but that too is now full of shouting, milling people.

"Go, David, go!" someone crows, then whoops like a cowboy.

I cut through them like a fullback, knocking reporters and the citizens of Tomichi to the ground and into each other. A jolt of pain shrieks up my leg with each step but I keep shoving forward. In my wake, even more mayhem erupts. Over it all, I can hear Kim shouting my name. She has her hands pressed into the small of my back, propelling me forward with even greater speed.

The courthouse lobby is empty but for the civilian security guards, who stand staring at the big glass doors leading outside with their mouths agape. "Call 911!" I yell at them. "There's been an escape!" And then I'm shoving through the glass, too, with Kim still pushing at my back. Just ahead of me is the fat deputy from the courtroom. He's yelling into the radio mounted on his shoulder as he struggles to force his bulk into a sprint down the courthouse steps. Fifty feet ahead is Fast. He's moving in an easy jog across the wide lawn, across the sidewalk, and into the street. Then Kim passes me, almost knocking me down with her shoulder.

I stagger and windmill on the steps, jabbing wildly at the ground with the crutch as I try to keep from falling. It's not a matter of controlling the pain anymore—the ankle is simply failing. Kim blows past the deputy, too, taking the steps in such a rush it looks like she's in low-level flight.

Fast looks over his shoulder and sees Kim hot on his heels. He seems to shake his head amusedly, but he picks up the pace.

I follow as best I can. With each haphazard landing, my ankle threatens to buckle.

In the street now, Fast runs by the two TV vans with the lounging cameramen beside them. Then he passes my Land Cruiser where it's parked in front of a fire hydrant. I see it shake, rocking hard on its axles, as Oso bellows at the man sprinting by. The beast is slamming his snout through the four inches of open space on the driver's-side window. For an instant I wonder if he recognizes Fast as one of the men who'd shot him, if he has picked up Fast's scent through the few inches of open glass.

Up ahead, in the middle of the street, a pickup with no license plates idles just a hundred feet ahead of Fast. I can see the driver through the rear window. He's twisted around in the seat, watching Fast run toward him. A bandana or a scarf covers the lower part of his face. With Fast so close, and only a one-eyed woman anywhere near him, the driver doesn't seem to feel the need to reverse closer.

There's no way I can catch him, I realize as I struggle to make the turn into the street with the deputy huffing beside me. Fast is a hundred feet ahead and closing quickly on the pickup. I hear its engine rev. One of the cameramen has gotten a big camera up on his shoulder and is standing in the street, filming the town's fleeing prodigy being chased by a woman.

Kim sprints full-out in the street behind her enemy. As she gets close to where the beast is violently rocking my Land Cruiser, she reaches one hand into her pocket. For a moment I think she's feeling for some kind of a weapon, then it hits me—she's reaching for my truck's keys.

Kim abruptly skids to a stop beside my truck. She plunges the keys into the truck's door and rips it open. Oso stops bellowing and cocks his head at her. His ears are still laid back, his lips high and wrinkled with a snarl.

"Sic him, Oso!" she yells, pointing at Fast's back. "Get—!"

Oso doesn't wait for her to finish shouting. Before Kim can step out of the way, a hundred and fifty pounds of wild canine muscle drives into her chest, knocking her down in the street. The beast lands on top of her and pulls his bandaged leg high. He takes a lunge in Fast's direction, limping badly. I think, *He's going to get away!* But that's the last limp Oso makes. He shoves off the asphalt with all four paws, accelerating in a single bound, the excitement of the chase nullifying what must be a screaming pain from his wound. He shoots forward in an incredible burst of speed. Within ten paces he's moving faster than I've ever seen a creature move. The unraveling bandage trails out behind him like a bloody streamer.

Fast glances over his shoulder as he nears the pickup. The driver has opened the passenger-side door and the engine is revving even higher, ready with the pop of the clutch to carry him far away from the courts and justice. Then Fast looks again in disbelief.

I crash into Kim just as she's getting to her feet. We go down hard in a tangle. Both of us are so focused on Fast and Oso that we hadn't seen each other coming. I struggle to my feet first and almost collapse again when my ankle seems to fold in on itself. Catching myself with my hands on the Land Cruiser's fender, I hobble as quick as I can down the middle of the street after them.

The beast hits Fast like a heat-seeking missile. Those great white fangs lock onto the back of Fast's left thigh, and Oso's momentum carries him right through his prey, flipping Fast backwards and twisting and then slamming him down on the asphalt.

Behind us a shouting, swarming mass of people is spilling out of the courthouse and down onto the lawn. There are horrified shrieks as the spectators catch sight of what's happening in the street.

On top of him now, Oso swings his head. An inhuman scream fills the air, eclipsing all the others. It comes from Fast. The dog's jaws are locked on his thigh. Oso is slinging his head from side to side, sending the big man grating back and forth across the pavement. Fast tries to roll halfway over to beat at Oso's flat skull with his fist, but the beast just swings him in a new direction.

The pickup's driver leaps out of the cab. He has a black bandana pulled up over his face and a gun in one hand. He stares at the mauling on the pavement behind his truck—*what looks like a fucking bear just ripping the shit out of his boss*—then looks at me hobbling toward him with my crutch held high in the air like a club. *Boss be damned*—the driver jumps back in the cab and smokes the tires out of there.

I come up yelling Oso's name and *"Parada! Parada!"* Stop! He doesn't hear. The dog is still jerking the man's body over the pavement. Fast has given up trying to punch Oso's head and is now digging his torn fingertips into the asphalt, trying to drag himself away. His screams have turned to moans. He's begging.

Wincing from the pain in my ankle, I kick the beast between the hind legs with the toe of my hiking boot. Oso's rear lifts into the air, then the beast releases his grip on Fast's thigh and pivots on me with unbelievable speed.

He faces me with bloody teeth and an evil hum coming from his chest as loud as a lawn mower. His eyes are yellow slits. They are as ancient and lethal as the devil's. "*Fácil,* Oso. Easy, boy," I tell him. Beside us, Fast's red hands, burned from the asphalt, flail weakly on the ground.

Slowly, Oso's lips sink over his teeth. The eyes widen just a little in recognition. And the heat drains out of them. I take his collar in my hand and pull him to the sidewalk, murmuring, "Easy, easy, easy."

Both cameramen, their machines perched on their shoulders, carefully approach Fast's writhing form. After filming him for a moment, they turn their cameras toward where I have Oso on the curb. But I crouch awkwardly on my bad ankle in front of him to block their view. I wave them away with my gun still in my hand and they turn back to Fast. They make no move to help him, to stop the thick red liquid from pooling beneath his leg. Their only concern is to get it all on tape. A crowd starts to gather. They stay well away from my bloody dog and me. The sound of sirens fills the air.

FORTY-FIVE

"ROBERTO'S COMING UP to Wyoming for a while. I called his parole officer and worked it out," I say. "Why don't you come, too?"

Kim looks at the ground and doesn't answer.

We're in front of the courthouse again, standing on the lawn, after having finished a second round of statements with police and prosecutors. It's early in the evening now. Most of the reporters have finally gone home or to their motel rooms after making their five o'clock broadcasts, although a few still linger where cameramen film them on the courthouse steps. Their numbers had exploded since Fast's attempt to escape just hours earlier. The news that the town's leading businessman had been arrested for murder and kidnapping had been just a statewide issue, but when he was mauled by a giant dog while trying to escape and subsequently hospitalized, well, that is a whole other matter. By tomorrow I expect the town to be full of journalists from all over the country. And I want to be far away from here.

One of the reporters—a pretty young blonde in a blue suit with a big hairdo—spots us. We're conspicuous even from a distance in our filthy clothes and me with the crutch. *A scar-faced man and a one-eyed woman,* I remember Kim had once joked, *no one will notice us.* The reporter waves for a cameraman to follow and starts heading our way across the grass.

"Hang on a minute." I hobble angrily toward them, punching the end of the crutch into the soft grass.

The reporter starts in with the questions while she's still twenty feet away.

"Mr. Burns! Is it true your dog is going to be destroyed? That you've been ordered to turn him over to Animal Control in the morning?"

It's true, but it's not going to happen. I'm taking him back to Wyoming tonight with Roberto and me. And as soon as we cross the state line, I'm going to buy him the biggest damn steak I can find.

I keep moving closer, saying nothing, until I can wave the crutch first in her face and then in the camera's lens. "I'm not making a fucking statement right now, or ever," I say, using the profanity to try to ensure they don't use this footage. But it probably doesn't matter—they can just bleep it out. "Now please leave us the fuck alone."

The pretty reporter looks stunned. Her bright painted lips hang open, displaying teeth unnaturally white. I doubt I've said anything she hasn't heard before, but she acts as if she's shocked to the core. I'm sure she's hoping to make me feel guilty for my outburst. She closes her mouth for a moment in an exaggerated pout, and then opens it to go ahead with her questions.

I wheel away and crutch back to Kim, who's trying to hide a smile.

"Did I scare them off?" I ask her, not turning around.

"I guess so. You sounded pretty ferocious over there, but maybe Oso needs to give you a few more lessons."

"Kim—" I start to say.

She interrupts me, looking over my shoulder. "She's going back to the steps, looking pissed. If you'd been nicer to her, you probably could have gotten a date."

"I'm hoping I've already got one."

Kim doesn't respond, but she's still smiling.

"Kim, I've got to get out of town now. For Oso and my brother. So please, will you come up to Wyoming with us? At least for an extended visit, until this place cools off?"

For the first time in my life I'm thinking about how nice it would be to share everything with someone else. The dawn and the dusk and every night under a down quilt on a soft bed, or better yet, out under the stars on the hard earth.

Kim stops smiling. Her good eye fixes on mine. "I don't think that's such a hot idea, Anton."

"Why not?"

The exhaustion is messing with my emotions. It's as if some demon inside me is picking up the feelings that are running around in my chest like playful cats and throwing them into the air to see what flies. Seconds ago it had been Love. Now the one that soars up into my throat is an unreasonable Anger. I feel my jaw getting tense.

"There are a lot of reasons." She raises one hand to

touch my chest when I start to interrupt. It grips my shirt. And then she sighs before continuing.

"Listen, Anton, there are things here I have to do. I have to file for an injunction against the Forest Service just to make absolutely sure they don't go ahead with the swap. I have to show them the ruin." Her face turns hard. "And I have to make damn sure the DA doesn't screw up Fast's case when he gets out of the hospital."

"That could be a while." Oso had done some serious damage.

She allows a smile. "Yes."

"Once you've dealt with the Forest Service, then will you come north? For a couple of weeks? There won't be a trial for a long time." With Fast's stature, it could be years.

Kim looks away from me, still holding my shirt in one fist. "All of this that's happened in these last days, Anton... I need some time to sort it all out. For so long all I've thought about is how I can use the law and the courts to ruin Fast. That's all my life has been about. Now, I don't know... I need to figure out what happened... where I go from here."

"We should do it together. Away from here. Come on. Come to Wyoming."

"Listen, Anton, we're totally different. I'm..." She sighs again and glances toward where the reporters continue to watch us.

"What?"

"Well, I'm really too tired to deal with this right now." She looks at me, then away again. "But to start with, this place is my home. I've got work to do here. Real work. For the valley. It wasn't all bullshit, you know. I do like this place. And you, you need to get out. Get your brother and your dog out of here. Get back to your job up in Wyoming, if you've still got one."

She means the last part as a joke but I'm not laughing. I try to swallow the anger. I have no right to expect anything from her. "Maybe Sheriff Munik would hire me," I say, trying to joke. "I could move here."

She takes her hand off my chest and touches my lips with her fingertips to silence me. "And I'm almost old enough to be your mother."

I speak through her fingers. "Bullshit, Kim. You're nine years older. Stop with that. Now tell me what you're really talking about."

Kim drops her fingers from my face. Her hands hang neatly at her sides, utterly still. Her head hangs down a little bit, too, but that soft brown eye drills right into my face with a surprising force.

"I'm a victim, kid," she says softly. "It's been twelve years and I'm still a victim. I still wake up at night screaming sometimes." She touches her eye patch. "I can't even love myself—how can you expect me to love you? And you're too much like your brother, you know. Too wild and free to be tied down by the things that bind me."

I want to say something like *You'd think after twelve years you'd let someone help*. But it's not my business to try to tell her what to do. I sense it would only drive her further away. I just make a gentle attempt: "Then let me untie you. Us climbers are pretty handy with knots."

"No." She smiles so gently that the anger in my chest is almost smothered. "I've been doing things my own way for too long. I've got to free myself." She looks past me and up, toward where Wild Fire Valley is hidden by the craggy foothills and the forests that cover them. The peak is visible, though. "But that doesn't mean I don't want you to visit me sometime. You'll be down here to climb in the valley, right? And to testify at Fast's trial?"

"Right."

With her gaze off my face, a little ember hisses within me. We've earned a shot together. I've earned some alone time with her. Now. I'm owed. But a more reasonable part of me knows that's bullshit. She owes me nothing. I'm just feeling like a rejected little kid. Trying to act like a grown-up, I step forward and hug her. My ankle burns as I put my weight on it and purposely grind it into the earth. The hug is warm and full-bodied—I don't care if the cameras behind us are rolling.

She feels so small and delicate in my arms. I'm aware of the bones in her back beneath my hands and her high breasts pushing against my chest through her dirty clothes. Aware of each breath she takes. I put my mouth against her ear and push her dark hair out of the way with my lips. I want to whisper something but don't know what would be appropriate. She holds me so tight that I have to breathe shallow, feeling the heat coursing through me, the creak of my bruised ribs, and the numbness in the small of my back.

"Goodbye, Anton."

"I'll be back, Kim. You're not the only one who can be tenacious."

ABOUT THE AUTHOR

CLINTON McKINZIE is the acclaimed author of THE EDGE OF JUSTICE and POINT OF LAW. His third novel, TRIAL BY ICE AND FIRE, is forthcoming from Delacorte Press. He was raised in Santa Monica and now lives in Colorado with his wife, son, and dog. Prior to becoming a writer, he worked as a peace officer and deputy district attorney in Denver. His passion is climbing alpine walls. Visit his website at www.clintonmckinzie.com.

ONE

FROM THE TRAILHEAD parking lot the couloir had looked like a narrow, radiant column rising out of a snowfield near the center of the dark mountain. Now that I'm on it, attached by the spike of my ax and the sharp points of my crampons, it appears more like a strip of caulking in a deep cut running down the mountain's face. Gray-black walls line the nearly vertical wound, broken and serrated as if the long gash had been made by a God-sized shank instead of a scalpel.

The snow in the couloir is wind blasted and sun baked, but so far this morning there is no wind and there is no sun. At this hour the night sky is just starting its fade into indigo. Soon pink and orange rays will spill down from Teewinot's summit spire and the wind will begin to moan through toothy gaps in the ridge above us.

I had almost forgotten how much I love these

early-morning ascents. How much I *need* this sense of exhilaration that comes enhanced by an inherent dread of heights and the dark.

Over the last six months I've allowed my passion for climbing mountains to be smothered by my work and an infatuation of a totally different, totally unexpected sort: for a pretty Denver newspaper reporter named Rebecca Hersh. As I plant my ax and kick my boots into the steep snow, I concentrate on the night's stillness and the dawn's coming colors. I ignore all thoughts of the recent trial, the failing romance, the weight of the pack on my back, and the burn of lactic acid in my butt and thighs.

The snow crunches with each high step, creating a syncopated rhythm that regulates my breathing. Over two steps I exhale, then I pause for a moment to suck in the cold, thin air.

As I inhale, I glance down at the young woman following me. She is cautiously placing her boots in the holds I've made. A purple fleece headband warms the tops of her ears and keeps the sweaty tendrils of blonde hair from her face. Above her head the pointed shapes of ski tips wave like antennae from where they're strapped to her pack. Although I'm a little wary of her, I'm also impressed that she hasn't once called for a rest. Not bad for a lawyer.

"How's it going, Cali?" I ask, trying not to pant too loud. The last six months have taken more than just a psychological toll.

"Fine." Her breath is as labored as mine but her teeth flash a smile in the darkness. "How much farther?"

Above me the couloir stretches upward for another two hundred yards before it fades into the vanishing stars. "Not much. Twenty minutes, I guess."

I kick another step into the snow with a plastic boot and think about where my wariness toward her comes from.

There is a slight twinge of guilt, as if I'm somehow betraying Rebecca by being alone with another woman in a place like this. A place where I feel so pumped up and alive. But this is, after all, just another job. Nothing to feel guilty about. I've baby-sat for lots of victims and witnesses before. Of course, none of them had asked me to take them into the mountains. But then I'd spent my college and grad-school summers dragging plenty of doctors and lawyers up Alaskan peaks.

This woman is different in other ways, too. It isn't just that she's good-looking or that she's semifamous. My wariness comes from the simple fact that she's strange. I can't figure her out. How many children of movie stars run from big-city glamour and move to a place like Wyoming? How many of them attend law school and then become small-town prosecutors when they're only twenty-six years old? How many of them like to spend their weekends jumping down dangerously steep snow with skinny boards locked to their feet?

The wariness, I decide, also comes from the way my boss at Wyoming's Division of Criminal Investigation told me to be careful with this one.

"For God's sake, don't screw it up!" Ross McGee had barked at me over the phone yesterday. "You're on thin fucking ice as it is."

I could picture him hunched at his desk in Cheyenne, looking like some demented Santa Claus in a pin-striped suit, and issuing a stern warning to his most troublesome elf.

"You know that's not my fault."

He responded with one of his signature phrases: "If

you're looking for sympathy, QuickDraw, look it up in the dictionary. It's between *shit* and *syphilis*."

I smile to myself as I stomp a boot through the snow's crust, thinking of the obscenities he'd bellow if he could see us right now.

The snow above has slid away in a few places and exposed sheets of iron-hard ice. When I'm unable to stab my ax's spike in at least a few inches, I traverse to the north side of the chute, hoping to find deeper stuff and safer footing. I don't want to waste time tying into a rope. Before long the sun will start heating the dark granite walls that flank the snow. Frozen water shoaling narrow cracks will melt and send rocks whistling down toward us. I unconsciously touch the scar on my left cheek with a gloved fingertip. I hate rockfall. It had branded me nearly a decade ago with a wound I took as a stern warning. My luck was used up a long time ago. I guess we have about an hour before the couloir becomes a shooting gallery.

Turning again to study the way she is steadily clumping up beneath me, I decide she's stable enough not to need a belay. But it would be more than embarrassing if she were to slip. Killing my ward would be a very bad way to mark my return to active duty.

"Watch out for the ice, Cali."

She responds with a feminine grunt: "Yeah."

The snow-filled chute extends down more than a thousand feet before it opens up into wider, more moderately angled slopes that continue another thousand feet to the tree line. Below me it glows in the half-light like a long, gray ribbon. The steep ribs of rock confine it on both sides. The angle averages a little more than fifty degrees, although looking down it appears nearly vertical. This optical illusion is accentuated by the fact that if you fall, you're going all the way. Well over a mile below us I can see the lights of the small marina on Jenny Lake.

I kick two more steps and pause again to breathe.

Yesterday, after McGee had told me the nature of the new assignment and warned me in his polite way not to screw it up, I entered Cali's name on Westlaw's news archives. Cali Morrow was the only child of Alana Reese, the so-called Reigning Queen of Hollywood and also the owner of an enormous ranch in Jackson Hole. Her birth was celebrated in the numerous articles I found not just because of her mother's fame, but also because of the oddity and tragedy of her paternity.

Her father had been a Forest Service smoke jumper who died in a fire two months before Cali's birth. He'd been sort of famous himself at the time, having been pictured on a *Life* magazine cover with a burning forest behind him. Apparently Alana had met him while vacationing at her ranch—he was a bit of local color for the actress. He soon became even more famous when an award-winning book called *Smoke Jump* was written about the fire that had taken his life.

Cali's childhood was detailed in numerous tabloid articles. Reading them, I'd been appalled that her childhood was so invaded by the public's obsession with celebrity. Even her preteen birthday parties made the news. And her mother didn't help things by making the occasions lavish, star-studded affairs.

I'd skimmed the articles, gleaning the essential facts.

Cali Morrow grew up in Santa Monica, California, attended a private school in Bel Air, spent her summers on her mom's ranch in Jackson Hole, and was the occasional child star of several TV movies. The critics called her teenage performances wooden and hoped she would improve with the years. But it seemed that upon her eighteenth birthday she made a determined effort to leave the spotlight her mother kept focused on her. Cali attended college at Brown University, where she was the captain of the women's ski team. She continued to return to Wyoming each summer, following in her father's footsteps by fighting fires on an elite Hot Shot ground crew, which was second in prestige and danger only to the parachuting smoke jumpers. Upon graduation she enrolled in law school at Michigan. Following that, just one year ago, she tried again to jump from the face of the earth by permanently moving to Wyoming and taking a job as a prosecutor with the County Attorney's Office.

"Some deranged piece of shit...tried to crawl through her window last night," McGee had told me over the phone, pausing in his peculiar manner to suck air into his emphysemic lungs. "A family friend walking by scared him off...but he left behind a stun gun and some duct tape.... You get the idea, lad? This asshole's serious."

"Any suspects?"

"No, not a sure thing, not yet...all I've heard about so far is a local cop...some guy she was dating but dumped recently.... That's the reason why...the County Attorney up there laid it at our feet...that and the fact that she's a prosecutor."

Although my office, Wyoming's Division of Criminal Investigation, is a statewide law enforcement agency primarily concerned with stopping the distribution of drugs, we are often brought in when a case is particularly important or complex or when there is a conflict of interest within a local police department. A conflict usually means you've got a cop or a local prosecutor for a victim or a suspect. Here there's both. You don't want a department investigating one of their own in a case like this.

Especially if the victim is a celebrity's daughter as well as a prosecutor.

"The ex's name is Charles Wokowski...and the County Attorney admits it's unlikely he's our boy," McGee continued. "But so far he's all we've got.... They call him Wook or Wookie, after some beast in a movie.... Not quite as flattering a nickname as yours, eh, Quick-Draw?"

"Don't call me that, fat man," I told him for the thousandth time. He responded only with what might have been a half-coughed chuckle before hanging up the phone.

After talking with McGee and conducting my quick Internet search, I'd looked up Cali's number at the Teton County Attorney's Office. When I told the spirited and un-lawyerlike voice on the other end of the line my name, she said, "Wow! Antonio Burns, huh. I can't believe they assigned *you* to watch my butt! Everybody's been talking about you, you know. You go by Anton, right? Or do you like—"

"Anton's fine," I'd interrupted.

I'm not famous. Not like her or her parents, anyway. For an uncomfortable amount of time, though, I've been notorious. And it has grown worse over the last six months, culminating in the media frenzy a few weeks ago when I was cross-examined for five of the longest days of my life. Any dirty laundry the defense attorneys could find or make up about me was fully aired after being carefully spun to put me in the worst possible light. And the jackals in the press (my Rebecca abstaining) ate up every scrap of it. *Three Cheyenne gang members shot in suspicious circumstances. Another man dead on a mountain. An Air Force colonel for a father who'd been court-martialed and was now living in South American exile. A drug-addicted brother, a killer too, recently escaped from prison.* I must have earned some truly shitty karma in a previous life.

When I didn't say anything else, Cali asked, "So when do you start looking for this creep?"

"Tomorrow. My boss is coming up too. With the help of another guy from DCI, I'm supposed to keep an eye on you when you're not in your office or in court."

"Great! You used to be a big mountain guide before you became a cop, right? How about skiing the east face of Teewinot in the morning? I've been trying to get someone to go with me all spring. Pick me up at three? Okay? In the morning?"

Maybe baby-sitting her wouldn't be so bad, I thought as I hung up the phone. God knows I've needed this kind of release for a while. It was high time I fed the creature my brother calls the Rat. He'd been gnawing away in my chest for far too long, begging for the adrenaline rush that nourishes his furry little body.

I reach the top of the couloir with Cali panting hard at my heels and leaning heavily on her ax. Once again, I'm impressed that she's made it without a single complaint. Whining had been one of the things that had ended my guiding career. The "office" in Alaska was unbelievably gorgeous, but the beauty of the place couldn't make up for the clients. Carrying their gear. Cooking their meals. Short-roping them up to grand summits that were defiled by their moans. Chasing after drug dealers with a badge in my wallet and a gun in my hand was a lot more fun, at least when it didn't involve lawsuits, cross-examination, and my picture in the paper.

The chute tops out at a break in the peak's southeastern ridge a few hundred feet short of the summit. A cornice has formed here, a twenty-foot cresting wave of snow. I move onto the broken field of talus to the left and pick my way above it, stepping carefully so as not to send rocks rolling down on Cali's head.

I dump my pack on a flat, rocky shelf that the previous afternoon's wind has swept free of snow. I turn and stare out at the brightening pastel sky to the east. In another few minutes the yellow orb of the sun will emerge over the low mountains on the other side of the valley. The daylight is already beginning to reveal the forests, meadows, and lakes in between. Although it's only late May, the land below us is already dry and brown—an omen of what everyone says will be another hot, fire-swept summer.

"It's all going to burn," Cali confirms as she comes up out of the chute and drops her own pack onto the rocks. The skis clatter against the aluminum avalanche shovel also strapped to the pack. With her hands resting on her knees and breathing hard, she adds, "This is wild. I can't believe you used to do this for a living."

"I can't believe you used to fight forest fires."

She grins. "You've been checking up on me, huh? I guess it's mutual then."

Despite the early-morning cold, she's wearing only a pair of black fleece leggings and a gray polypropylene shirt. Both are skintight and dark with sweat. Straightening up, she pulls a Gore-Tex shell from her pack and puts it on.

Her face is almost a perfect oval, rising from a pointed chin, and curving around prominent cheekbones. Her eyes are emerald green. Short blonde hair lifts from beneath the headband in a single curl.

On flat earth she might be considered a little plain because of a broad nose and too pointy a chin. But up on a mountain like this, with her eyes bright in the dawn and the smile on her lips, she could be modeling for a brand of expensive vodka. She'd sell a lot of it. I have to admit that my wariness toward her is thawing.

"Do you want to go all the way?" I point at the granite spire above us and to the right. It makes me feel a little strange, stopping short of the actual summit. My brother likes to say that the best place to be is where *the only way to get higher is to fall.*

"Hell no, Anton. Not unless we can ski down. I'm a skier, remember, not a rock jock like you."

To follow the spiny ridge up to the apex would take a lot more time and the use of the rope and other gear. I have all that in my pack but I'm relieved she doesn't want to continue. The rising sun is already starting to heat the couloir. Soon rocks will start screaming down and ripping through the snow.

I take out a bottle of sugary tea, drink some, then offer it to her.

"How are we going to do this?" she asks. At first I think she means the descent, but she continues, "How are you going to look after me and find this guy at the same time?"

"My partner and I will work the case when you're in your office or in court. You should be safe enough in both places. After work, I'll follow you around. Basically, I'll stalk you myself."

She makes a wry face. "Great."

"Don't worry about your privacy. I'll keep my distance as best I can."

She drinks half my tea. "No, that's all right. I don't have much to keep private these days. No boyfriend or anything. Not anymore. Besides, I want to hear firsthand about that wild shootout in Cheyenne."

I smile back but without any pleasure and don't respond.

After a minute she asks, "Do you have any idea who's doing this?"

"I heard there's a possible suspect. Your ex-boyfriend. Wokowski or Wookie or something like that."

She shrugs. "Wook. Sergeant Charles Wokowski. I don't know if it's him or not. I probably shouldn't have mentioned his name to my boss—I only did because everyone knows we haven't been getting along. A month ago, before we broke up, I would have said there's no way it could be him. Now, I don't know . . . Wook's been acting pretty weird around me lately. And the County Attorney's pissed off at him because of an excessive-force case."

Most stalkers I've dealt with were ex-boyfriends or ex-husbands, so it makes sense to give him a very hard look. Although with her being a celebrity, some random freak who would be tougher to find could have easily fixated on her. I hope that isn't the case because it will require a lot more work. But I don't want it to be a cop either. Arresting fellow officers is dangerous—I should know. At DCI we frequently have to investigate cops for a variety of allegations. They are always armed and know the rules of the game too well. And arresting a cop never fails to stir up a political maelstrom. But I also know that cops all too often become infatuated with their former lovers. Cops are so used to being dominant and in control that sometimes they can't take it when they're rejected.

I push away a thought about Rebecca and ask, "Tell me a little more about him."

She shrugs again. "He's with the Teton County Sheriff's Office. He's a big deal in the department. A leader, kind of. Maybe the next sheriff. Everybody looks up to him. They would protect him. But I just can't believe it's him. It's not his style. He's an in-your-face guy, not some sicko who'd try to crawl in my window with a stun gun." As she says this she shivers.

Then she drinks some more from my bottle, fixing me with those green eyes. "He can be a mean bastard, though. He never touched me in anger or anything, but he looked like he wanted to a couple of times. When we broke up last month he said he wished we were both dead. Is that a threat or what? A guy I dated in law school said the same thing once. What do you think?"

I hesitate for a moment. Despite her saying it isn't his style, this Wokowski is already looking pretty good for it. "It sounds like you have lousy taste in men."

She hands me back the now-empty bottle and laughs. "I'm sorry to hear you say that, Anton. I was beginning to like you."

I smile too. "I guess that proves it."

I'm not sure if she's flirting or just screwing around. Either way, it makes me think of Rebecca again. We'd been living together in Denver for the last six months, the first three of which I was on mandatory leave and the second three during which I was the primary witness in the trial of the state's governor-elect. Our life in her apartment started out great. We visited my family in Argentina for Christmas. Back in Denver I climbed and skied the Front Range while she worked at the paper. Then a few weeks ago—just as the trial fell apart and I began to doubt the last flimsy strands of faith I had in the law as an instrument of justice—everything changed. There were sudden and totally uncharacteristic crying jags as well as questions of my long-term intentions asked with searching eyes.

I feel like I don't know her anymore. She'd once been the most stable woman I'd ever known. So poised and confident. She'd been my life preserver when I was tumbling down rapids. Now we've become cautiously formal with each other, where a few months earlier we were as happy and exuberant together as a couple of puppies.

I tried to call her late last night only to discover that she wasn't answering the phone. And reporters always answer the phone, no matter what the hour. It wasn't until after I'd left a message—probably not concealing my irritation very well—that I realized my name had been taken off her answering machine.

Screw it. Focus on where you are now, Ant. Look around. There's no better place than this.

"Are you going to confront Wook?" Cali asks, bringing me back.

"Maybe. First I want to talk to some people, see the report on the attempted break-in, and find out more about what's going on. Then I'll see about talking to him."

She puts on a pair of amber-tinted glasses that only half hide her eyes. "I know everyone says you're a badass, Anton. But take my word for it—you'll want some backup around if you get in his face."

I don't bother trying to refute the undeserved reputation. I'd done enough of that on the witness stand. Instead I just nod and say, "Okay."

After a few minutes' rest we unstrap the skis from our packs. I walk out onto the rocks to one side of the cornice and study the chute below, trying to fix the dangerous gray patches of ice in my mind. I don't want to make a mistake today. It isn't just because of McGee's warning about not screwing it up, but also because it's been a long time since I've skied anything this steep. The first few hundred feet of the couloir are about ten degrees steeper than anything I've done in years. A fall here could easily be fatal. I would slide faster and faster, bouncing off the couloir's stony walls that stand like the brown-stained teeth lining some great beast's mouth. There would be no way to self-arrest on something this steep. The rock and ice and snow would chew me up until it vomited out what was left in the forest twenty-five hundred feet below.

Fear wraps its arms around me, embracing me with a cold but familiar hug.

As I stare down I hear a faint whispering. It doesn't come from the rising wind beginning to rush over this high notch in the ridge but from somewhere deep inside my chest. The Rat is calling. He's hungry for a meal, that surge of adrenaline required to calm and sate him. He's starting to feed.

"How are we going to do this?" This time Cali means the descent. Her voice is sharper, her face a little paler with excitement. "I haven't done much off-piste, you know. Nothing like *this.*"

"Jump turns. Don't even think about pointing your skis downhill." I say this more to myself than to her. She'd been the captain of her college ski team so she's probably a far better skier than I. But because I'm supposed to be the former big mountain guide as well as the state cop who's protecting her, I add, "I'll go first." It seems like the gentlemanly thing to do. Maybe I'll somehow be able to stop her if she falls.

My heart rate is starting to accelerate. The thought of flying from the cornice's lip, of my stomach floating up into my throat, of the thirty-foot free fall through space and then leaping down the steep chute below, makes the Rat begin to sing with something approaching delirium.

"I hope your edges are sharp," I tell her as I finger my own.

Looking me in the eye, she picks up one of her skis and holds it before her face. She grins then sticks out her tongue.

"Don't—" I start to say, realizing what she's about to do.

But she ignores me. Her pink tongue touches the ski's metal edge and she licks a short distance along it. Then she spits in the snow at her feet. A red stain appears. "Okay?" she says. "They're sharp."

I shake my head. This girl is full of surprises. She's going to be a lot of trouble. But she's not at all reserved, not at all like Rebecca in recent days. The Rat is delighted—he thinks he's found a new friend.

I check my bindings to be sure the DIN setting is maxed out. A prerelease would be fatal. Then we both click in and slide out, snowplowing, onto the wave of wind-packed snow. Leaning over our quivering poles, we try one more time to examine the couloir below. But it's hard to see from this angle on top of the cornice. There's just the sloping forest far below. And beyond that, more than a vertical mile down, is the blue water of Jenny Lake. It feels like with a powerful enough leap I might be able to splash into it. Cannonball among the white shapes of the small fishing boats that are already starting to dot the lake.

I look over at Cali and she's staring back at me. Still grinning with a bit of blood reddening her lower lip. Despite her sunglasses, I see white all the way around the jade irises. I can almost hear her heart beating over the pounding roar of my own. The adrenal glands are squeezing out their sweet juice. The sky has turned Wyoming blue—the kind of blue that's neon through my own colored lenses.

"Still want to do this?" I ask, smiling back now.

"Hell yes!" she shouts.

The Rat is howling some frantic, mad chant. Enticing me to *Jump! Jump! Jump!* And I do it, too scared to scream, too ecstatic to whoop, trying to just focus on leaning forward and fighting the instinctive reaction to slump back. If I hit the snow with anything but my skis springing beneath my hips I will bounce out into space. Into the forest. Into the lake. I stretch out my arms and the poles that are clenched in my fists like frail wings.

Suddenly, in midflight and with the wind tearing at my clothes, the fear blows away. It's replaced by absolute rapture. The adrenaline shoots through my veins as if it's being plunged there by an enormous syringe. I'm truly flying, like an eagle in the heavens, soaring far out above the dry earth.

But somewhere buried deep beneath the thrill and the rush is a sense of foreboding. If I could see just a week into the future, I might imagine my wings being plucked clean off. I might imagine falling hard and fast then crashing—breaking right through the planet's crust. Right into the fire that some people say burns below.